A Graphic Novel from

The Land of Stories

Goldilocks

Wanted Dead or Alive

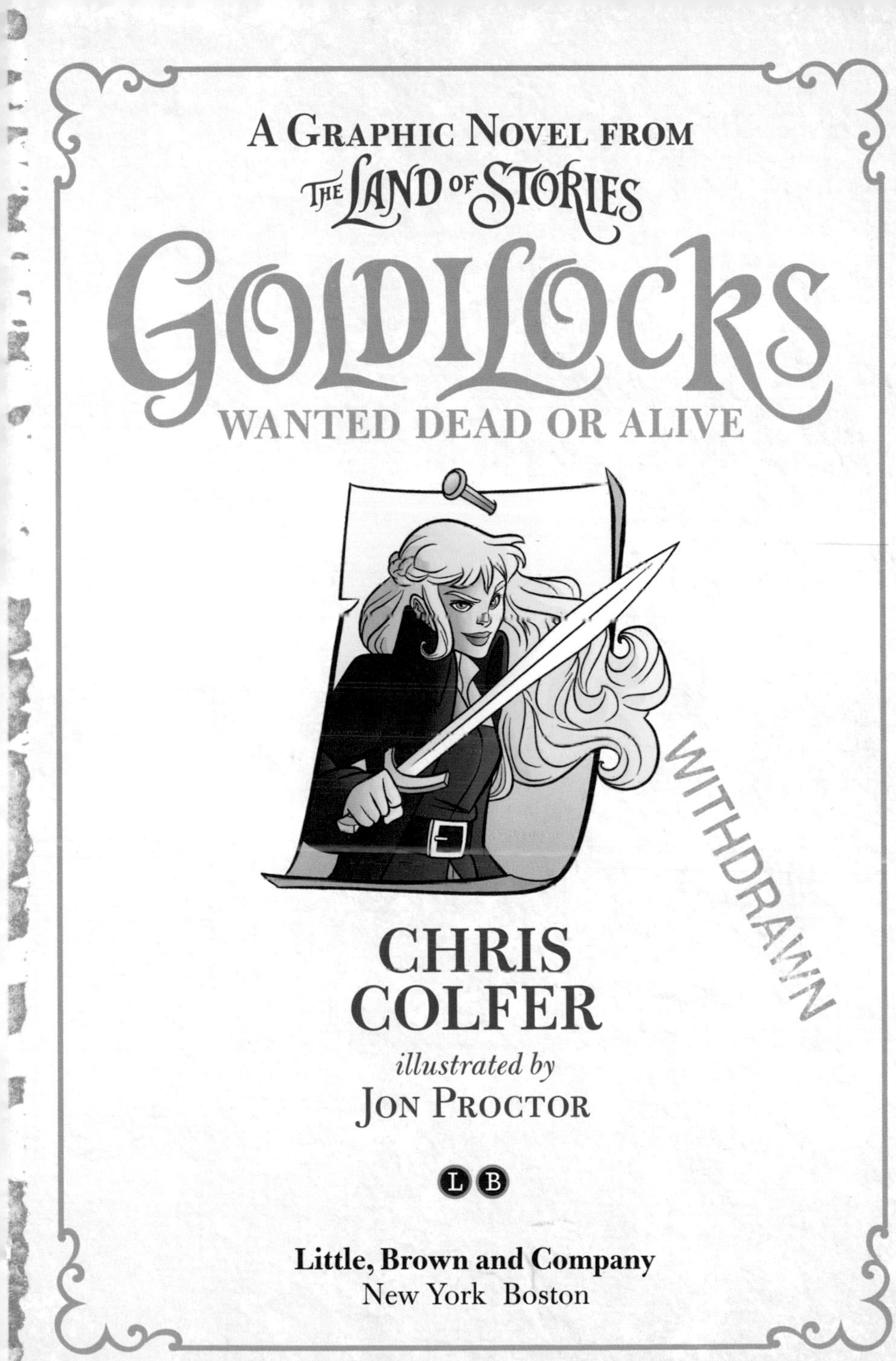

CHRIS COLFER

illustrated by

Jon Proctor

LB

Little, Brown and Company

New York Boston

About This Book

This book was edited by Alvina Ling and designed by Christina Quintero and Ching N. Chan. The production was supervised by Virginia Lawther, and the production editor was Jen Graham. The text was set in CCComicrazy, and the display type is Bulmer MT Std.

Text copyright © 2021 by Christopher Colfer
Illustrations copyright © 2021 by Lisa K. Weber and Jon Proctor

Lettering by Maria Caritas, Dwi Febri Novita, Dies Caya of Caravan Studio.

Cover illustration copyright © 2021 by Lisa K. Weber and Jon Proctor.
Cover design by Ching N. Chan.
Cover copyright © 2021 by Hachette Book Group, Inc.

Little, Brown and Company
Hachette Book Group
1290 Avenue of the Americas, New York, NY 10104
Visit us at LBYR.com

First Edition: June 2021

Little, Brown and Company is a division of Hachette Book Group, Inc.
The Little, Brown name and logo are trademarks of Hachette Book Group, Inc.

The publisher is not responsible for websites (or their content) that are not owned by the publisher.

Library of Congress Cataloging-in-Publication Data

Names: Colfer, Chris, 1990– author. | Proctor, Jon, illustrator. | Weber, Lisa K., illustrator.

Title: Goldilocks: wanted dead or alive / Chris Colfer; illustrations by Jon Proctor [and] Lisa K. Weber.

Description: First edition. | New York: Little, Brown and Company, 2021. | Series: Land of stories | Summary: When King Charming and his brothers set out to purge the Dwarf Forests of outlaws and rule it themselves, they must face the most feared outlaw, Goldilocks—and then, their wives.

Identifiers: LCCN 2020008478 | ISBN 9780316355933 (hardcover) | ISBN 9780316355957 (paperback) | ISBN 9780316355926 (ebook) | ISBN 9780316355971 (ebook other)

Subjects: CYAC: Kings, queens, rulers, etc.—Fiction. | Robbers and outlaws—Fiction. | Brothers—Fiction. | Characters in literature—Fiction.

Classification: LCC PZ7.C677474 Gol 2021 | DDC [Fic]—dc23

LC record available at https://lccn.loc.gov/2020008478

ISBNs: 978-0-316-35593-3 (hardcover), 978-0-316-35595-7 (pbk.),
978-0-316-35592-6 (ebook), 978-0-316-42706-7 (ebook), 978-0-316-42707-4 (ebook)

PRINTED IN CHINA

APS

Hardcover: 10 9 8 7 6 5 4 3 2 1

Paperback: 10 9 8 7 6 5 4 3 2 1

To Pam,
for being a hero to so many.
Thank you for helping
me fight my battles.

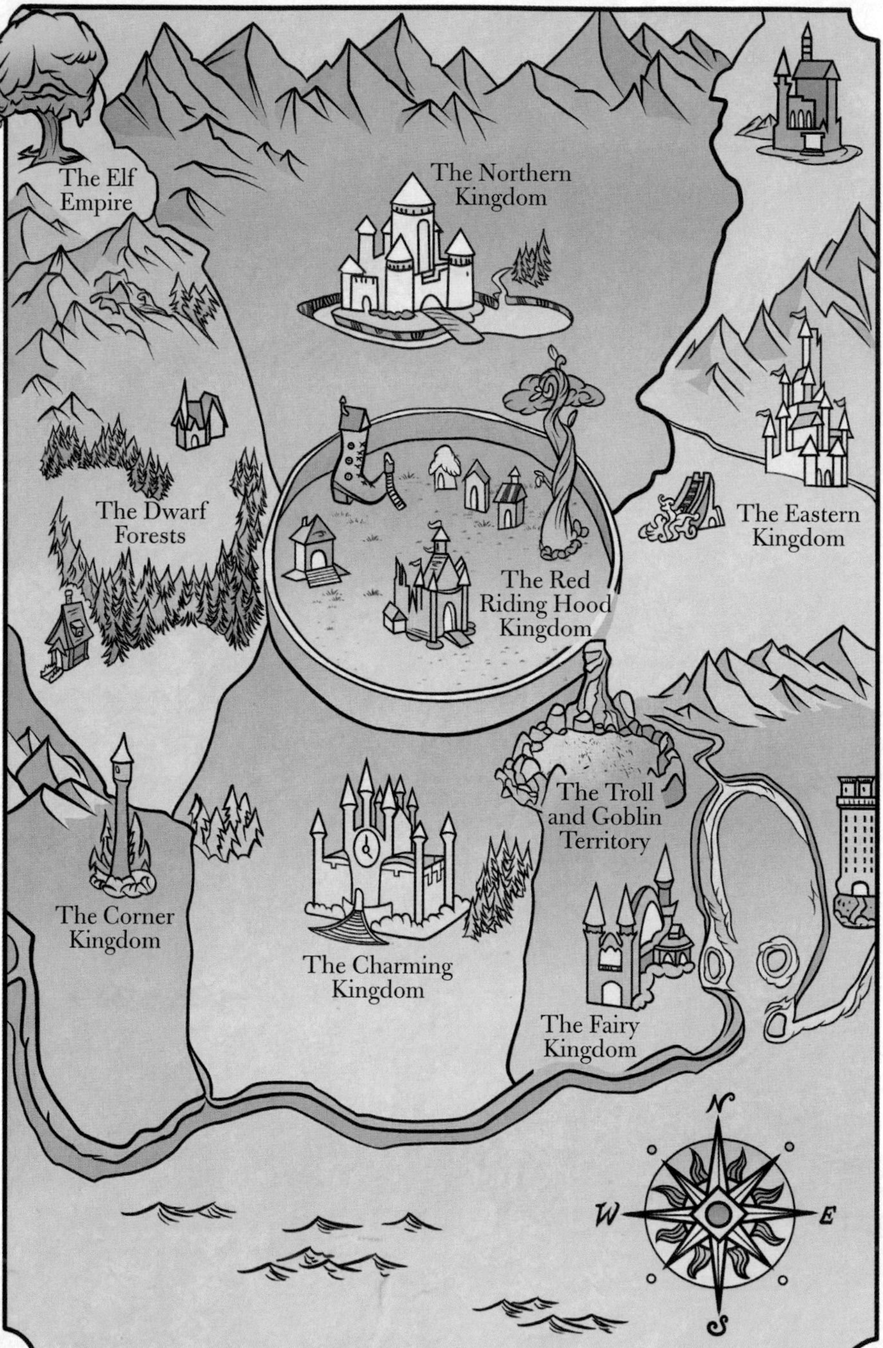

The Elf Empire
The Northern Kingdom
The Dwarf Forests
The Eastern Kingdom
The Red Riding Hood Kingdom
The Troll and Goblin Territory
The Corner Kingdom
The Charming Kingdom
The Fairy Kingdom
N
W
E
S

The kingdoms of the fairy-tale world are enjoying a much-needed period of peace. After the imprisonment of her evil stepmother, Snow White inherited her father's throne and was crowned queen of the Northern Kingdom. In the Eastern Kingdom, Queen Sleeping Beauty and her people have finally awoken from the terrible one-hundred-year sleeping curse. In the south, the Charming Kingdom has been in a constant state of celebration since King Chance Charming married his beloved consort, Queen Cinderella.

In the southwest, Queen Rapunzel established the Corner Kingdom after inheriting land from the witch who infamously imprisoned her in a tower. The Red Riding Hood Kingdom was founded by a large farming community that successfully separated from the Northern Kingdom. They elected Red Riding Hood as their queen, and her first royal act was naming the nation after herself.

The Fairy Godmother and her Fairy Council oversee the majestic Fairy Kingdom in the southeast. Together, the fairies and the kingdoms of man have created the Happily Ever After Assembly—a coalition that maintains peace and prosperity throughout the land.

While the humans and fairies are united in diplomacy, not all territories in the fairy-tale world have been invited to their union. After centuries of rambunctious behavior, the troll and goblin populations have been confined to the Troll and Goblin Territory deep underground in the east. The elves live in the secluded Elf Empire in the northwest. The majority of the west is occupied by the Dwarf Forests, where criminals are allowed to roam free from laws and convictions.

Despite the vast range of people and creatures living in the fairy-tale world, there is nothing threatening the harmony between borders in any way…

Yet.

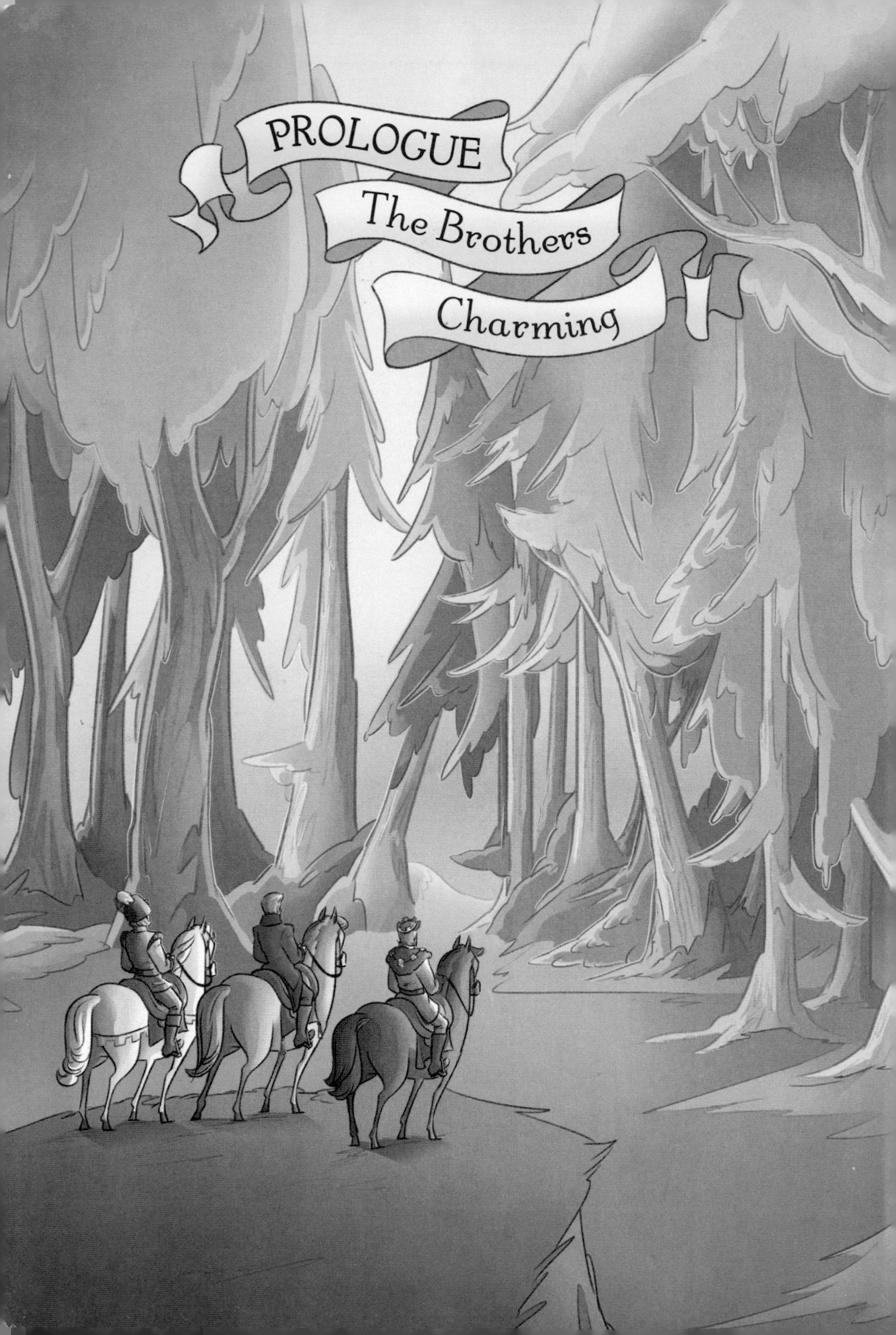
PROLOGUE
The Brothers
Charming

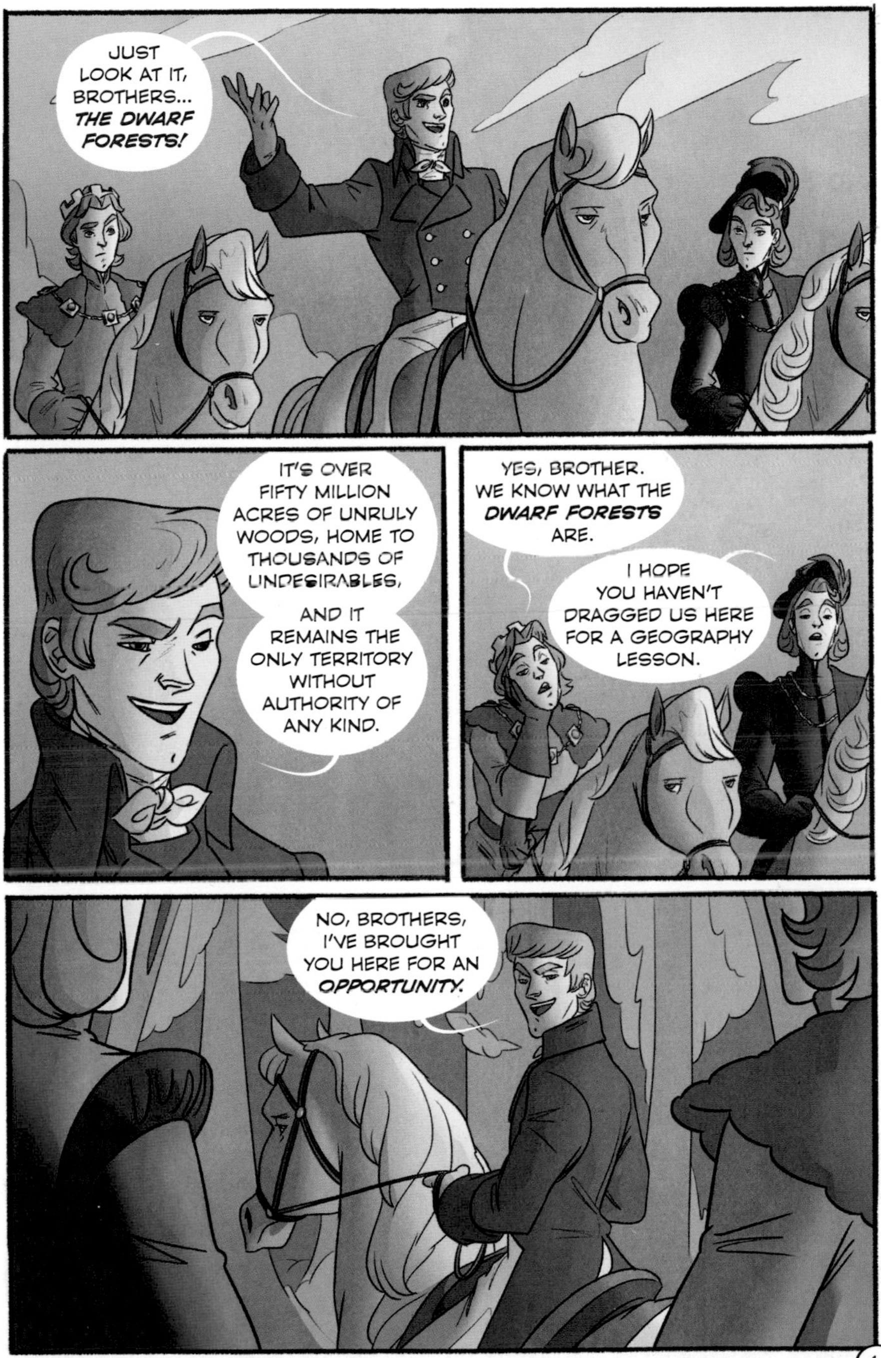
JUST LOOK AT IT, BROTHERS... THE DWARF FORESTS!
IT'S OVER FIFTY MILLION ACRES OF UNRULY WOODS, HOME TO THOUSANDS OF UNDESIRABLES,
AND IT REMAINS THE ONLY TERRITORY WITHOUT AUTHORITY OF ANY KIND.
YES, BROTHER. WE KNOW WHAT THE DWARF FORESTS ARE.
I HOPE YOU HAVEN'T DRAGGED US HERE FOR A GEOGRAPHY LESSON.
NO, BROTHERS, I'VE BROUGHT YOU HERE FOR AN OPPORTUNITY.

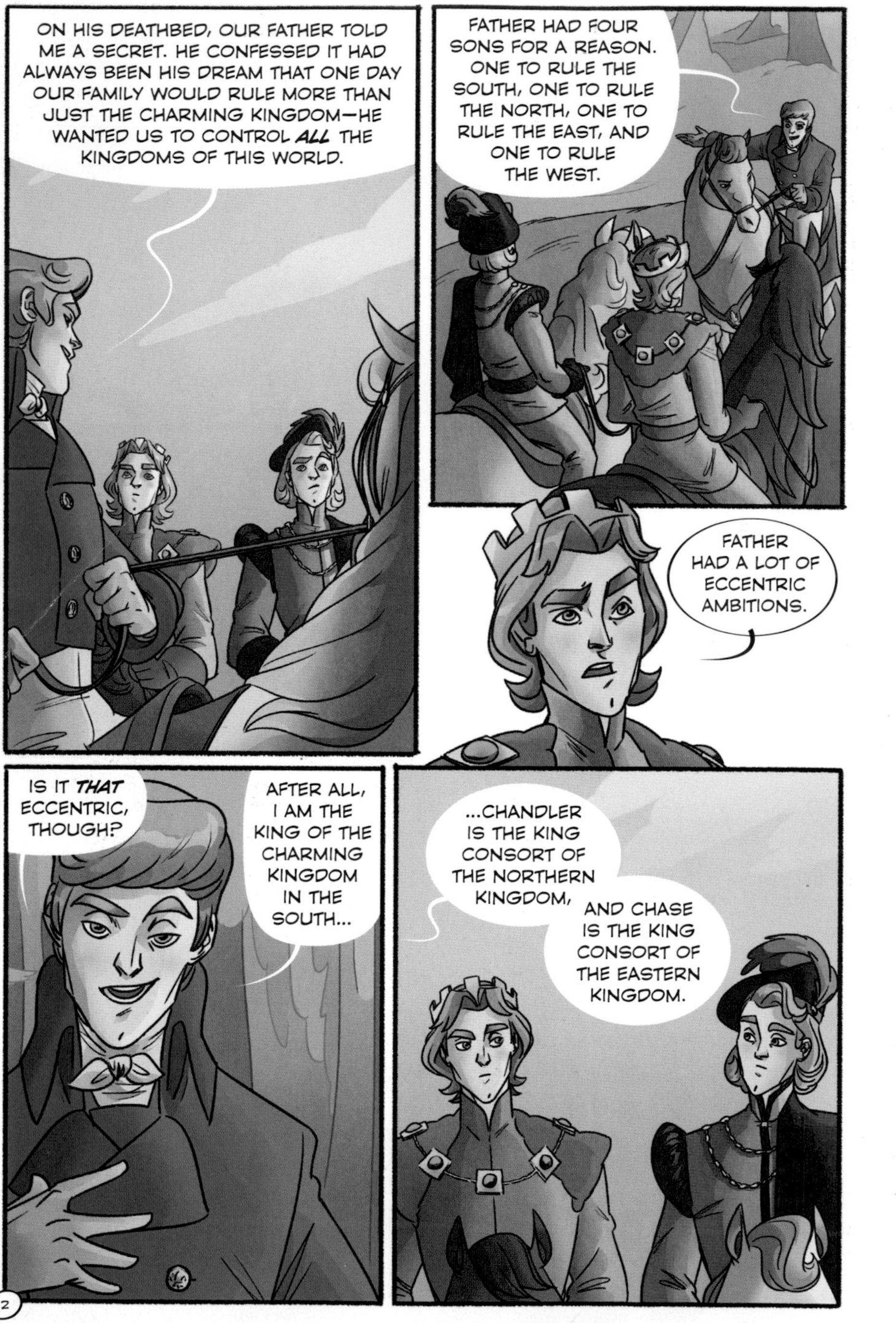

ON HIS DEATHBED, OUR FATHER TOLD ME A SECRET. HE CONFESSED IT HAD ALWAYS BEEN HIS DREAM THAT ONE DAY OUR FAMILY WOULD RULE MORE THAN JUST THE CHARMING KINGDOM—HE WANTED US TO CONTROL ***ALL*** THE KINGDOMS OF THIS WORLD.
FATHER HAD FOUR SONS FOR A REASON. ONE TO RULE THE SOUTH, ONE TO RULE THE NORTH, ONE TO RULE THE EAST, AND ONE TO RULE THE WEST.
FATHER HAD A LOT OF ECCENTRIC AMBITIONS.
IS IT ***THAT*** ECCENTRIC, THOUGH?
AFTER ALL, I AM THE KING OF THE CHARMING KINGDOM IN THE SOUTH...
...CHANDLER IS THE KING CONSORT OF THE NORTHERN KINGDOM,
AND CHASE IS THE KING CONSORT OF THE EASTERN KINGDOM.

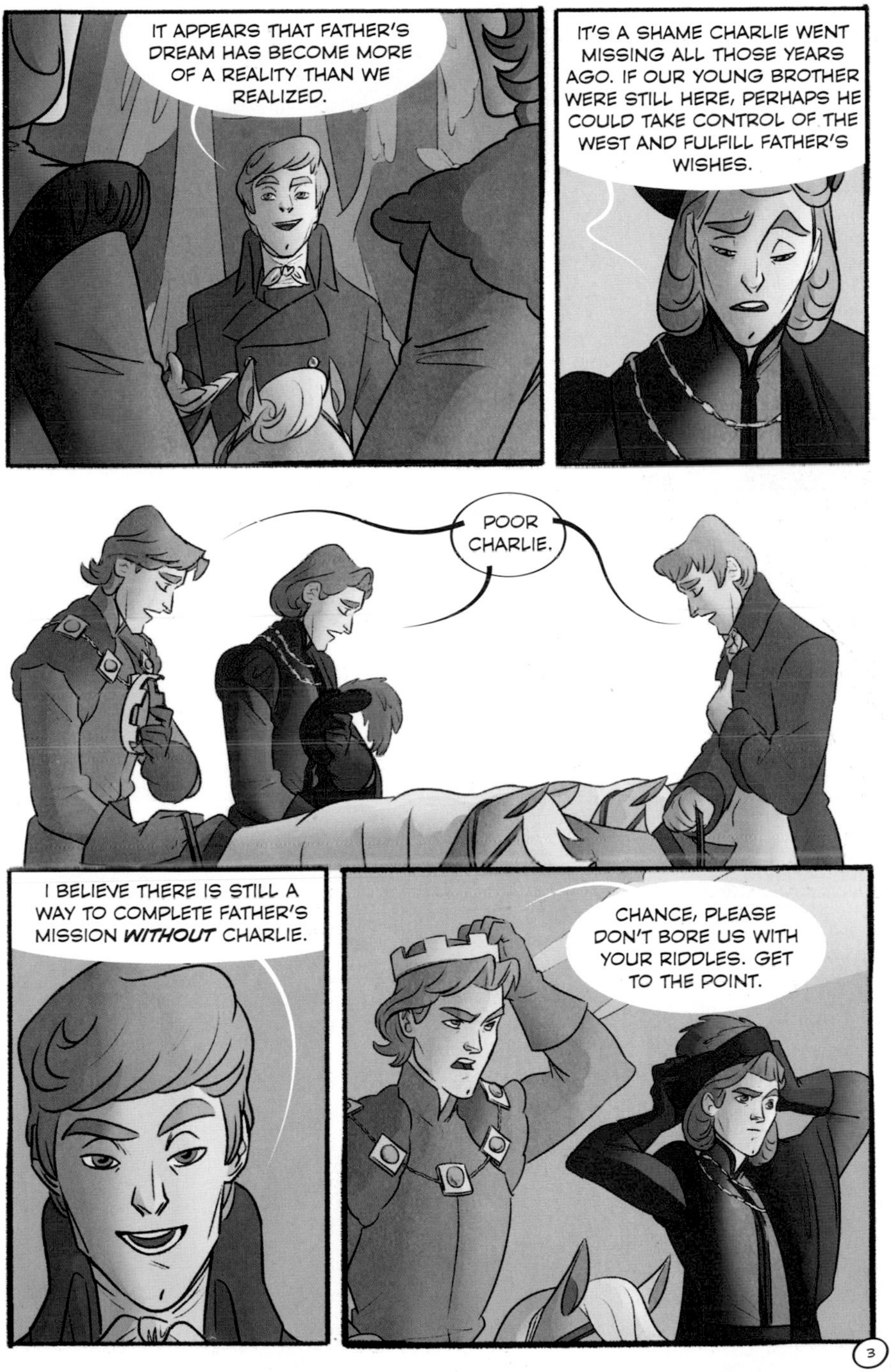

IT APPEARS THAT FATHER'S DREAM HAS BECOME MORE OF A REALITY THAN WE REALIZED.
IT'S A SHAME CHARLIE WENT MISSING ALL THOSE YEARS AGO. IF OUR YOUNG BROTHER WERE STILL HERE, PERHAPS HE COULD TAKE CONTROL OF THE WEST AND FULFILL FATHER'S WISHES.
POOR CHARLIE.
I BELIEVE THERE IS STILL A WAY TO COMPLETE FATHER'S MISSION ***WITHOUT*** CHARLIE.
CHANCE, PLEASE DON'T BORE US WITH YOUR RIDDLES. GET TO THE POINT.

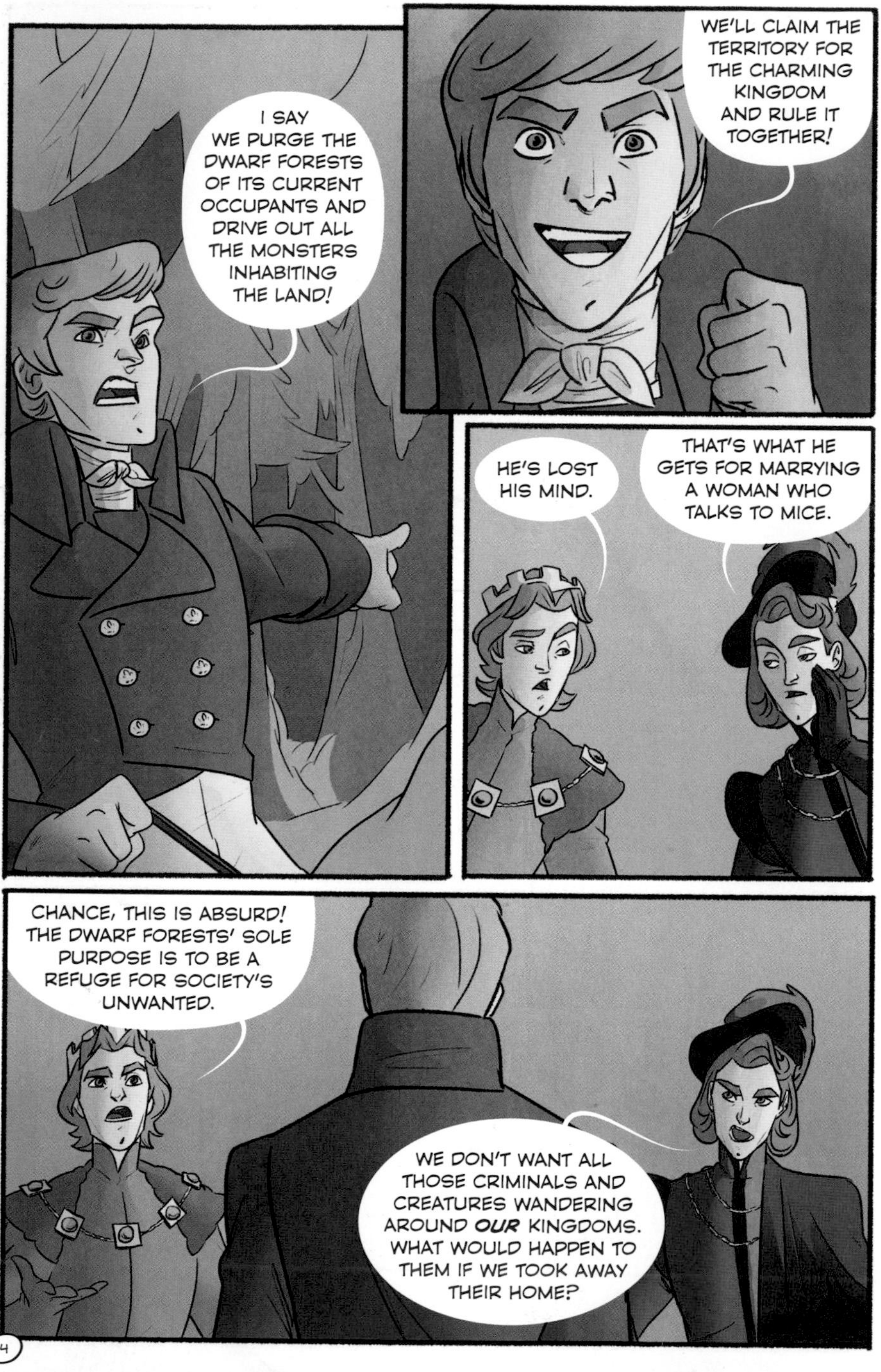
I SAY WE PURGE THE DWARF FORESTS OF ITS CURRENT OCCUPANTS AND DRIVE OUT ALL THE MONSTERS INHABITING THE LAND!
WE'LL CLAIM THE TERRITORY FOR THE CHARMING KINGDOM AND RULE IT TOGETHER!
HE'S LOST HIS MIND.
THAT'S WHAT HE GETS FOR MARRYING A WOMAN WHO TALKS TO MICE.
CHANCE, THIS IS ABSURD! THE DWARF FORESTS' SOLE PURPOSE IS TO BE A REFUGE FOR SOCIETY'S UNWANTED.
WE DON'T WANT ALL THOSE CRIMINALS AND CREATURES WANDERING AROUND *OUR* KINGDOMS. WHAT WOULD HAPPEN TO THEM IF WE TOOK AWAY THEIR HOME?

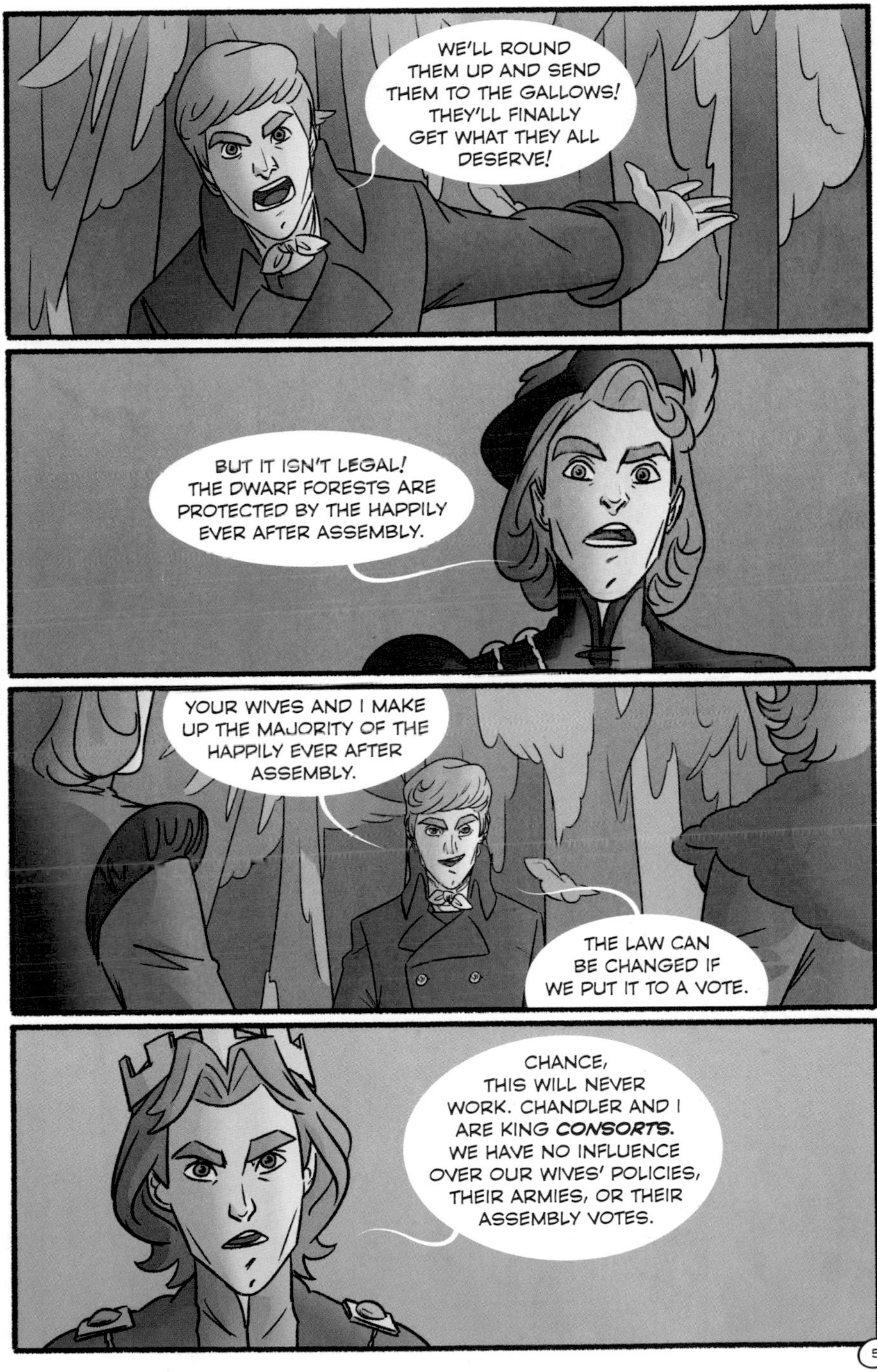
WE'LL ROUND THEM UP AND SEND THEM TO THE GALLOWS! THEY'LL FINALLY GET WHAT THEY ALL DESERVE!
BUT IT ISN'T LEGAL! THE DWARF FORESTS ARE PROTECTED BY THE HAPPILY EVER AFTER ASSEMBLY.
YOUR WIVES AND I MAKE UP THE MAJORITY OF THE HAPPILY EVER AFTER ASSEMBLY.
THE LAW CAN BE CHANGED IF WE PUT IT TO A VOTE.
CHANCE, THIS WILL NEVER WORK. CHANDLER AND I ARE KING ***CONSORTS.*** WE HAVE NO INFLUENCE OVER OUR WIVES' POLICIES, THEIR ARMIES, OR THEIR ASSEMBLY VOTES.

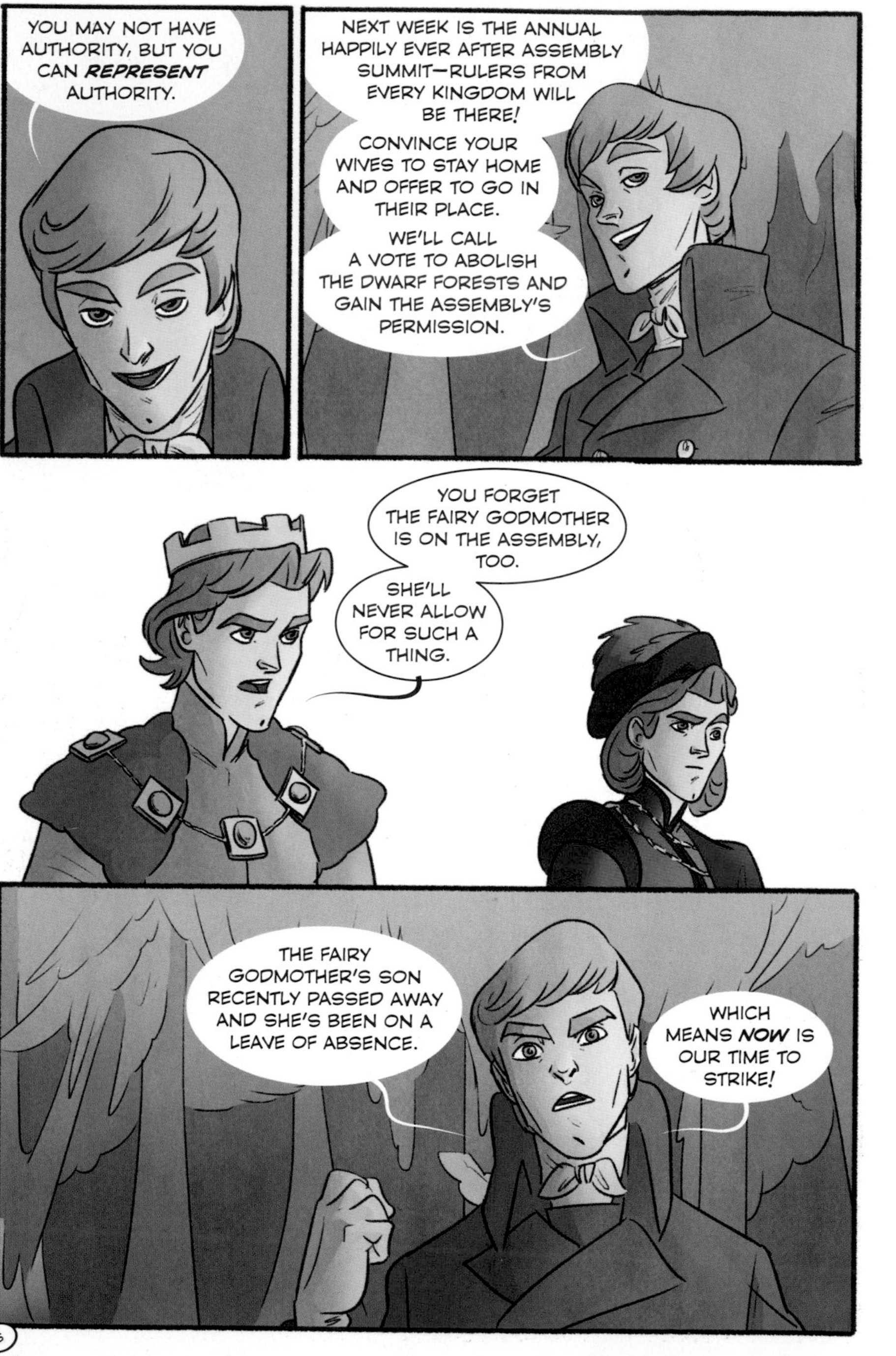
YOU MAY NOT HAVE AUTHORITY, BUT YOU CAN *REPRESENT* AUTHORITY.
NEXT WEEK IS THE ANNUAL HAPPILY EVER AFTER ASSEMBLY SUMMIT—RULERS FROM EVERY KINGDOM WILL BE THERE!
CONVINCE YOUR WIVES TO STAY HOME AND OFFER TO GO IN THEIR PLACE.
WE'LL CALL A VOTE TO ABOLISH THE DWARF FORESTS AND GAIN THE ASSEMBLY'S PERMISSION.
YOU FORGET THE FAIRY GODMOTHER IS ON THE ASSEMBLY, TOO.
SHE'LL NEVER ALLOW FOR SUCH A THING.
THE FAIRY GODMOTHER'S SON RECENTLY PASSED AWAY AND SHE'S BEEN ON A LEAVE OF ABSENCE.
WHICH MEANS *NOW* IS OUR TIME TO STRIKE!

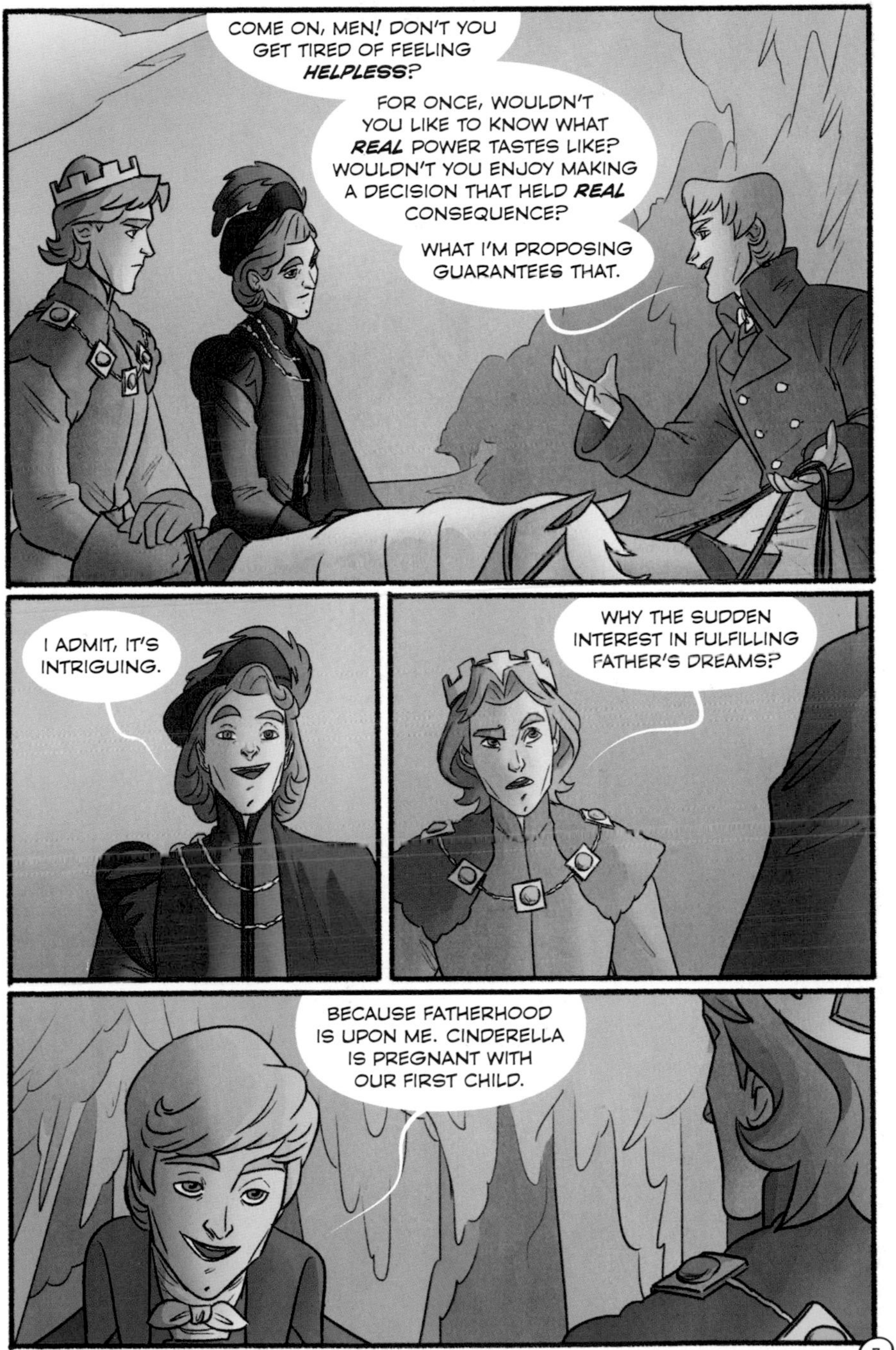
COME ON, MEN! DON'T YOU GET TIRED OF FEELING *HELPLESS*?
FOR ONCE, WOULDN'T YOU LIKE TO KNOW WHAT *REAL* POWER TASTES LIKE? WOULDN'T YOU ENJOY MAKING A DECISION THAT HELD *REAL* CONSEQUENCE?
WHAT I'M PROPOSING GUARANTEES THAT.
I ADMIT, IT'S INTRIGUING.
WHY THE SUDDEN INTEREST IN FULFILLING FATHER'S DREAMS?
BECAUSE FATHERHOOD IS UPON ME. CINDERELLA IS PREGNANT WITH OUR FIRST CHILD.

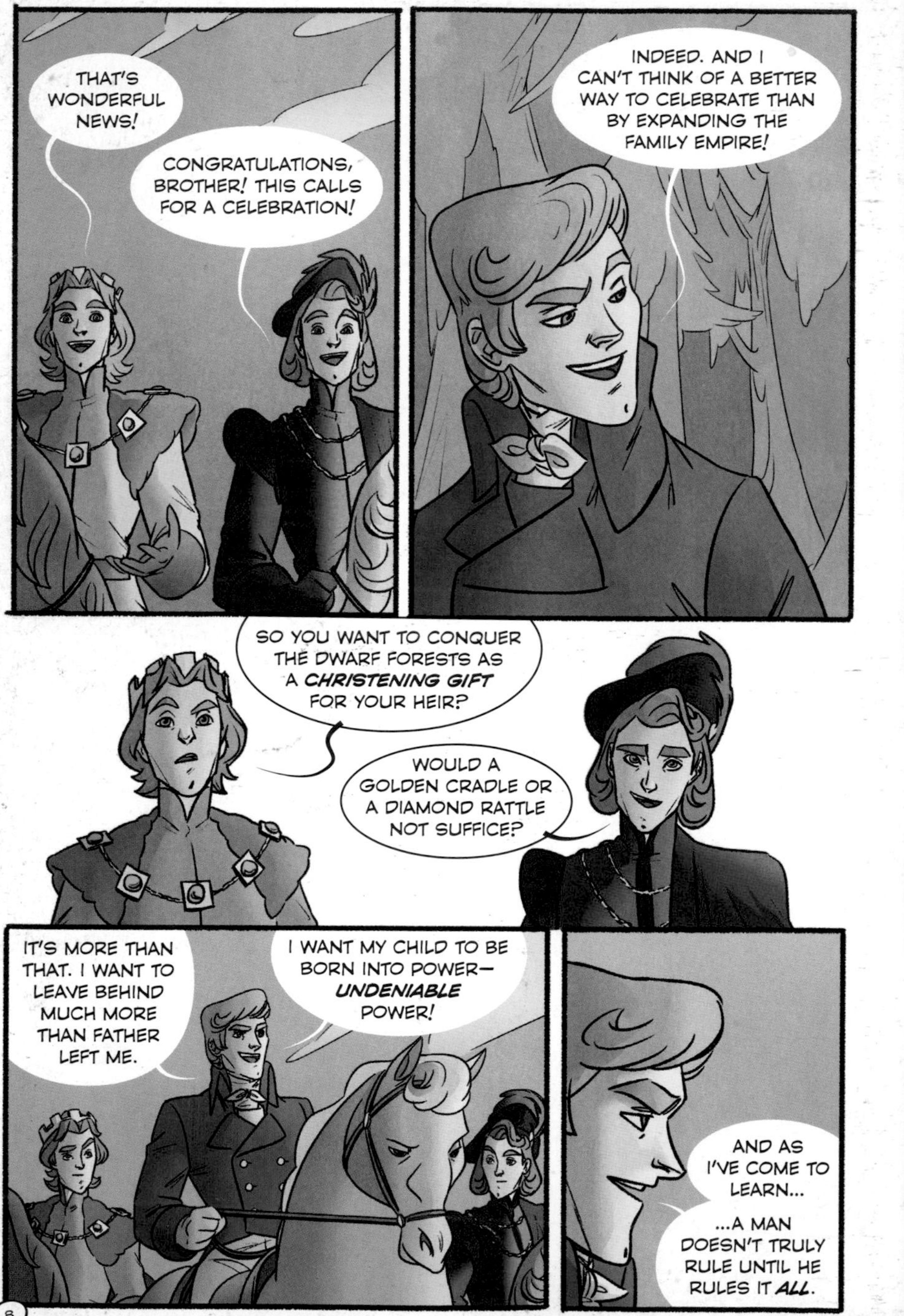
THAT'S WONDERFUL NEWS!
CONGRATULATIONS, BROTHER! THIS CALLS FOR A CELEBRATION!
INDEED. AND I CAN'T THINK OF A BETTER WAY TO CELEBRATE THAN BY EXPANDING THE FAMILY EMPIRE!
SO YOU WANT TO CONQUER THE DWARF FORESTS AS A *CHRISTENING GIFT* FOR YOUR HEIR?
WOULD A GOLDEN CRADLE OR A DIAMOND RATTLE NOT SUFFICE?
IT'S MORE THAN THAT. I WANT TO LEAVE BEHIND MUCH MORE THAN FATHER LEFT ME.
I WANT MY CHILD TO BE BORN INTO POWER— *UNDENIABLE* POWER!
AND AS I'VE COME TO LEARN...
...A MAN DOESN'T TRULY RULE UNTIL HE RULES IT *ALL*.

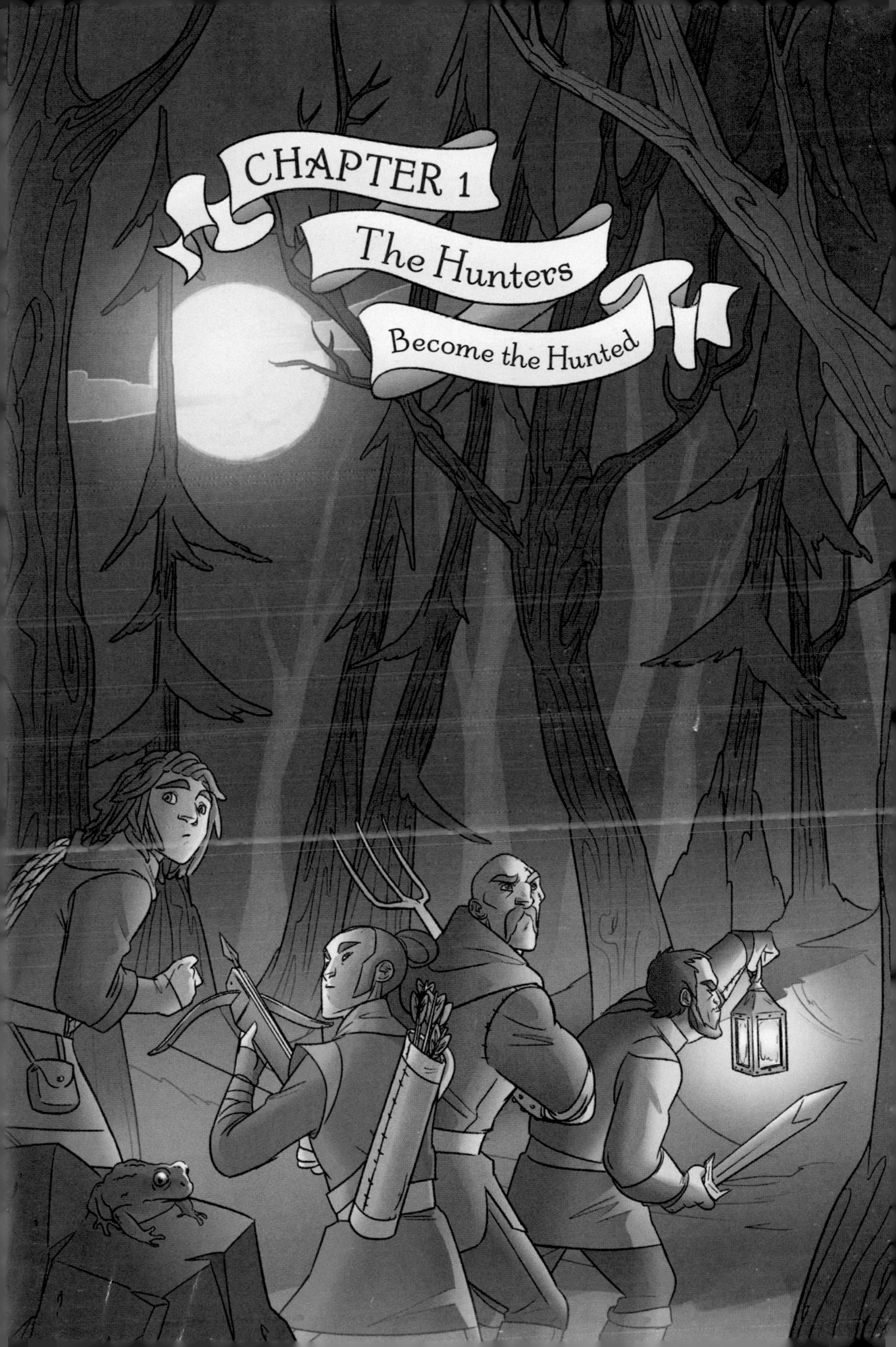
CHAPTER 1
The Hunters
Become the Hunted

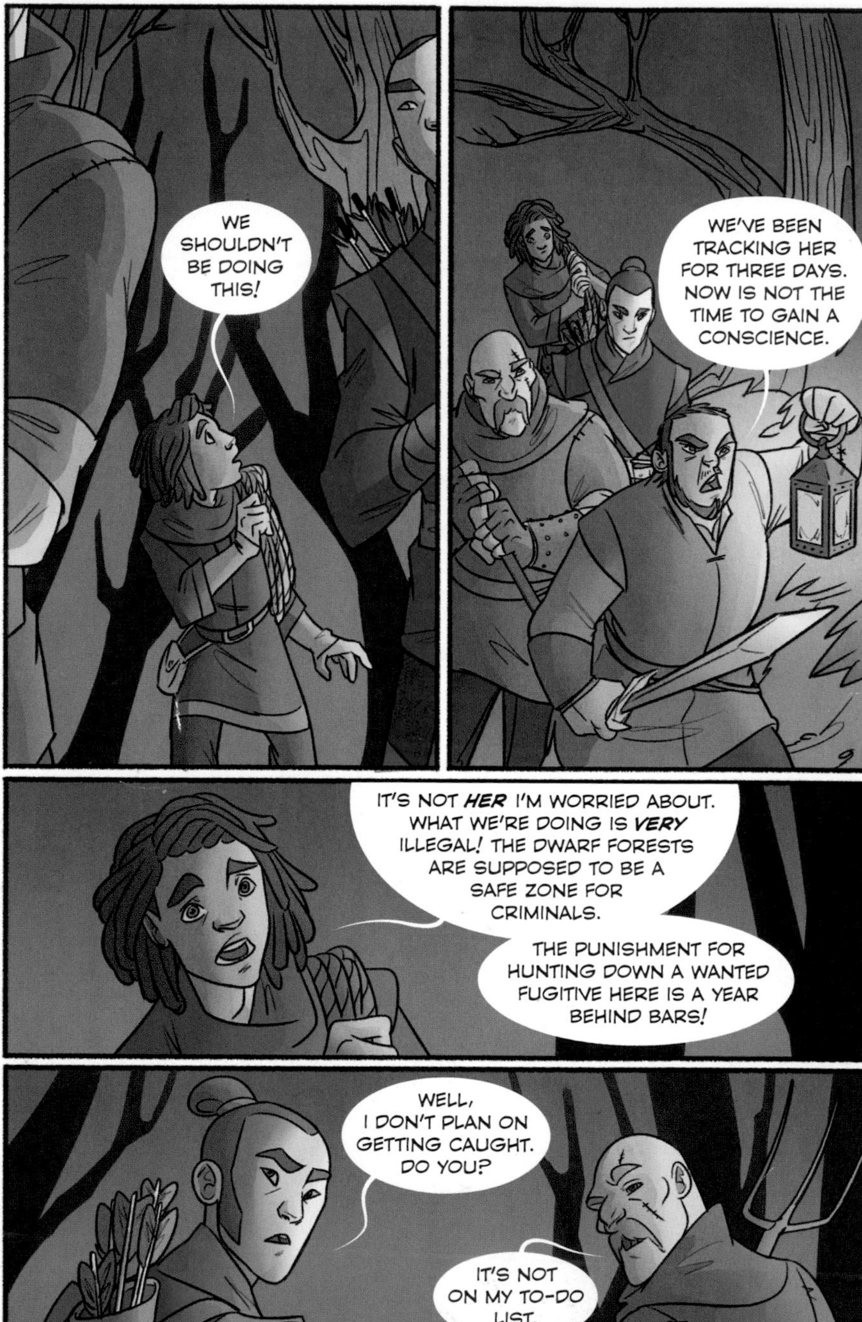
WE SHOULDN'T BE DOING THIS!
WE'VE BEEN TRACKING HER FOR THREE DAYS. NOW IS NOT THE TIME TO GAIN A CONSCIENCE.
IT'S NOT HER I'M WORRIED ABOUT. WHAT WE'RE DOING IS VERY ILLEGAL! THE DWARF FORESTS ARE SUPPOSED TO BE A SAFE ZONE FOR CRIMINALS.
THE PUNISHMENT FOR HUNTING DOWN A WANTED FUGITIVE HERE IS A YEAR BEHIND BARS!
WELL, I DON'T PLAN ON GETTING CAUGHT. DO YOU?
IT'S NOT ON MY TO-DO LIST.

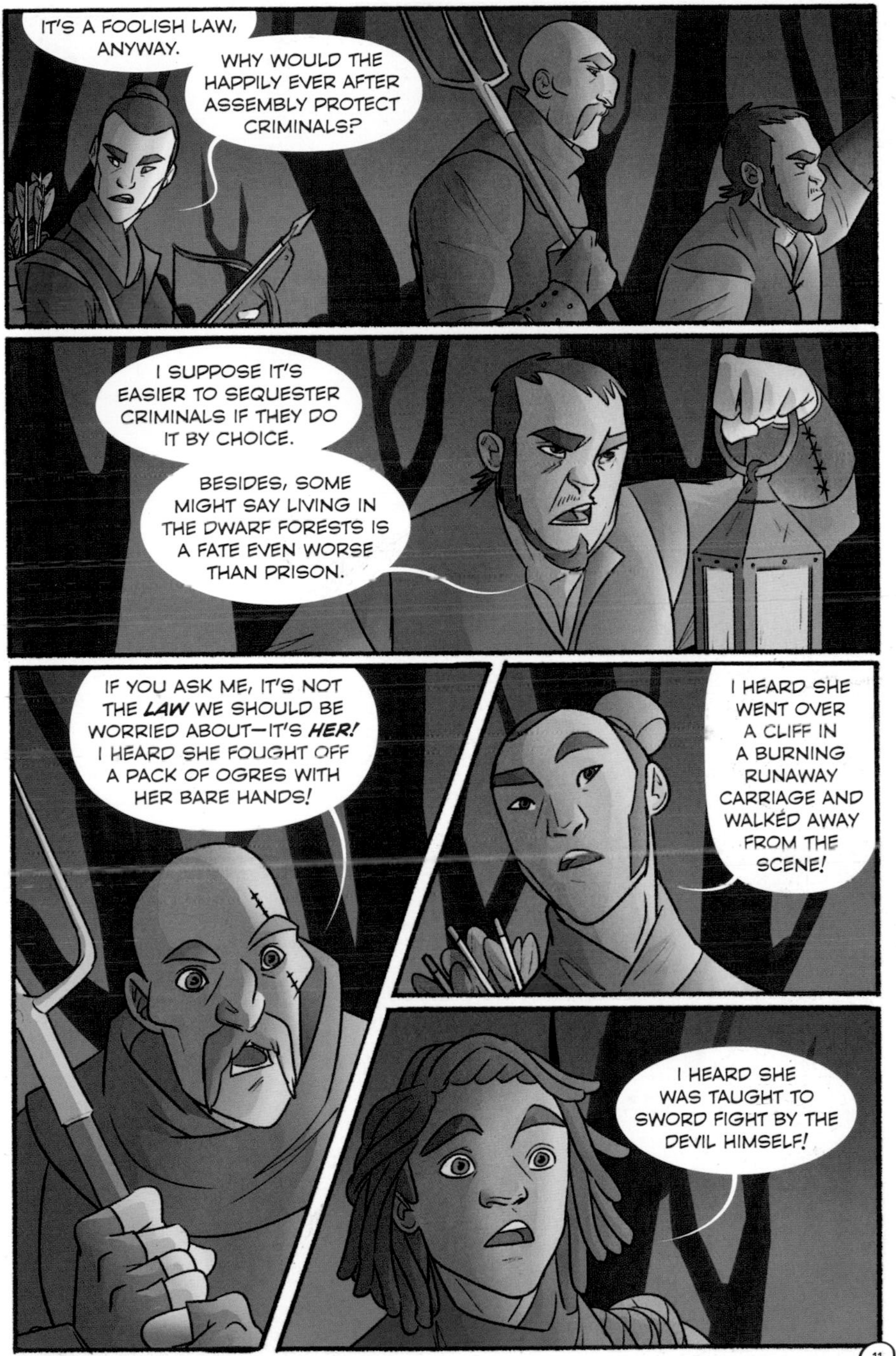
IT'S A FOOLISH LAW, ANYWAY.
WHY WOULD THE HAPPILY EVER AFTER ASSEMBLY PROTECT CRIMINALS?
I SUPPOSE IT'S EASIER TO SEQUESTER CRIMINALS IF THEY DO IT BY CHOICE.
BESIDES, SOME MIGHT SAY LIVING IN THE DWARF FORESTS IS A FATE EVEN WORSE THAN PRISON.
IF YOU ASK ME, IT'S NOT THE *LAW* WE SHOULD BE WORRIED ABOUT—IT'S ***HER!*** I HEARD SHE FOUGHT OFF A PACK OF OGRES WITH HER BARE HANDS!
I HEARD SHE WENT OVER A CLIFF IN A BURNING RUNAWAY CARRIAGE AND WALKED AWAY FROM THE SCENE!
I HEARD SHE WAS TAUGHT TO SWORD FIGHT BY THE DEVIL HIMSELF!

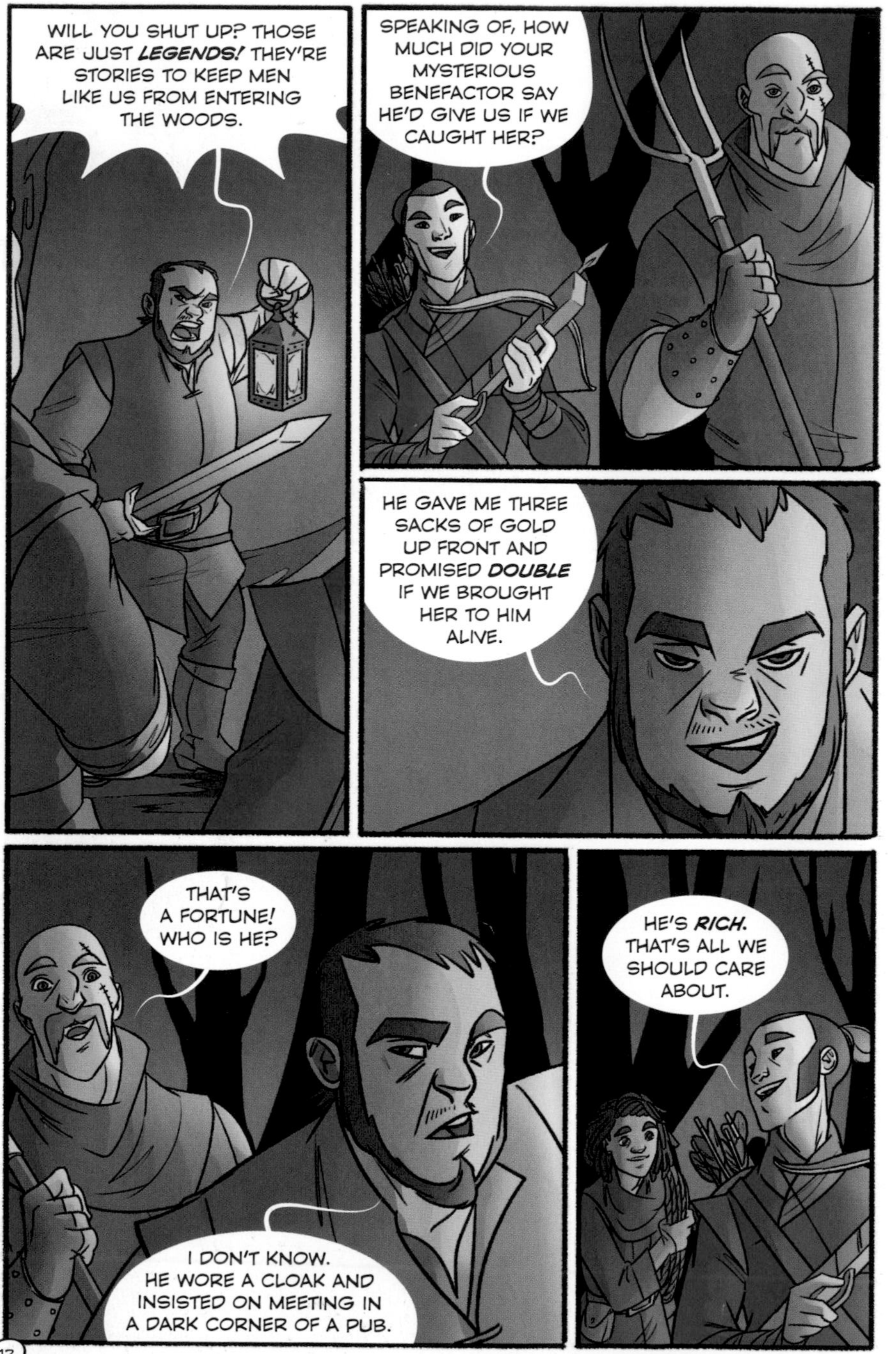
WILL YOU SHUT UP? THOSE ARE JUST *LEGENDS!* THEY'RE STORIES TO KEEP MEN LIKE US FROM ENTERING THE WOODS.
SPEAKING OF, HOW MUCH DID YOUR MYSTERIOUS BENEFACTOR SAY HE'D GIVE US IF WE CAUGHT HER?
HE GAVE ME THREE SACKS OF GOLD UP FRONT AND PROMISED *DOUBLE* IF WE BROUGHT HER TO HIM ALIVE.
THAT'S A FORTUNE! WHO IS HE?
I DON'T KNOW. HE WORE A CLOAK AND INSISTED ON MEETING IN A DARK CORNER OF A PUB.
HE'S *RICH.* THAT'S ALL WE SHOULD CARE ABOUT.

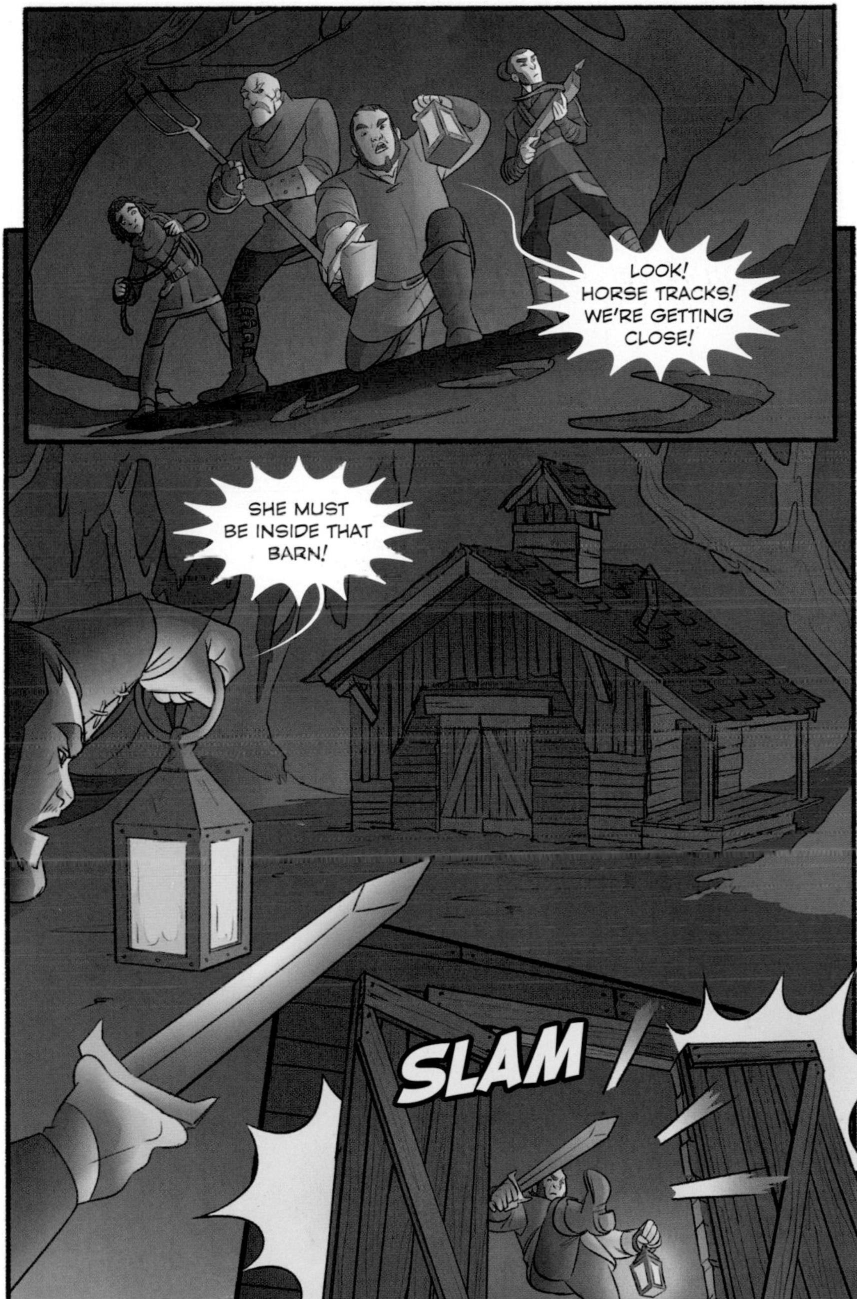
LOOK! HORSE TRACKS! WE'RE GETTING CLOSE!
SHE MUST BE INSIDE THAT BARN!
SLAM

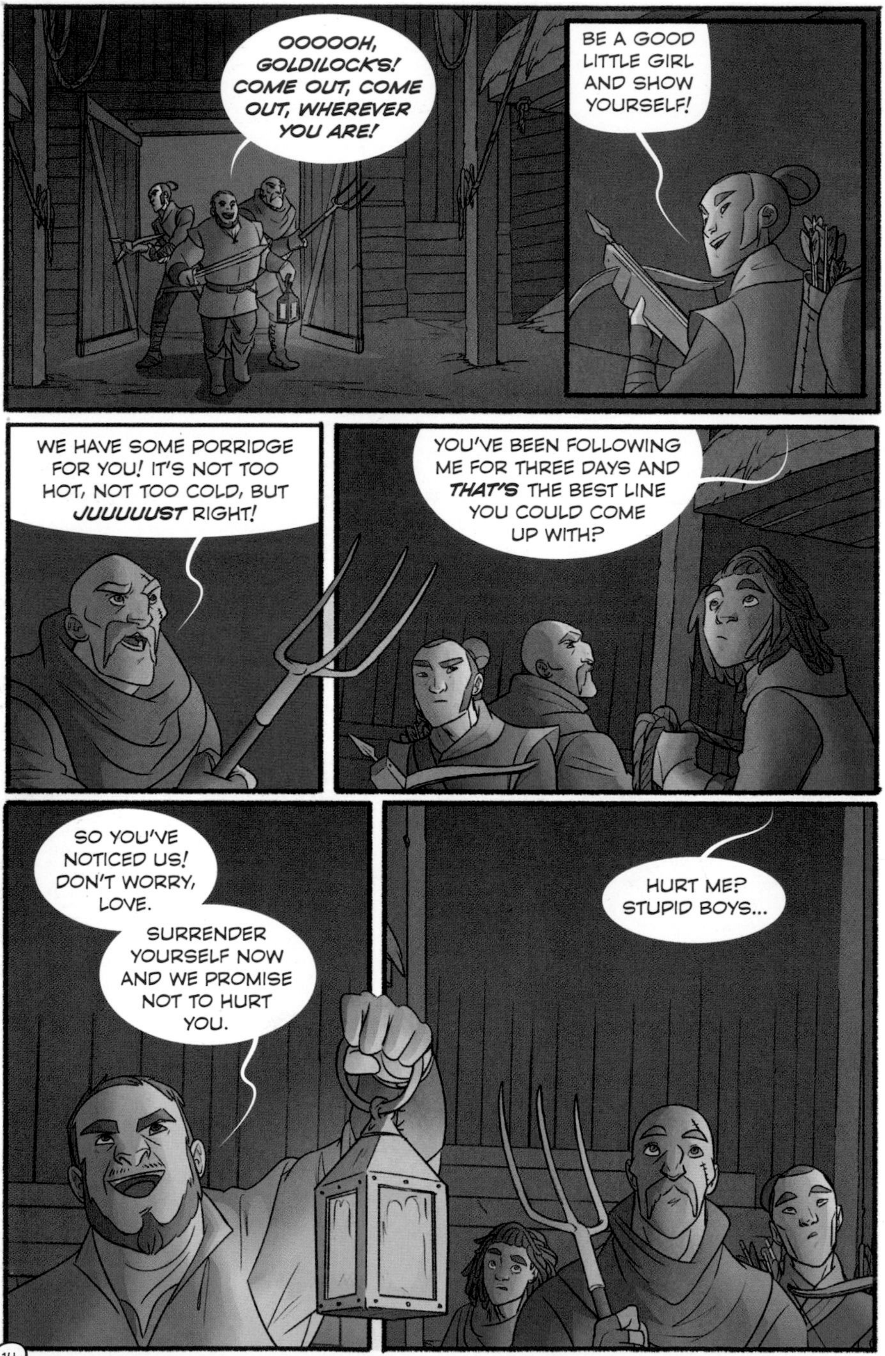
OOOOOOH, GOLDILOCKS! COME OUT, COME OUT, WHEREVER YOU ARE!
BE A GOOD LITTLE GIRL AND SHOW YOURSELF!
WE HAVE SOME PORRIDGE FOR YOU! IT'S NOT TOO HOT, NOT TOO COLD, BUT *JUUUUUST* RIGHT!
YOU'VE BEEN FOLLOWING ME FOR THREE DAYS AND *THAT'S* THE BEST LINE YOU COULD COME UP WITH?
SO YOU'VE NOTICED US! DON'T WORRY, LOVE.
SURRENDER YOURSELF NOW AND WE PROMISE NOT TO HURT YOU.
HURT ME? STUPID BOYS...

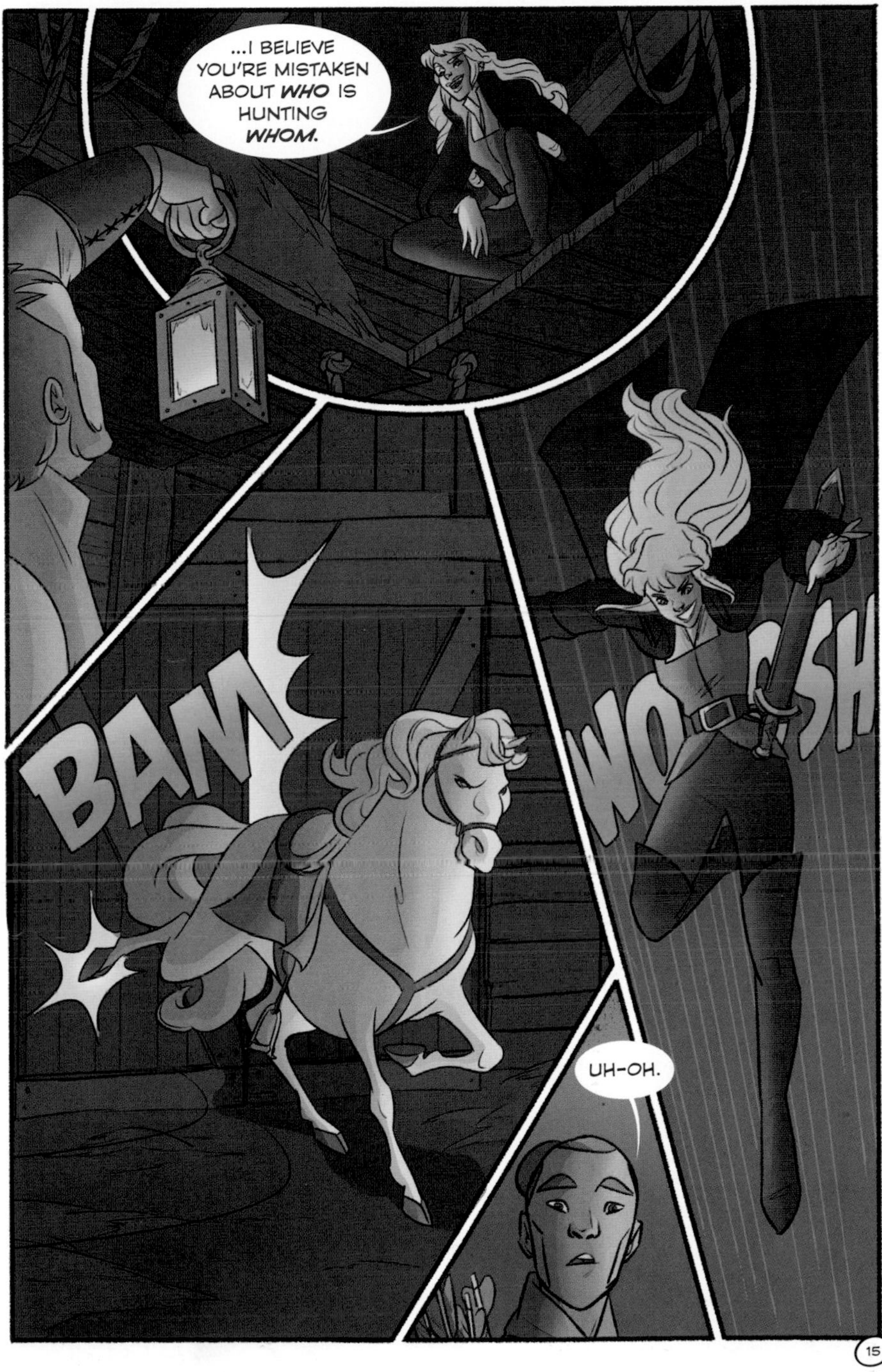
...I BELIEVE YOU'RE MISTAKEN ABOUT *WHO* IS HUNTING *WHOM*.
BAM
UH-OH.

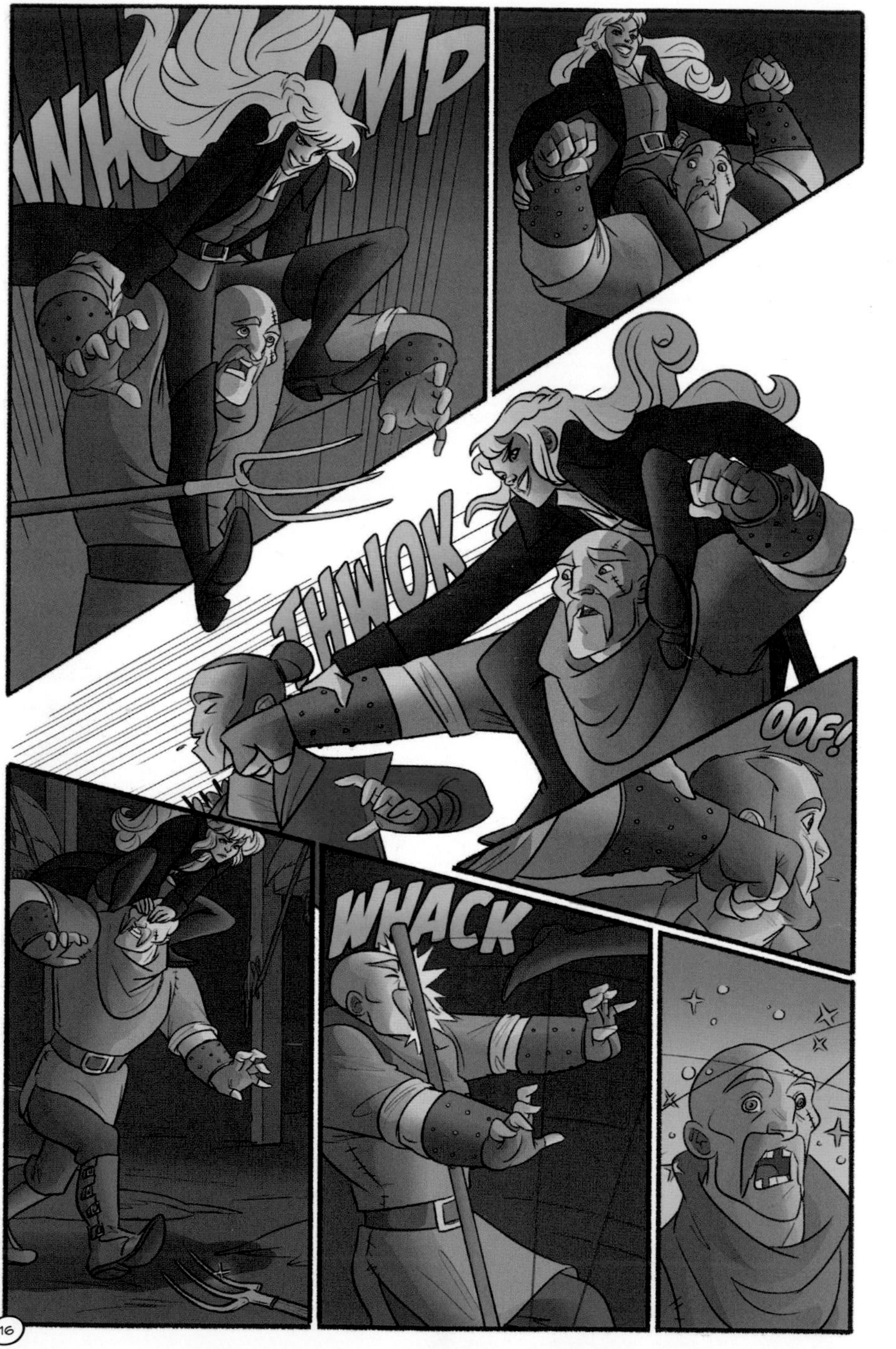
WHOOMP
THWOK
OOF!
WHACK

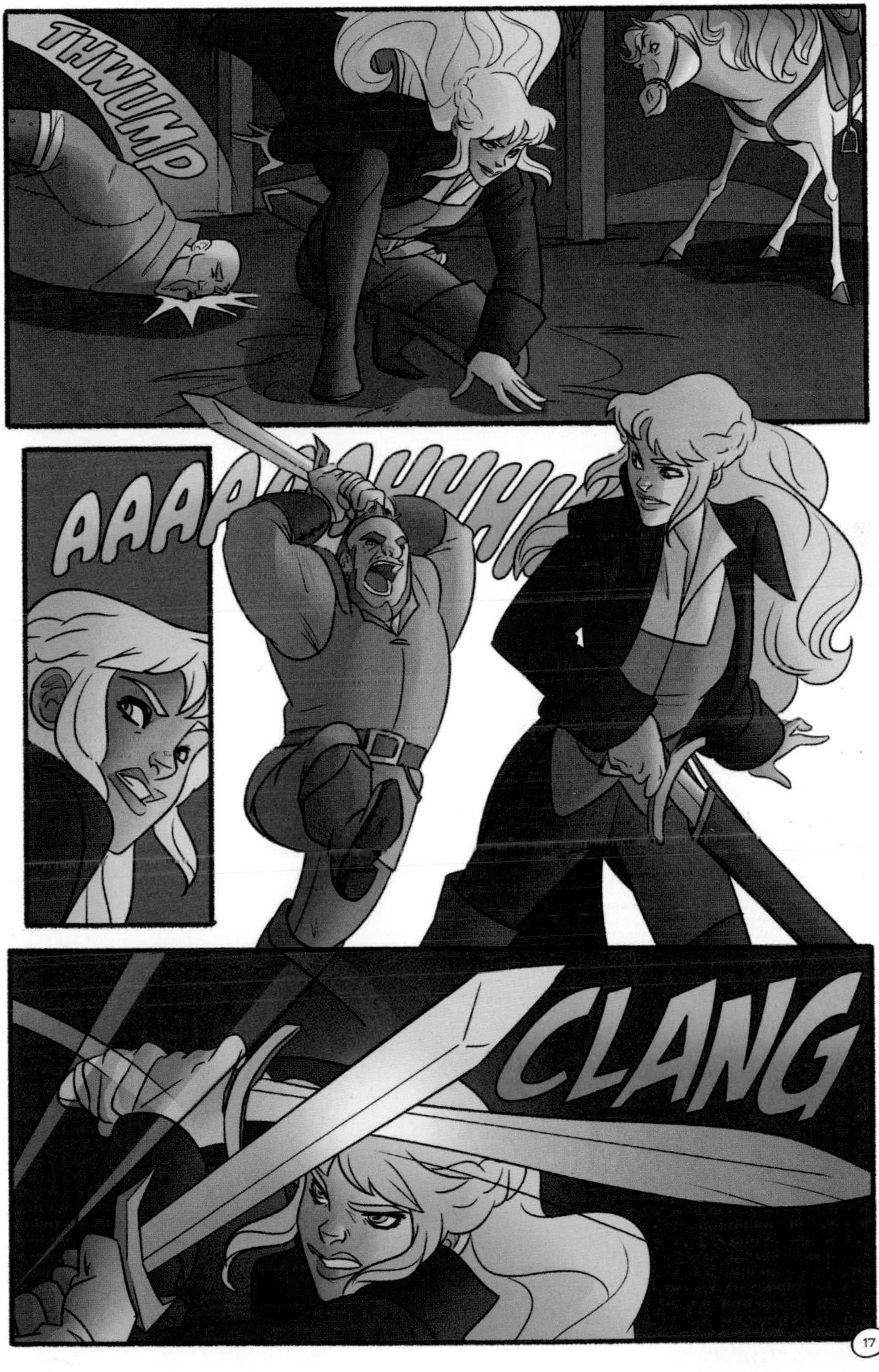
THWUMP
AAAAHHHH
CLANG

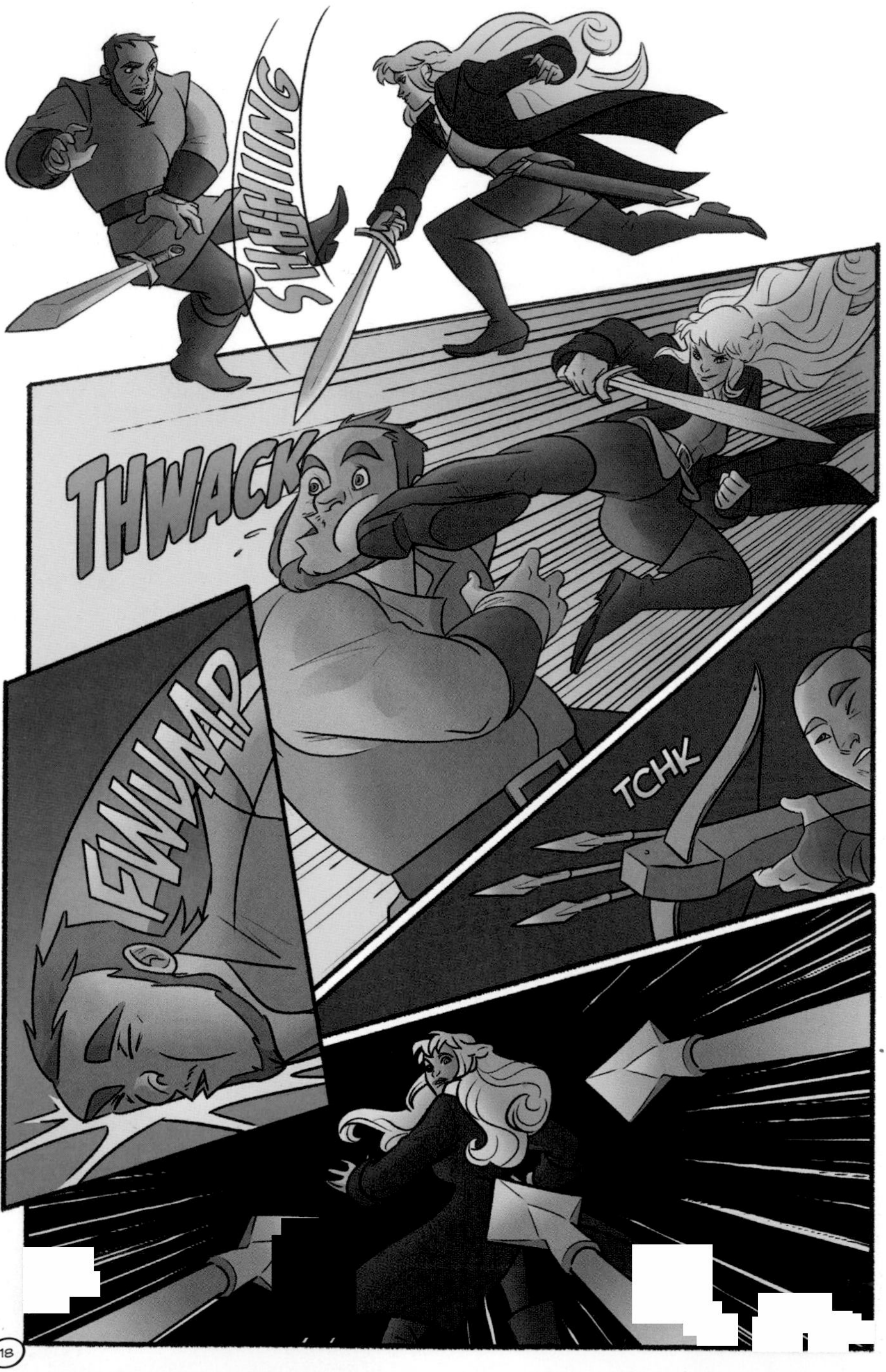
SHHIING
THWACK
TCHK
FWUMP

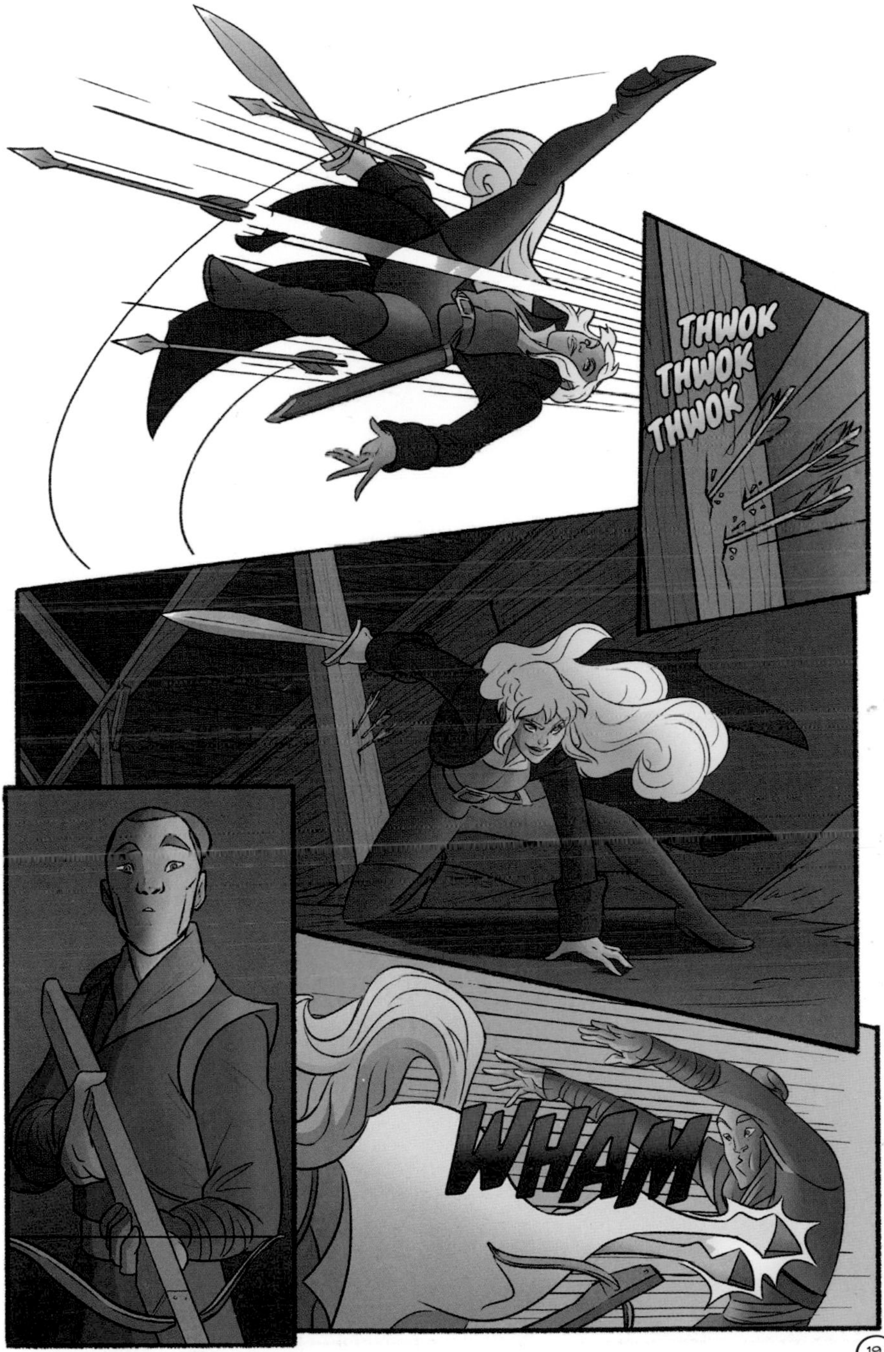
THWOK
THWOK
THWOK
WHAM

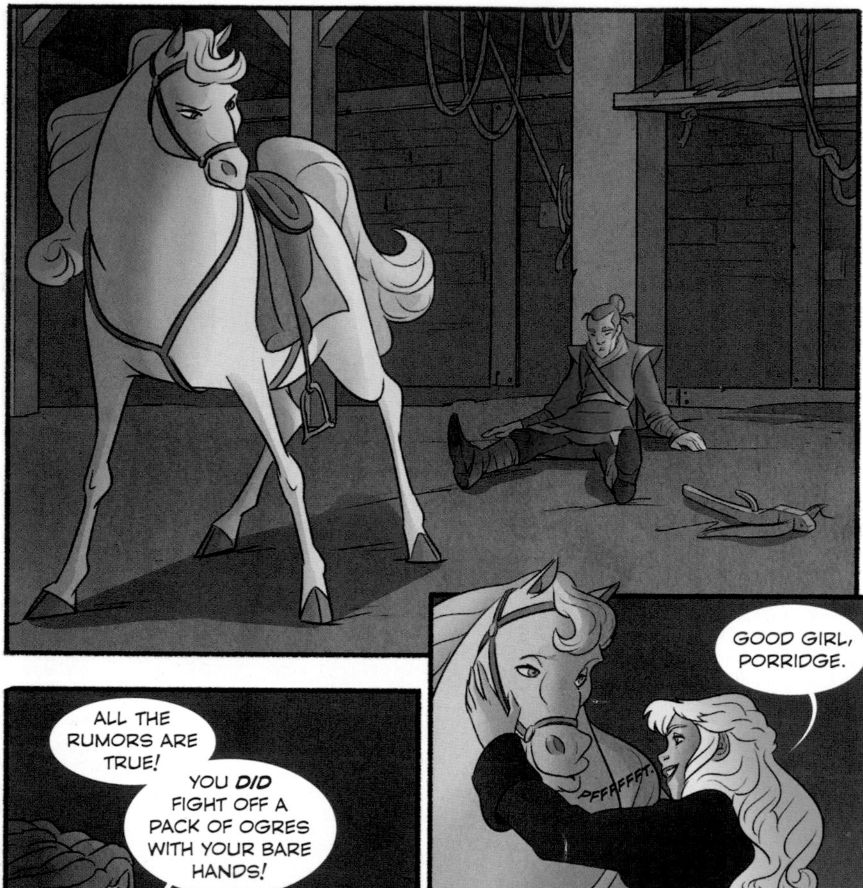
GOOD GIRL, PORRIDGE.
PFFFFFFT.
ALL THE RUMORS ARE TRUE!
YOU **DID** FIGHT OFF A PACK OF OGRES WITH YOUR BARE HANDS!
YES.
YOU REALLY WENT OVER A CLIFF IN A BURNING CARRIAGE!
YES.

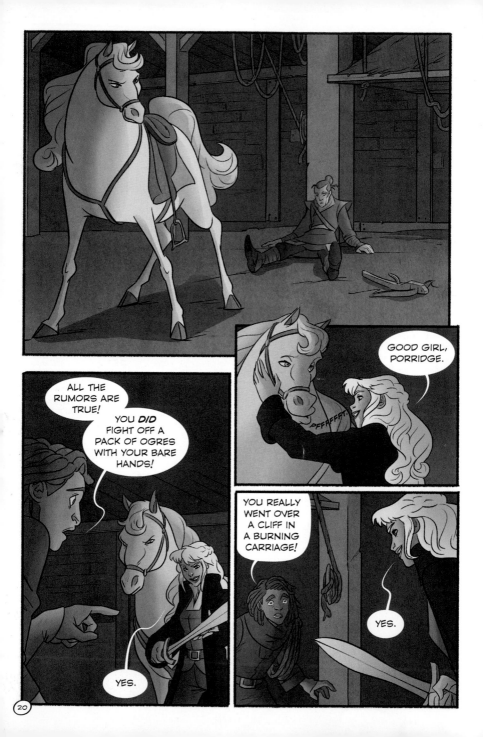

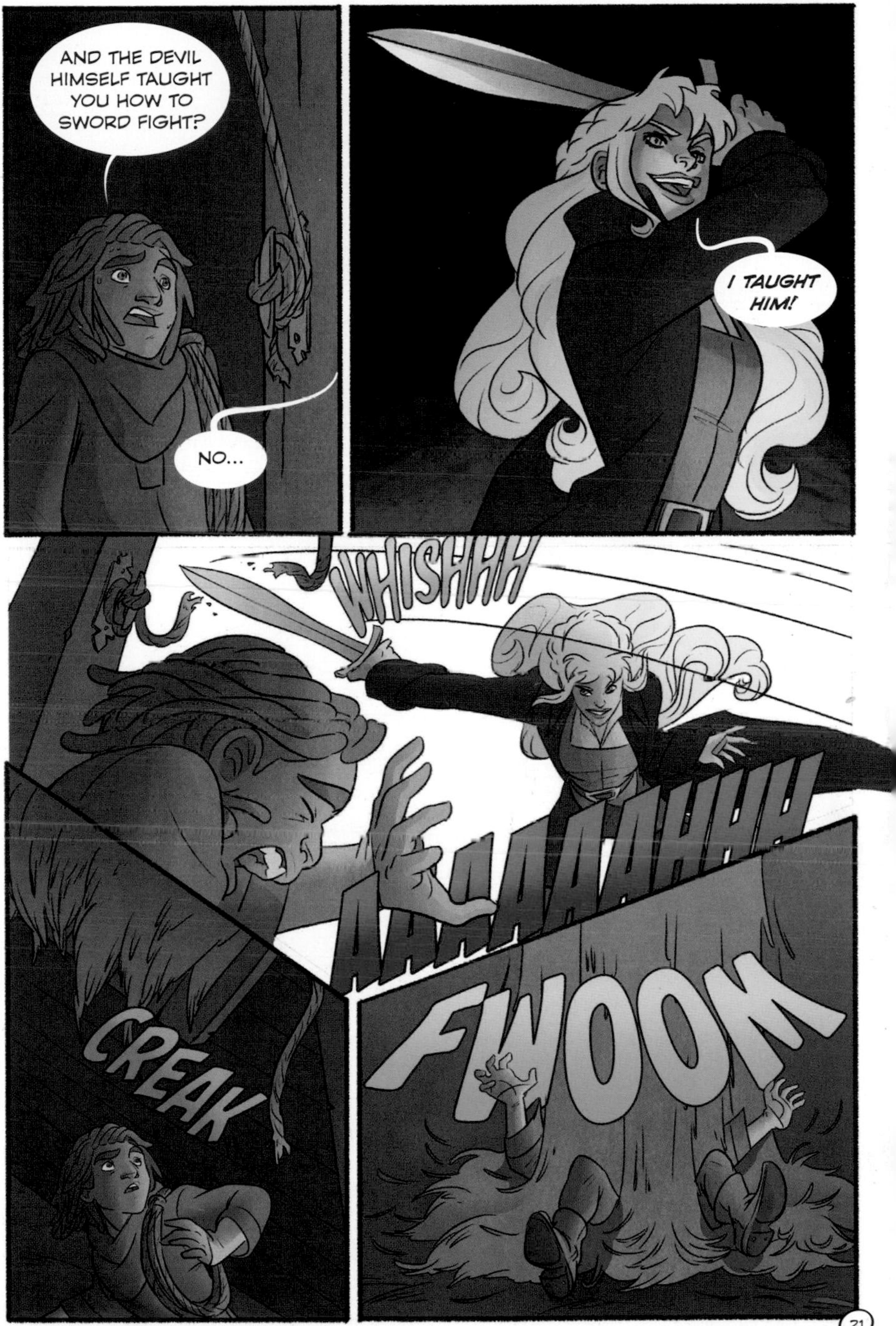
AND THE DEVIL HIMSELF TAUGHT YOU HOW TO SWORD FIGHT?
NO...
I TAUGHT HIM!
WHISHHH
AAAAAAHHHH
CREAK
FWOOM

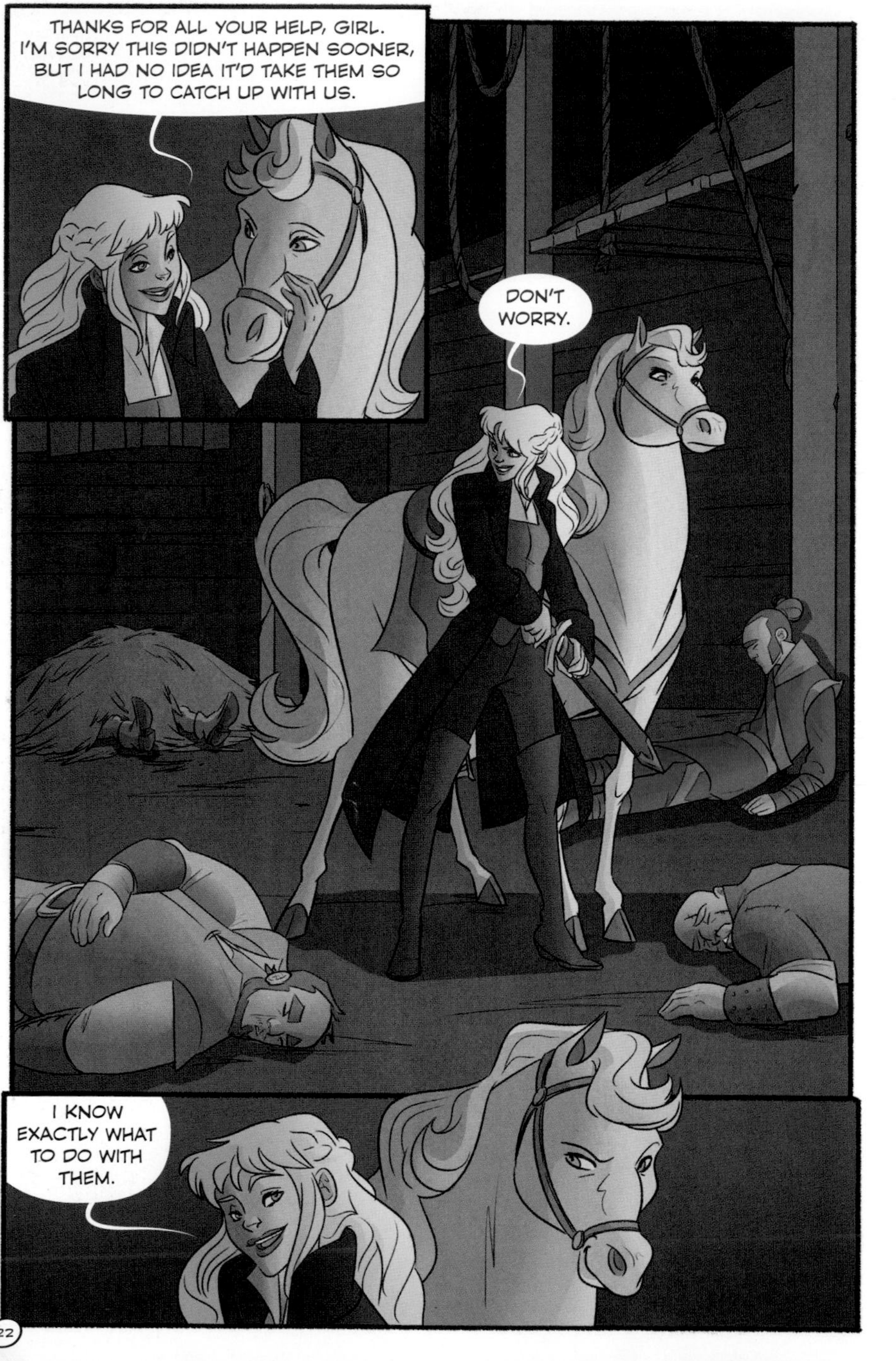
THANKS FOR ALL YOUR HELP, GIRL. I'M SORRY THIS DIDN'T HAPPEN SOONER, BUT I HAD NO IDEA IT'D TAKE THEM SO LONG TO CATCH UP WITH US.
DON'T WORRY.
I KNOW EXACTLY WHAT TO DO WITH THEM.

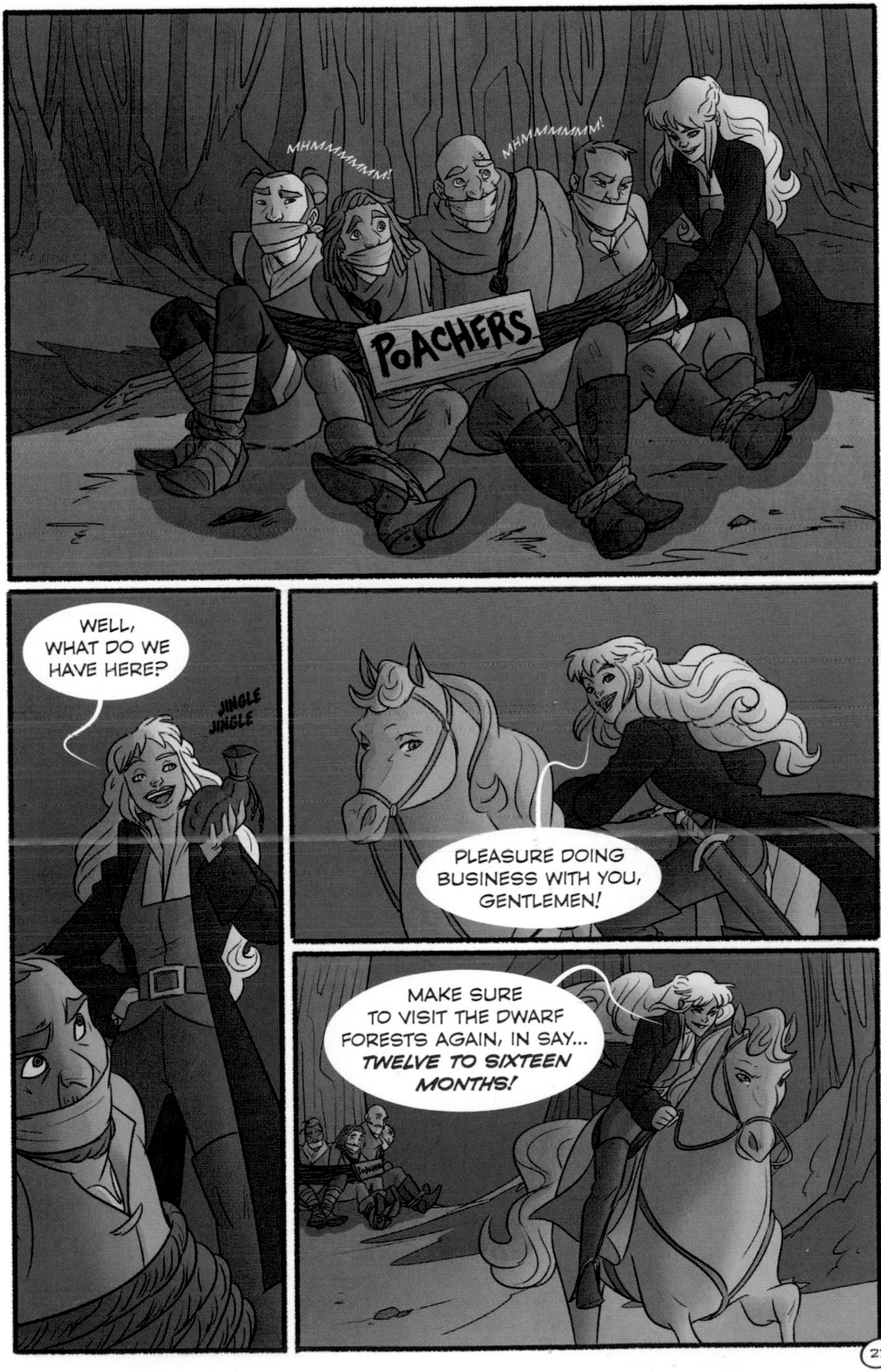
MHMMMMMMM!
MHMMMMMMM!
POACHERS
WELL, WHAT DO WE HAVE HERE?
JINGLE JINGLE
PLEASURE DOING BUSINESS WITH YOU, GENTLEMEN!
MAKE SURE TO VISIT THE DWARF FORESTS AGAIN, IN SAY... *TWELVE TO SIXTEEN MONTHS!*

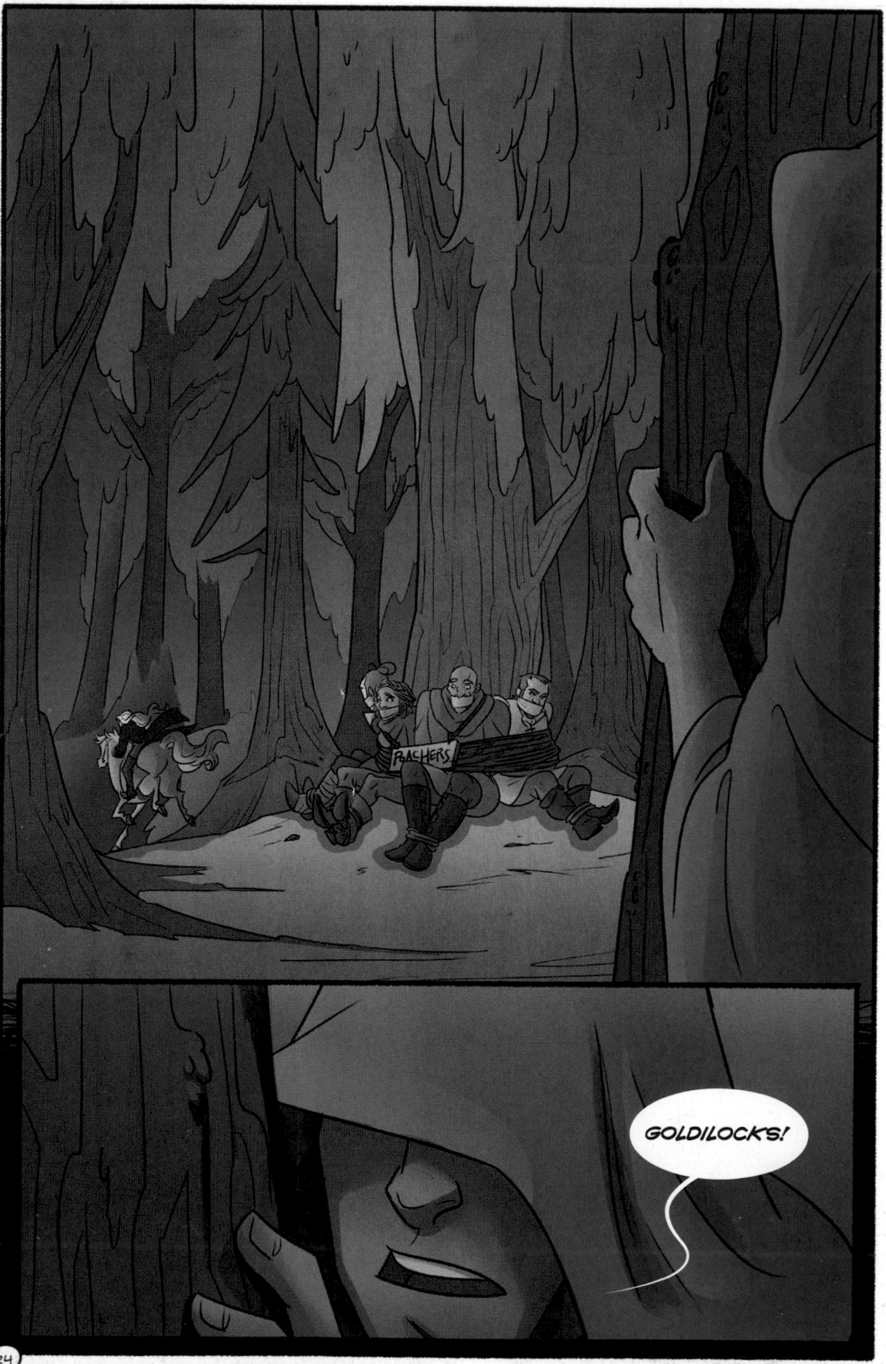
POACHERS
GOLDILOCKS!

CHAPTER 2
The Witch in the Woods

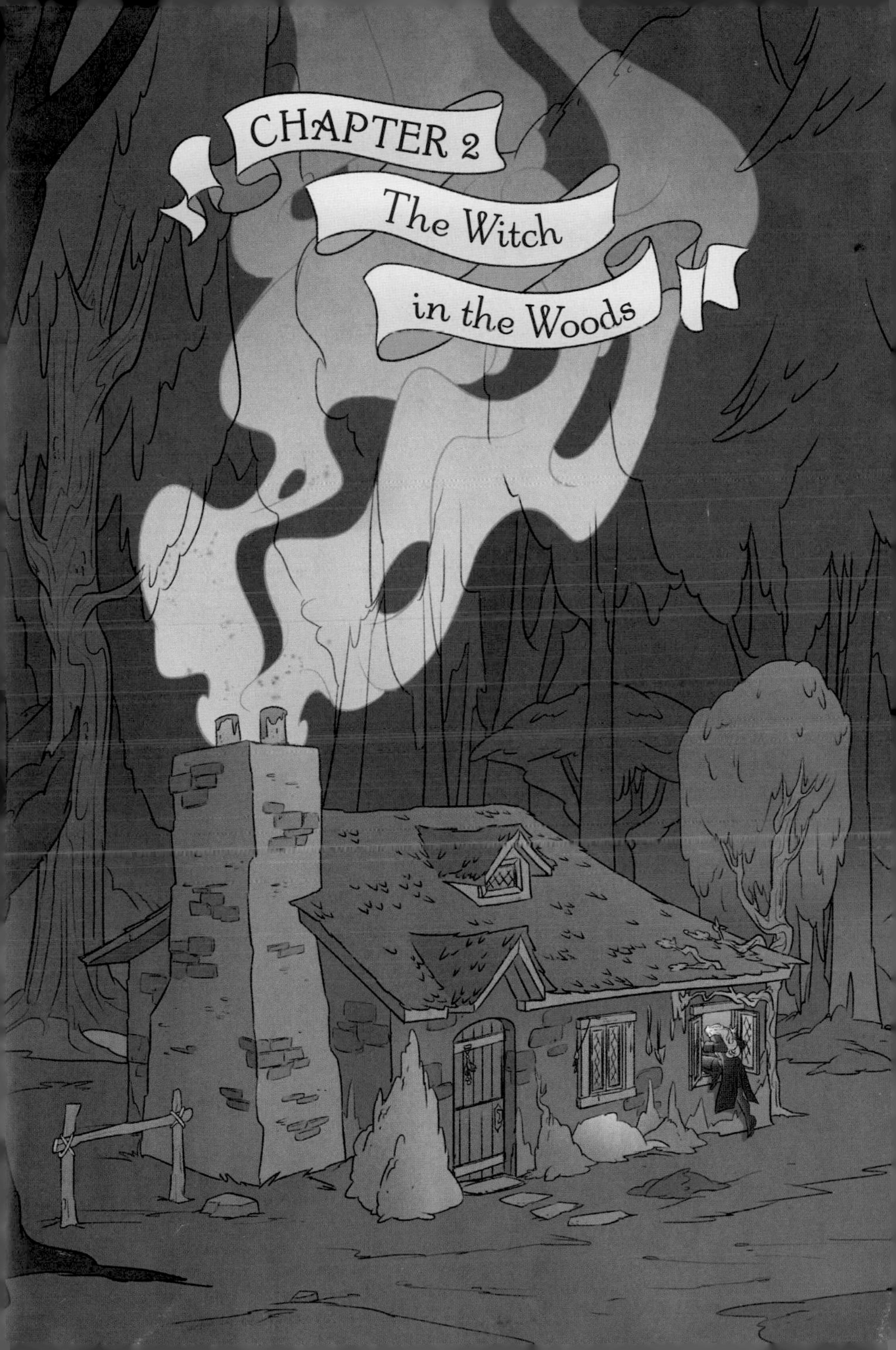

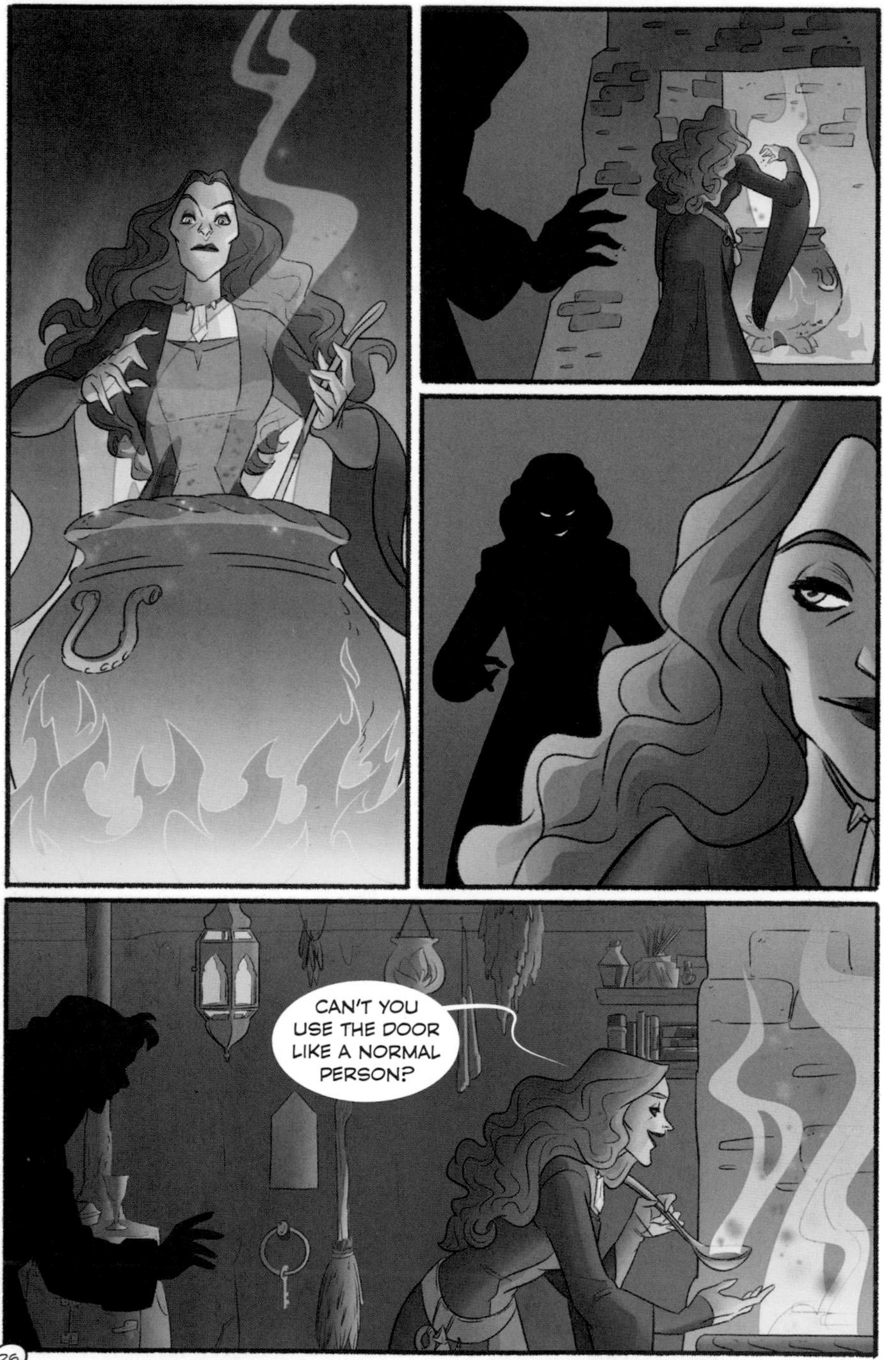
CAN'T YOU USE THE DOOR LIKE A NORMAL PERSON?

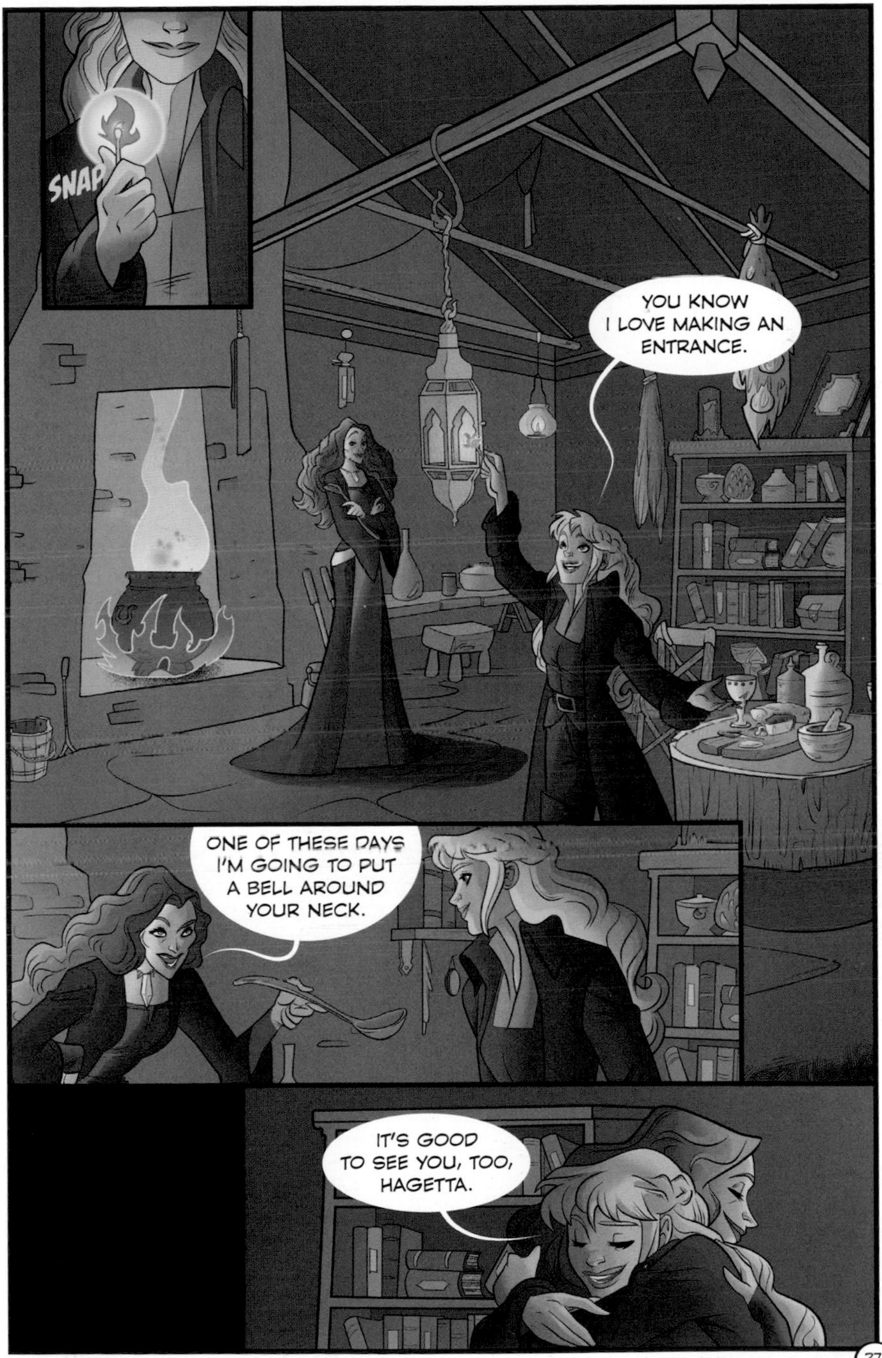
SNAP
YOU KNOW I LOVE MAKING AN ENTRANCE.
ONE OF THESE DAYS I'M GOING TO PUT A BELL AROUND YOUR NECK.
IT'S GOOD TO SEE YOU, TOO, HAGETTA.

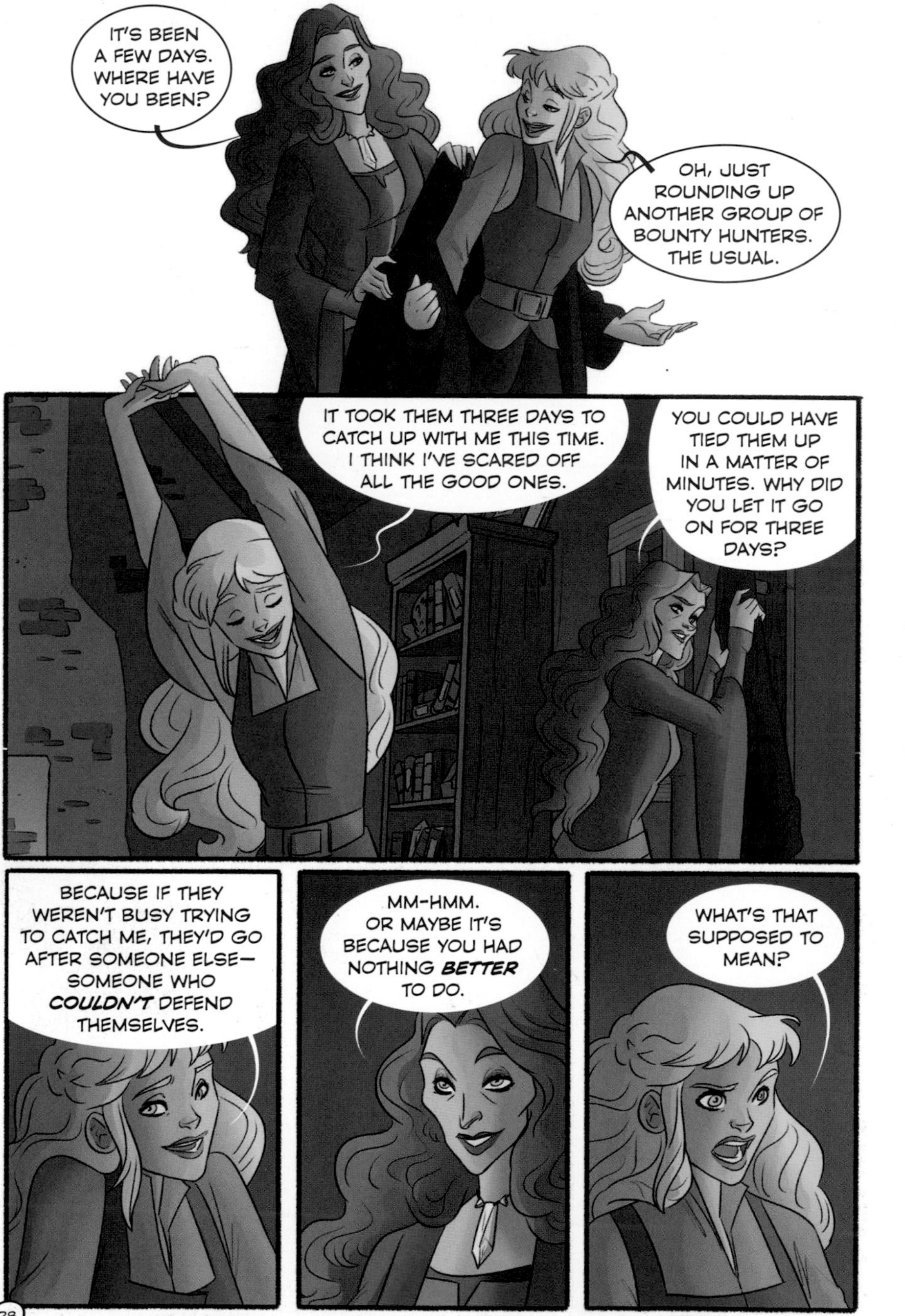
IT'S BEEN A FEW DAYS. WHERE HAVE YOU BEEN?
OH, JUST ROUNDING UP ANOTHER GROUP OF BOUNTY HUNTERS. THE USUAL.
IT TOOK THEM THREE DAYS TO CATCH UP WITH ME THIS TIME. I THINK I'VE SCARED OFF ALL THE GOOD ONES.
YOU COULD HAVE TIED THEM UP IN A MATTER OF MINUTES. WHY DID YOU LET IT GO ON FOR THREE DAYS?
BECAUSE IF THEY WEREN'T BUSY TRYING TO CATCH ME, THEY'D GO AFTER SOMEONE ELSE— SOMEONE WHO ***COULDN'T*** DEFEND THEMSELVES.
MM-HMM. OR MAYBE IT'S BECAUSE YOU HAD NOTHING ***BETTER*** TO DO.
WHAT'S THAT SUPPOSED TO MEAN?

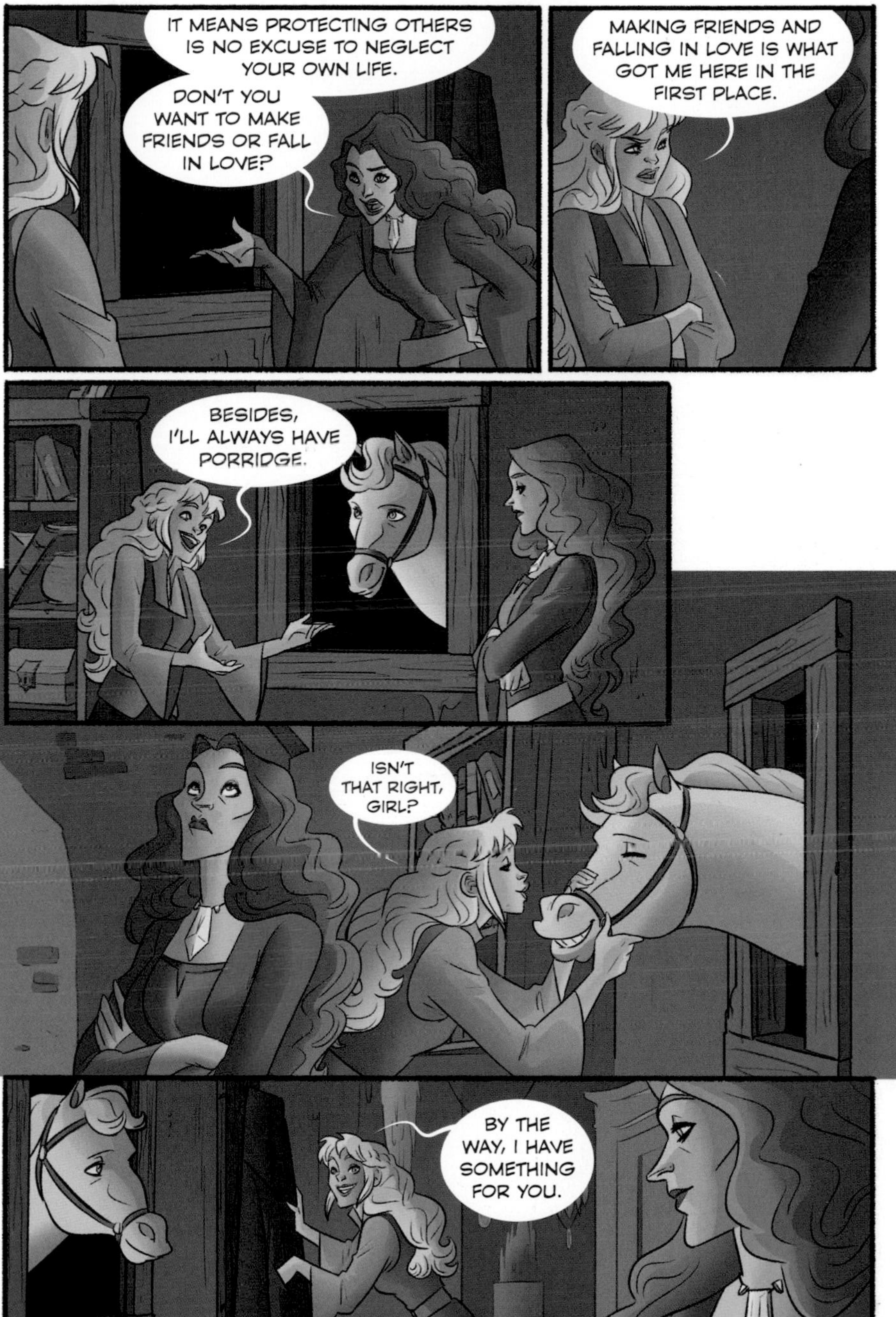
IT MEANS PROTECTING OTHERS IS NO EXCUSE TO NEGLECT YOUR OWN LIFE.
DON'T YOU WANT TO MAKE FRIENDS OR FALL IN LOVE?
MAKING FRIENDS AND FALLING IN LOVE IS WHAT GOT ME HERE IN THE FIRST PLACE.
BESIDES, I'LL ALWAYS HAVE PORRIDGE.
ISN'T THAT RIGHT, GIRL?
BY THE WAY, I HAVE SOMETHING FOR YOU.

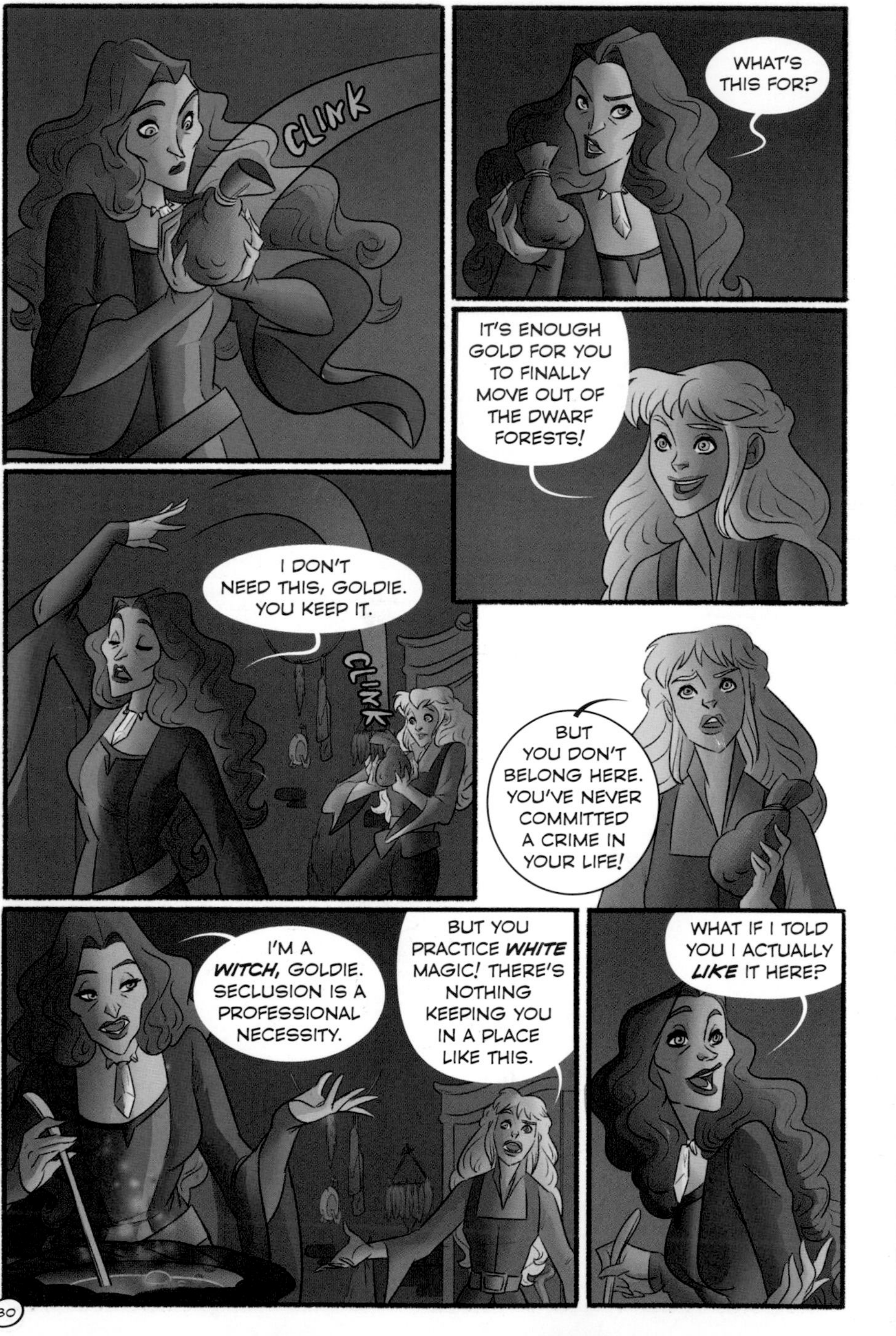
CLINK
WHAT'S THIS FOR?
IT'S ENOUGH GOLD FOR YOU TO FINALLY MOVE OUT OF THE DWARF FORESTS!
I DON'T NEED THIS, GOLDIE. YOU KEEP IT.
CLINK
BUT YOU DON'T BELONG HERE. YOU'VE NEVER COMMITTED A CRIME IN YOUR LIFE!
I'M A WITCH, GOLDIE. SECLUSION IS A PROFESSIONAL NECESSITY.
BUT YOU PRACTICE WHITE MAGIC! THERE'S NOTHING KEEPING YOU IN A PLACE LIKE THIS.
WHAT IF I TOLD YOU I ACTUALLY LIKE IT HERE?

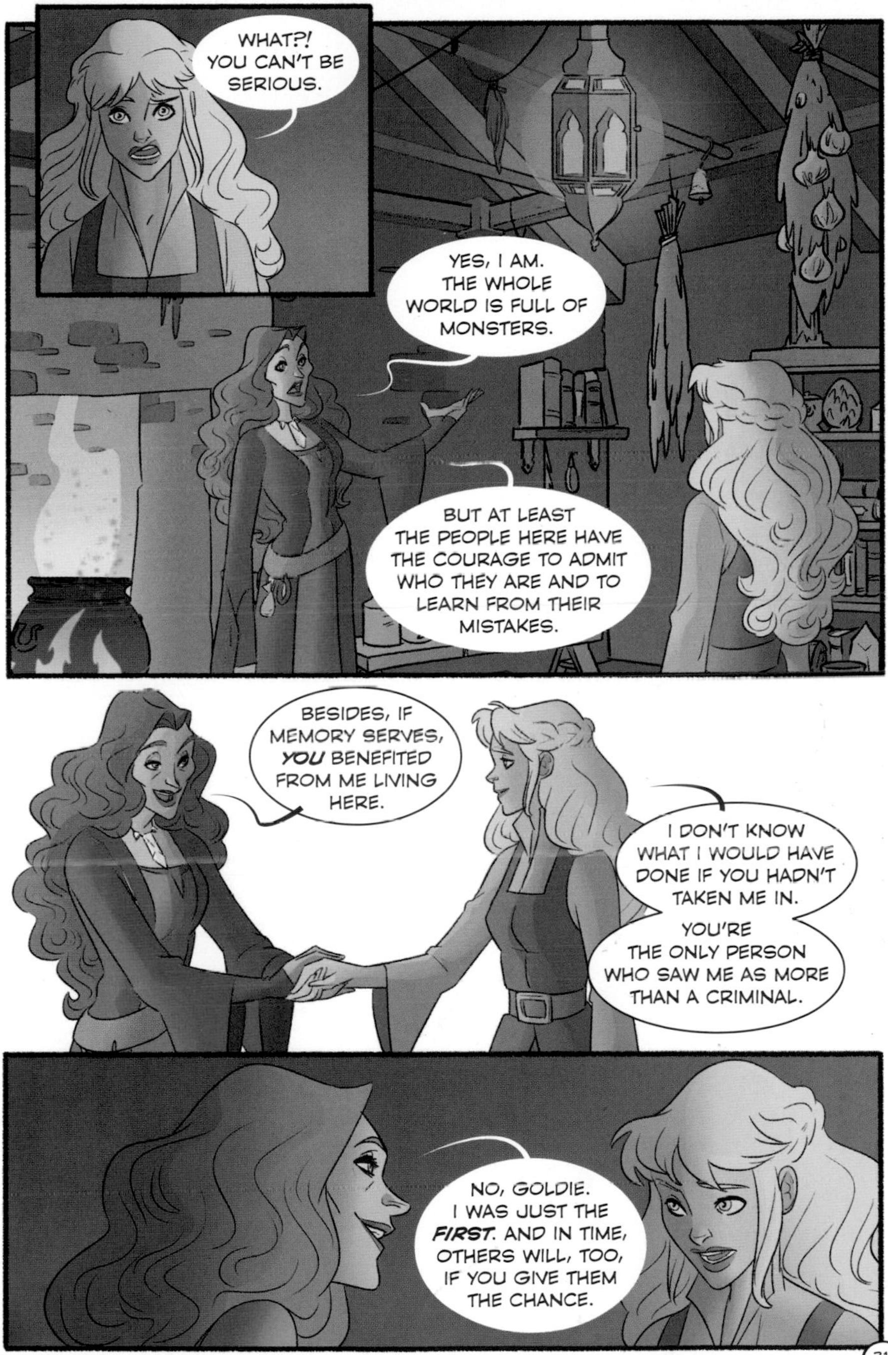
WHAT?! YOU CAN'T BE SERIOUS.
YES, I AM. THE WHOLE WORLD IS FULL OF MONSTERS.
BUT AT LEAST THE PEOPLE HERE HAVE THE COURAGE TO ADMIT WHO THEY ARE AND TO LEARN FROM THEIR MISTAKES.
BESIDES, IF MEMORY SERVES, *YOU* BENEFITED FROM ME LIVING HERE.
I DON'T KNOW WHAT I WOULD HAVE DONE IF YOU HADN'T TAKEN ME IN.
YOU'RE THE ONLY PERSON WHO SAW ME AS MORE THAN A CRIMINAL.
NO, GOLDIE. I WAS JUST THE *FIRST*. AND IN TIME, OTHERS WILL, TOO, IF YOU GIVE THEM THE CHANCE.

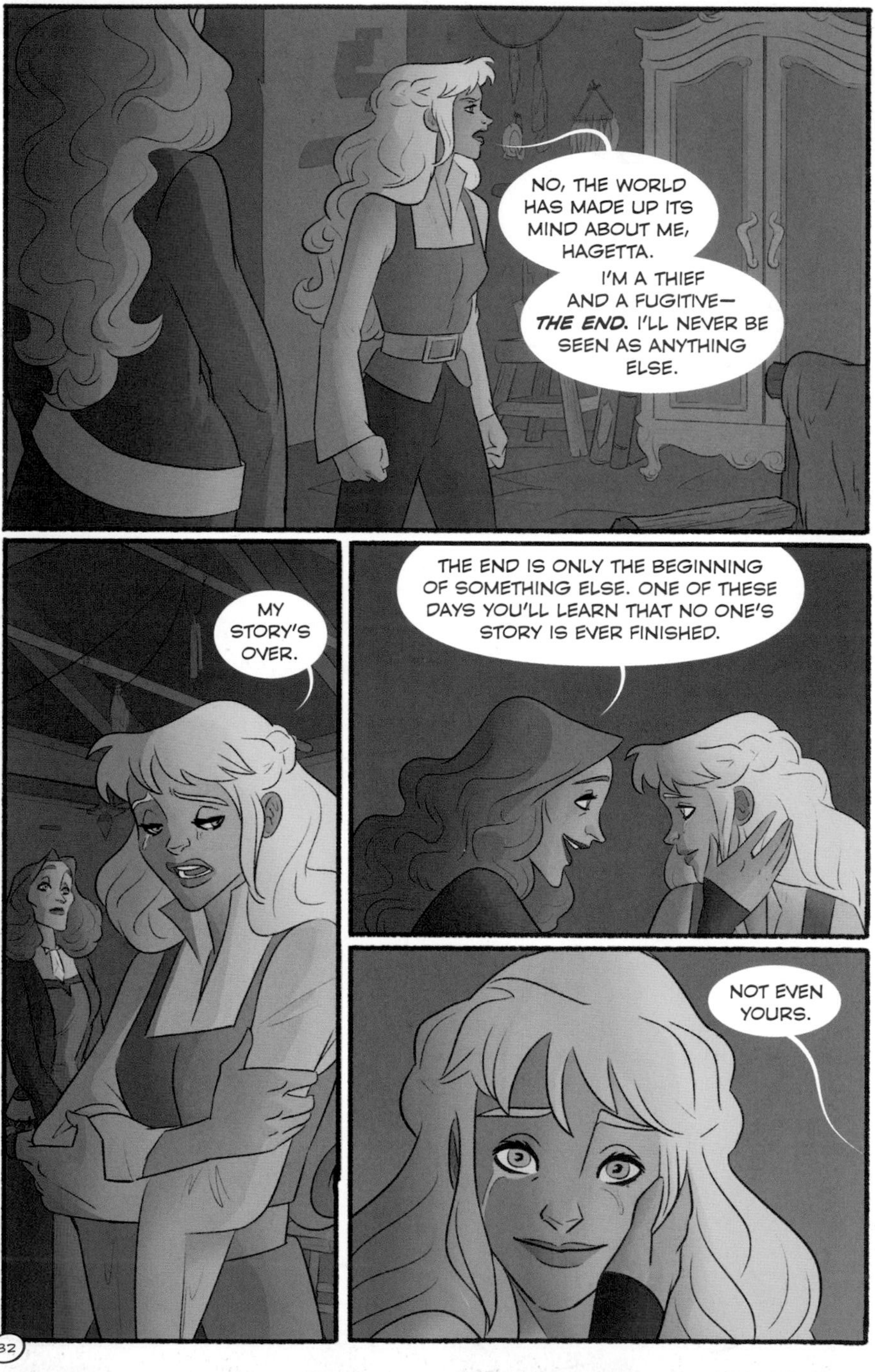
NO, THE WORLD HAS MADE UP ITS MIND ABOUT ME, HAGETTA.
I'M A THIEF AND A FUGITIVE— **THE END.** I'LL NEVER BE SEEN AS ANYTHING ELSE.
MY STORY'S OVER.
THE END IS ONLY THE BEGINNING OF SOMETHING ELSE. ONE OF THESE DAYS YOU'LL LEARN THAT NO ONE'S STORY IS EVER FINISHED.
NOT EVEN YOURS.

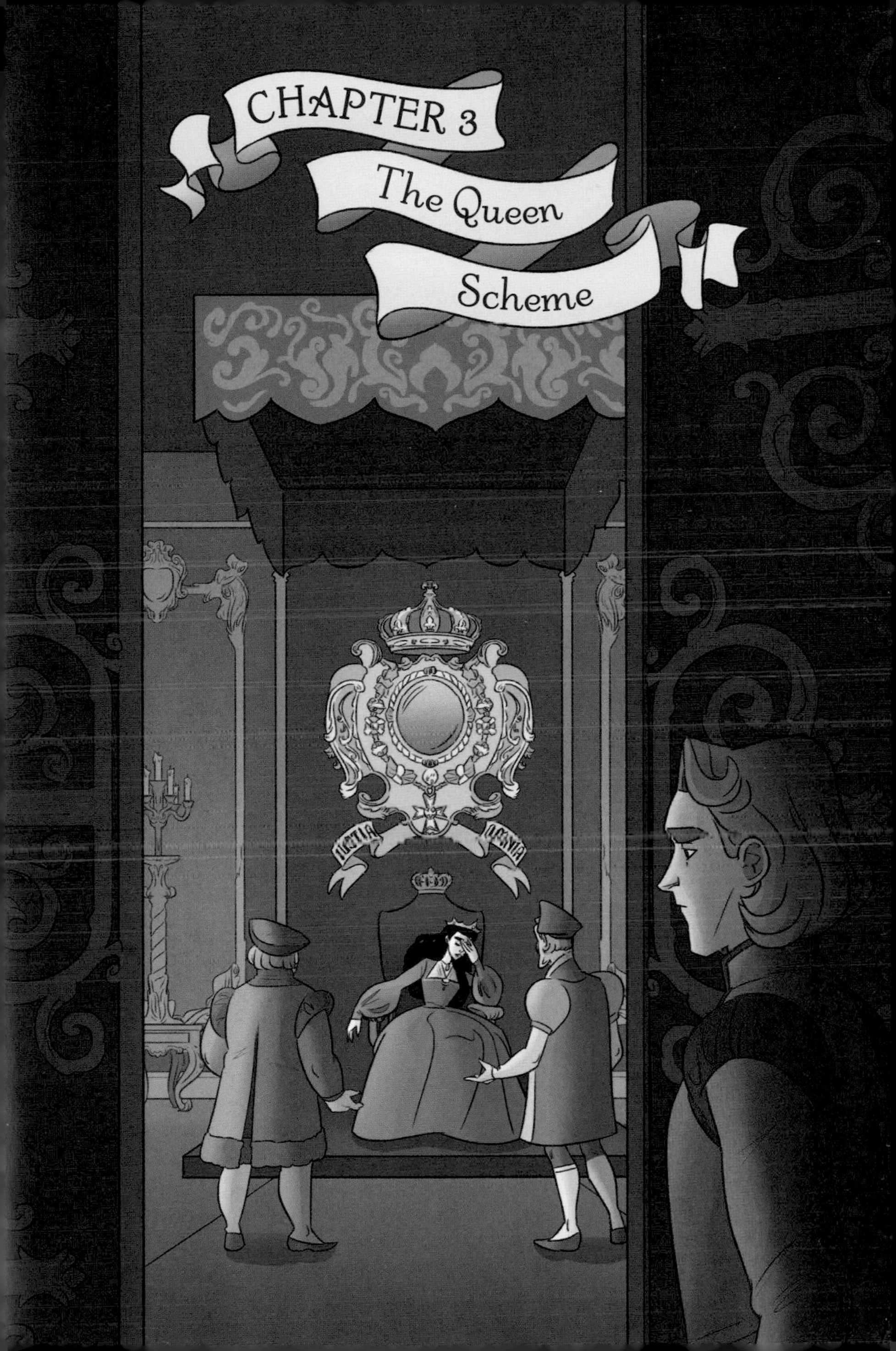
CHAPTER 3
The Queen
Scheme

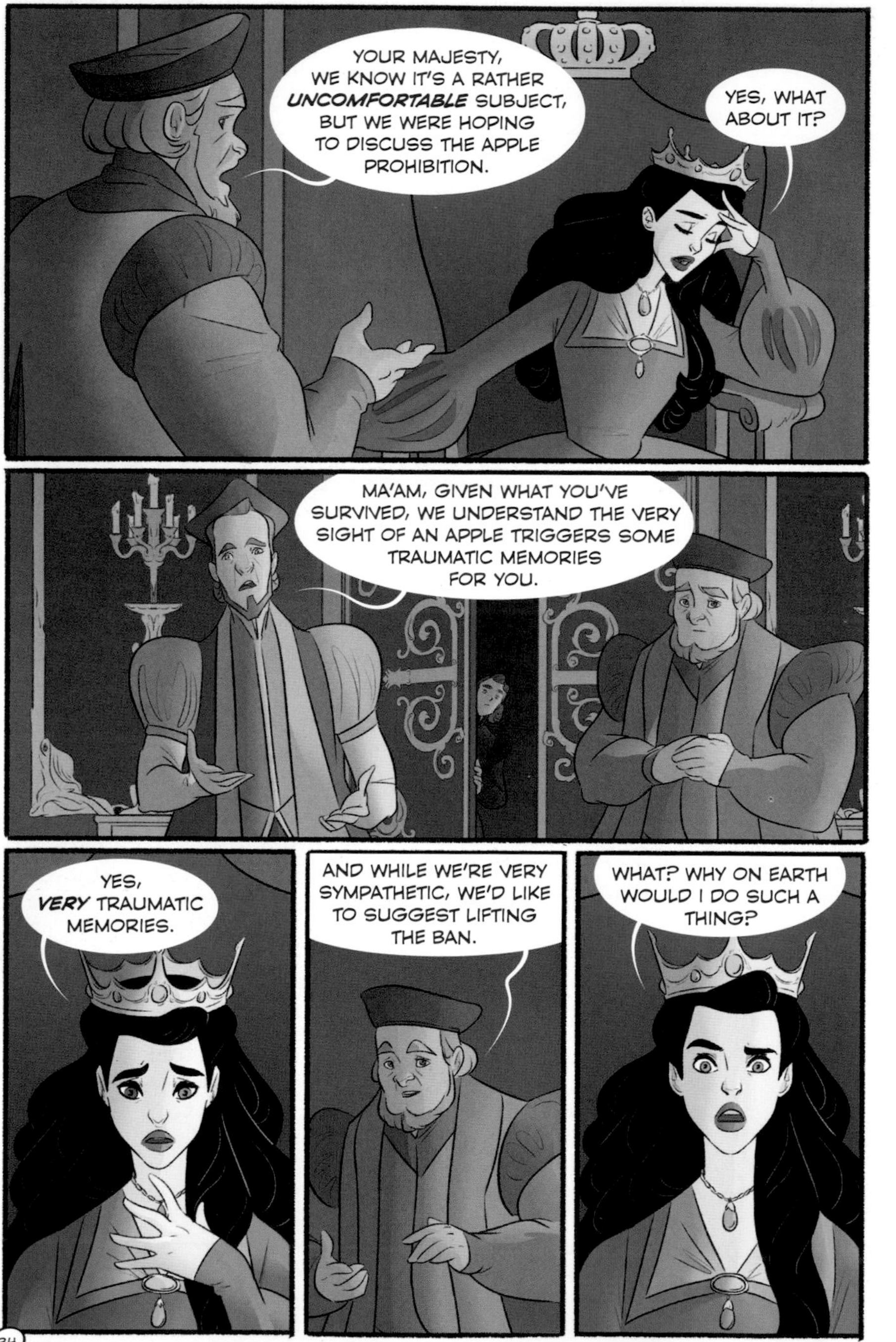
YOUR MAJESTY, WE KNOW IT'S A RATHER *UNCOMFORTABLE* SUBJECT, BUT WE WERE HOPING TO DISCUSS THE APPLE PROHIBITION.
YES, WHAT ABOUT IT?
MA'AM, GIVEN WHAT YOU'VE SURVIVED, WE UNDERSTAND THE VERY SIGHT OF AN APPLE TRIGGERS SOME TRAUMATIC MEMORIES FOR YOU.
YES, *VERY* TRAUMATIC MEMORIES.
AND WHILE WE'RE VERY SYMPATHETIC, WE'D LIKE TO SUGGEST LIFTING THE BAN.
WHAT? WHY ON EARTH WOULD I DO SUCH A THING?

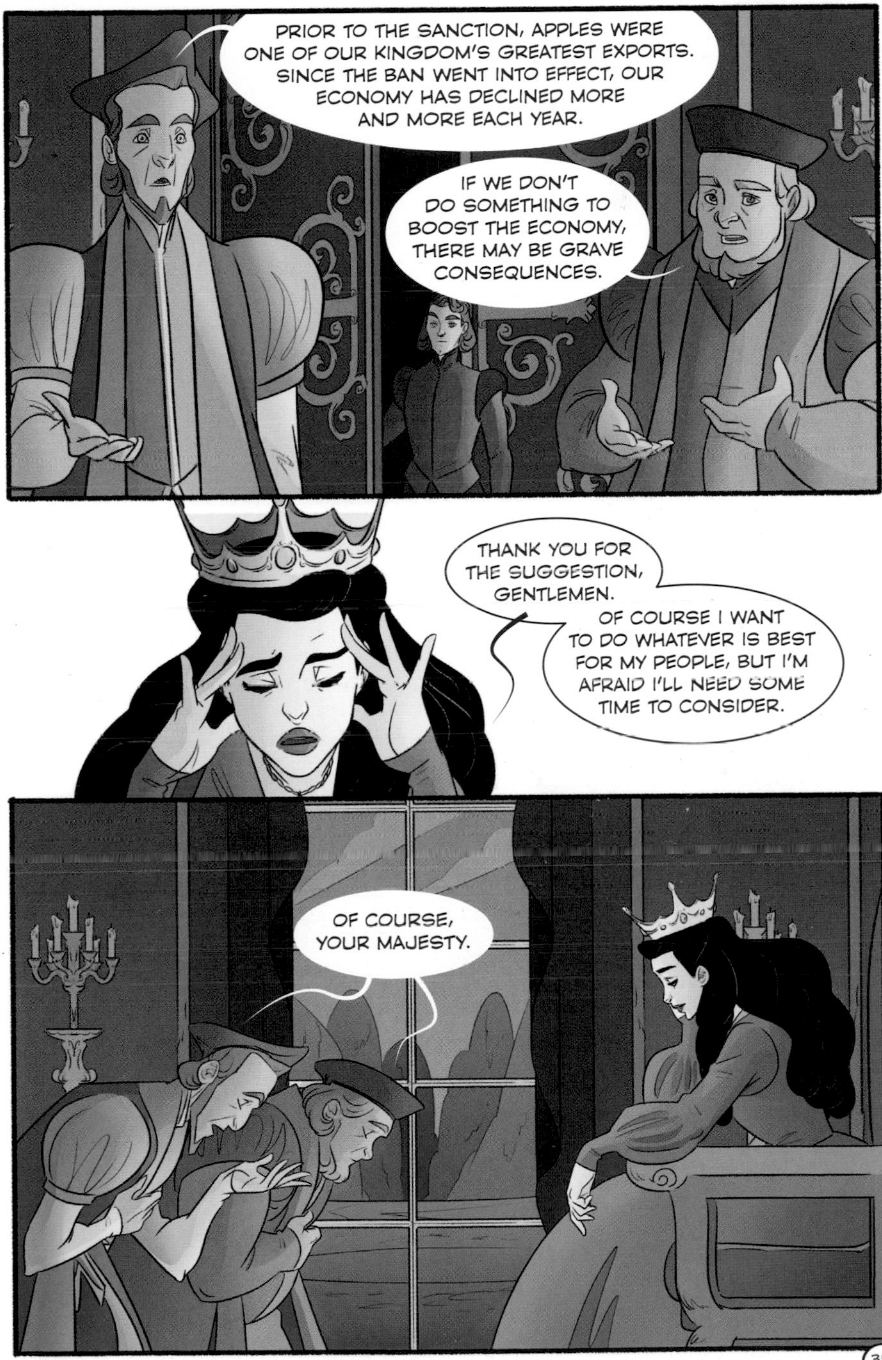
PRIOR TO THE SANCTION, APPLES WERE ONE OF OUR KINGDOM'S GREATEST EXPORTS. SINCE THE BAN WENT INTO EFFECT, OUR ECONOMY HAS DECLINED MORE AND MORE EACH YEAR.
IF WE DON'T DO SOMETHING TO BOOST THE ECONOMY, THERE MAY BE GRAVE CONSEQUENCES.
THANK YOU FOR THE SUGGESTION, GENTLEMEN.
OF COURSE I WANT TO DO WHATEVER IS BEST FOR MY PEOPLE, BUT I'M AFRAID I'LL NEED SOME TIME TO CONSIDER.
OF COURSE, YOUR MAJESTY.

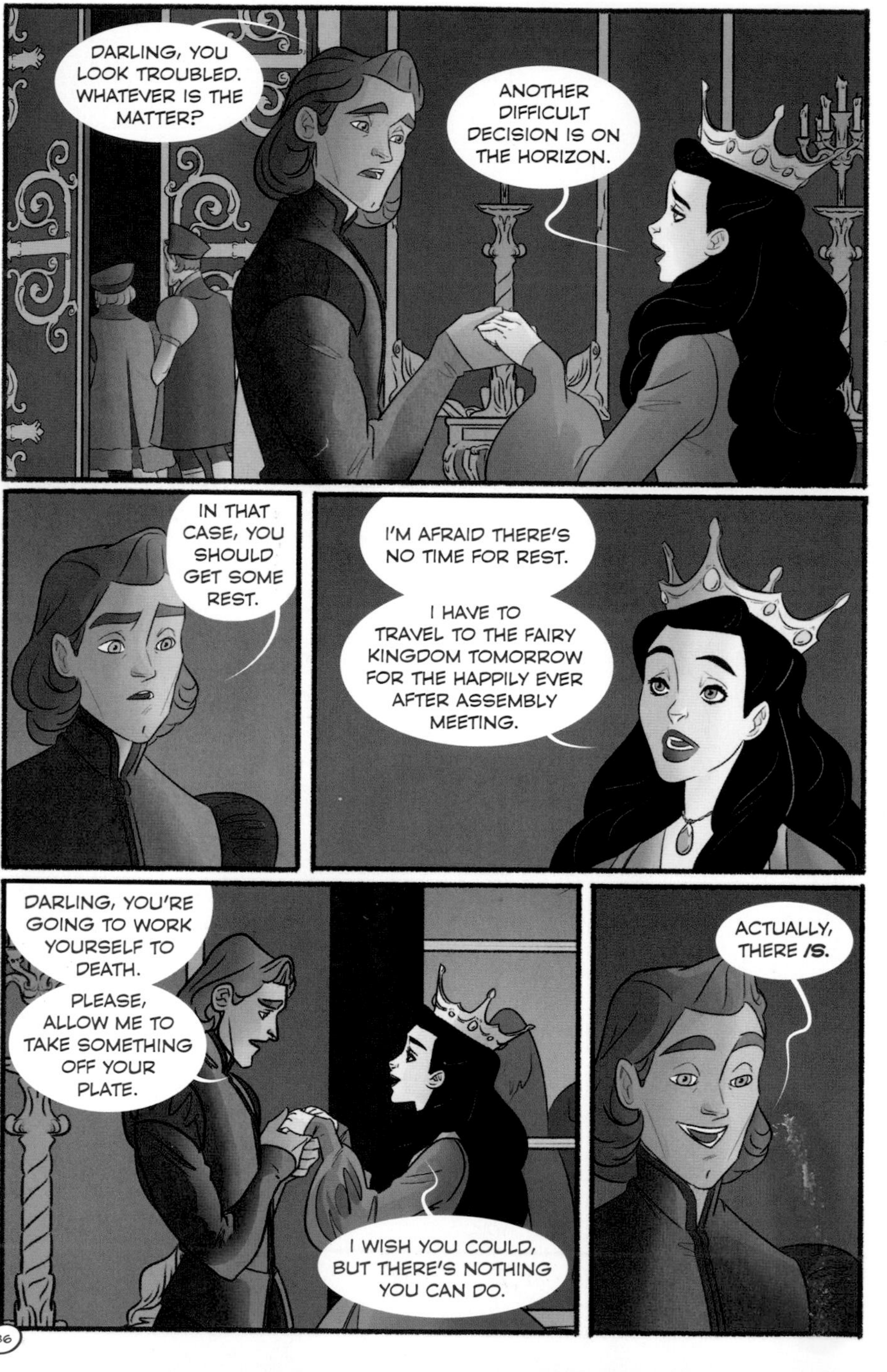
DARLING, YOU LOOK TROUBLED. WHATEVER IS THE MATTER?
ANOTHER DIFFICULT DECISION IS ON THE HORIZON.
IN THAT CASE, YOU SHOULD GET SOME REST.
I'M AFRAID THERE'S NO TIME FOR REST.
I HAVE TO TRAVEL TO THE FAIRY KINGDOM TOMORROW FOR THE HAPPILY EVER AFTER ASSEMBLY MEETING.
DARLING, YOU'RE GOING TO WORK YOURSELF TO DEATH.
PLEASE, ALLOW ME TO TAKE SOMETHING OFF YOUR PLATE.
I WISH YOU COULD, BUT THERE'S NOTHING YOU CAN DO.
ACTUALLY, THERE *IS*.

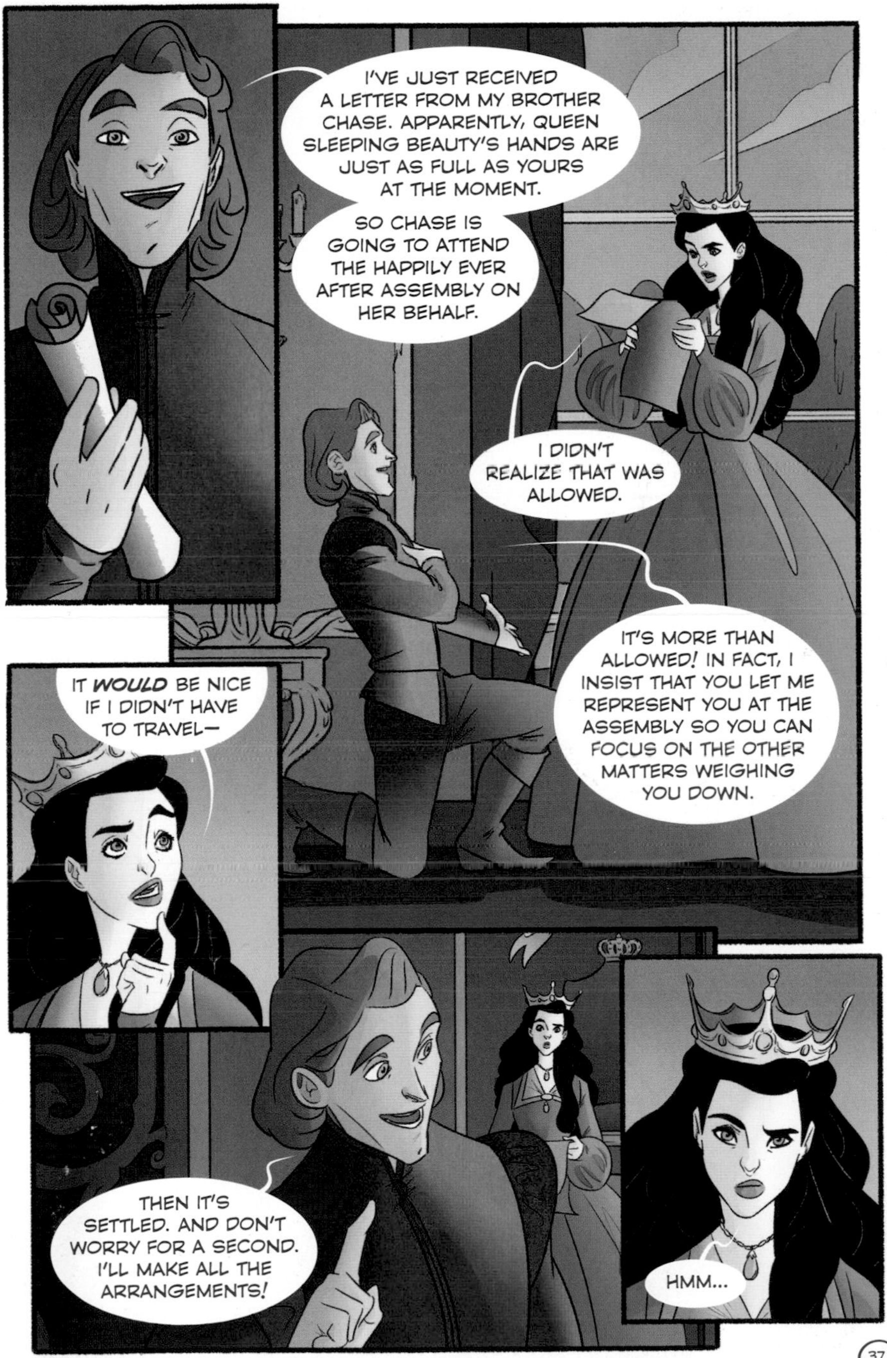
I'VE JUST RECEIVED A LETTER FROM MY BROTHER CHASE. APPARENTLY, QUEEN SLEEPING BEAUTY'S HANDS ARE JUST AS FULL AS YOURS AT THE MOMENT.
SO CHASE IS GOING TO ATTEND THE HAPPILY EVER AFTER ASSEMBLY ON HER BEHALF.
I DIDN'T REALIZE THAT WAS ALLOWED.
IT'S MORE THAN ALLOWED! IN FACT, I INSIST THAT YOU LET ME REPRESENT YOU AT THE ASSEMBLY SO YOU CAN FOCUS ON THE OTHER MATTERS WEIGHING YOU DOWN.
IT ***WOULD*** BE NICE IF I DIDN'T HAVE TO TRAVEL—
THEN IT'S SETTLED. AND DON'T WORRY FOR A SECOND. I'LL MAKE ALL THE ARRANGEMENTS!
HMM...

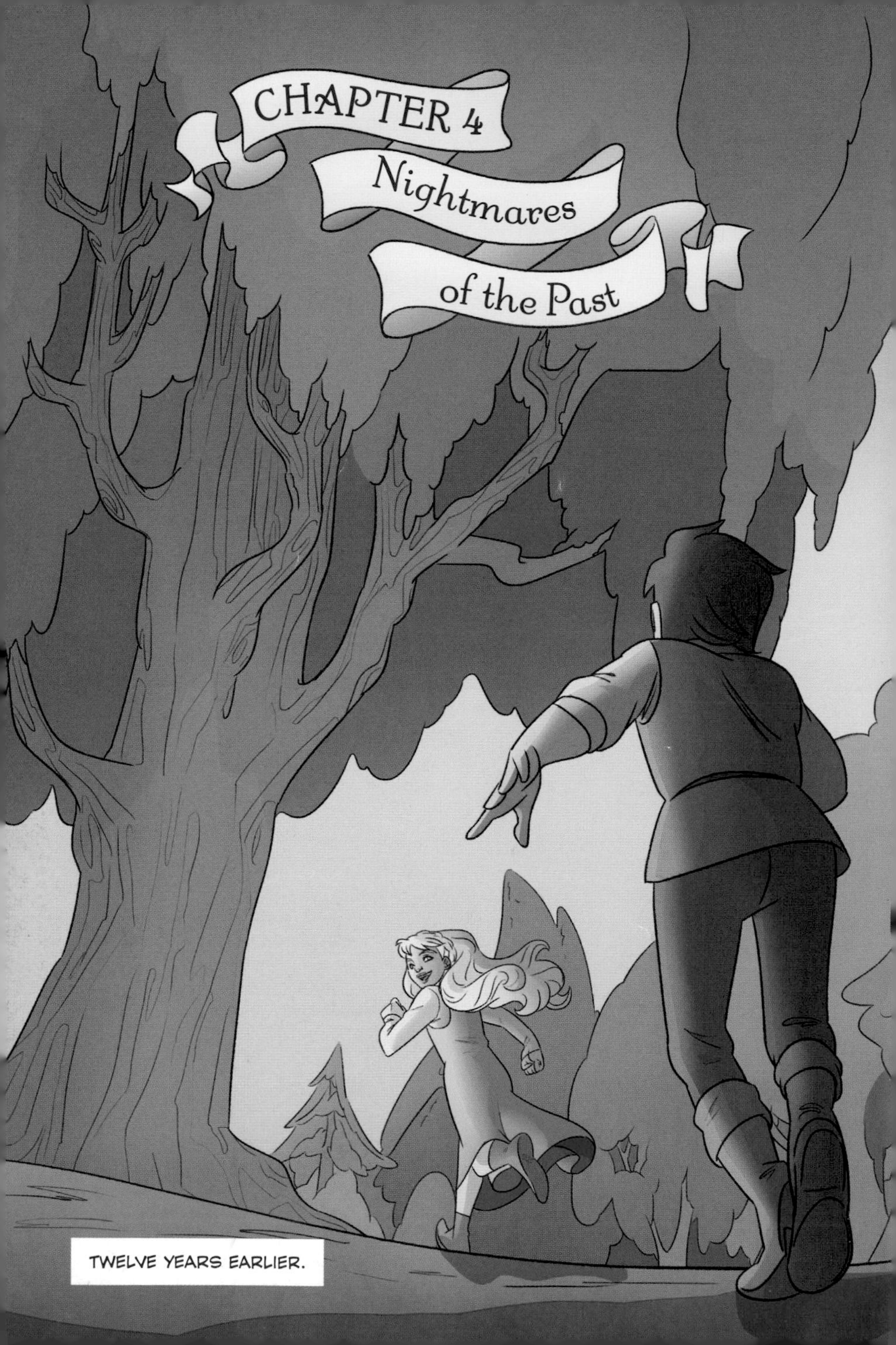
CHAPTER 4
Nightmares of the Past
TWELVE YEARS EARLIER.

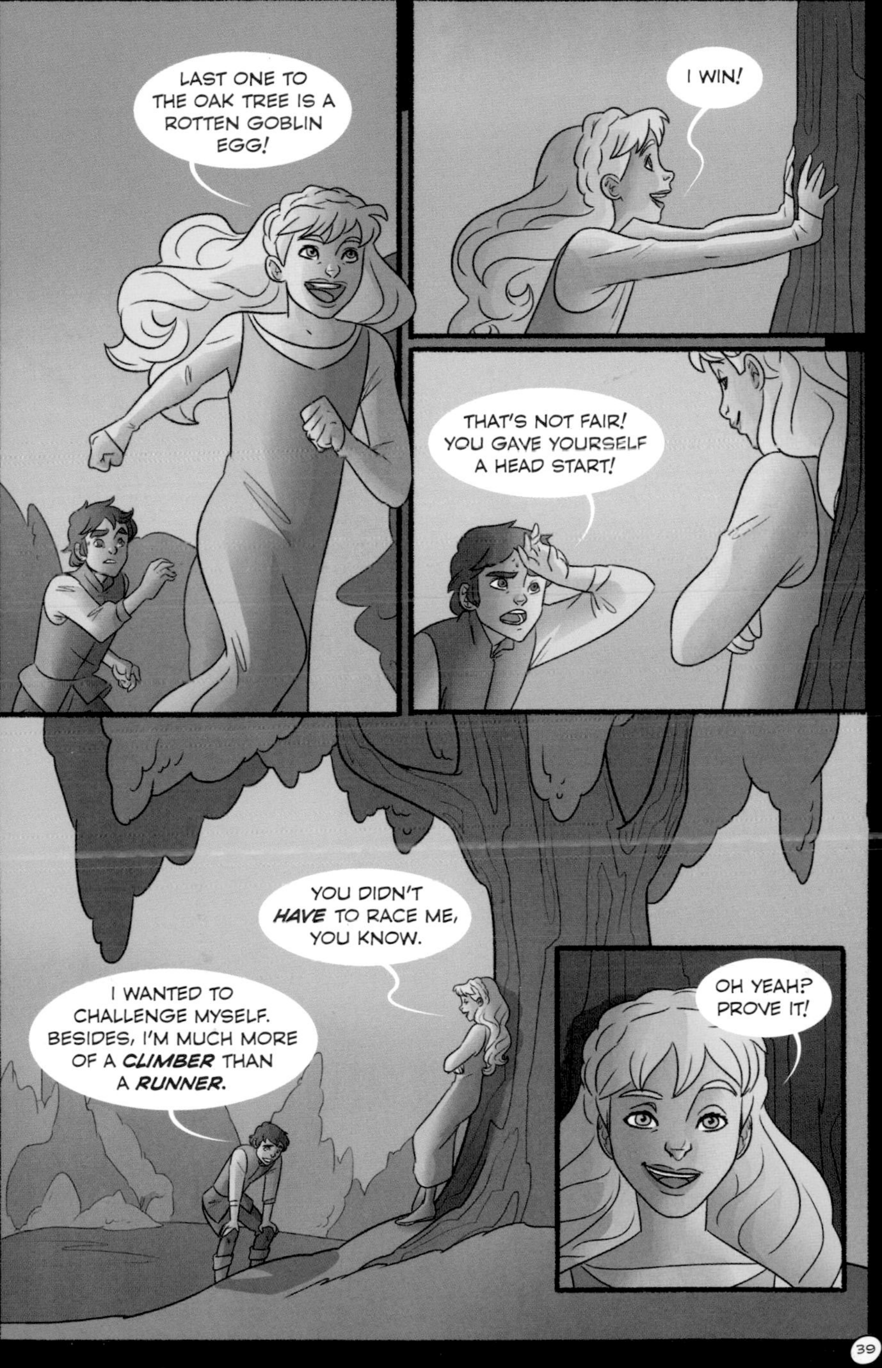
LAST ONE TO THE OAK TREE IS A ROTTEN GOBLIN EGG!
I WIN!
THAT'S NOT FAIR! YOU GAVE YOURSELF A HEAD START!
YOU DIDN'T *HAVE* TO RACE ME, YOU KNOW.
I WANTED TO CHALLENGE MYSELF. BESIDES, I'M MUCH MORE OF A *CLIMBER* THAN A *RUNNER*.
OH YEAH? PROVE IT!

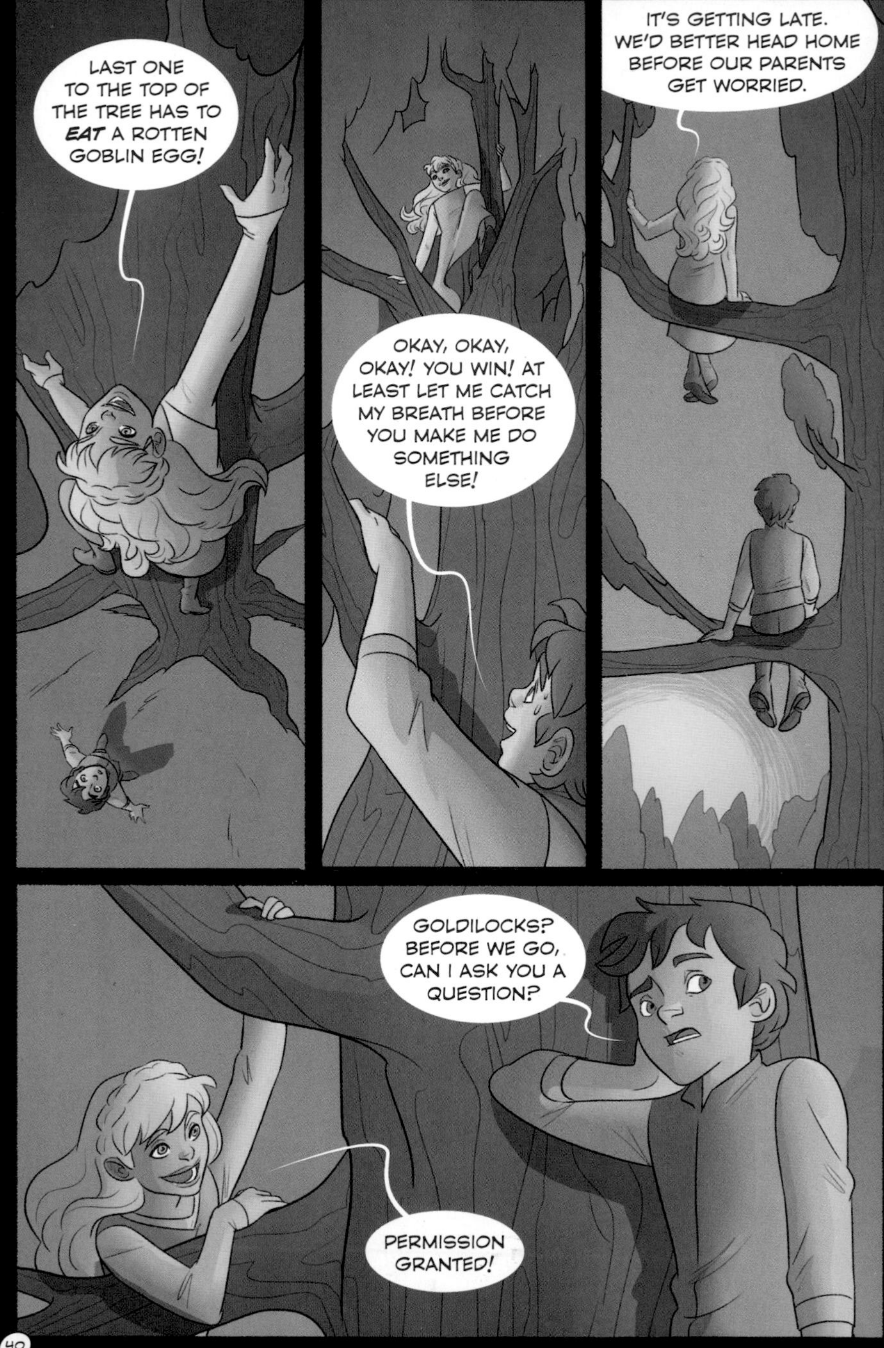
LAST ONE TO THE TOP OF THE TREE HAS TO *EAT* A ROTTEN GOBLIN EGG!
OKAY, OKAY, OKAY! YOU WIN! AT LEAST LET ME CATCH MY BREATH BEFORE YOU MAKE ME DO SOMETHING ELSE!
IT'S GETTING LATE. WE'D BETTER HEAD HOME BEFORE OUR PARENTS GET WORRIED.
GOLDILOCKS? BEFORE WE GO, CAN I ASK YOU A QUESTION?
PERMISSION GRANTED!

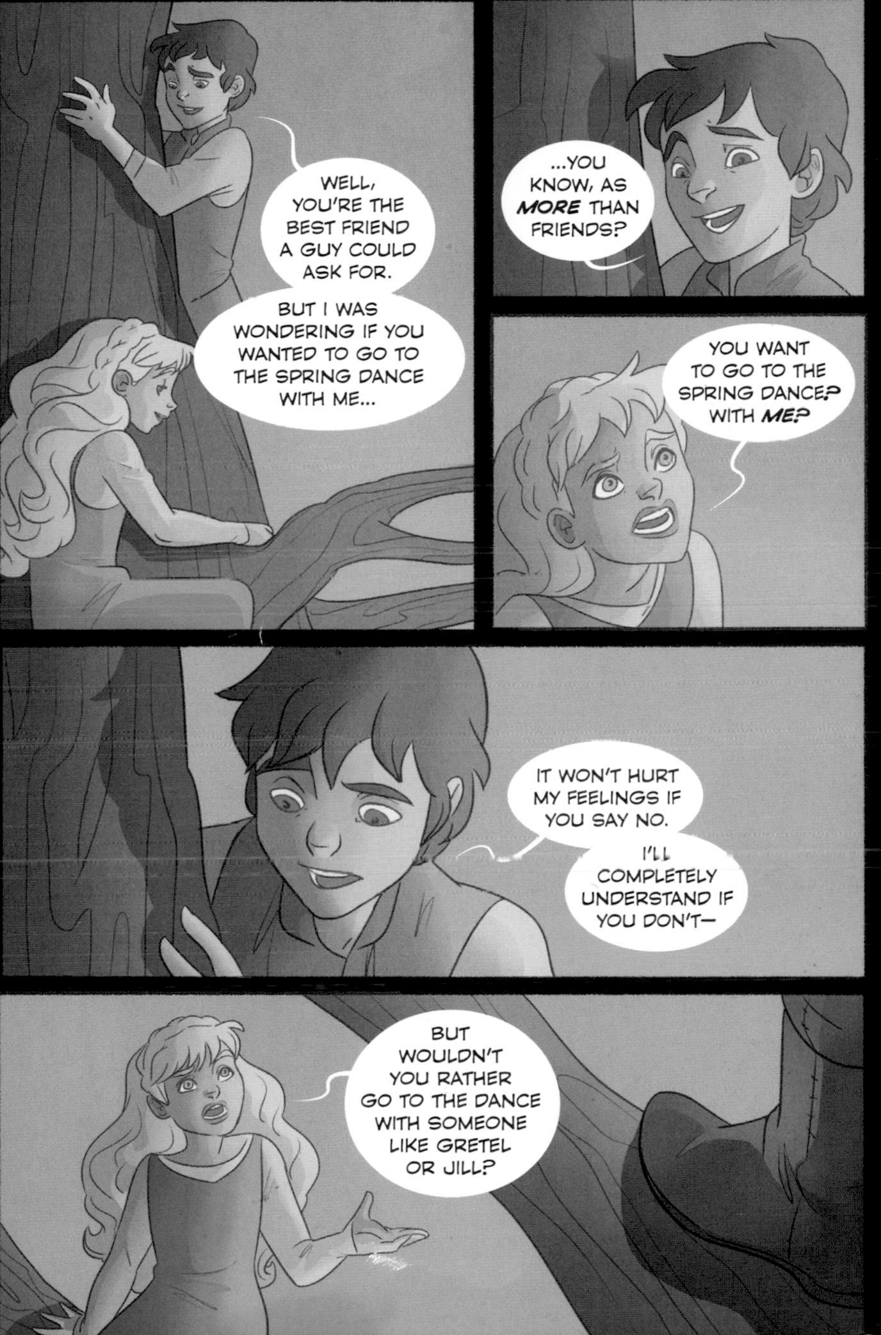
WELL, YOU'RE THE BEST FRIEND A GUY COULD ASK FOR.
BUT I WAS WONDERING IF YOU WANTED TO GO TO THE SPRING DANCE WITH ME...
...YOU KNOW, AS *MORE* THAN FRIENDS?
YOU WANT TO GO TO THE SPRING DANCE? WITH *ME?*
IT WON'T HURT MY FEELINGS IF YOU SAY NO.
I'LL COMPLETELY UNDERSTAND IF YOU DON'T—
BUT WOULDN'T YOU RATHER GO TO THE DANCE WITH SOMEONE LIKE GRETEL OR JILL?

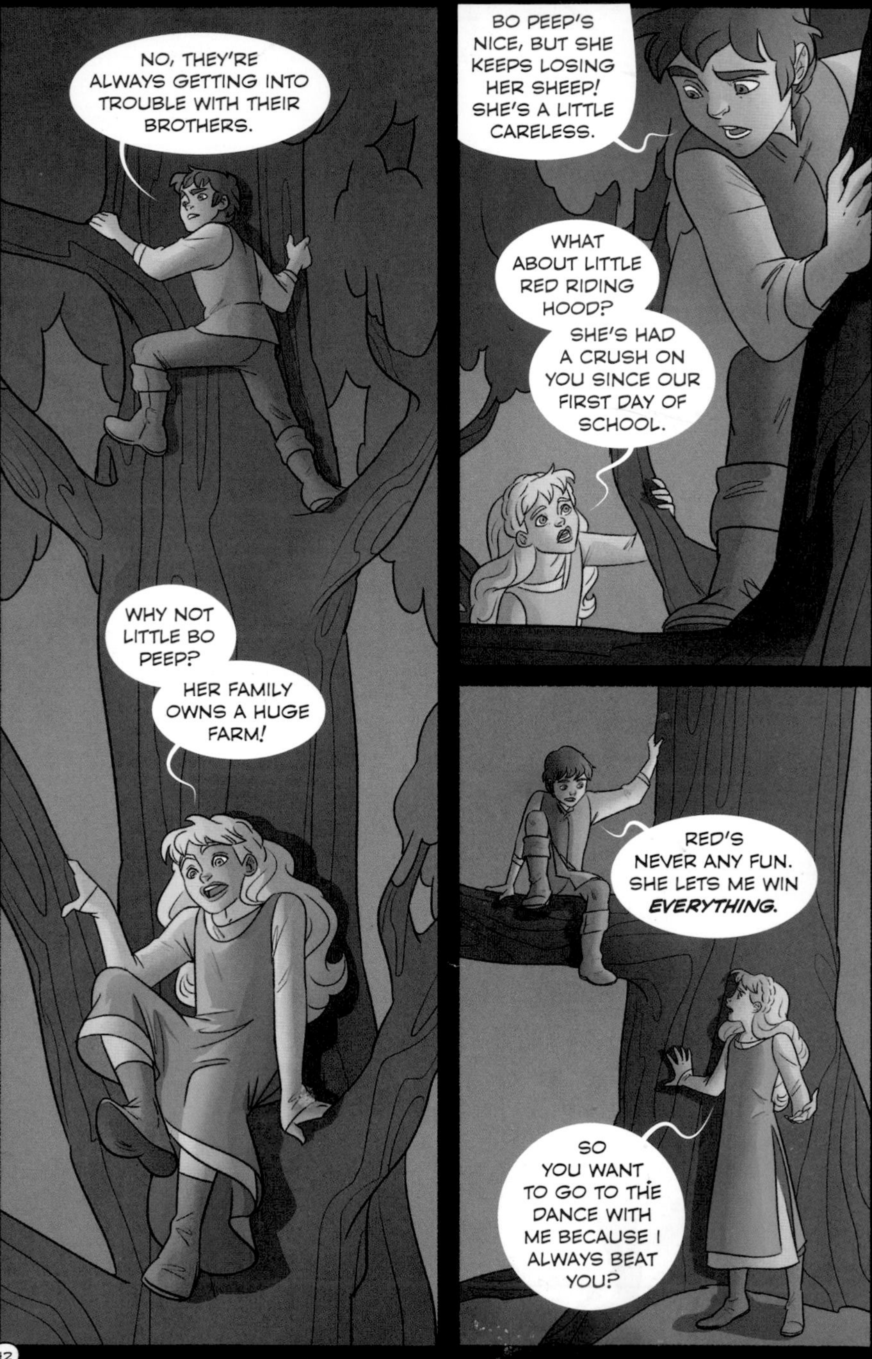
NO, THEY'RE ALWAYS GETTING INTO TROUBLE WITH THEIR BROTHERS.
WHY NOT LITTLE BO PEEP?
HER FAMILY OWNS A HUGE FARM!
BO PEEP'S NICE, BUT SHE KEEPS LOSING HER SHEEP! SHE'S A LITTLE CARELESS.
WHAT ABOUT LITTLE RED RIDING HOOD?
SHE'S HAD A CRUSH ON YOU SINCE OUR FIRST DAY OF SCHOOL.
RED'S NEVER ANY FUN. SHE LETS ME WIN ***EVERYTHING***.
SO YOU WANT TO GO TO THE DANCE WITH ME BECAUSE I ALWAYS BEAT YOU?

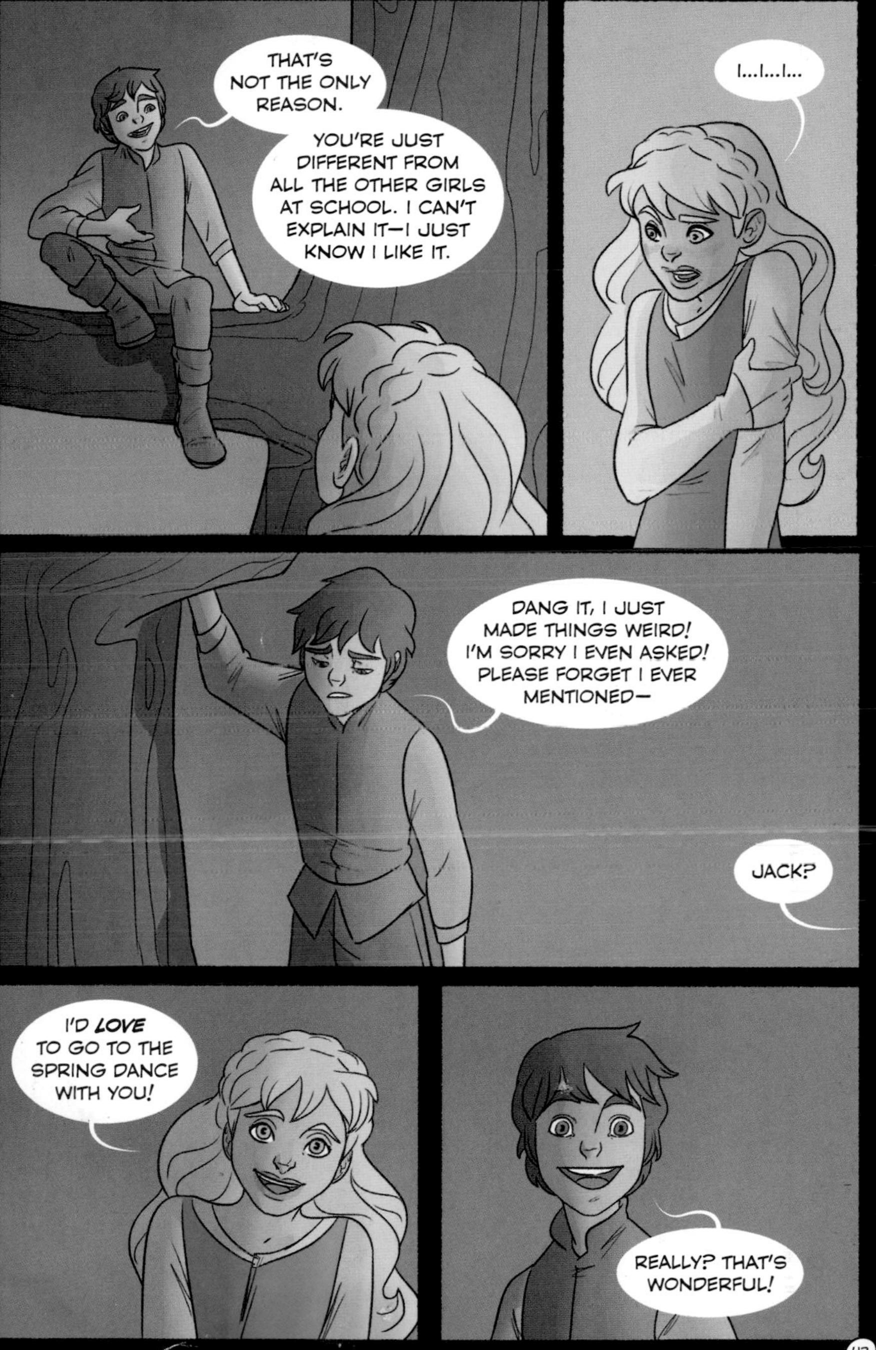
THAT'S NOT THE ONLY REASON.
YOU'RE JUST DIFFERENT FROM ALL THE OTHER GIRLS AT SCHOOL. I CAN'T EXPLAIN IT—I JUST KNOW I LIKE IT.
I...I...I...
DANG IT, I JUST MADE THINGS WEIRD! I'M SORRY I EVEN ASKED! PLEASE FORGET I EVER MENTIONED—
JACK?
I'D ***LOVE*** TO GO TO THE SPRING DANCE WITH YOU!
REALLY? THAT'S WONDERFUL!

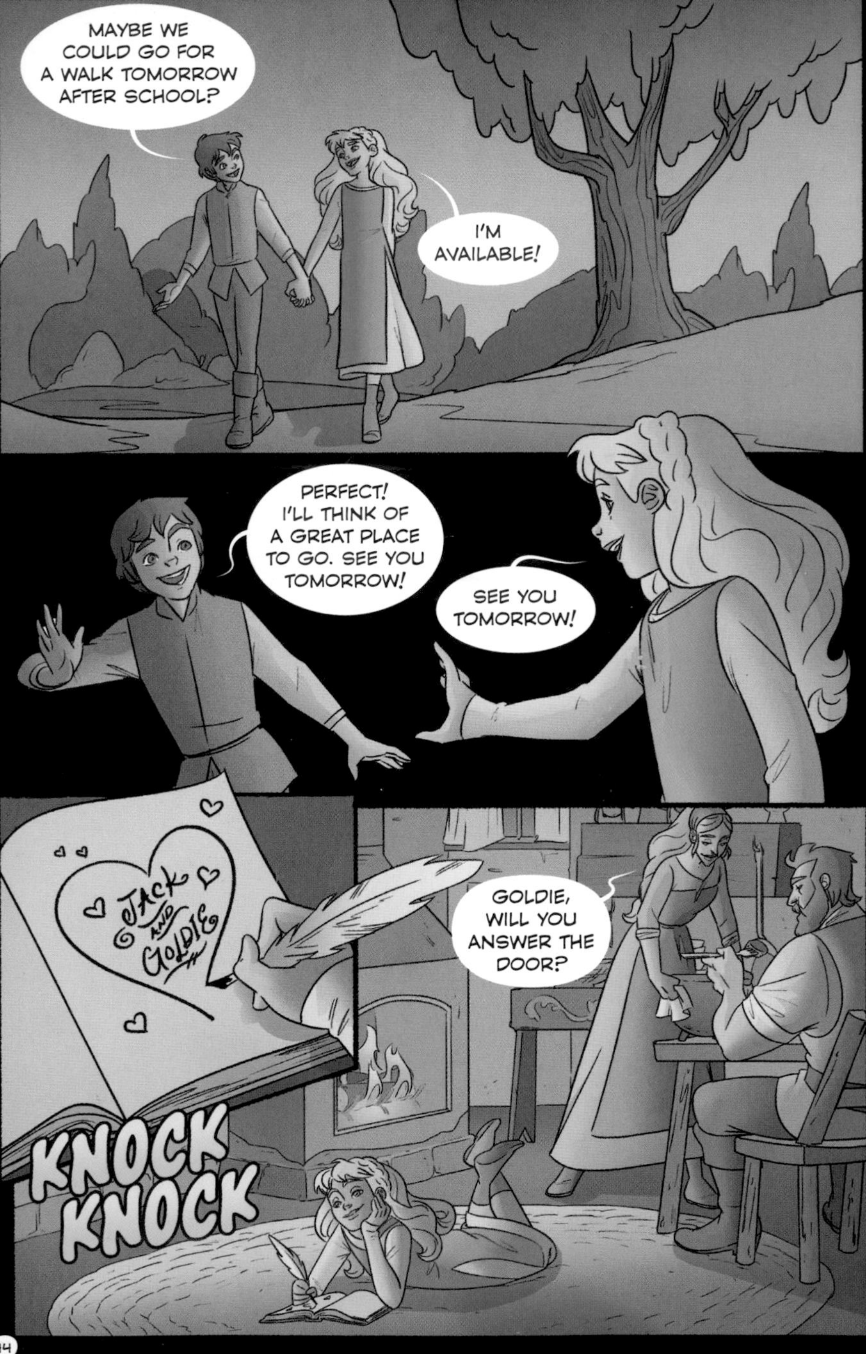
MAYBE WE COULD GO FOR A WALK TOMORROW AFTER SCHOOL?
I'M AVAILABLE!
PERFECT! I'LL THINK OF A GREAT PLACE TO GO. SEE YOU TOMORROW!
SEE YOU TOMORROW!
JACK AND GOLDIE
GOLDIE, WILL YOU ANSWER THE DOOR?
KNOCK KNOCK

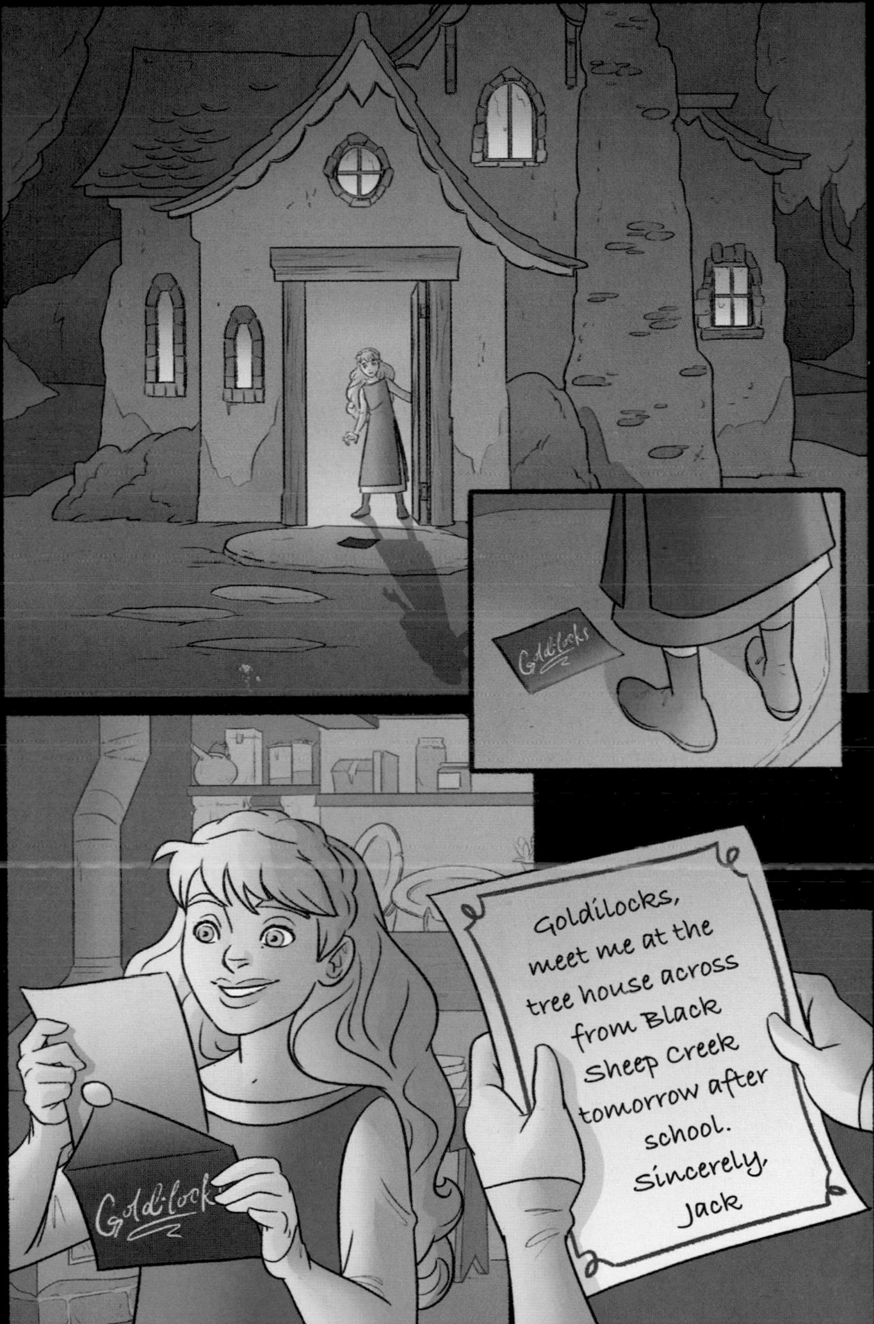
Goldilocks
Goldilocks
Goldilocks, meet me at the tree house across from Black Sheep Creek tomorrow after school. Sincerely, Jack

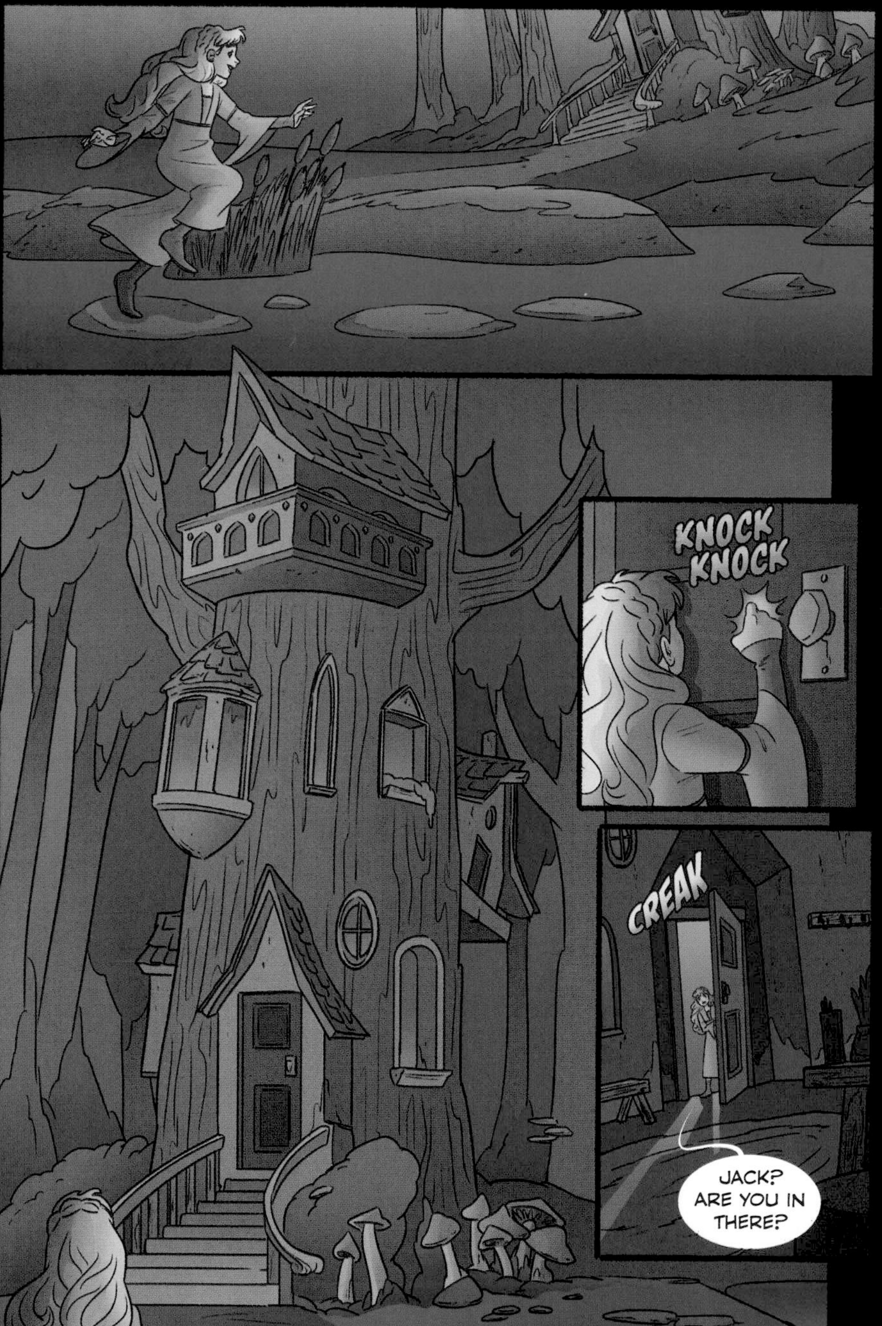

KNOCK KNOCK
CREAK
JACK? ARE YOU IN THERE?

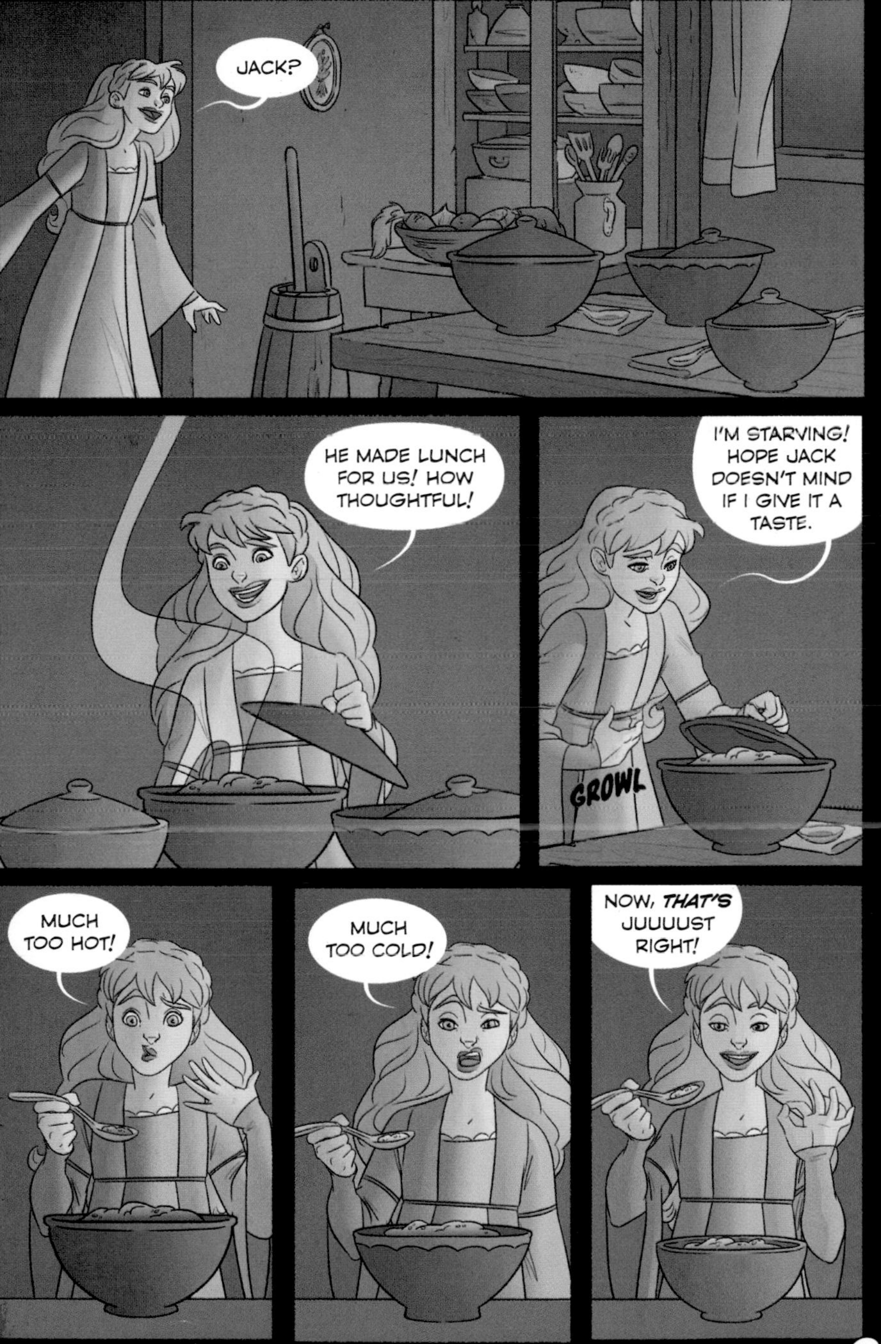
JACK?
HE MADE LUNCH FOR US! HOW THOUGHTFUL!
I'M STARVING! HOPE JACK DOESN'T MIND IF I GIVE IT A TASTE.
GROWL
MUCH TOO HOT!
MUCH TOO COLD!
NOW, *THAT'S* JUUUUST RIGHT!

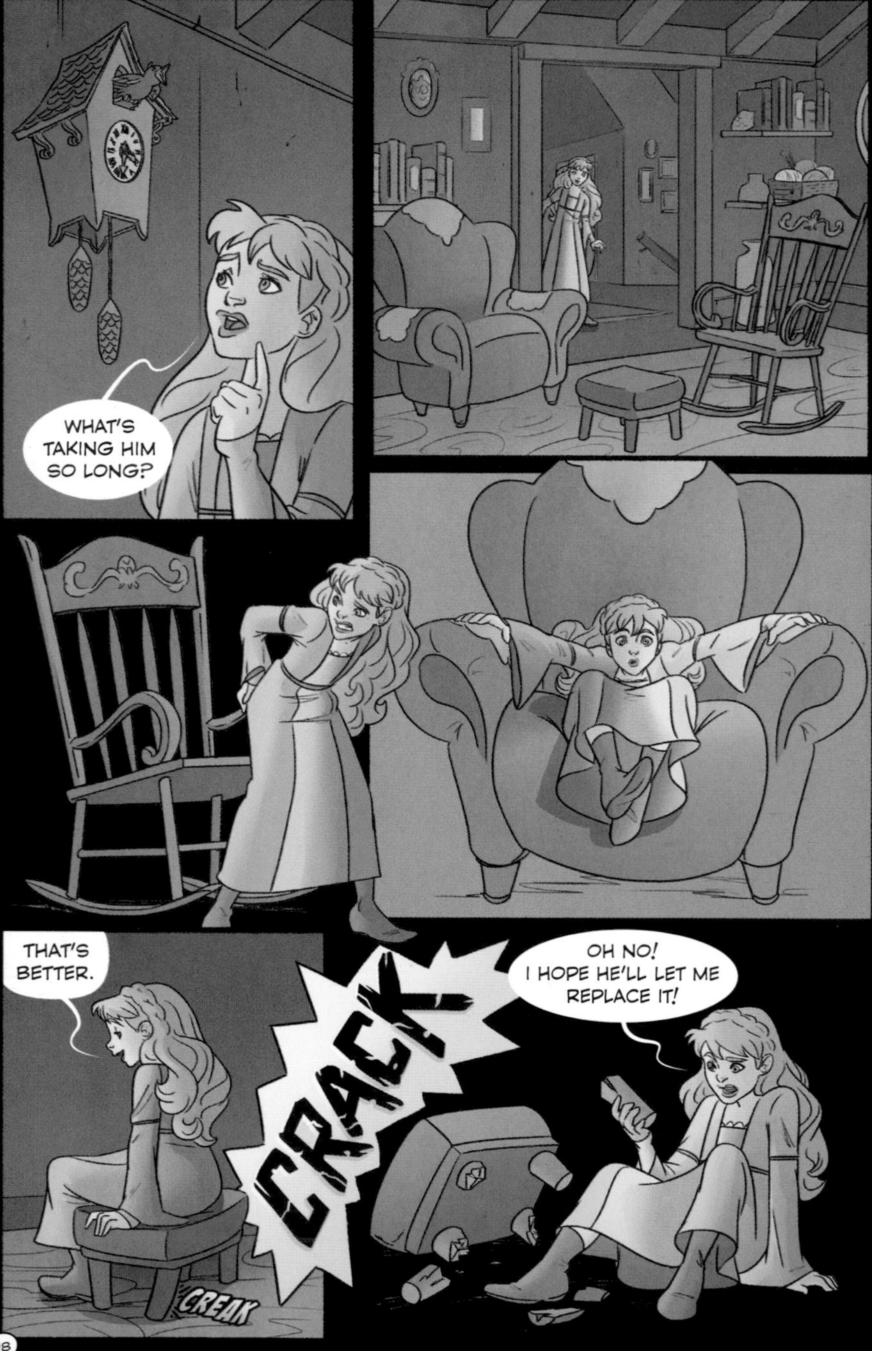
WHAT'S TAKING HIM SO LONG?
THAT'S BETTER.
CRACK
CREAK
OH NO! I HOPE HE'LL LET ME REPLACE IT!

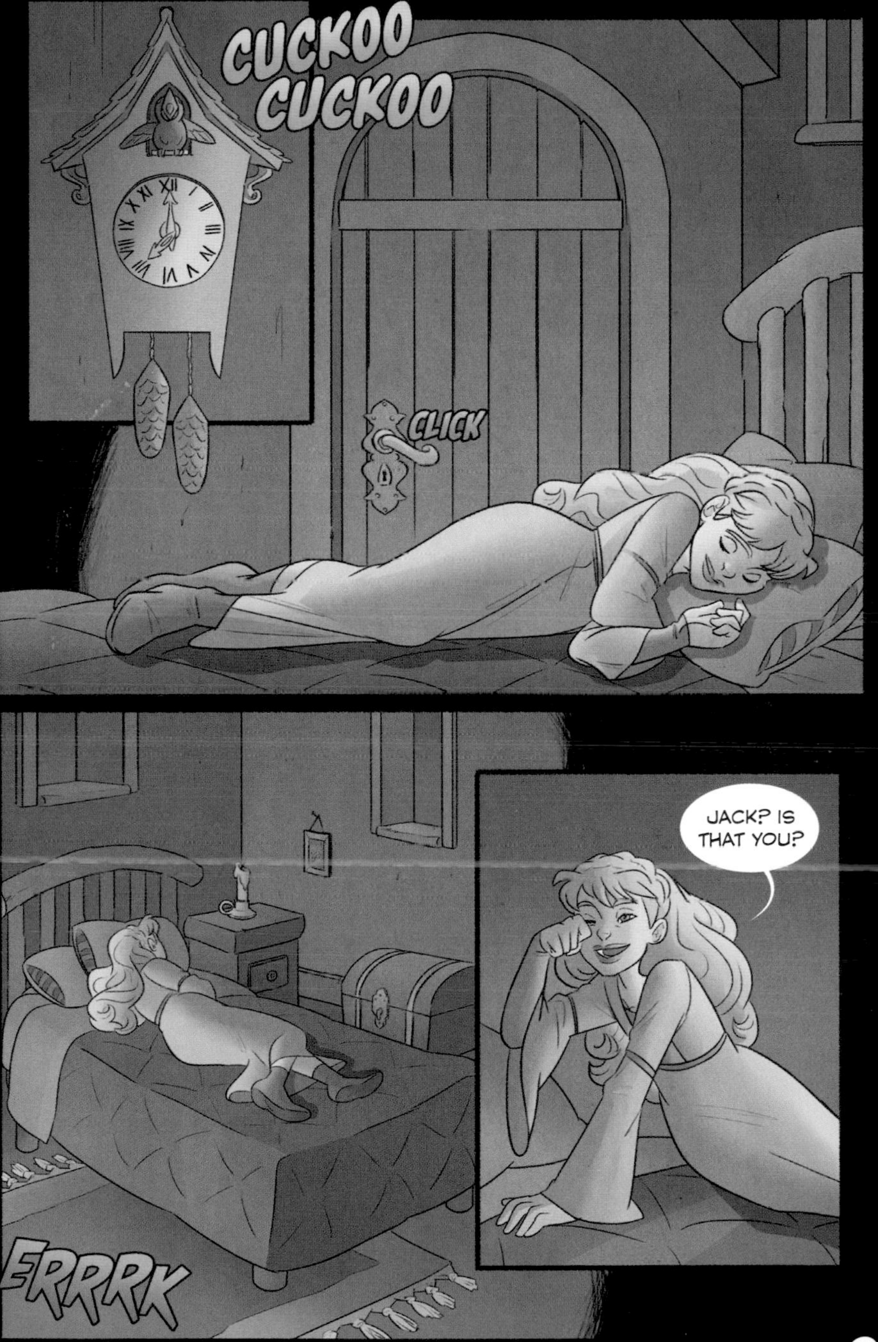
CUCKOO
CUCKOO
CLICK
ERRRK
JACK? IS THAT YOU?

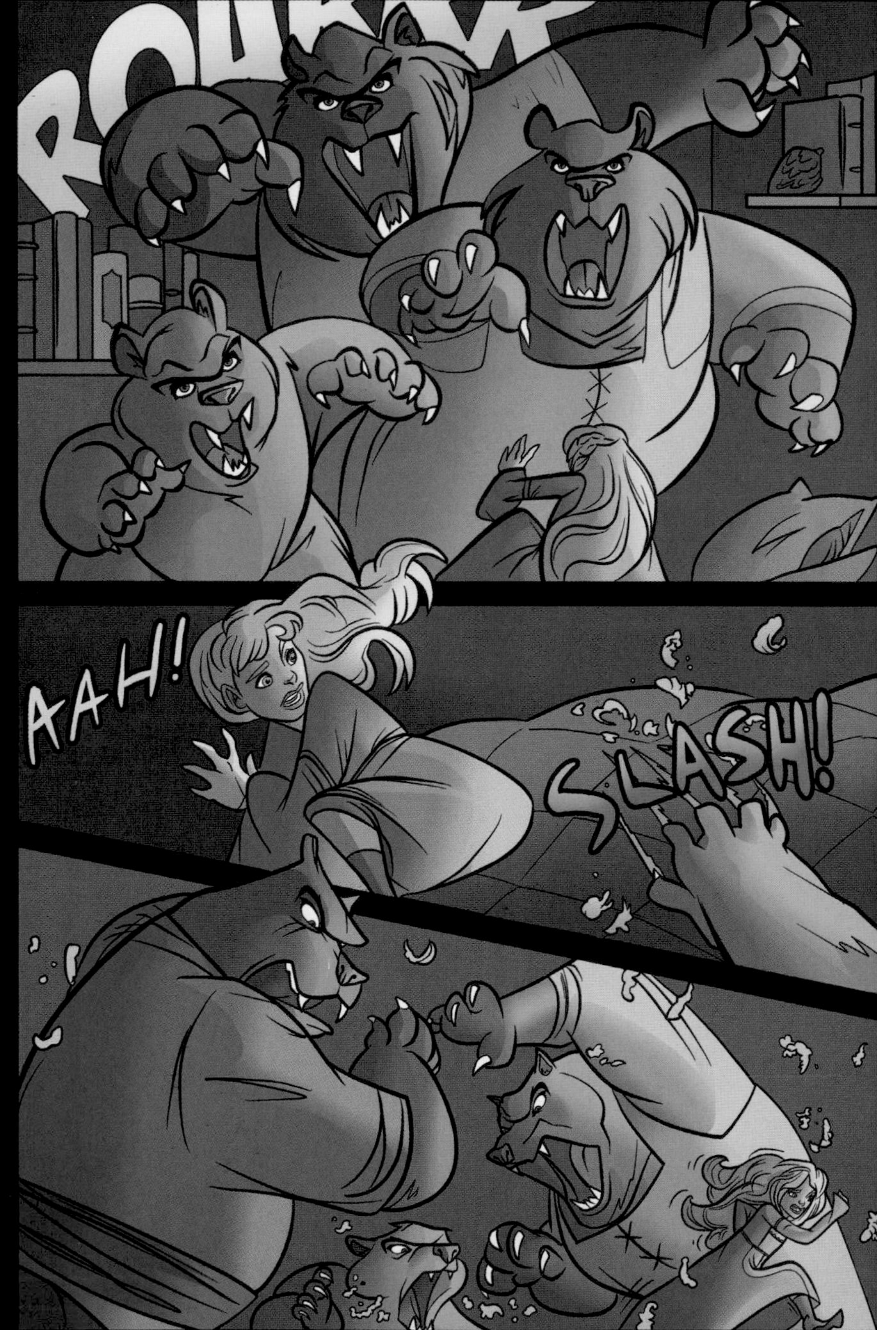
AAH!
SLASH!

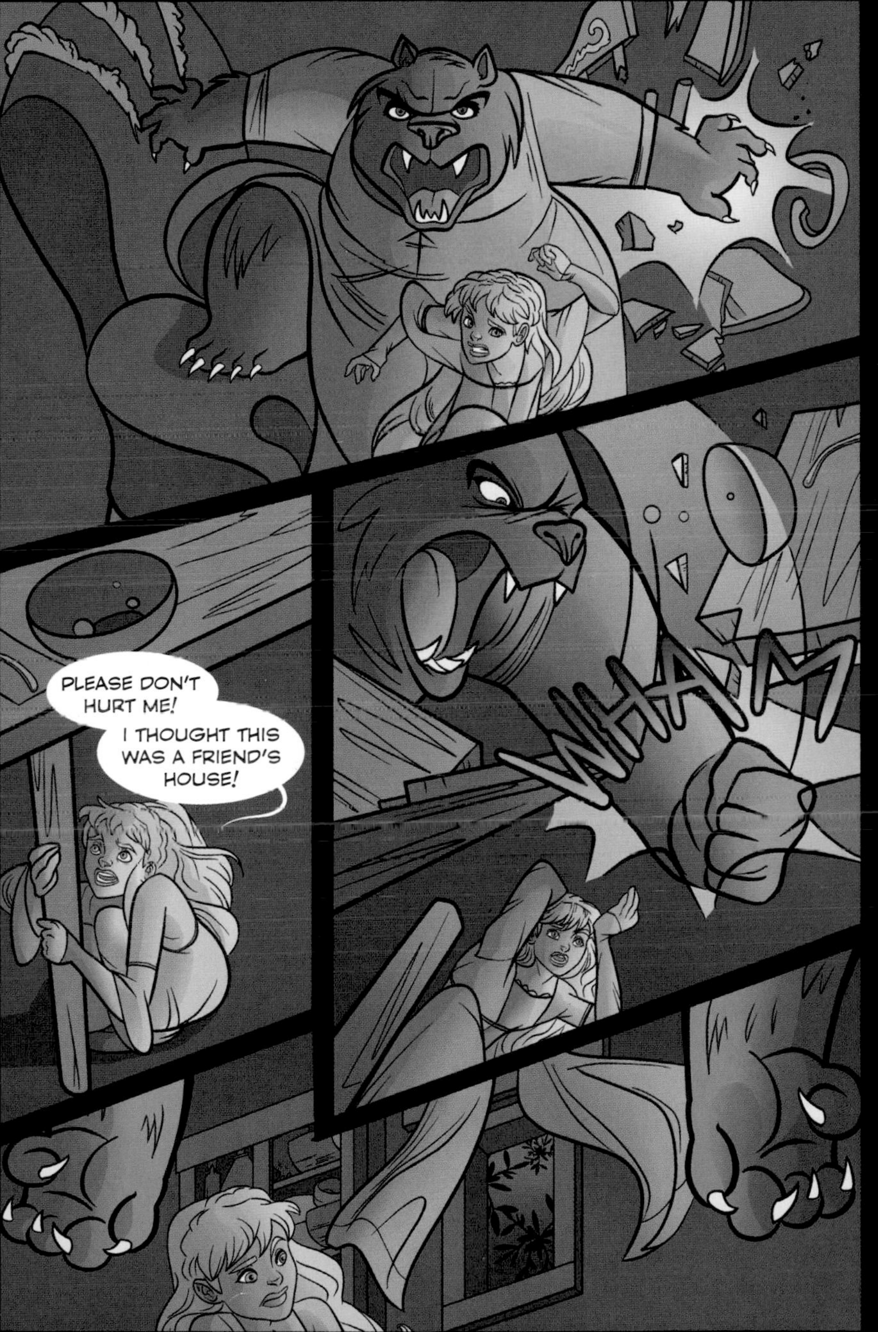
PLEASE DON'T HURT ME!
I THOUGHT THIS WAS A FRIEND'S HOUSE!
WHAM

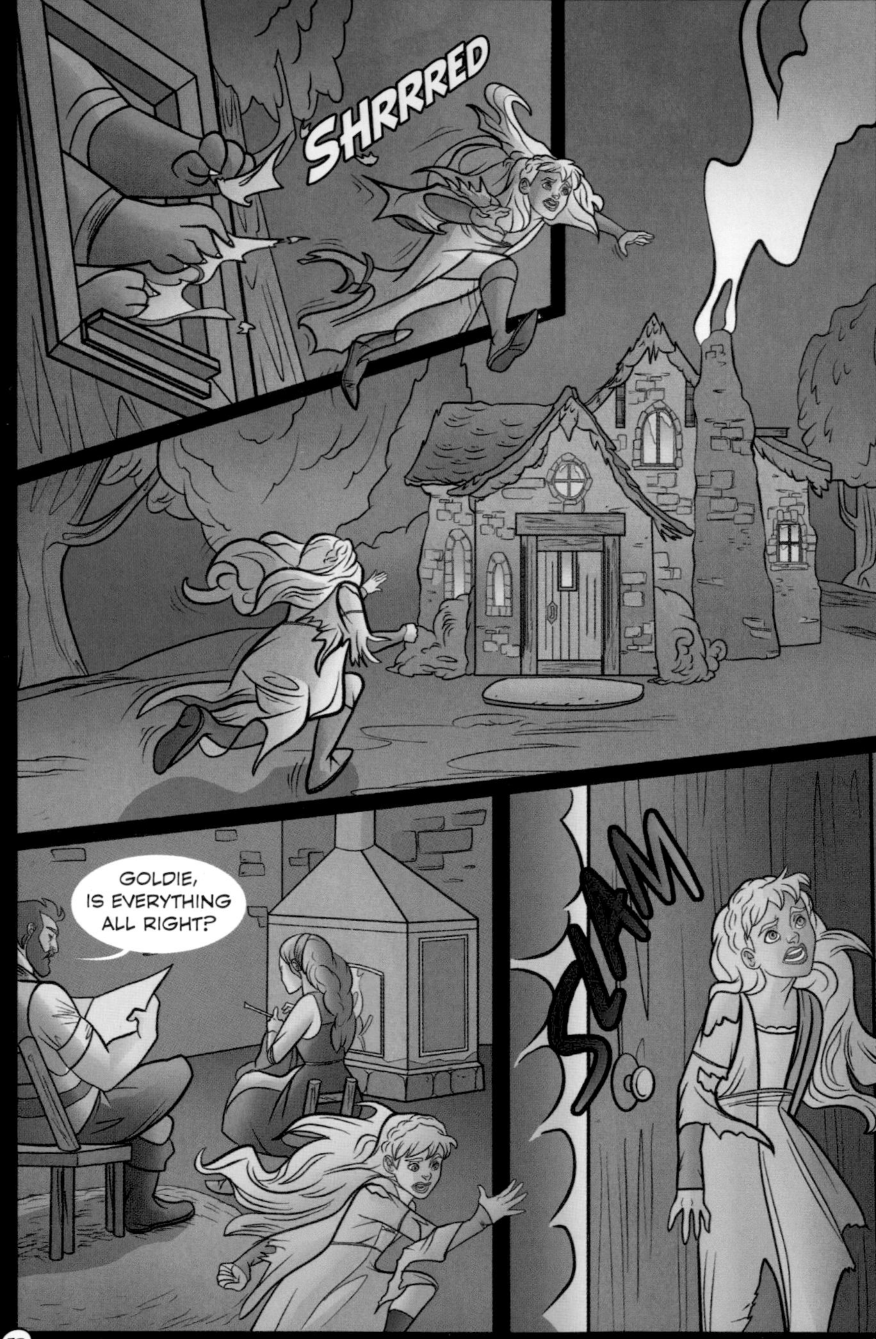
SHRRRED
GOLDIE, IS EVERYTHING ALL RIGHT?
SLAM

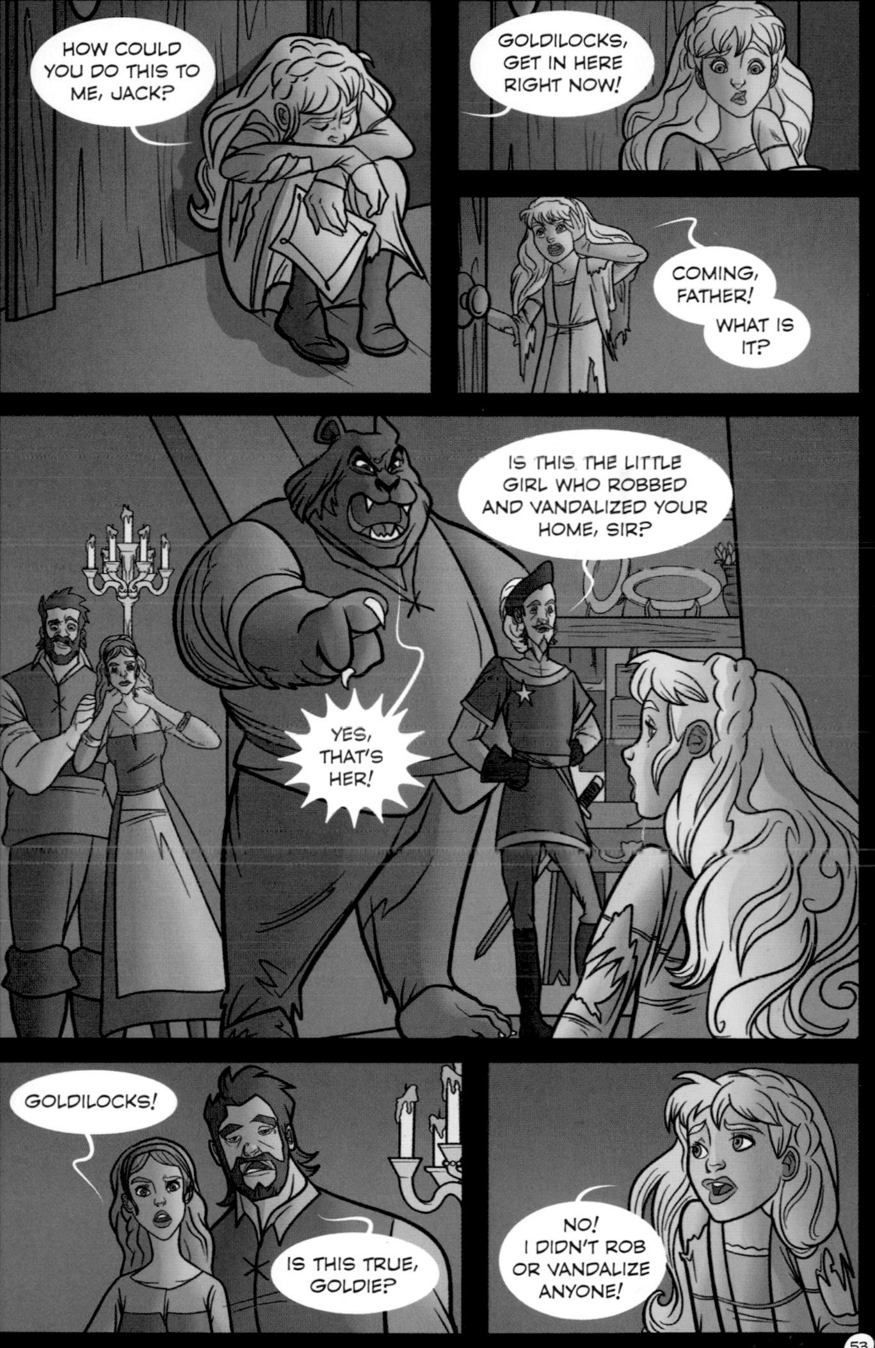
HOW COULD YOU DO THIS TO ME, JACK?
GOLDILOCKS, GET IN HERE RIGHT NOW!
COMING, FATHER!
WHAT IS IT?
IS THIS THE LITTLE GIRL WHO ROBBED AND VANDALIZED YOUR HOME, SIR?
YES, THAT'S HER!
GOLDILOCKS!
IS THIS TRUE, GOLDIE?
NO! I DIDN'T ROB OR VANDALIZE ANYONE!

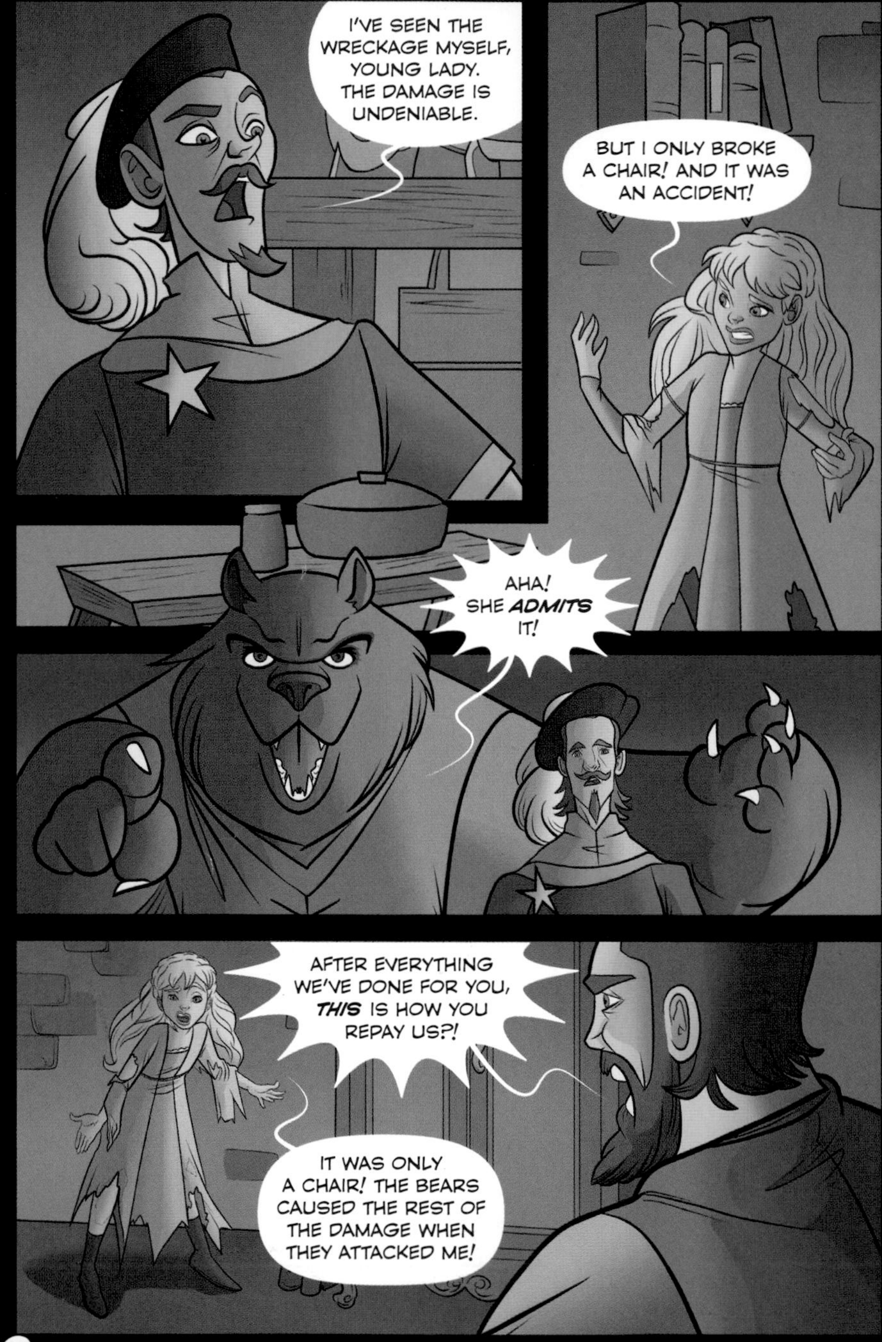
I'VE SEEN THE WRECKAGE MYSELF, YOUNG LADY. THE DAMAGE IS UNDENIABLE.
BUT I ONLY BROKE A CHAIR! AND IT WAS AN ACCIDENT!
AHA! SHE ADMITS IT!
AFTER EVERYTHING WE'VE DONE FOR YOU, THIS IS HOW YOU REPAY US?!
IT WAS ONLY A CHAIR! THE BEARS CAUSED THE REST OF THE DAMAGE WHEN THEY ATTACKED ME!

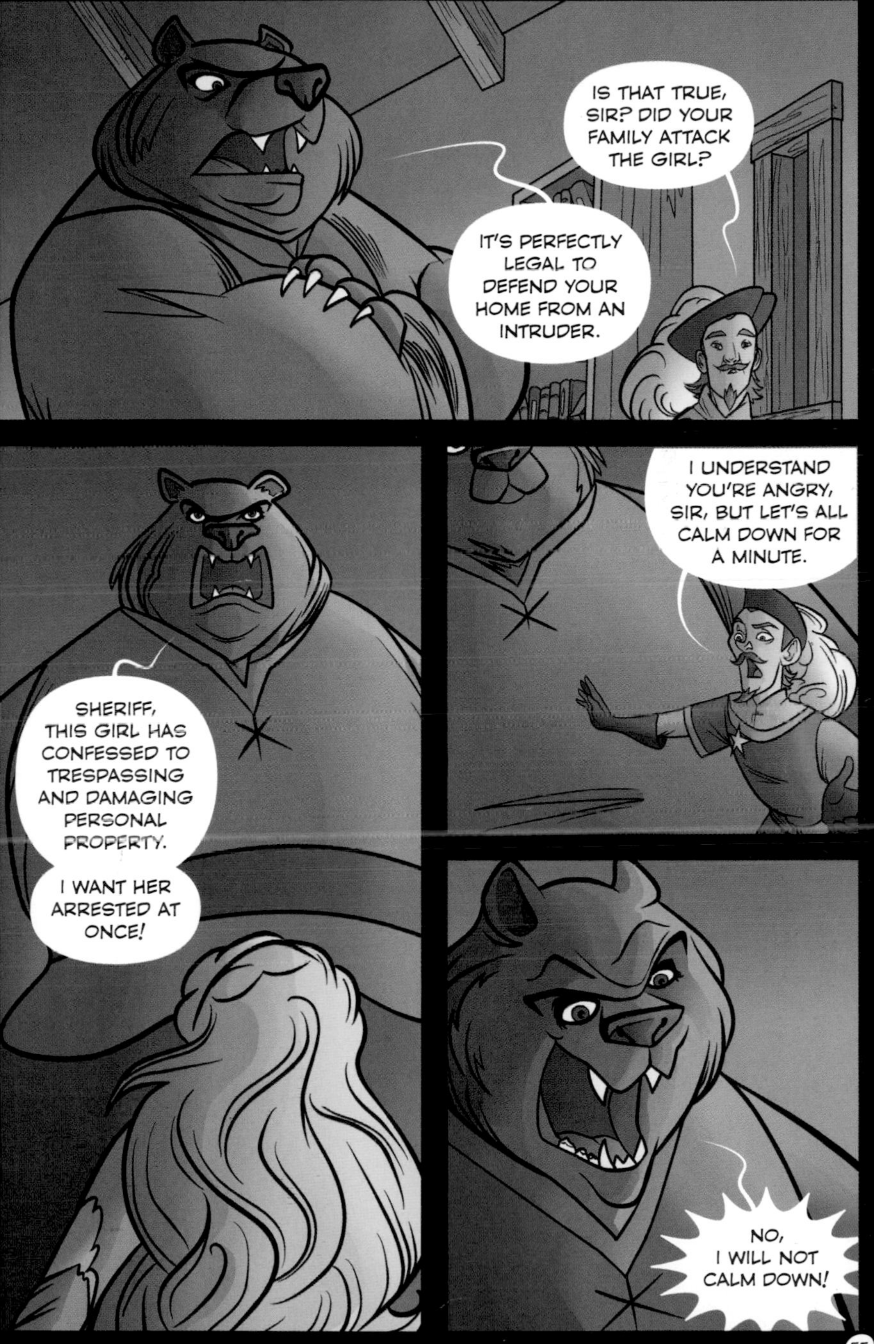
IS THAT TRUE, SIR? DID YOUR FAMILY ATTACK THE GIRL?
IT'S PERFECTLY LEGAL TO DEFEND YOUR HOME FROM AN INTRUDER.
SHERIFF, THIS GIRL HAS CONFESSED TO TRESPASSING AND DAMAGING PERSONAL PROPERTY.
I WANT HER ARRESTED AT ONCE!
I UNDERSTAND YOU'RE ANGRY, SIR, BUT LET'S ALL CALM DOWN FOR A MINUTE.
NO, I WILL NOT CALM DOWN!

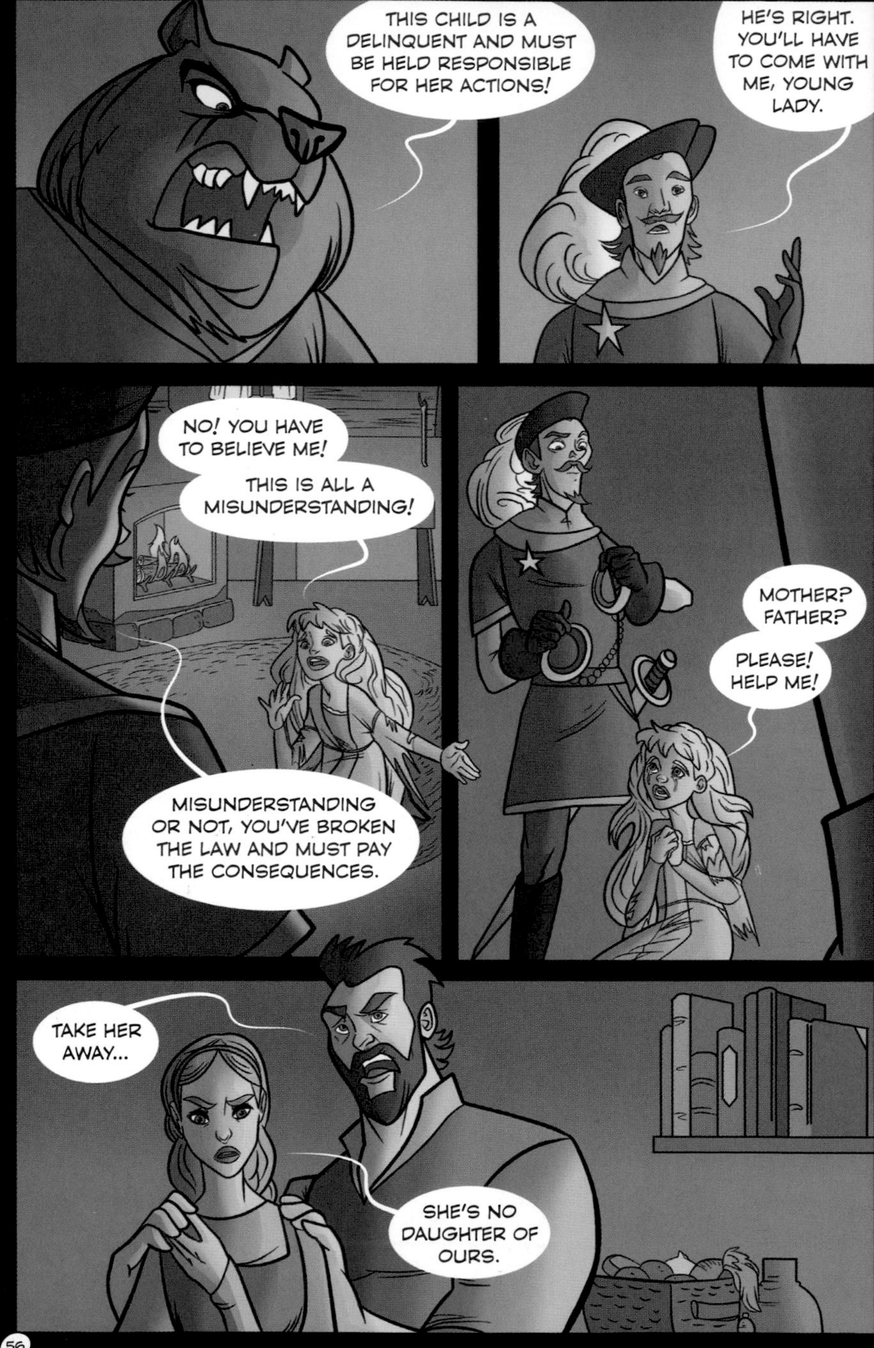
THIS CHILD IS A DELINQUENT AND MUST BE HELD RESPONSIBLE FOR HER ACTIONS!
HE'S RIGHT. YOU'LL HAVE TO COME WITH ME, YOUNG LADY.
NO! YOU HAVE TO BELIEVE ME!
THIS IS ALL A MISUNDERSTANDING!
MISUNDERSTANDING OR NOT, YOU'VE BROKEN THE LAW AND MUST PAY THE CONSEQUENCES.
MOTHER? FATHER?
PLEASE! HELP ME!
TAKE HER AWAY...
SHE'S NO DAUGHTER OF OURS.

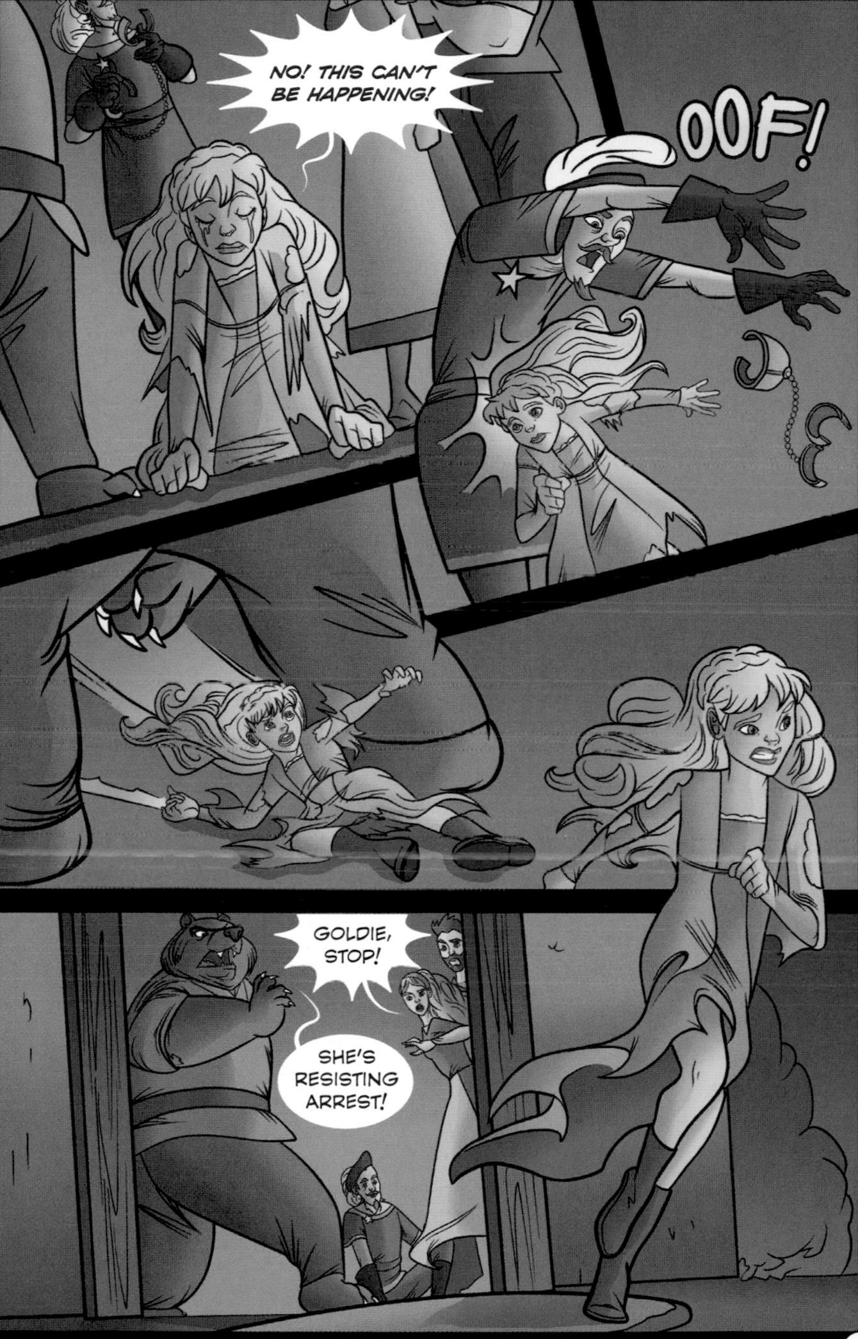
NO! THIS CAN'T BE HAPPENING!
OOF!
GOLDIE, STOP!
SHE'S RESISTING ARREST!

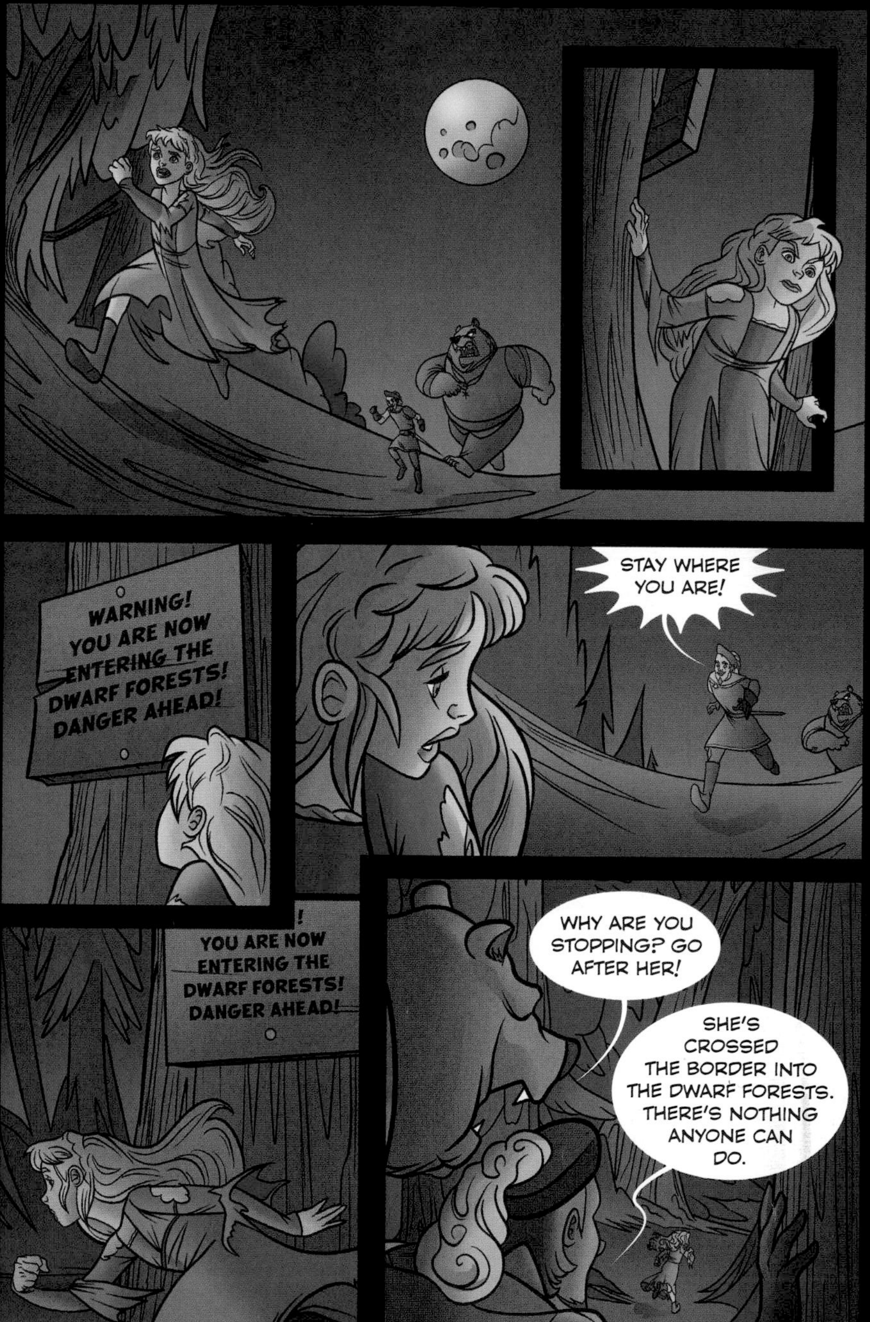

WARNING! YOU ARE NOW ENTERING THE DWARF FORESTS! DANGER AHEAD!
STAY WHERE YOU ARE!
! YOU ARE NOW ENTERING THE DWARF FORESTS! DANGER AHEAD!
WHY ARE YOU STOPPING? GO AFTER HER!
SHE'S CROSSED THE BORDER INTO THE DWARF FORESTS. THERE'S NOTHING ANYONE CAN DO.

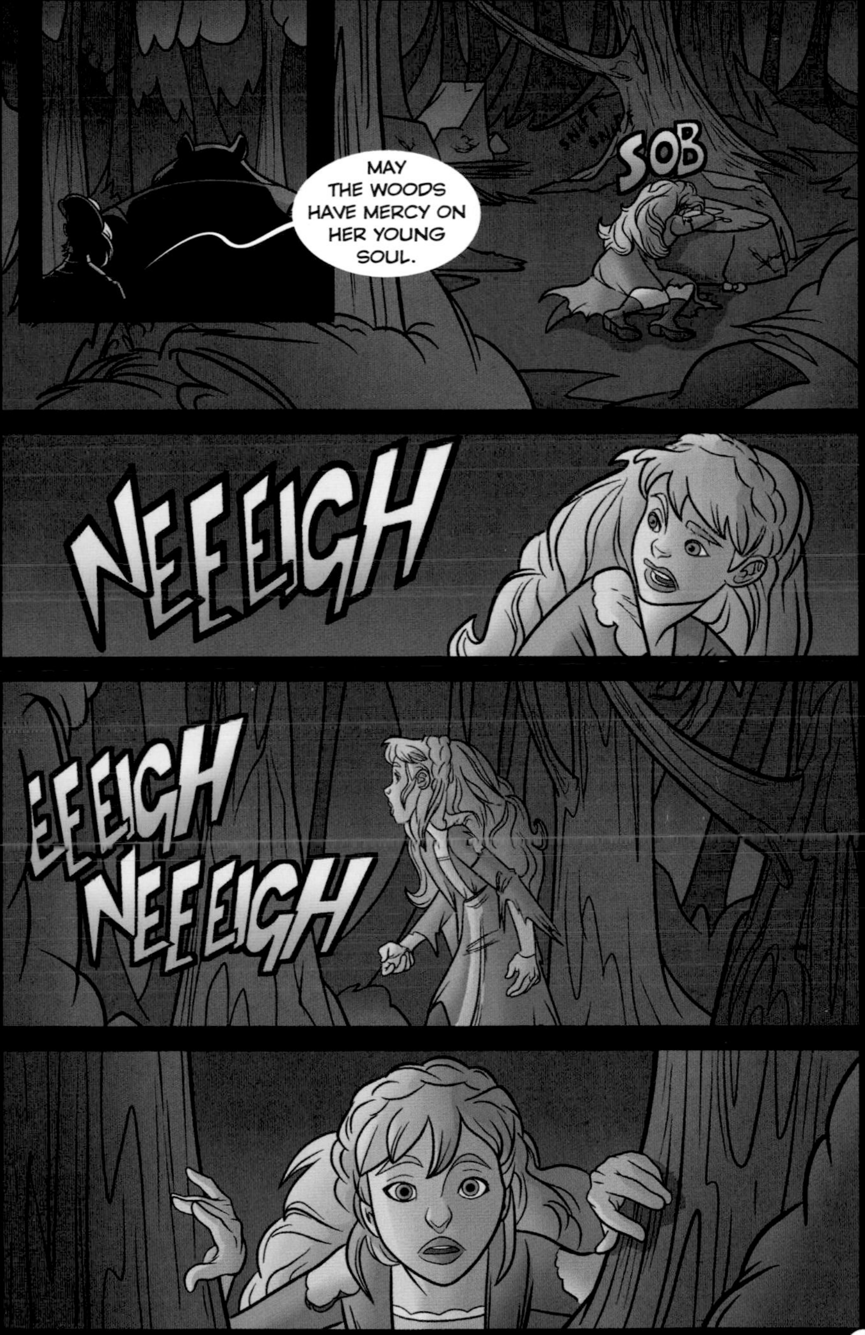
MAY THE WOODS HAVE MERCY ON HER YOUNG SOUL.
SOB
NEE EIGH
EE EIGH
NEE EIGH

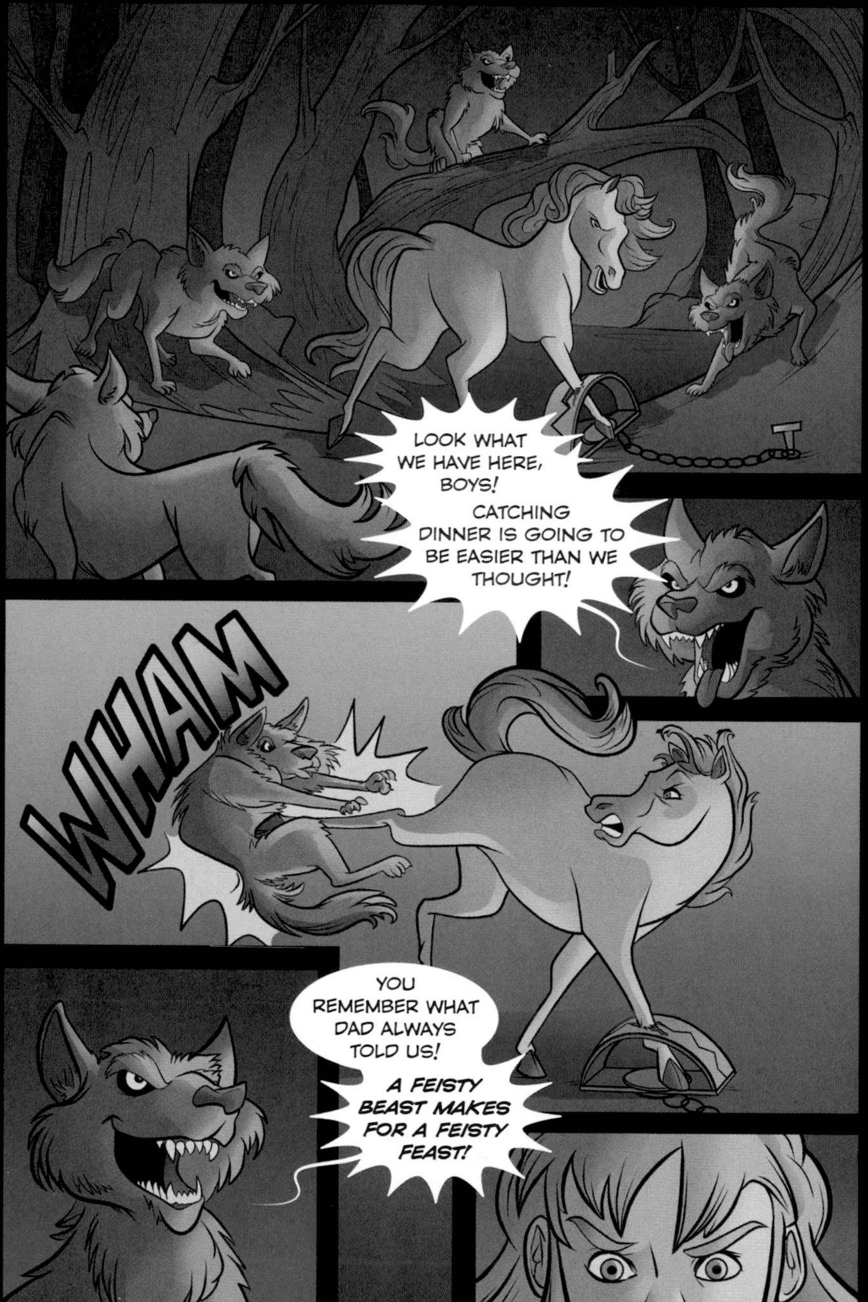
LOOK WHAT WE HAVE HERE, BOYS!
CATCHING DINNER IS GOING TO BE EASIER THAN WE THOUGHT!
WHAM
YOU REMEMBER WHAT DAD ALWAYS TOLD US!
A FEISTY BEAST MAKES FOR A FEISTY FEAST!

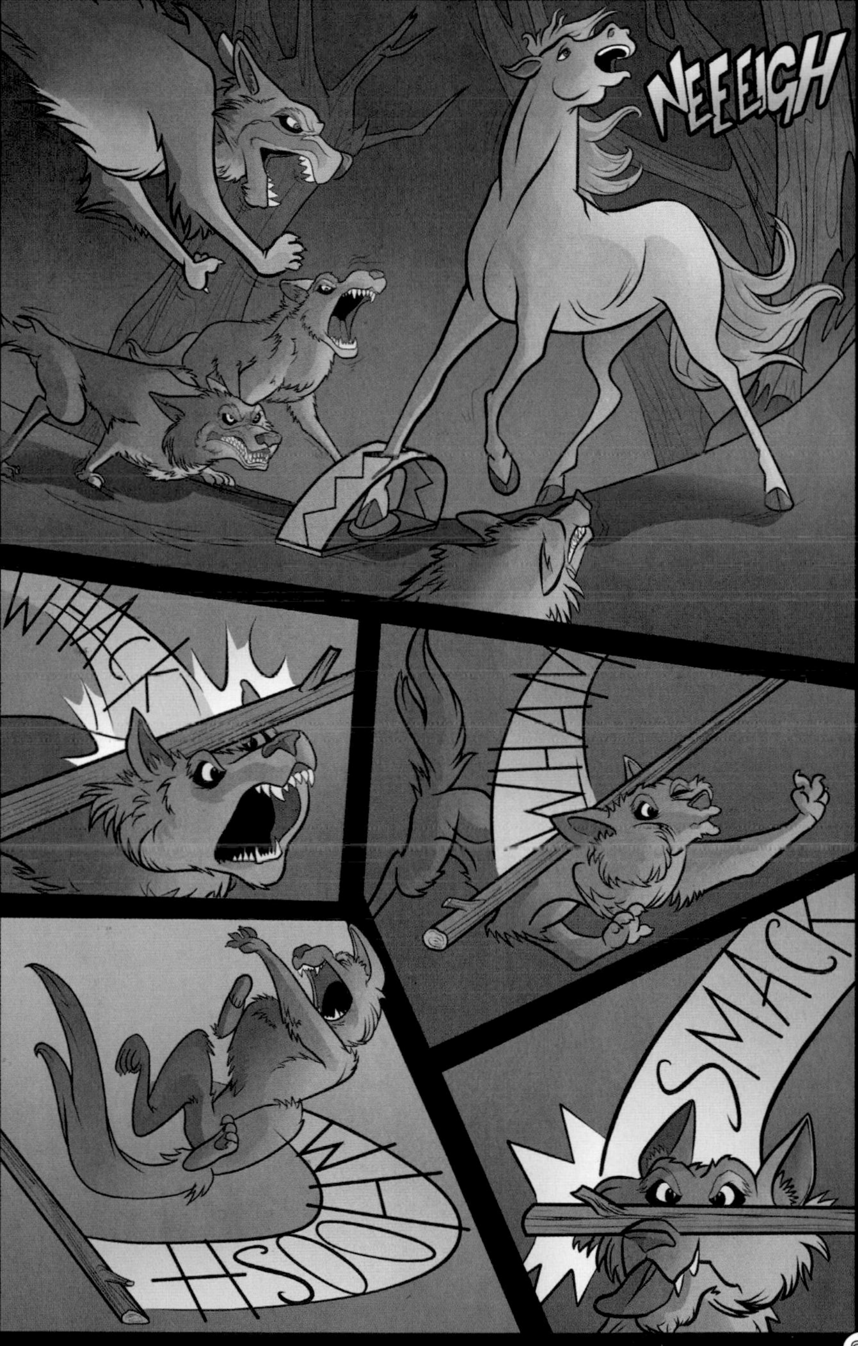
NEEEIGH
WHACK
WHAM
SMACK
WHOOSH

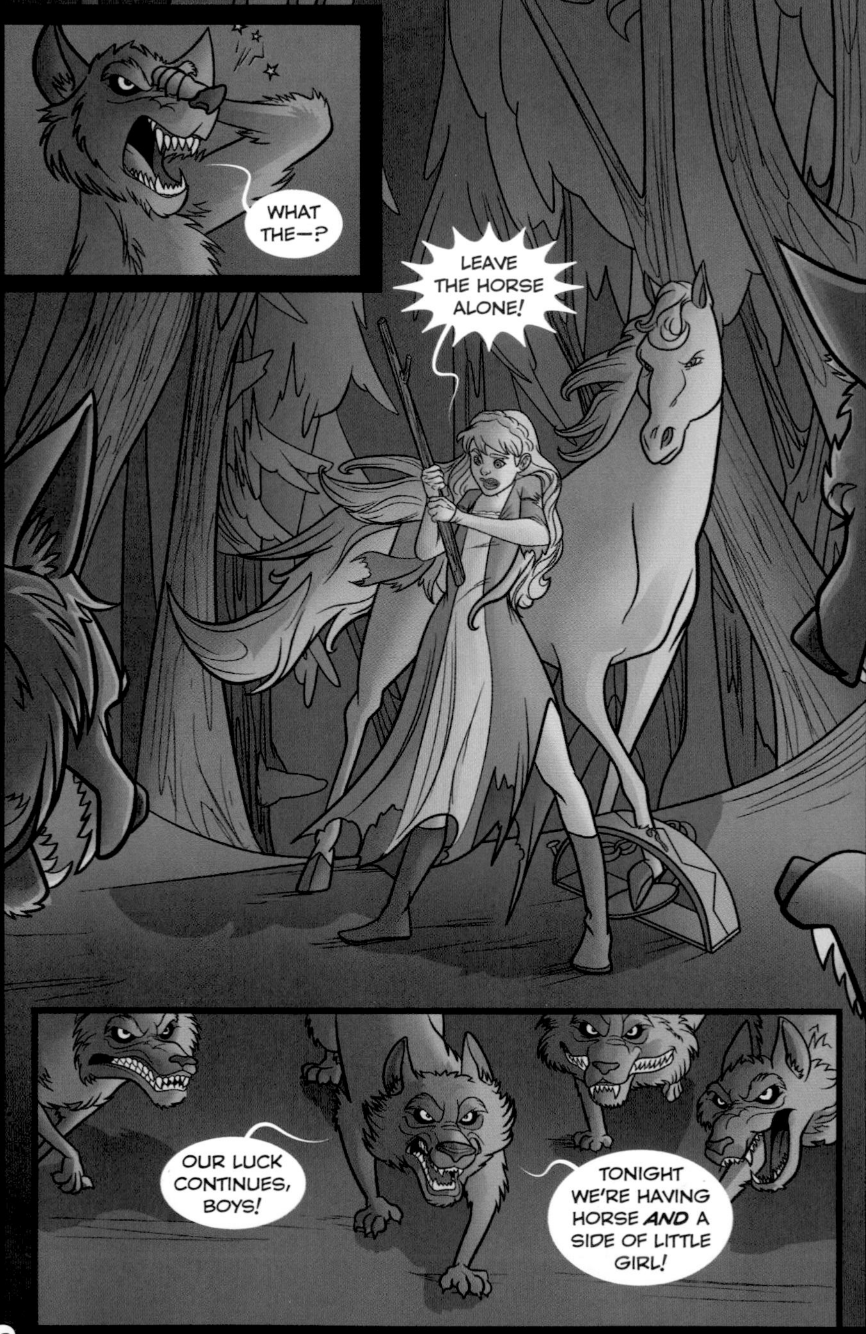
WHAT THE—?
LEAVE THE HORSE ALONE!
OUR LUCK CONTINUES, BOYS!
TONIGHT WE'RE HAVING HORSE *AND* A SIDE OF LITTLE GIRL!

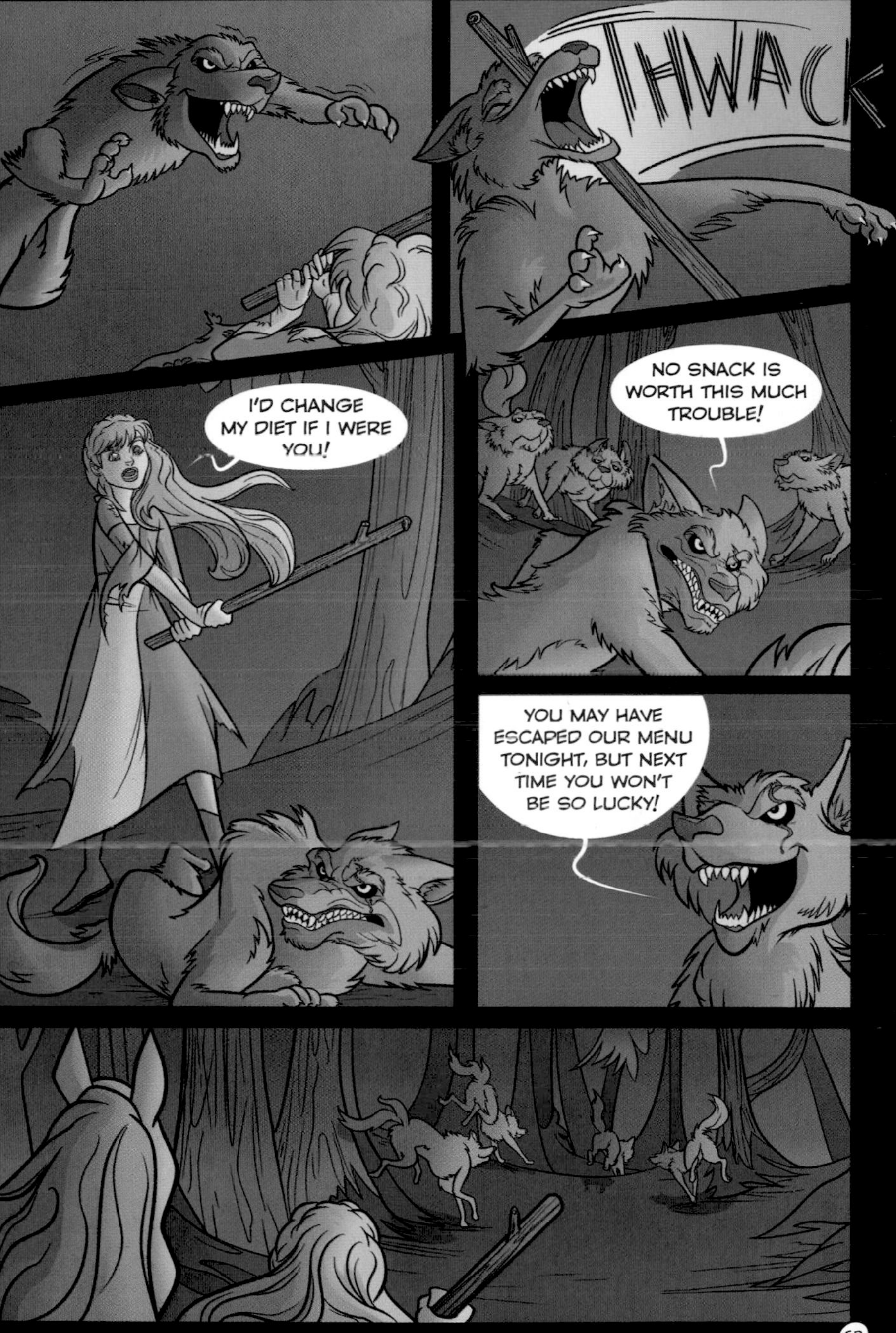
THWACK
I'D CHANGE MY DIET IF I WERE YOU!
NO SNACK IS WORTH THIS MUCH TROUBLE!
YOU MAY HAVE ESCAPED OUR MENU TONIGHT, BUT NEXT TIME YOU WON'T BE SO LUCKY!

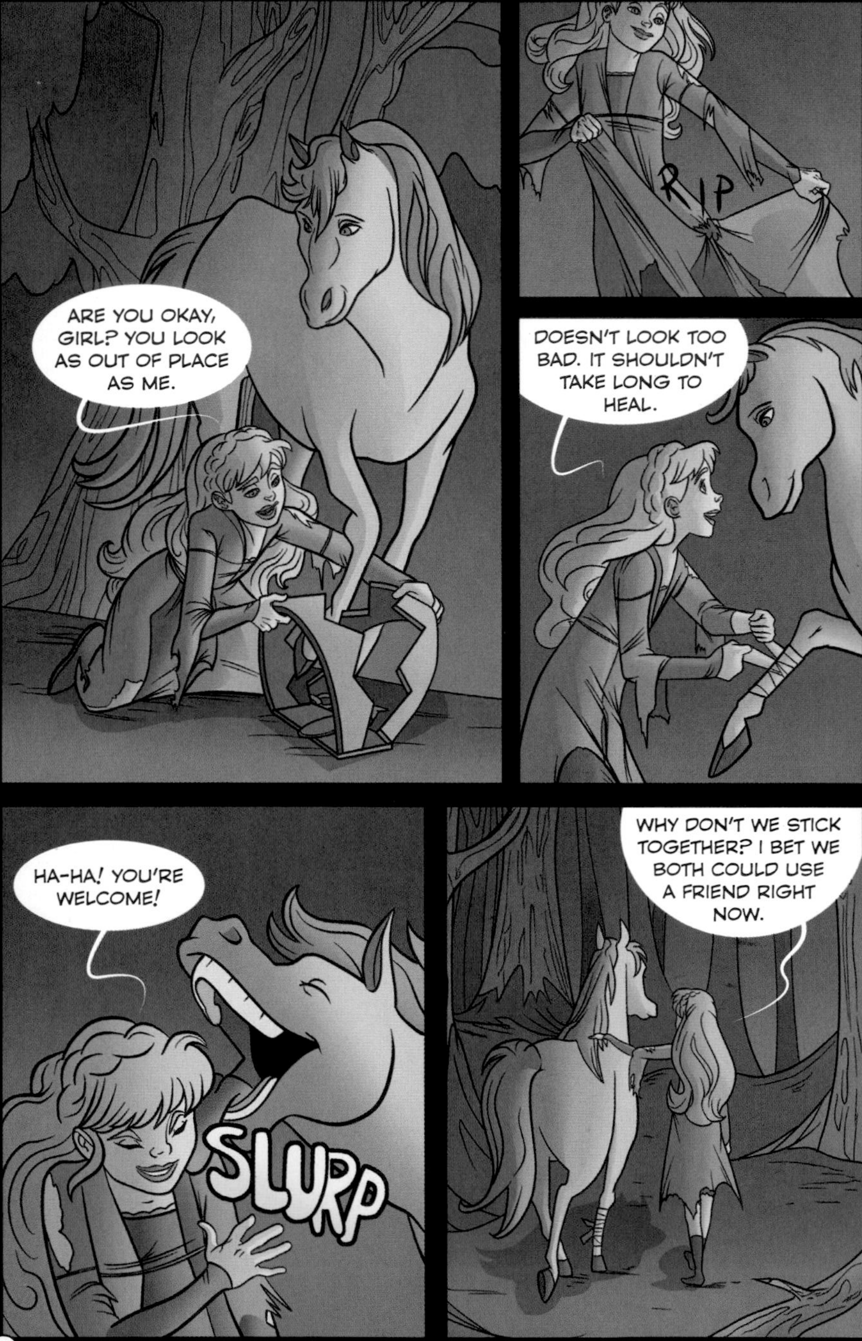
RIP
ARE YOU OKAY, GIRL? YOU LOOK AS OUT OF PLACE AS ME.
DOESN'T LOOK TOO BAD. IT SHOULDN'T TAKE LONG TO HEAL.
SLURP
HA-HA! YOU'RE WELCOME!
WHY DON'T WE STICK TOGETHER? I BET WE BOTH COULD USE A FRIEND RIGHT NOW.

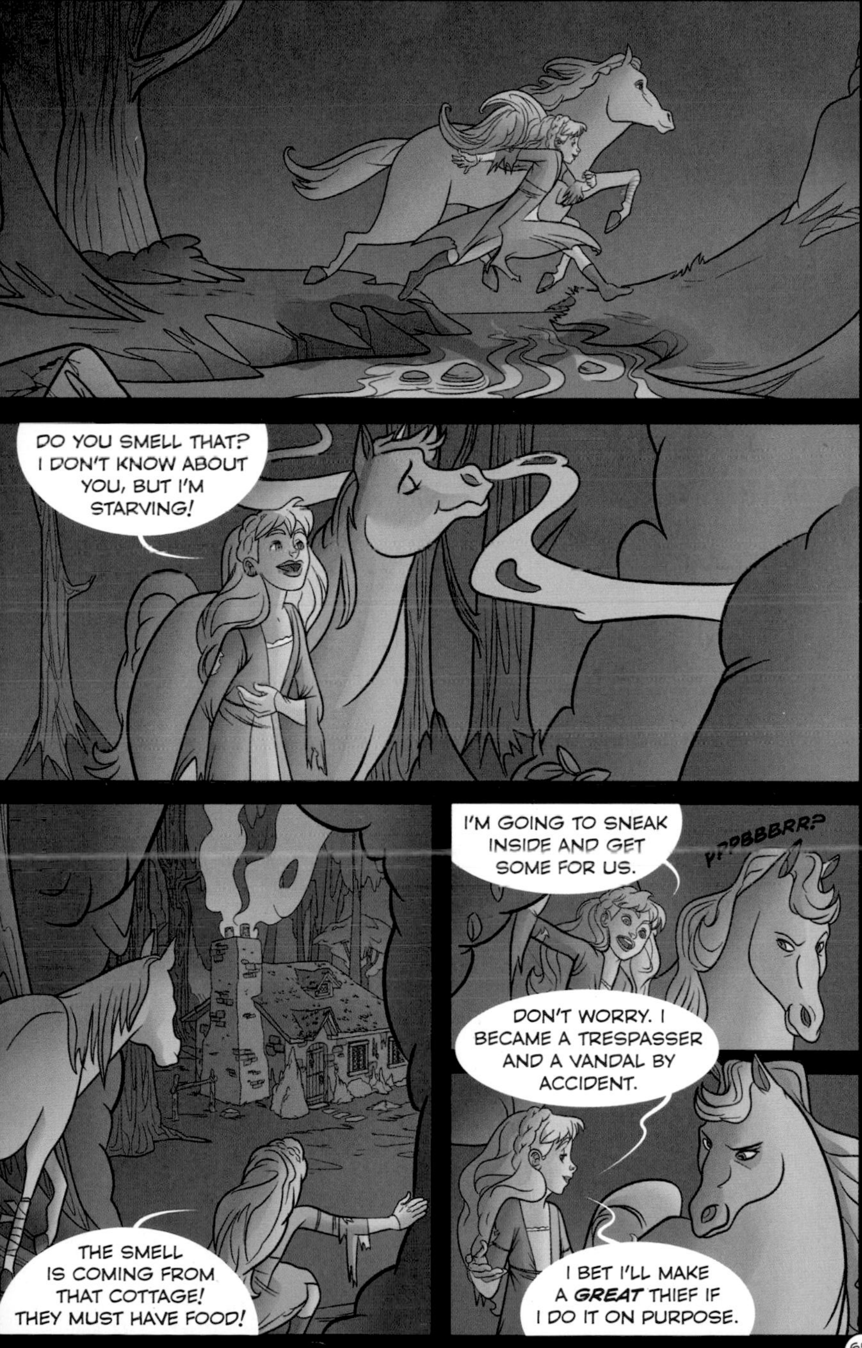

DO YOU SMELL THAT? I DON'T KNOW ABOUT YOU, BUT I'M STARVING!
THE SMELL IS COMING FROM THAT COTTAGE! THEY MUST HAVE FOOD!
I'M GOING TO SNEAK INSIDE AND GET SOME FOR US.
PPPBBBRR?
DON'T WORRY. I BECAME A TRESPASSER AND A VANDAL BY ACCIDENT.
I BET I'LL MAKE A ***GREAT*** THIEF IF I DO IT ON PURPOSE.

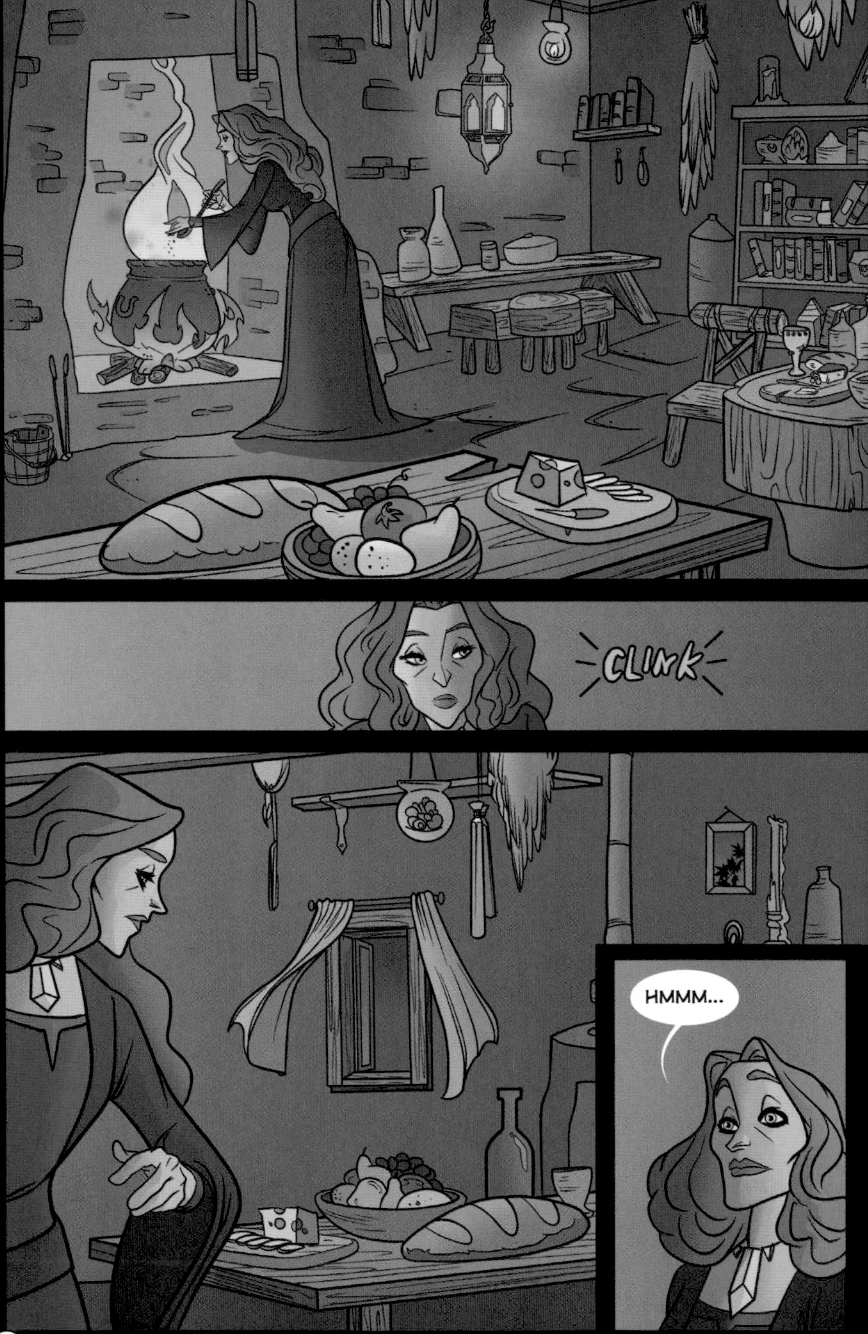
CLINK
HMMM...

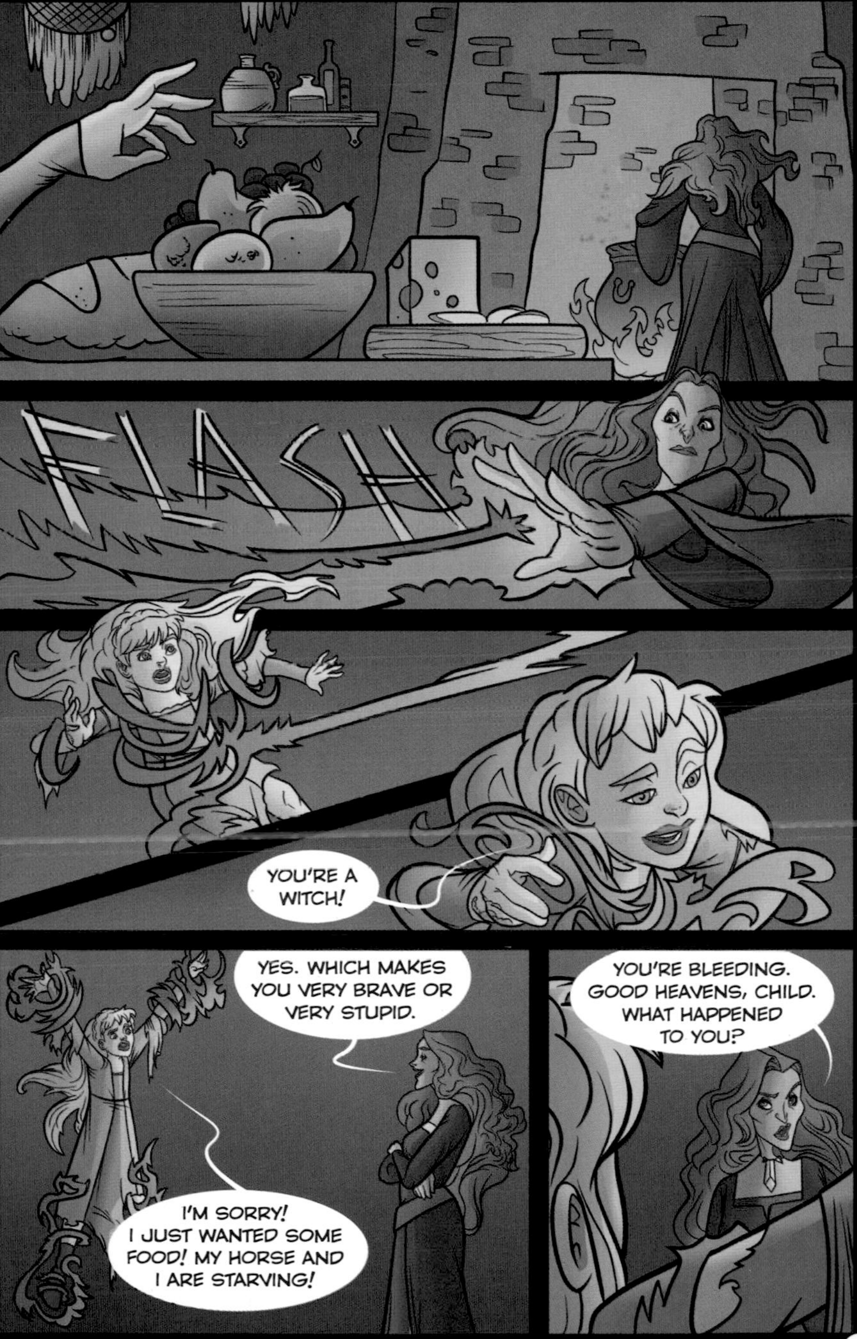
FLASH
YOU'RE A WITCH!
YES. WHICH MAKES YOU VERY BRAVE OR VERY STUPID.
I'M SORRY! I JUST WANTED SOME FOOD! MY HORSE AND I ARE STARVING!
YOU'RE BLEEDING. GOOD HEAVENS, CHILD. WHAT HAPPENED TO YOU?

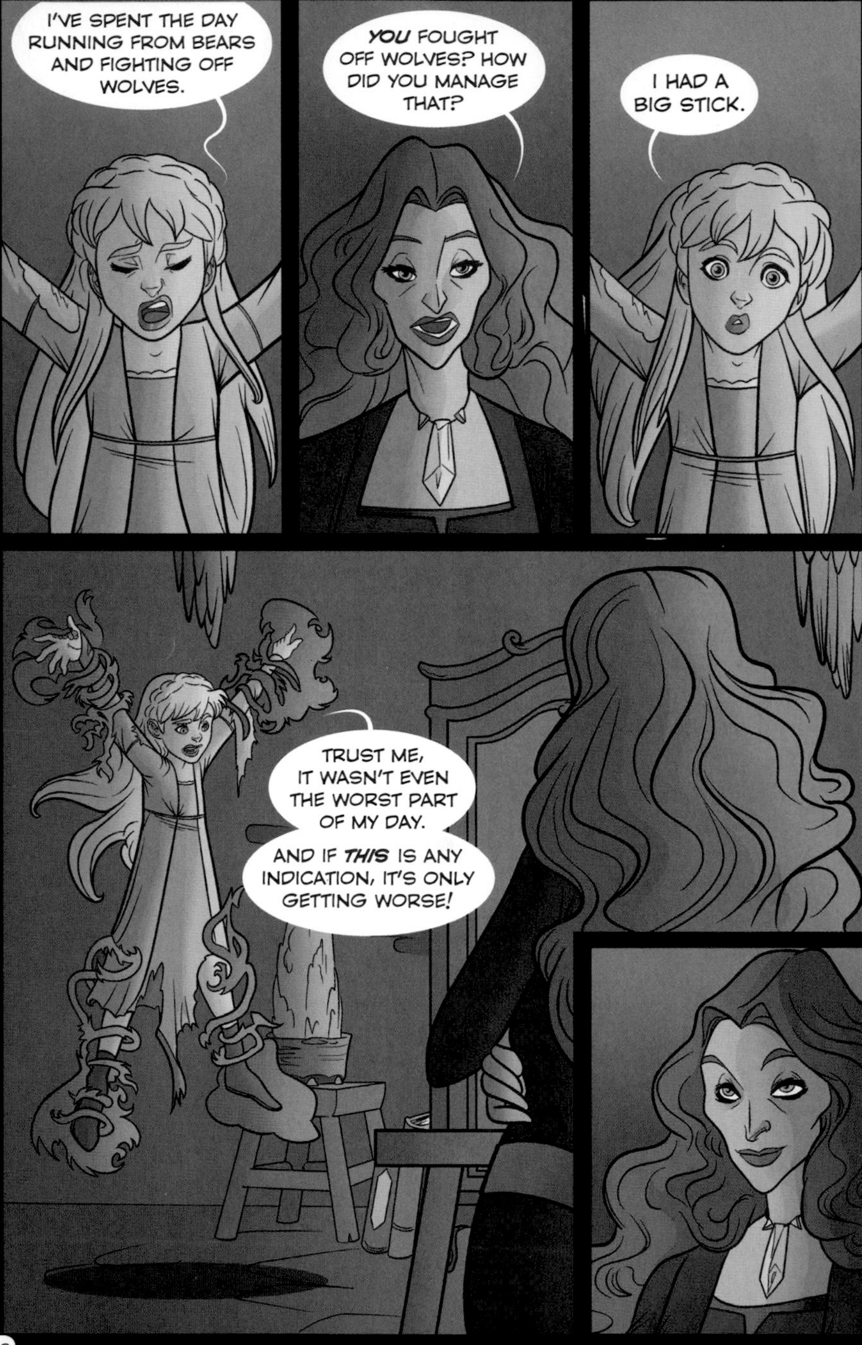
I'VE SPENT THE DAY RUNNING FROM BEARS AND FIGHTING OFF WOLVES.
YOU FOUGHT OFF WOLVES? HOW DID YOU MANAGE THAT?
I HAD A BIG STICK.
TRUST ME, IT WASN'T EVEN THE WORST PART OF MY DAY.
AND IF THIS IS ANY INDICATION, IT'S ONLY GETTING WORSE!

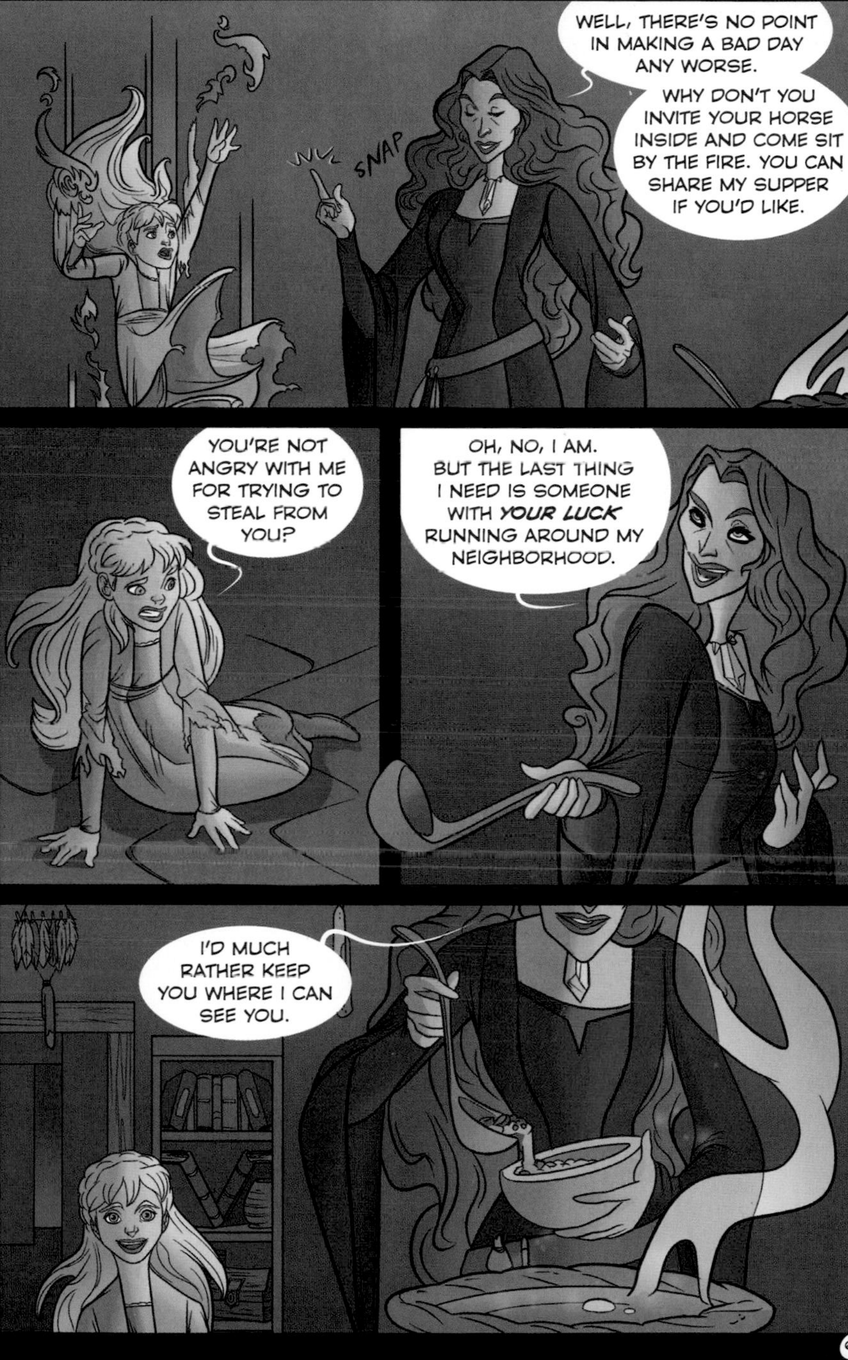
SNAP
WELL, THERE'S NO POINT IN MAKING A BAD DAY ANY WORSE.
WHY DON'T YOU INVITE YOUR HORSE INSIDE AND COME SIT BY THE FIRE. YOU CAN SHARE MY SUPPER IF YOU'D LIKE.
YOU'RE NOT ANGRY WITH ME FOR TRYING TO STEAL FROM YOU?
OH, NO, I AM. BUT THE LAST THING I NEED IS SOMEONE WITH *YOUR LUCK* RUNNING AROUND MY NEIGHBORHOOD.
I'D MUCH RATHER KEEP YOU WHERE I CAN SEE YOU.

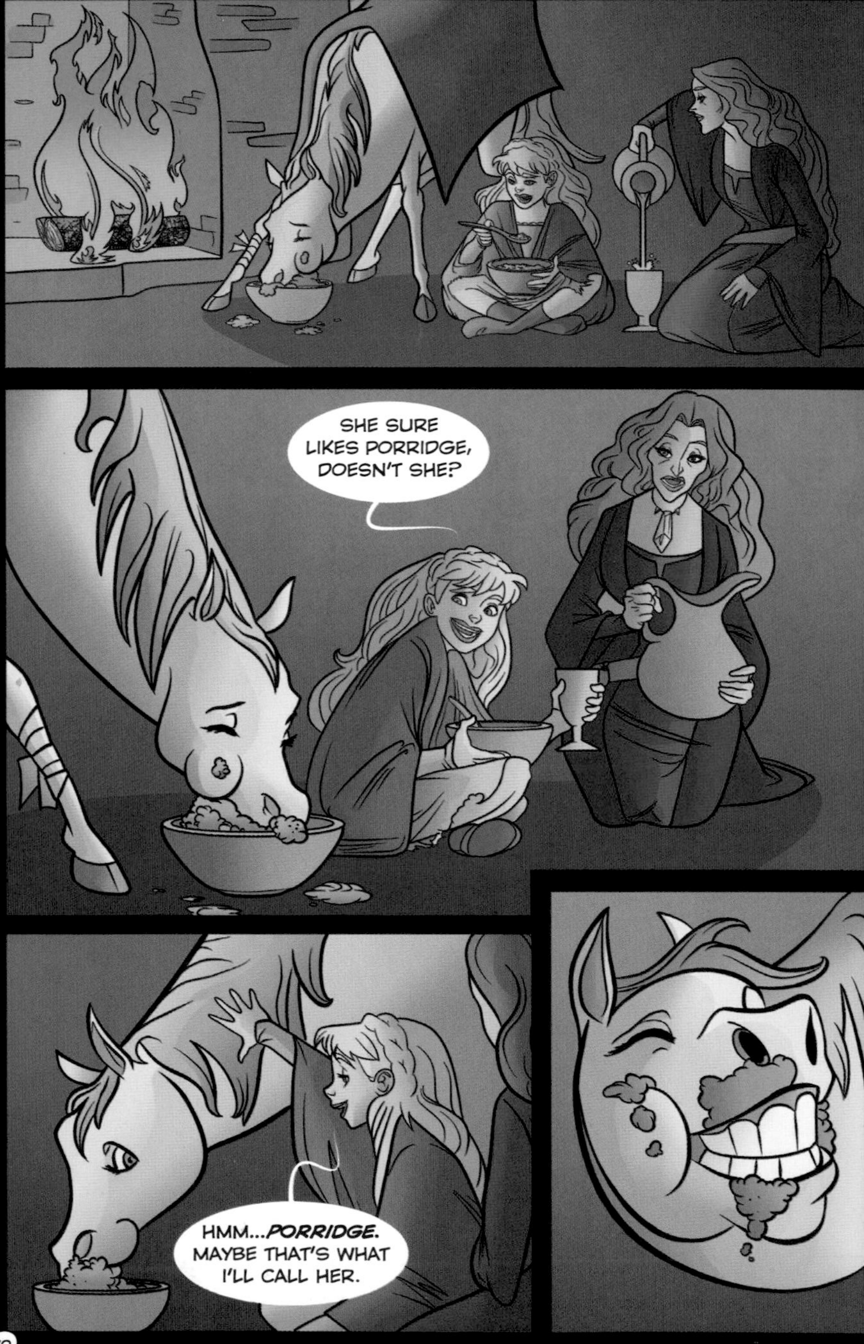
SHE SURE LIKES PORRIDGE, DOESN'T SHE?
HMM...PORRIDGE. MAYBE THAT'S WHAT I'LL CALL HER.

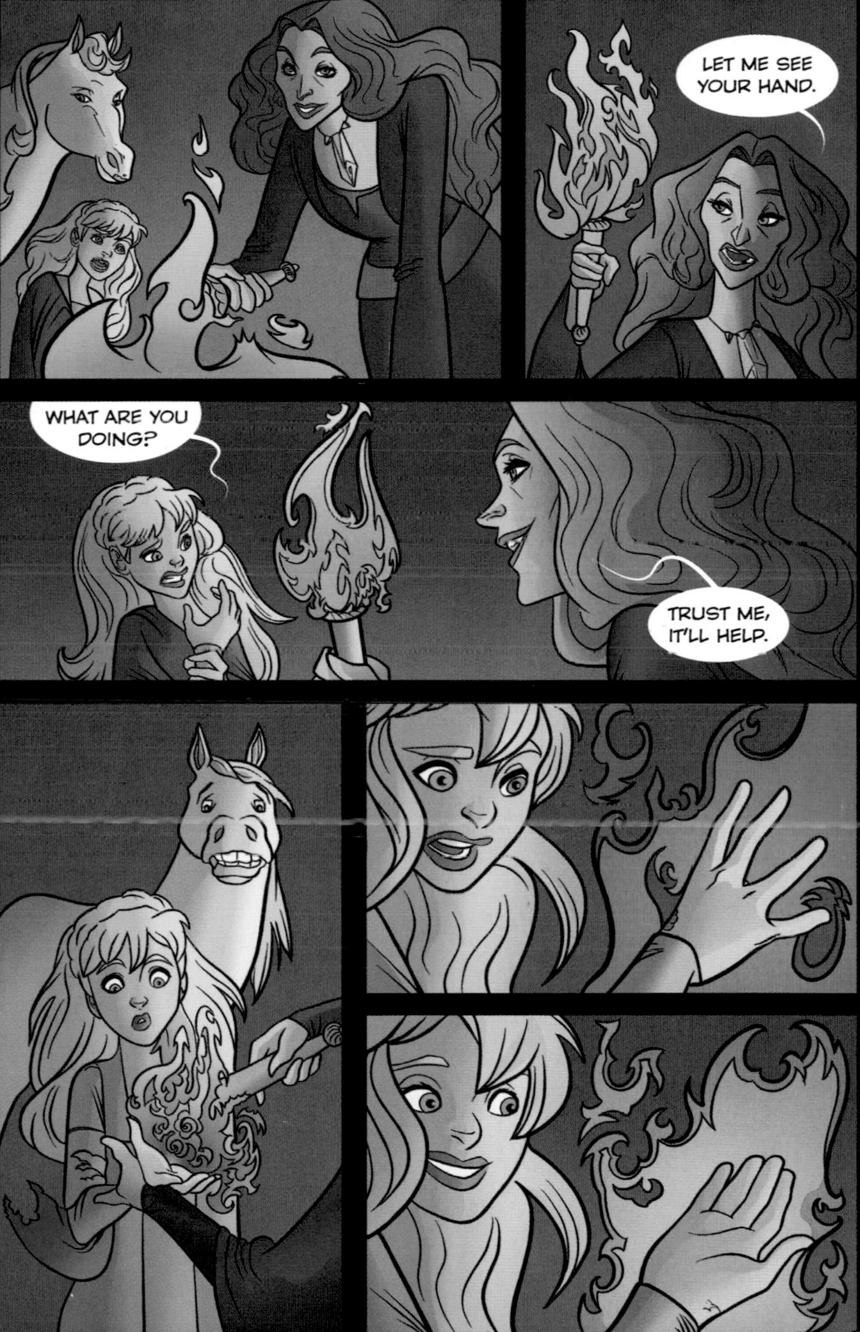
LET ME SEE YOUR HAND.
WHAT ARE YOU DOING?
TRUST ME, IT'LL HELP.

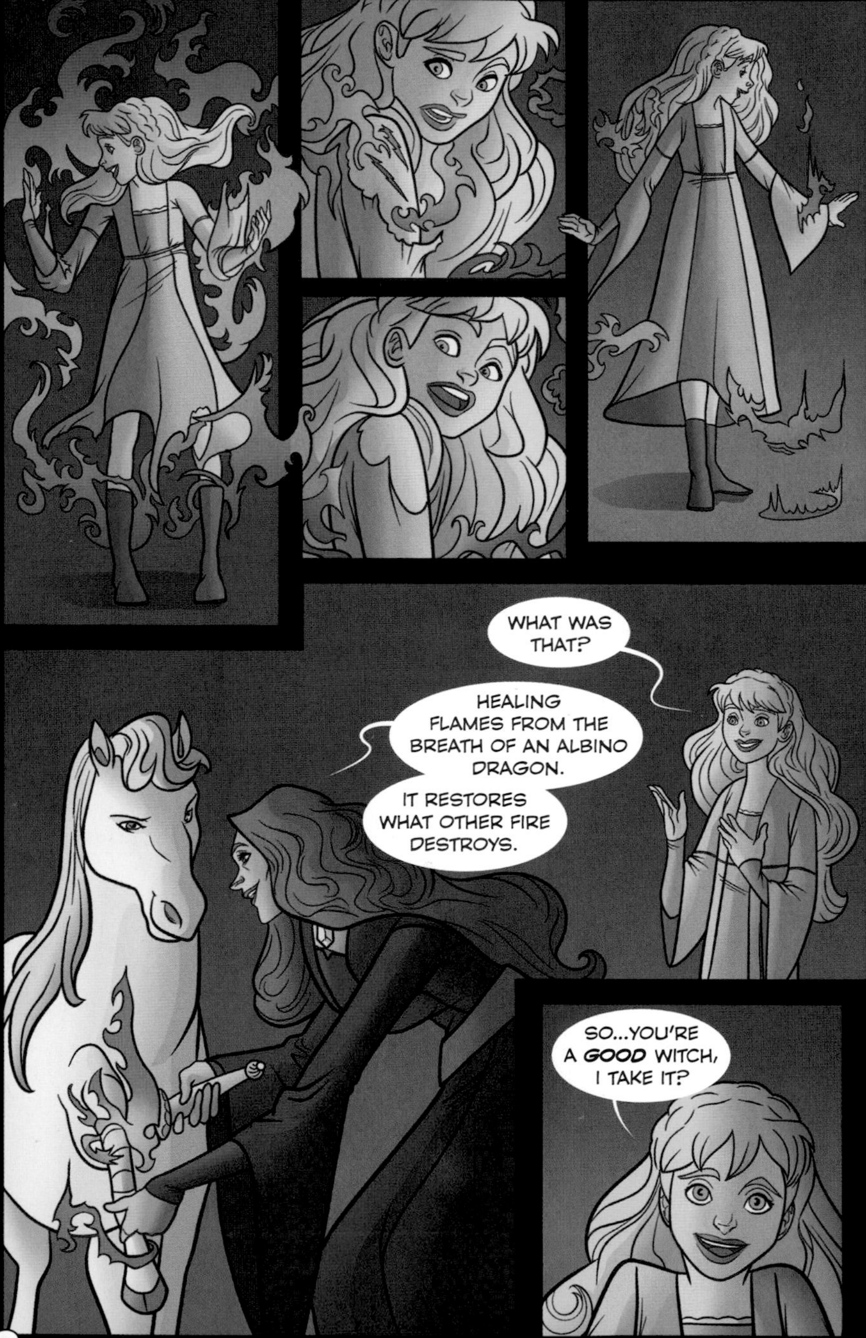
WHAT WAS THAT?
HEALING FLAMES FROM THE BREATH OF AN ALBINO DRAGON.
IT RESTORES WHAT OTHER FIRE DESTROYS.
SO...YOU'RE A **GOOD** WITCH, I TAKE IT?

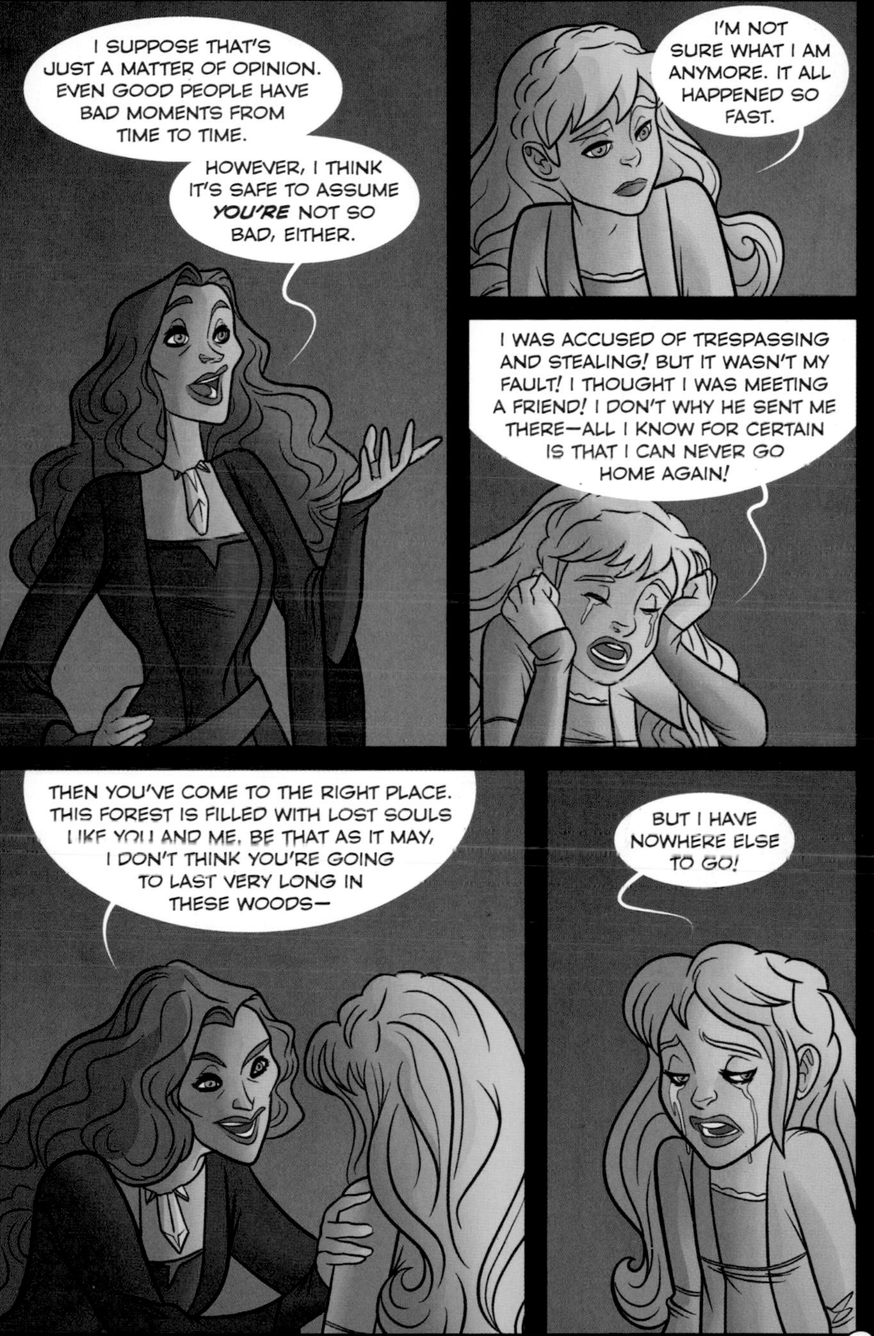
I SUPPOSE THAT'S JUST A MATTER OF OPINION. EVEN GOOD PEOPLE HAVE BAD MOMENTS FROM TIME TO TIME.
HOWEVER, I THINK IT'S SAFE TO ASSUME *YOU'RE* NOT SO BAD, EITHER.
I'M NOT SURE WHAT I AM ANYMORE. IT ALL HAPPENED SO FAST.
I WAS ACCUSED OF TRESPASSING AND STEALING! BUT IT WASN'T MY FAULT! I THOUGHT I WAS MEETING A FRIEND! I DON'T WHY HE SENT ME THERE—ALL I KNOW FOR CERTAIN IS THAT I CAN NEVER GO HOME AGAIN!
THEN YOU'VE COME TO THE RIGHT PLACE. THIS FOREST IS FILLED WITH LOST SOULS LIKE YOU AND ME. BE THAT AS IT MAY, I DON'T THINK YOU'RE GOING TO LAST VERY LONG IN THESE WOODS—
BUT I HAVE NOWHERE ELSE TO GO!

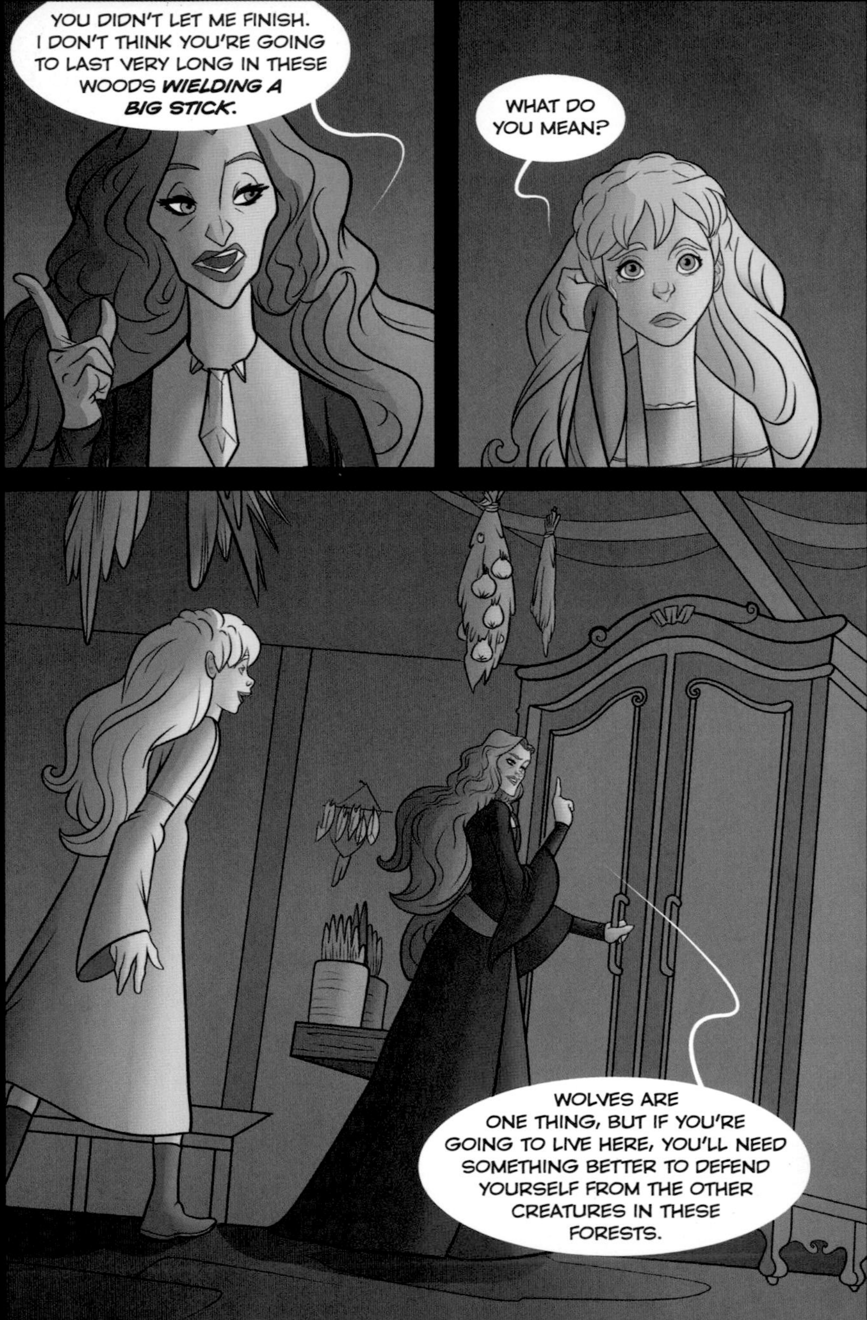
YOU DIDN'T LET ME FINISH. I DON'T THINK YOU'RE GOING TO LAST VERY LONG IN THESE WOODS ***WIELDING A BIG STICK***.
WHAT DO YOU MEAN?
WOLVES ARE ONE THING, BUT IF YOU'RE GOING TO LIVE HERE, YOU'LL NEED SOMETHING BETTER TO DEFEND YOURSELF FROM THE OTHER CREATURES IN THESE FORESTS.

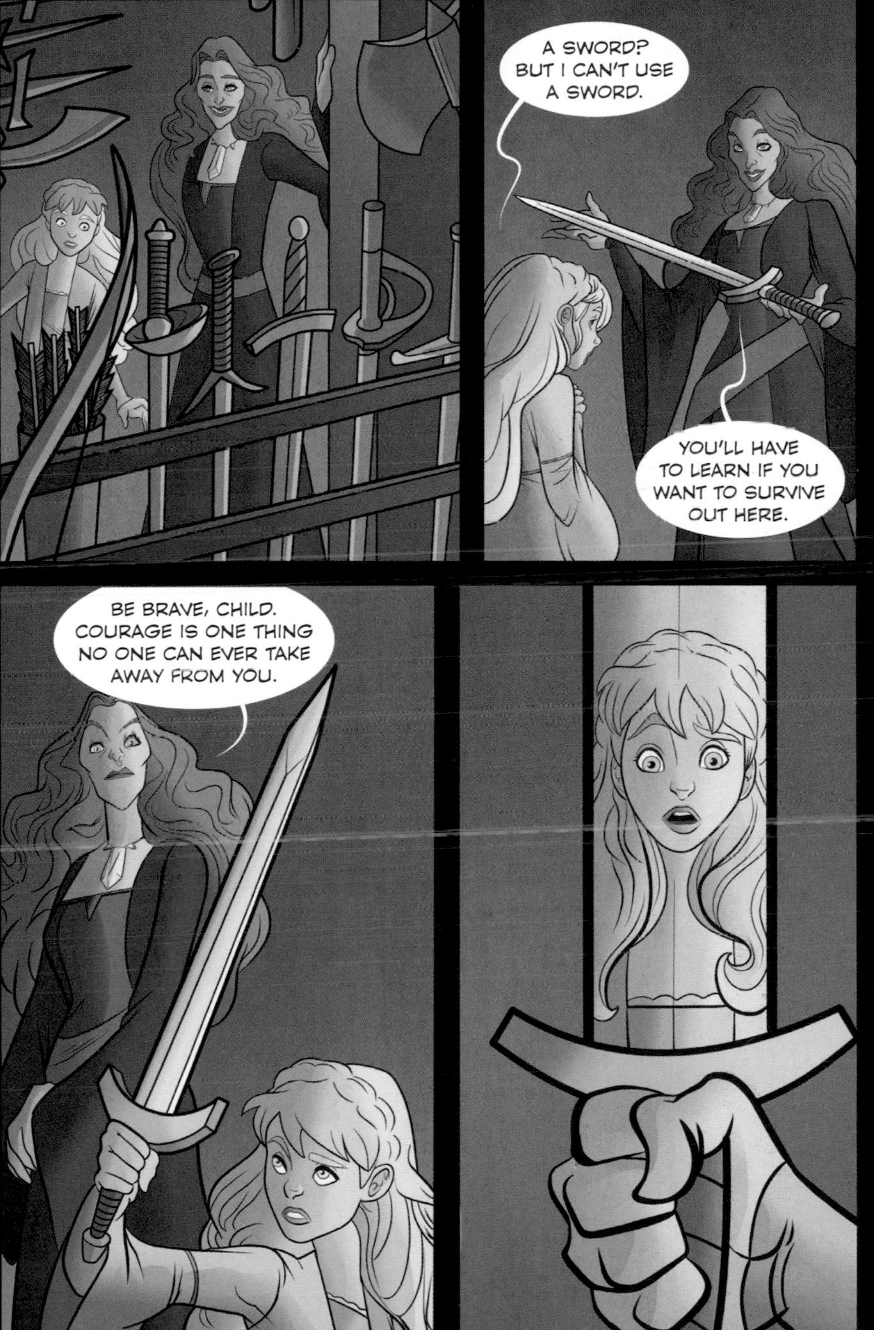
A SWORD? BUT I CAN'T USE A SWORD.
YOU'LL HAVE TO LEARN IF YOU WANT TO SURVIVE OUT HERE.
BE BRAVE, CHILD. COURAGE IS ONE THING NO ONE CAN EVER TAKE AWAY FROM YOU.

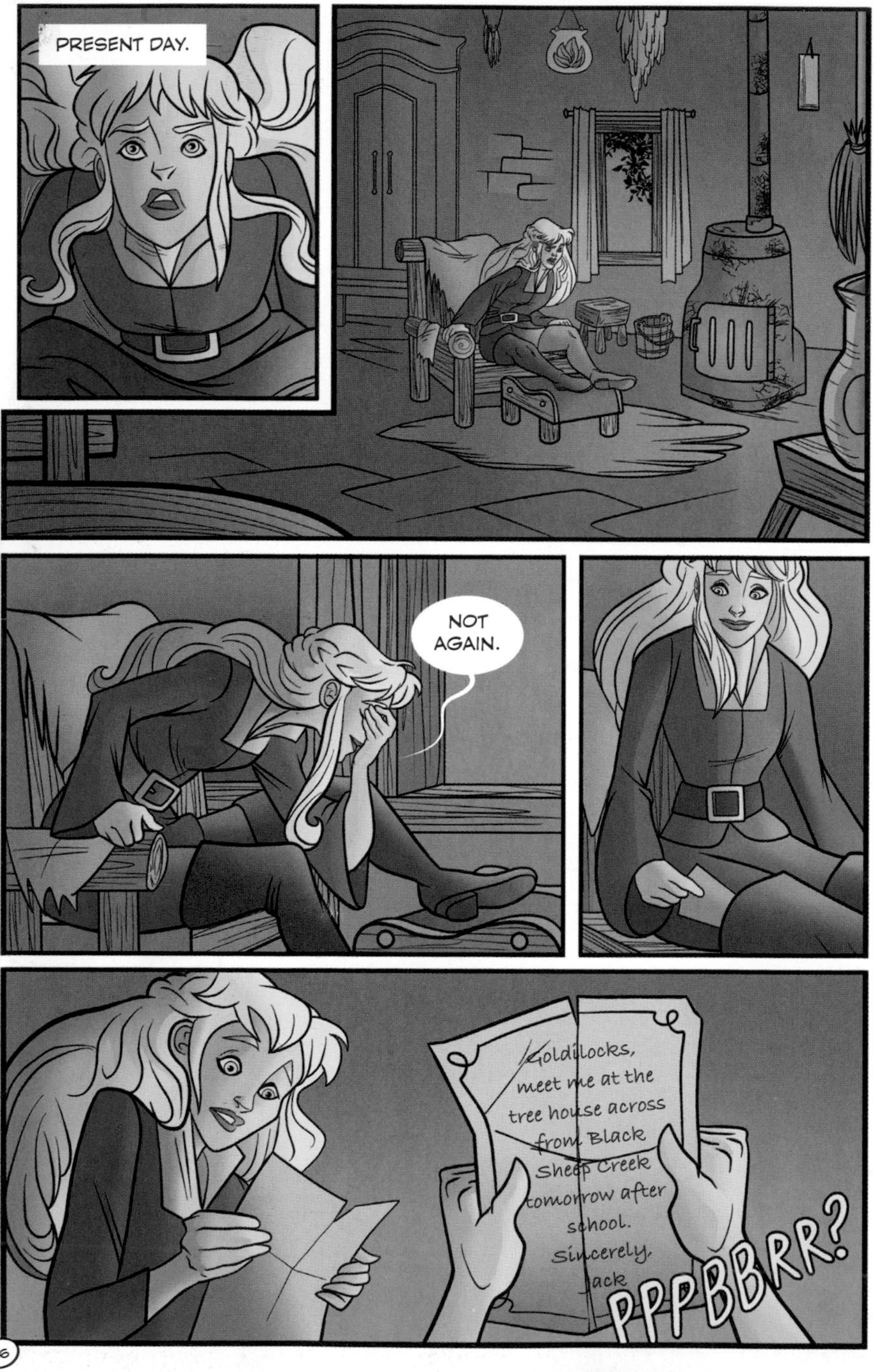
PRESENT DAY.
NOT AGAIN.
Goldilocks, meet me at the tree house across from Black Sheep Creek tomorrow after school. Sincerely, Jack
PPPBBRR?

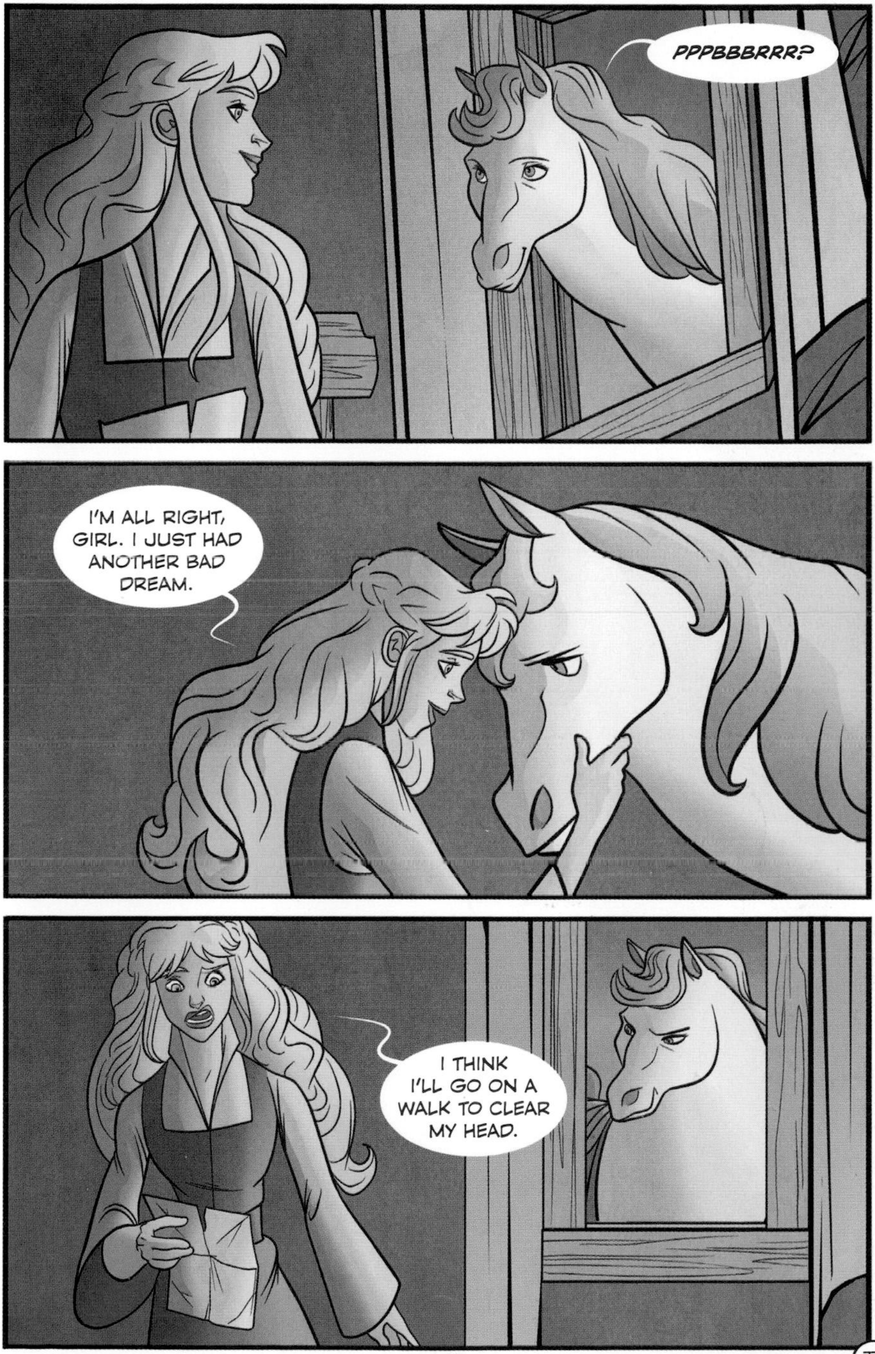
PPPBBBRRR?
I'M ALL RIGHT, GIRL. I JUST HAD ANOTHER BAD DREAM.
I THINK I'LL GO ON A WALK TO CLEAR MY HEAD.

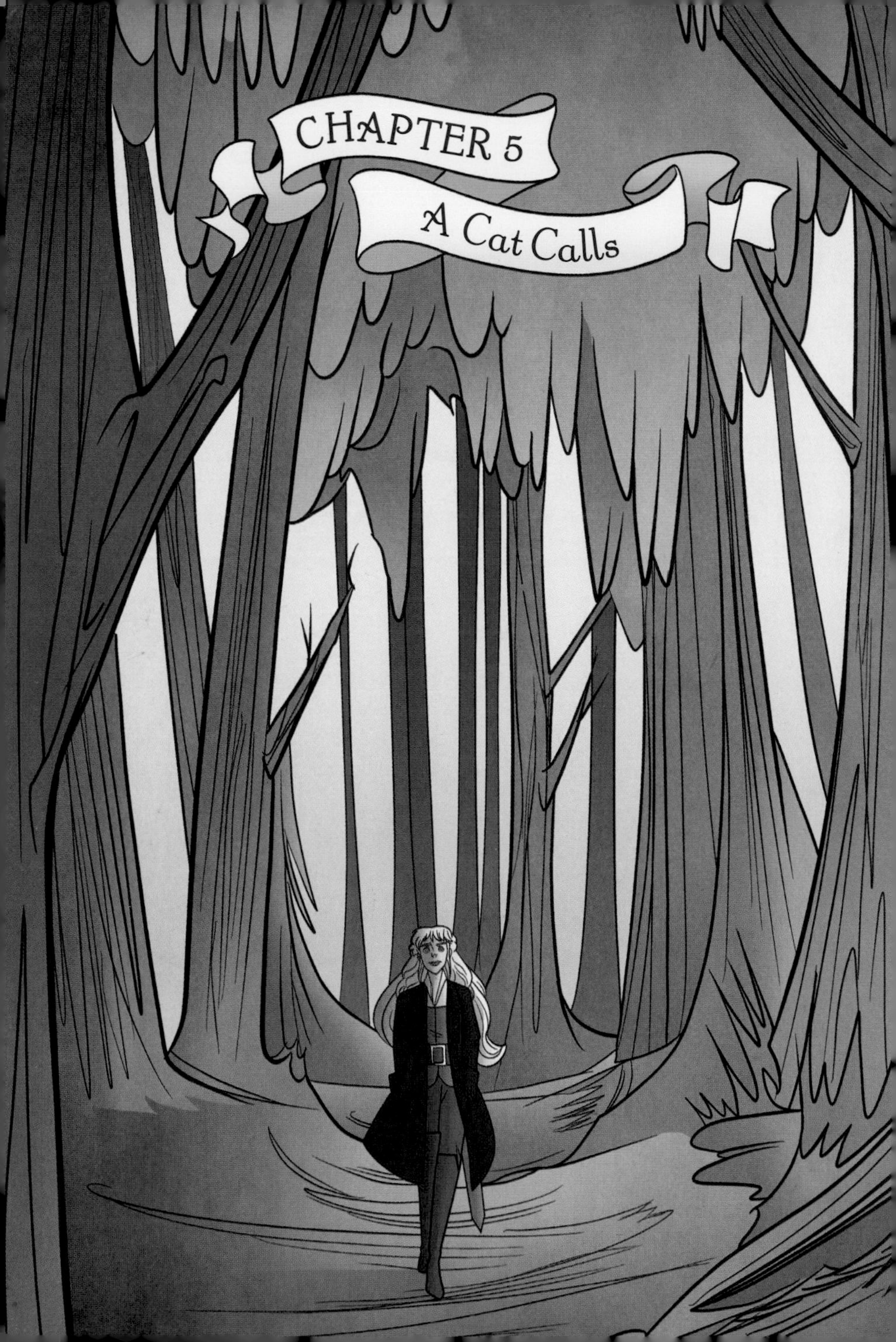
CHAPTER 5
A Cat Calls

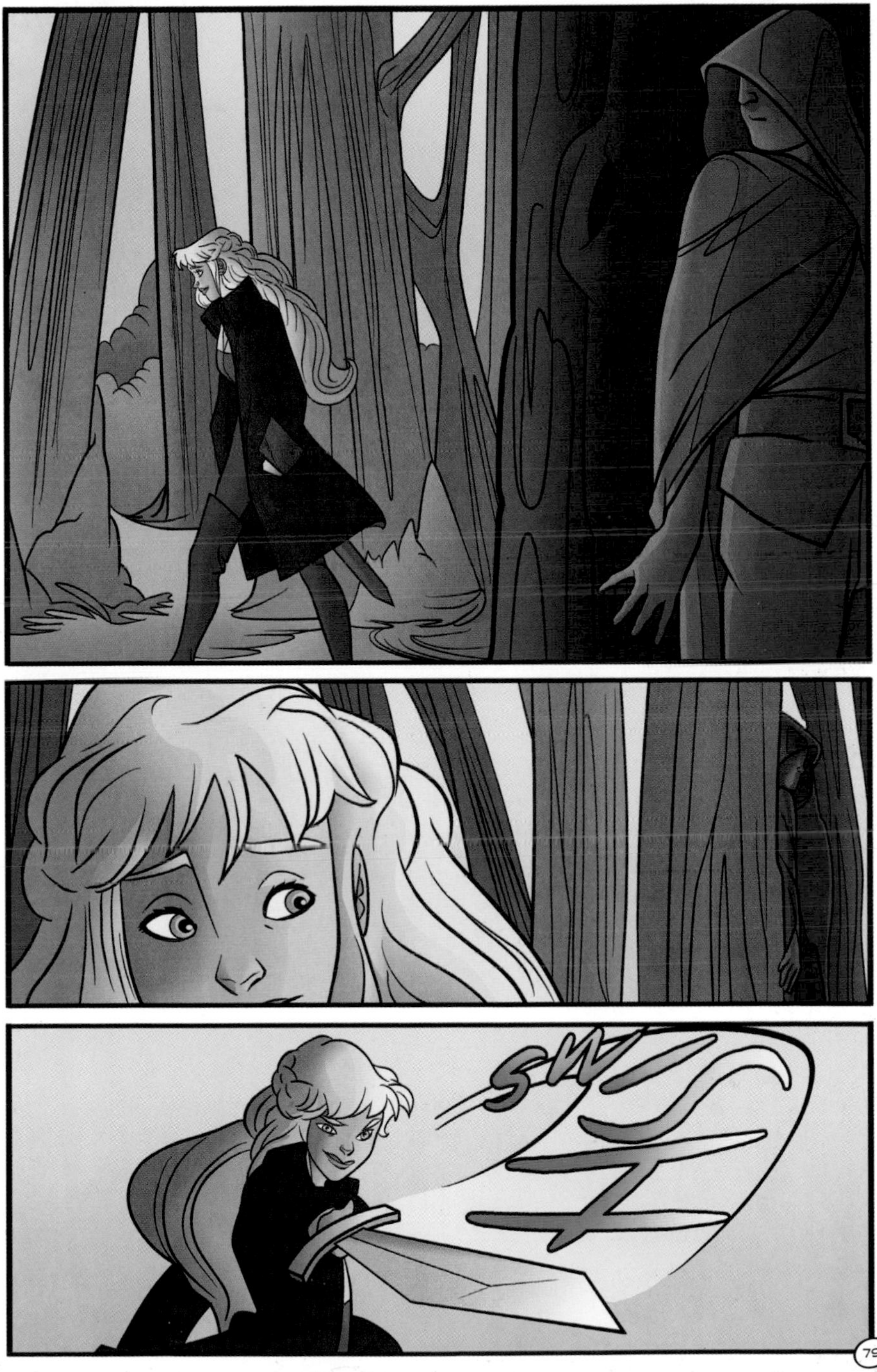
SWISH

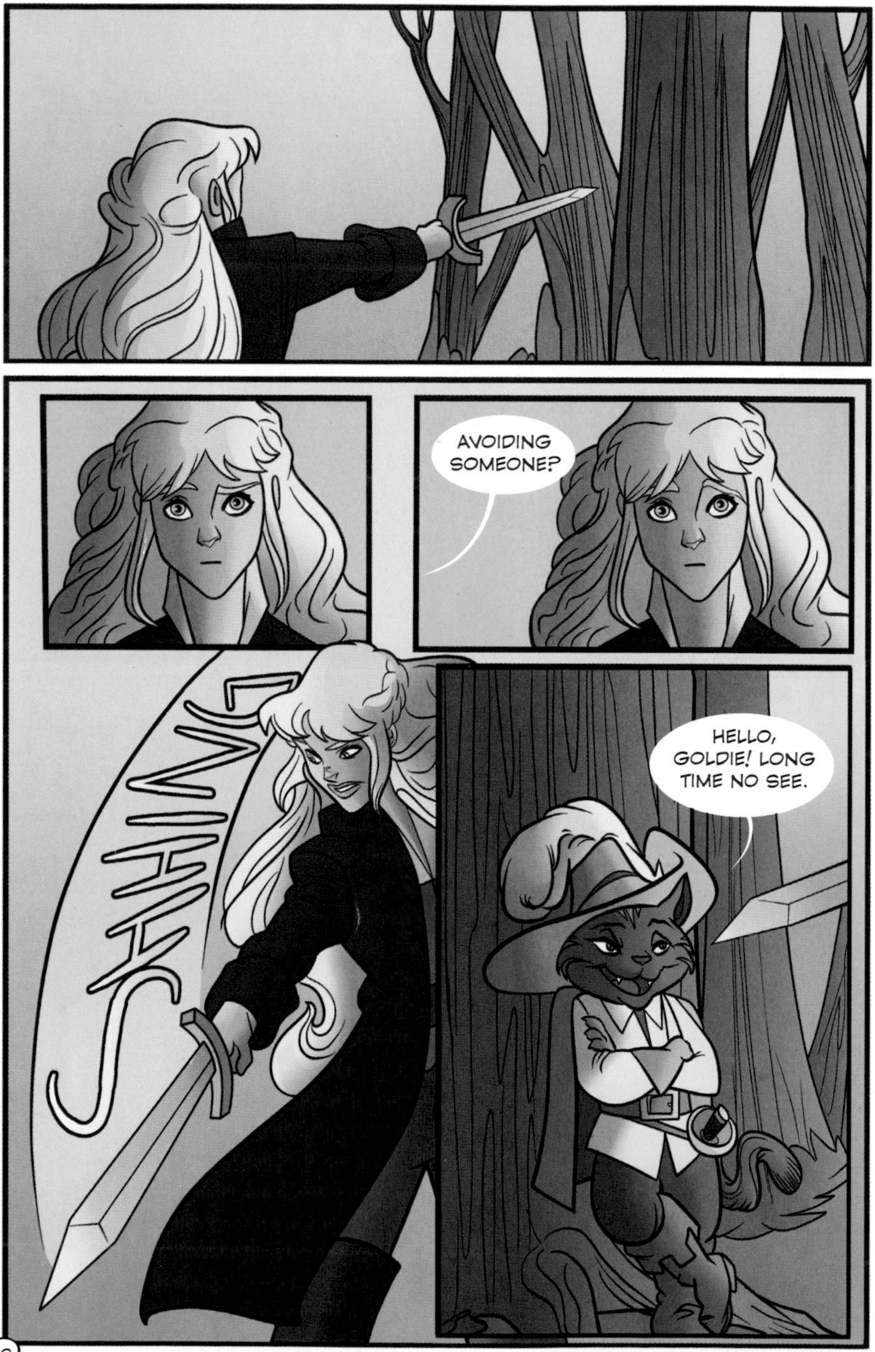
AVOIDING SOMEONE?
SHHING
HELLO, GOLDIE! LONG TIME NO SEE.

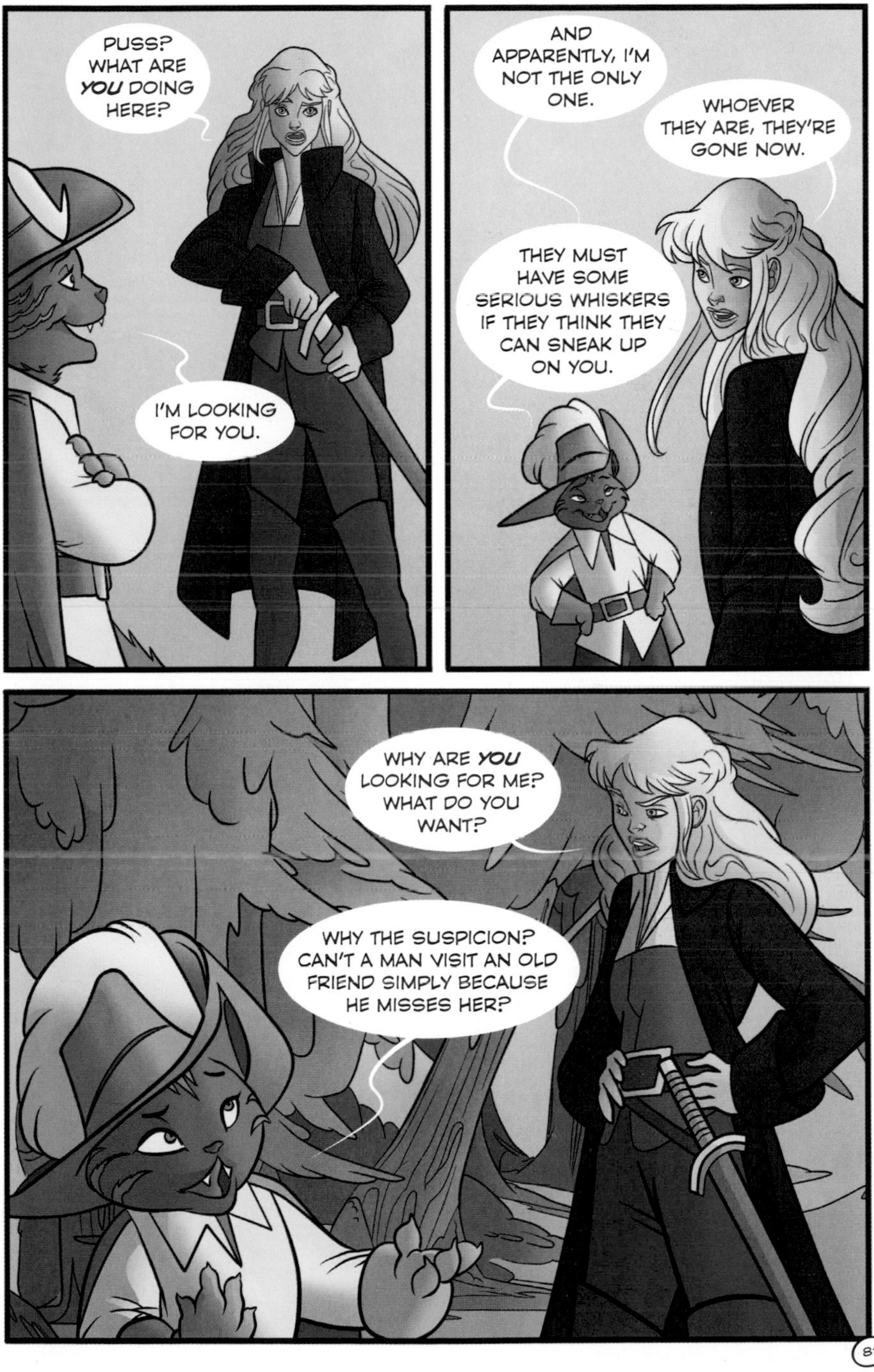
PUSS? WHAT ARE *YOU* DOING HERE?
I'M LOOKING FOR YOU.
AND APPARENTLY, I'M NOT THE ONLY ONE.
WHOEVER THEY ARE, THEY'RE GONE NOW.
THEY MUST HAVE SOME SERIOUS WHISKERS IF THEY THINK THEY CAN SNEAK UP ON YOU.
WHY ARE *YOU* LOOKING FOR ME? WHAT DO YOU WANT?
WHY THE SUSPICION? CAN'T A MAN VISIT AN OLD FRIEND SIMPLY BECAUSE HE MISSES HER?

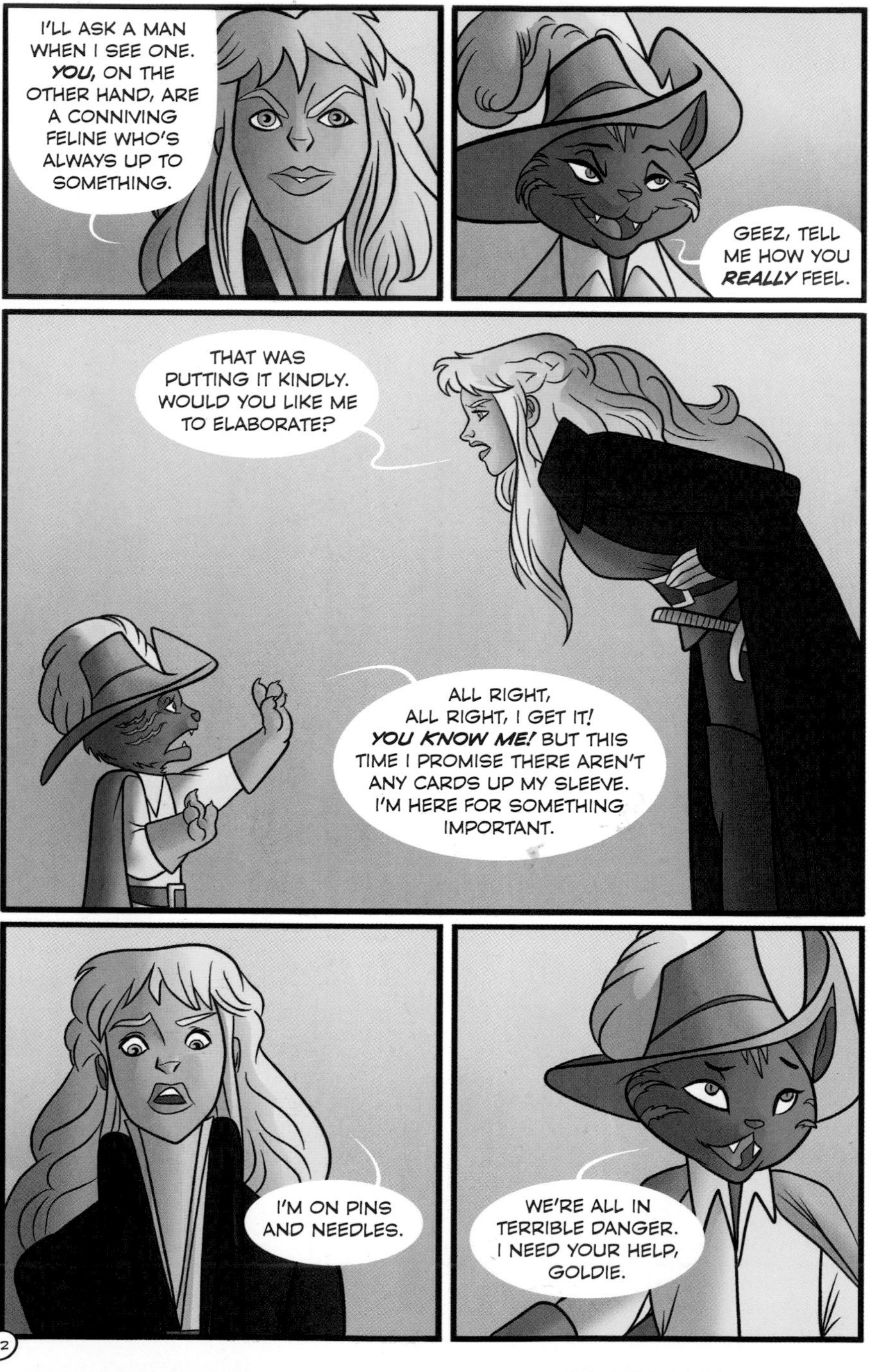
I'LL ASK A MAN WHEN I SEE ONE. *YOU,* ON THE OTHER HAND, ARE A CONNIVING FELINE WHO'S ALWAYS UP TO SOMETHING.
GEEZ, TELL ME HOW YOU *REALLY* FEEL.
THAT WAS PUTTING IT KINDLY. WOULD YOU LIKE ME TO ELABORATE?
ALL RIGHT, ALL RIGHT, I GET IT! *YOU KNOW ME!* BUT THIS TIME I PROMISE THERE AREN'T ANY CARDS UP MY SLEEVE. I'M HERE FOR SOMETHING IMPORTANT.
I'M ON PINS AND NEEDLES.
WE'RE ALL IN TERRIBLE DANGER. I NEED YOUR HELP, GOLDIE.

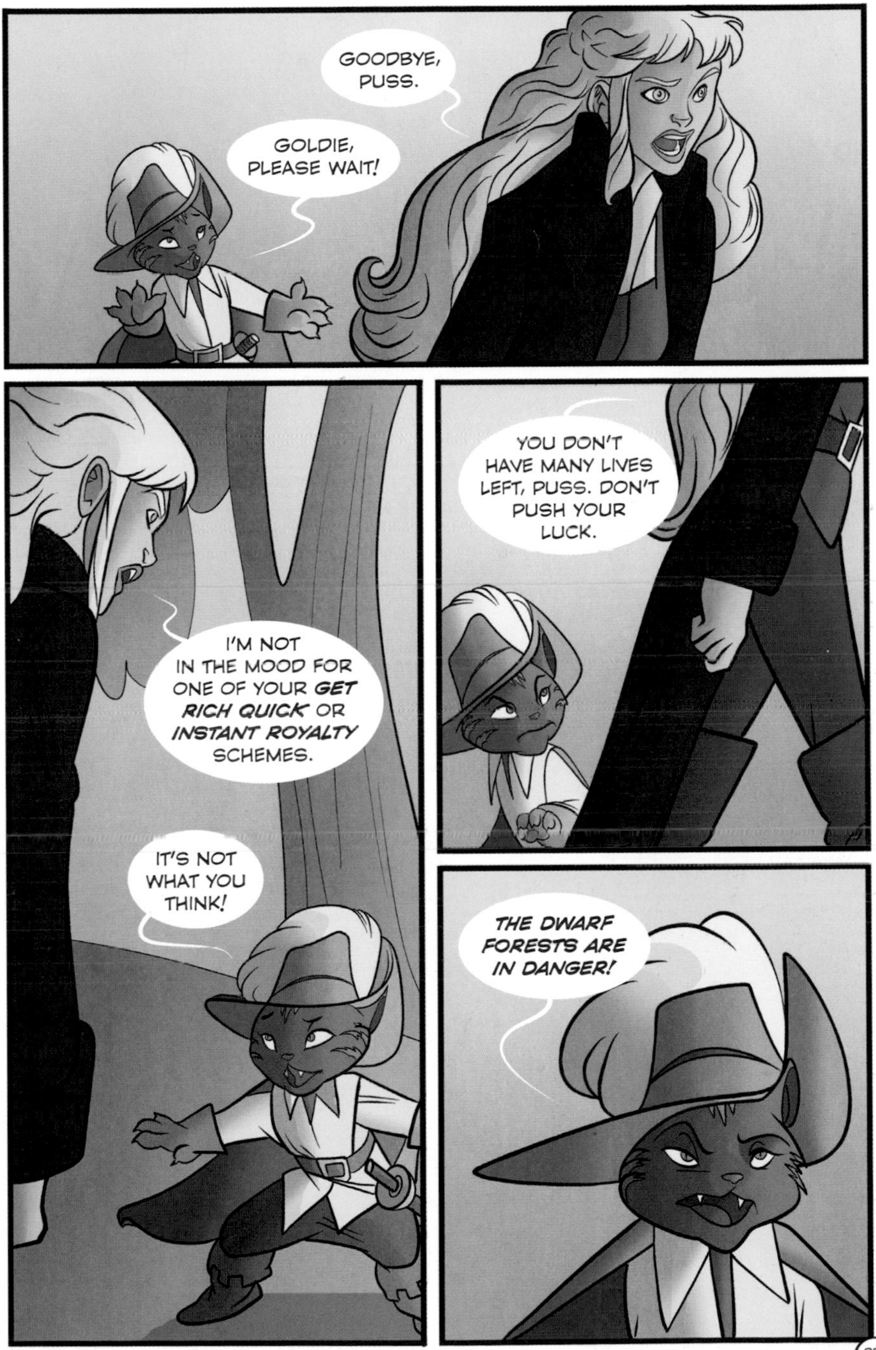
GOODBYE, PUSS.
GOLDIE, PLEASE WAIT!
I'M NOT IN THE MOOD FOR ONE OF YOUR **GET RICH QUICK** OR **INSTANT ROYALTY** SCHEMES.
IT'S NOT WHAT YOU THINK!
YOU DON'T HAVE MANY LIVES LEFT, PUSS. DON'T PUSH YOUR LUCK.
THE DWARF FORESTS ARE IN DANGER!

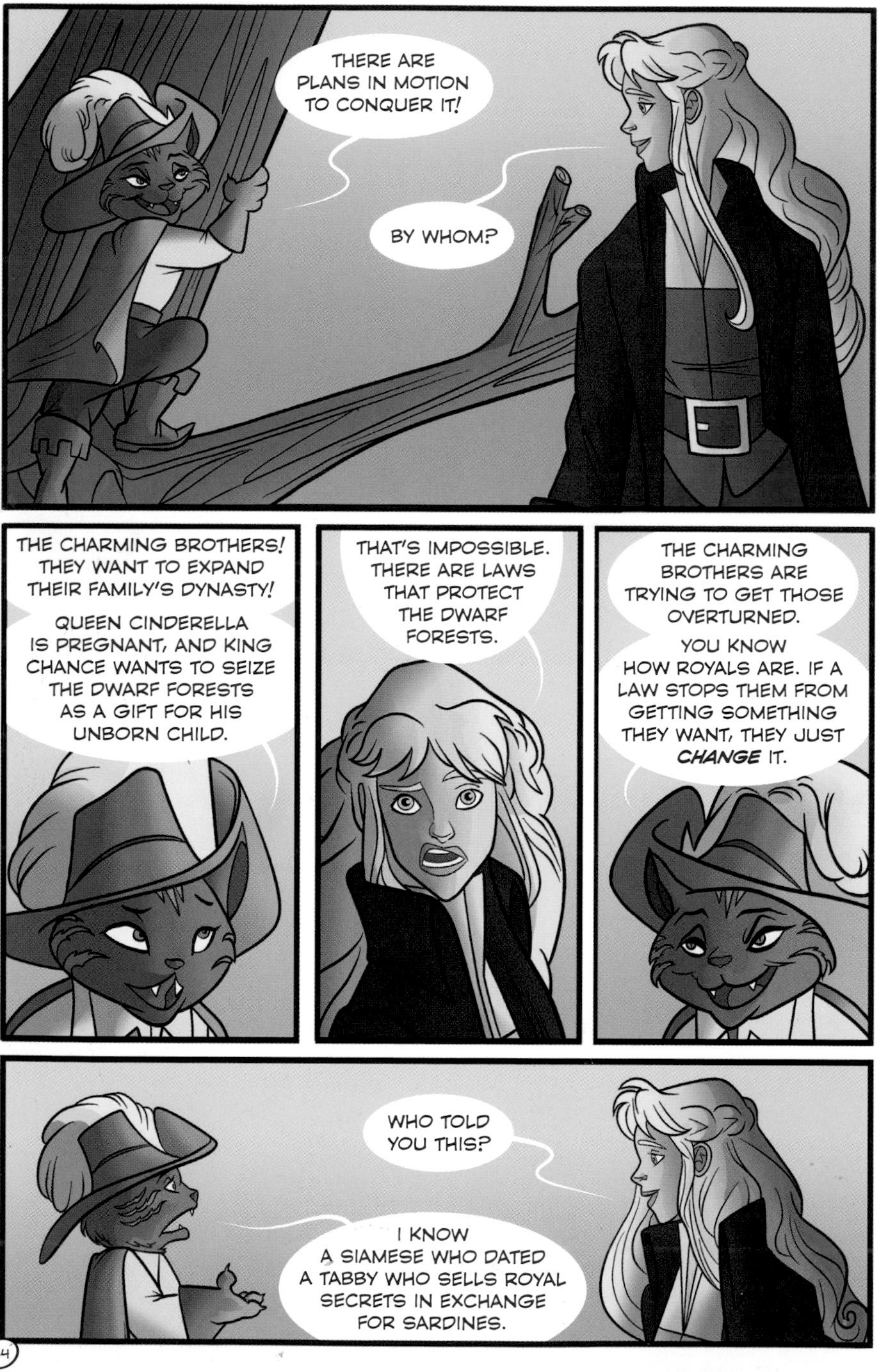
THERE ARE PLANS IN MOTION TO CONQUER IT!
BY WHOM?
THE CHARMING BROTHERS! THEY WANT TO EXPAND THEIR FAMILY'S DYNASTY!
QUEEN CINDERELLA IS PREGNANT, AND KING CHANCE WANTS TO SEIZE THE DWARF FORESTS AS A GIFT FOR HIS UNBORN CHILD.
THAT'S IMPOSSIBLE. THERE ARE LAWS THAT PROTECT THE DWARF FORESTS.
THE CHARMING BROTHERS ARE TRYING TO GET THOSE OVERTURNED.
YOU KNOW HOW ROYALS ARE. IF A LAW STOPS THEM FROM GETTING SOMETHING THEY WANT, THEY JUST ***CHANGE*** IT.
WHO TOLD YOU THIS?
I KNOW A SIAMESE WHO DATED A TABBY WHO SELLS ROYAL SECRETS IN EXCHANGE FOR SARDINES.

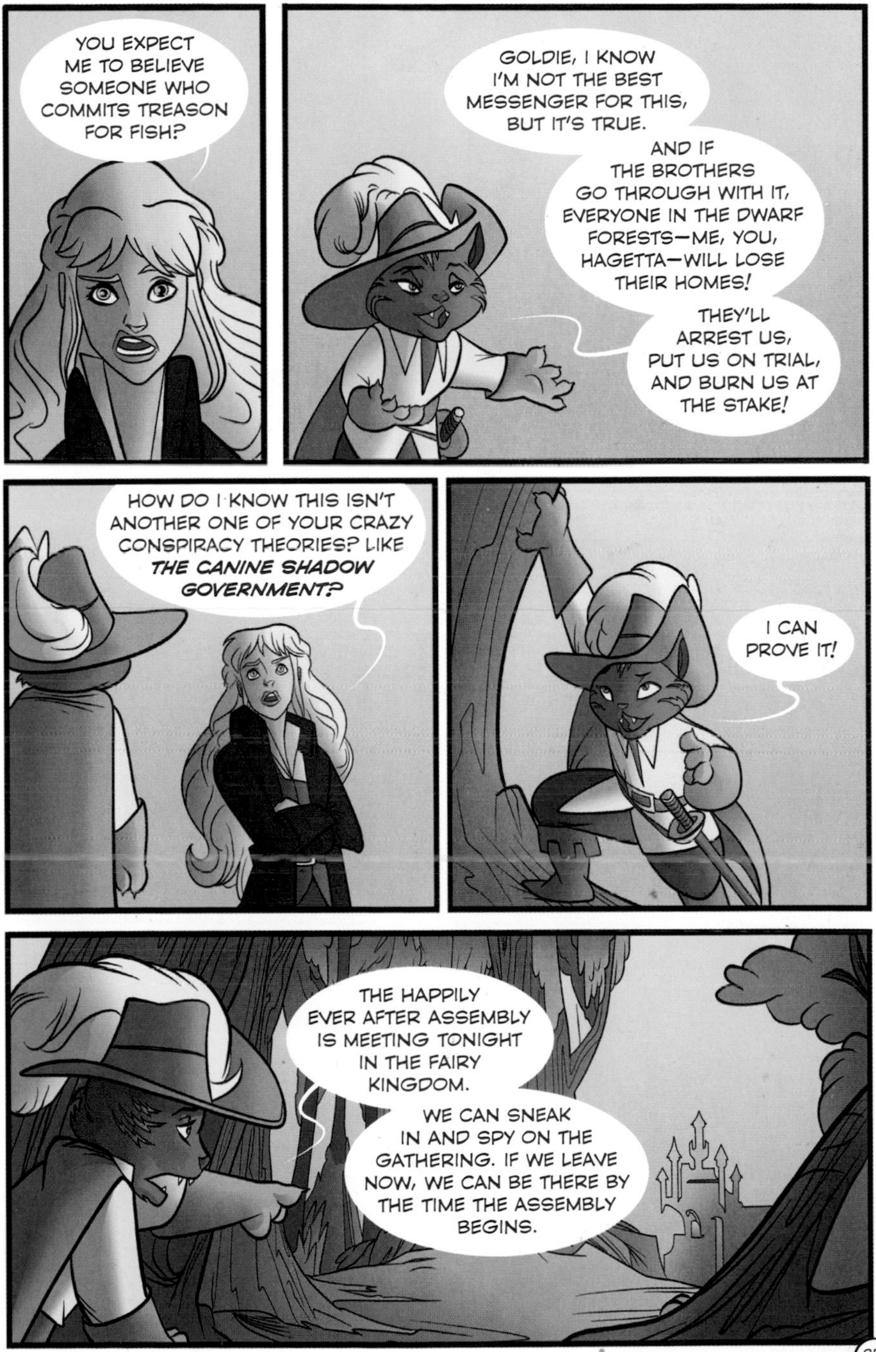
YOU EXPECT ME TO BELIEVE SOMEONE WHO COMMITS TREASON FOR FISH?
GOLDIE, I KNOW I'M NOT THE BEST MESSENGER FOR THIS, BUT IT'S TRUE.
AND IF THE BROTHERS GO THROUGH WITH IT, EVERYONE IN THE DWARF FORESTS—ME, YOU, HAGETTA—WILL LOSE THEIR HOMES!
THEY'LL ARREST US, PUT US ON TRIAL, AND BURN US AT THE STAKE!
HOW DO I KNOW THIS ISN'T ANOTHER ONE OF YOUR CRAZY CONSPIRACY THEORIES? LIKE *THE CANINE SHADOW GOVERNMENT?*
I CAN PROVE IT!
THE HAPPILY EVER AFTER ASSEMBLY IS MEETING TONIGHT IN THE FAIRY KINGDOM.
WE CAN SNEAK IN AND SPY ON THE GATHERING. IF WE LEAVE NOW, WE CAN BE THERE BY THE TIME THE ASSEMBLY BEGINS.

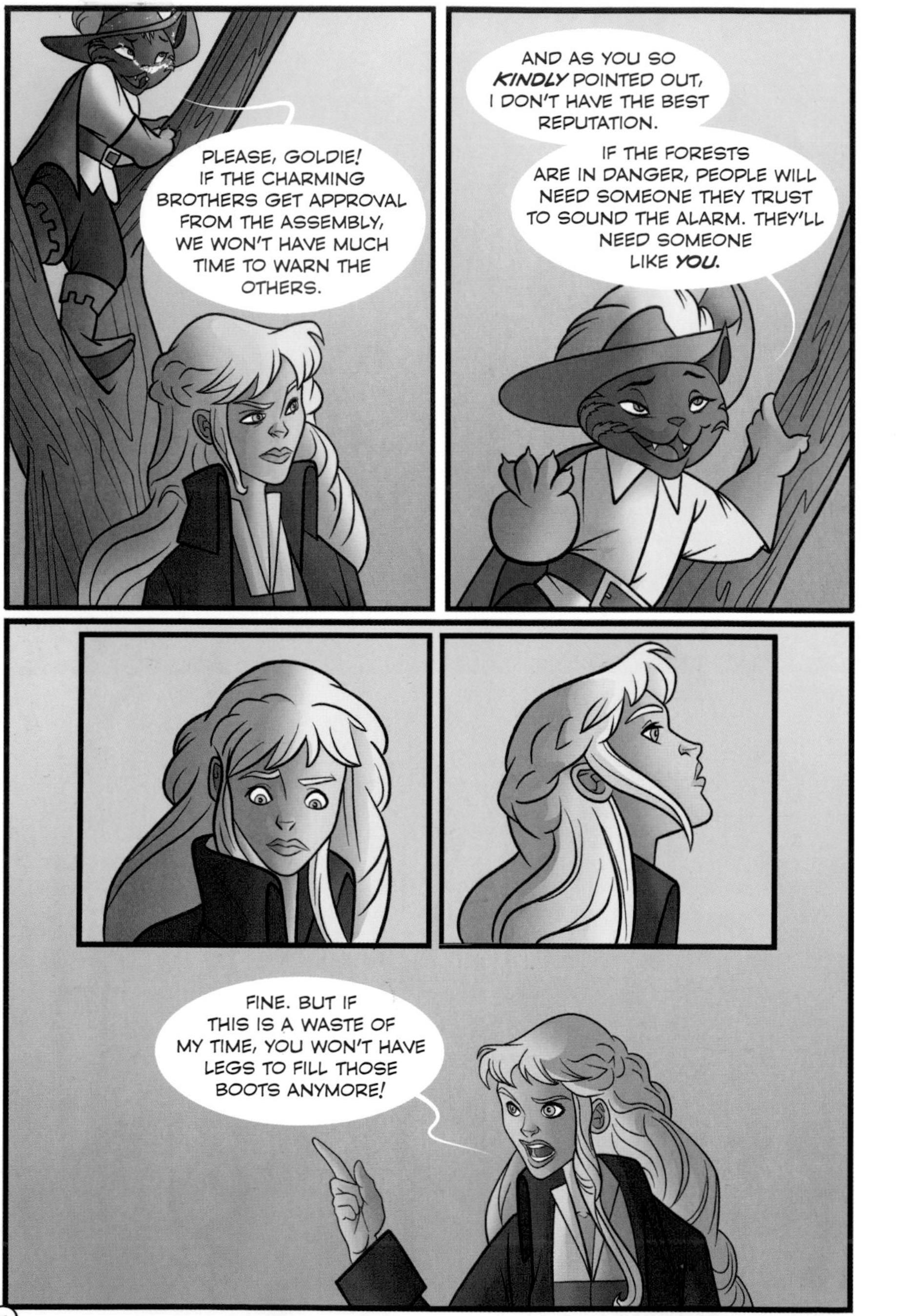
PLEASE, GOLDIE! IF THE CHARMING BROTHERS GET APPROVAL FROM THE ASSEMBLY, WE WON'T HAVE MUCH TIME TO WARN THE OTHERS.
AND AS YOU SO KINDLY POINTED OUT, I DON'T HAVE THE BEST REPUTATION.
IF THE FORESTS ARE IN DANGER, PEOPLE WILL NEED SOMEONE THEY TRUST TO SOUND THE ALARM. THEY'LL NEED SOMEONE LIKE YOU.
FINE. BUT IF THIS IS A WASTE OF MY TIME, YOU WON'T HAVE LEGS TO FILL THOSE BOOTS ANYMORE!

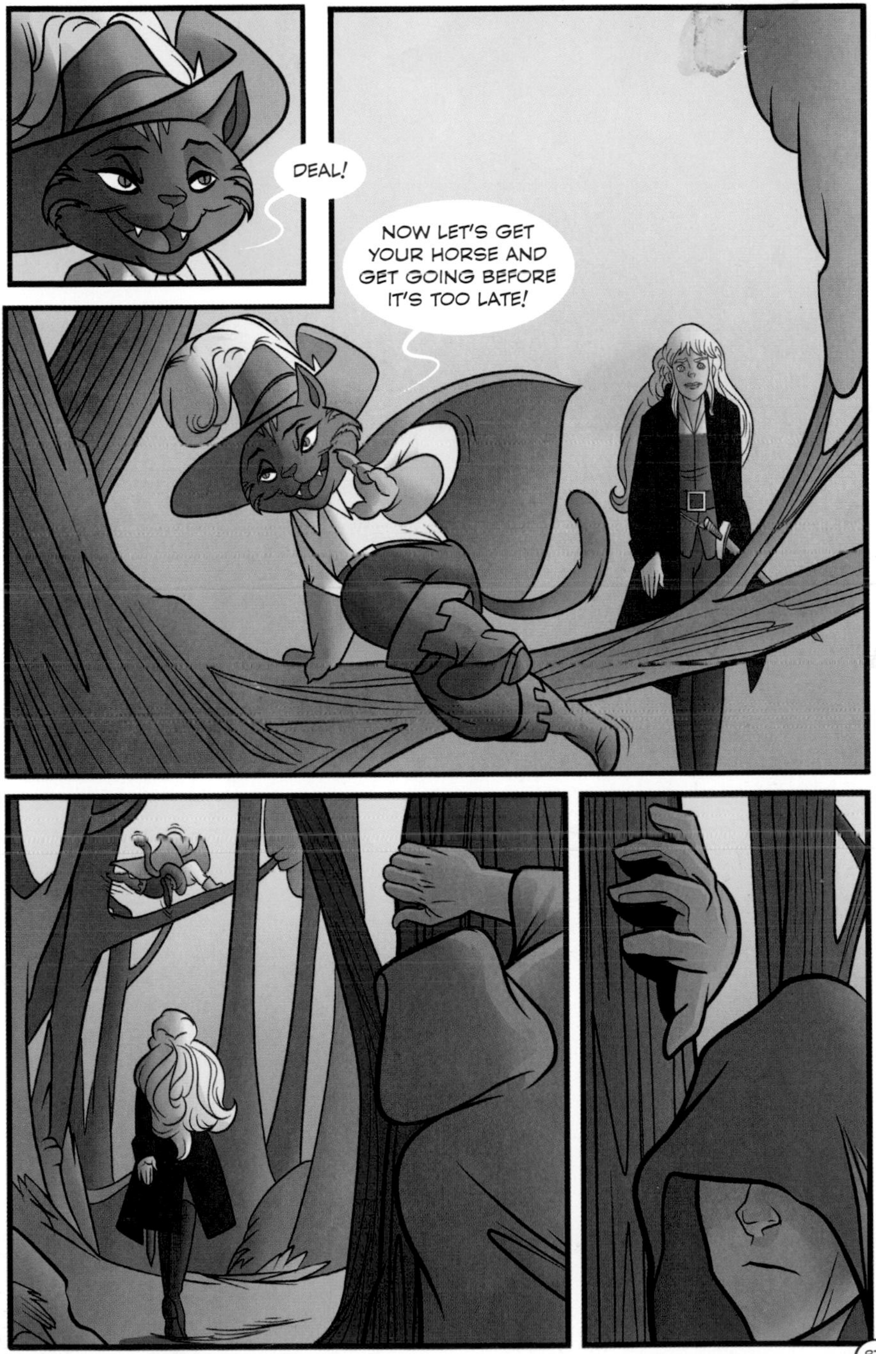
DEAL!
NOW LET'S GET YOUR HORSE AND GET GOING BEFORE IT'S TOO LATE!

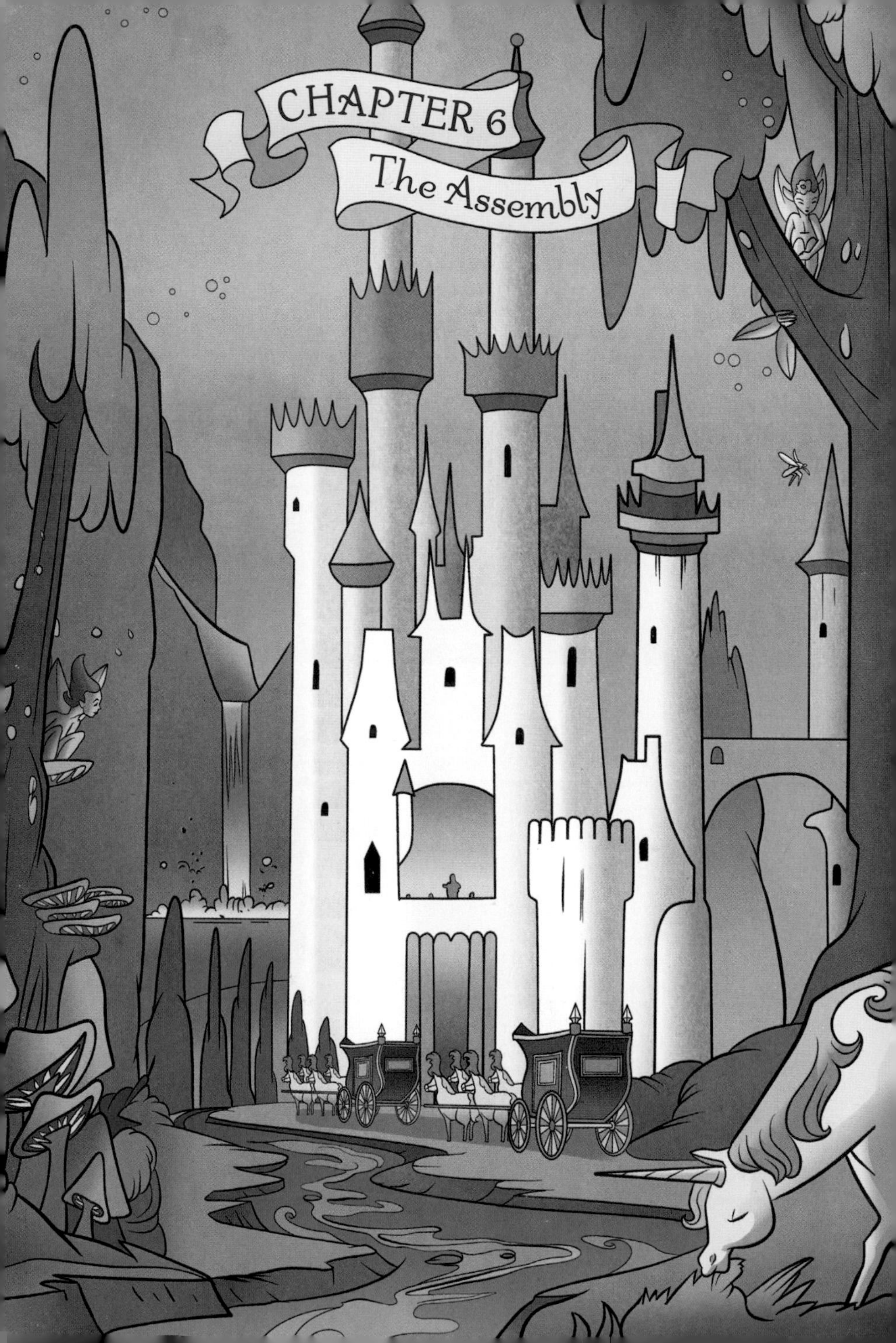
CHAPTER 6
The Assembly

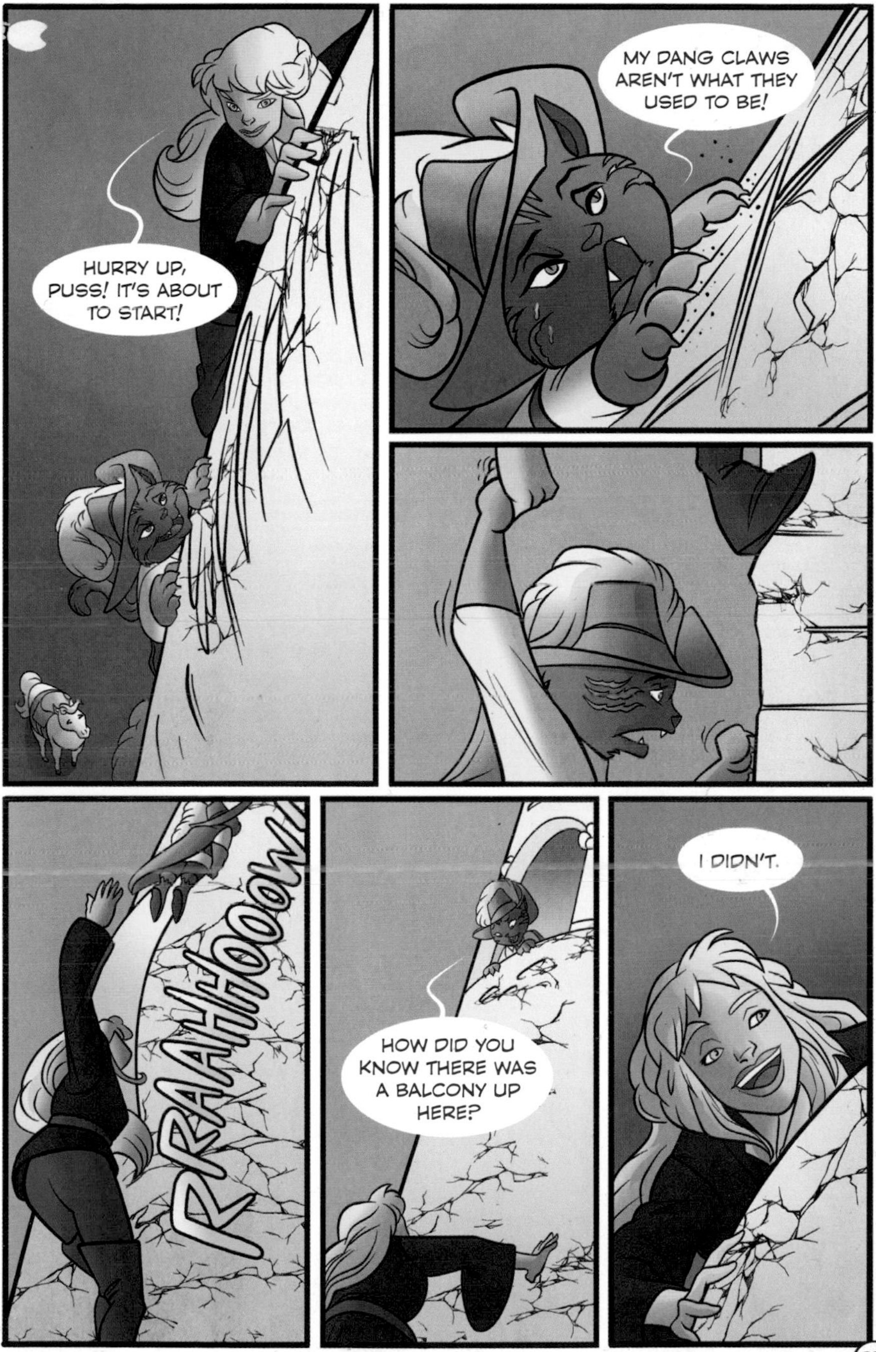
HURRY UP, PUSS! IT'S ABOUT TO START!
MY DANG CLAWS AREN'T WHAT THEY USED TO BE!
RRAAHHOOOW!
HOW DID YOU KNOW THERE WAS A BALCONY UP HERE?
I DIDN'T.

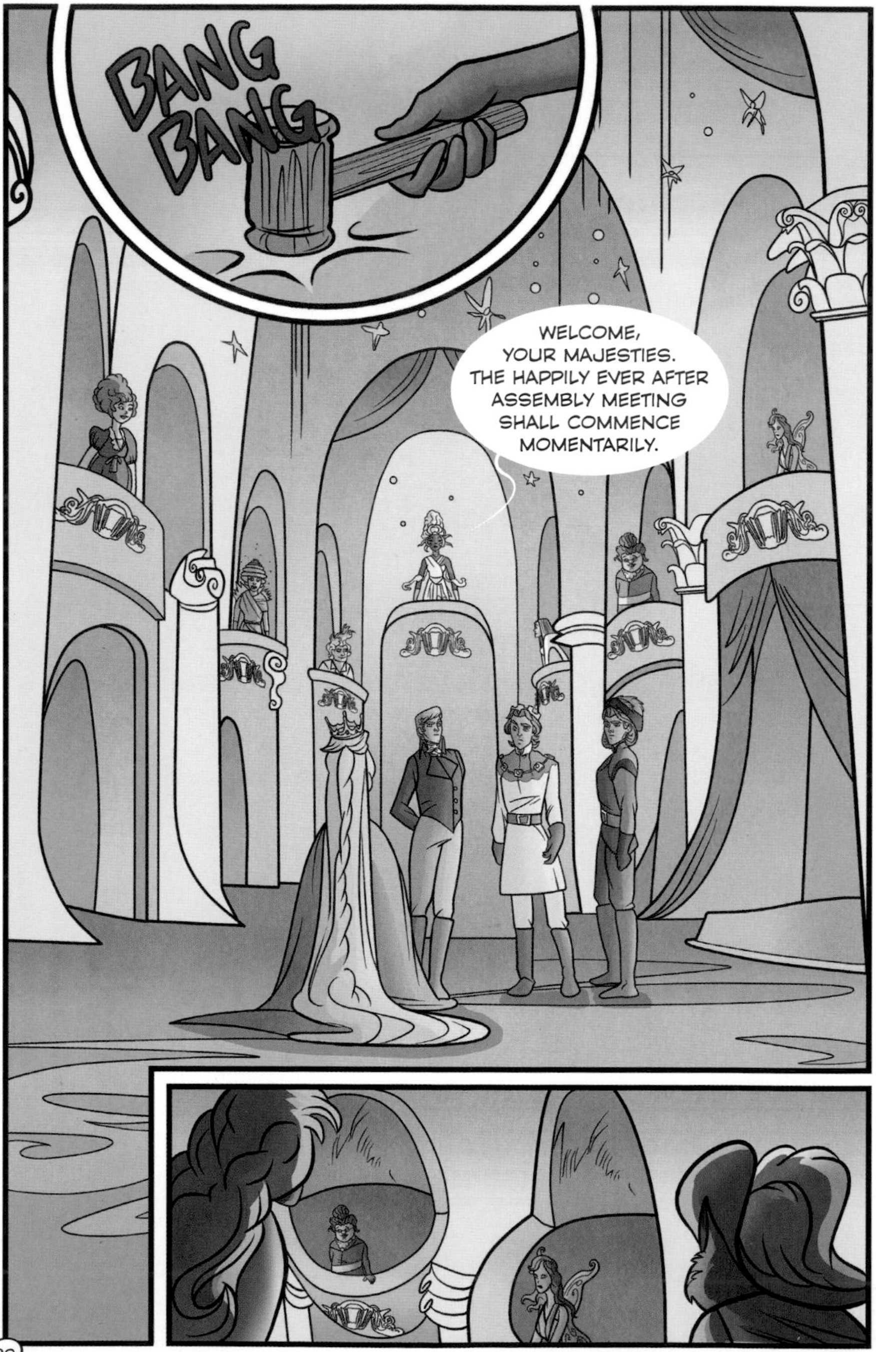
BANG BANG
WELCOME, YOUR MAJESTIES. THE HAPPILY EVER AFTER ASSEMBLY MEETING SHALL COMMENCE MOMENTARILY.

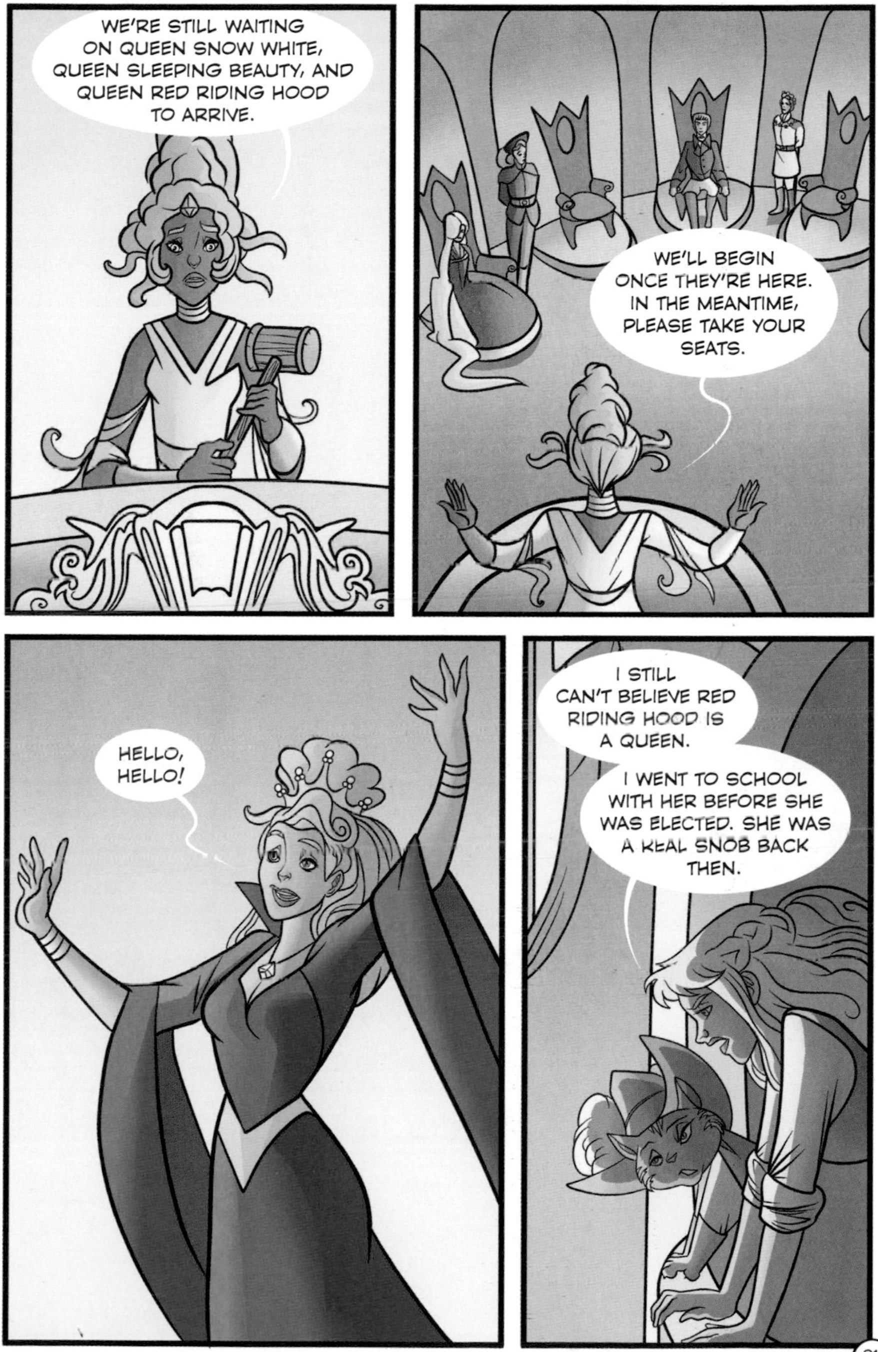
WE'RE STILL WAITING ON QUEEN SNOW WHITE, QUEEN SLEEPING BEAUTY, AND QUEEN RED RIDING HOOD TO ARRIVE.
WE'LL BEGIN ONCE THEY'RE HERE. IN THE MEANTIME, PLEASE TAKE YOUR SEATS.
HELLO, HELLO!
I STILL CAN'T BELIEVE RED RIDING HOOD IS A QUEEN.
I WENT TO SCHOOL WITH HER BEFORE SHE WAS ELECTED. SHE WAS A REAL SNOB BACK THEN.

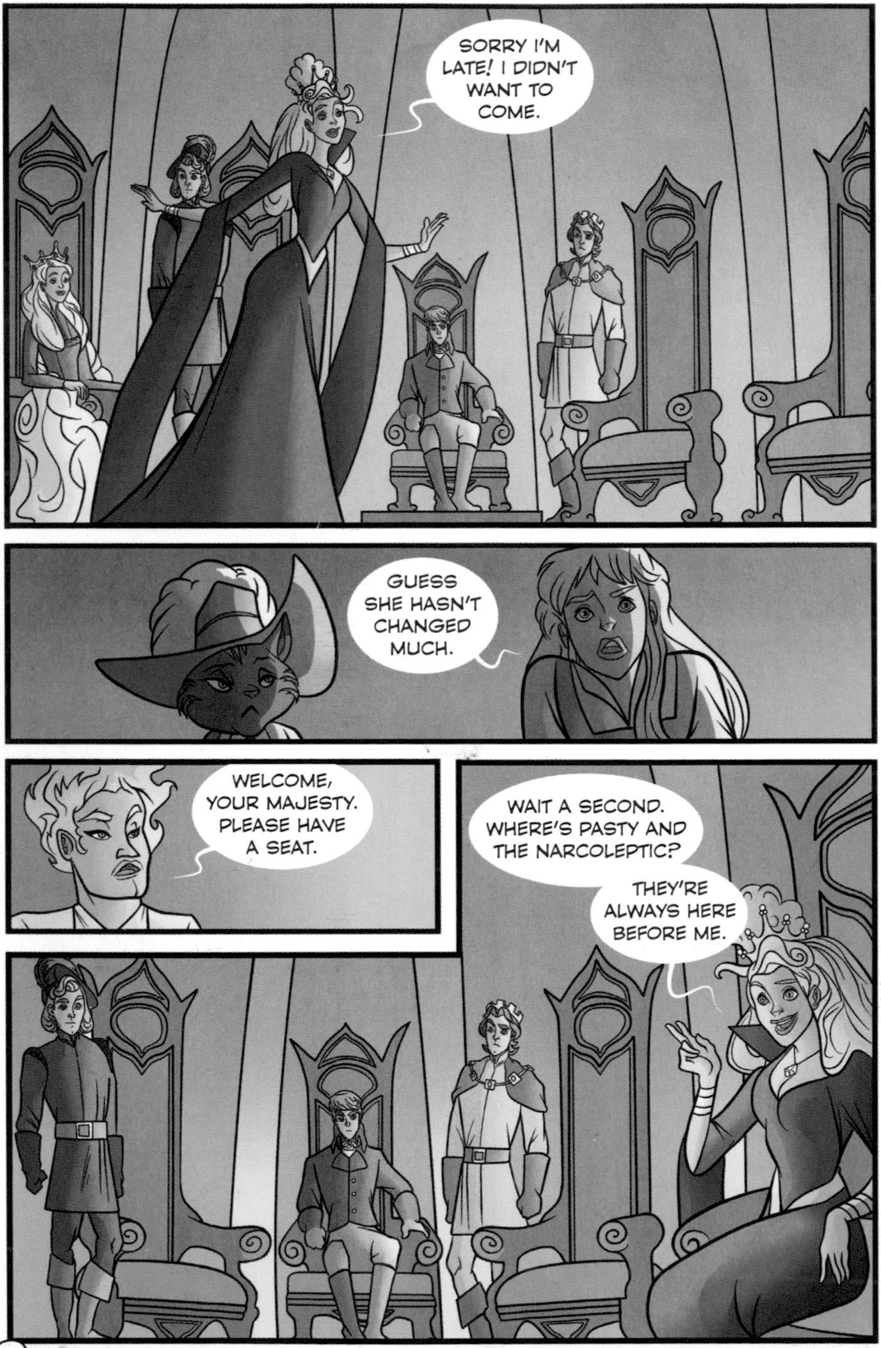
SORRY I'M LATE! I DIDN'T WANT TO COME.
GUESS SHE HASN'T CHANGED MUCH.
WELCOME, YOUR MAJESTY. PLEASE HAVE A SEAT.
WAIT A SECOND. WHERE'S PASTY AND THE NARCOLEPTIC?
THEY'RE ALWAYS HERE BEFORE ME.

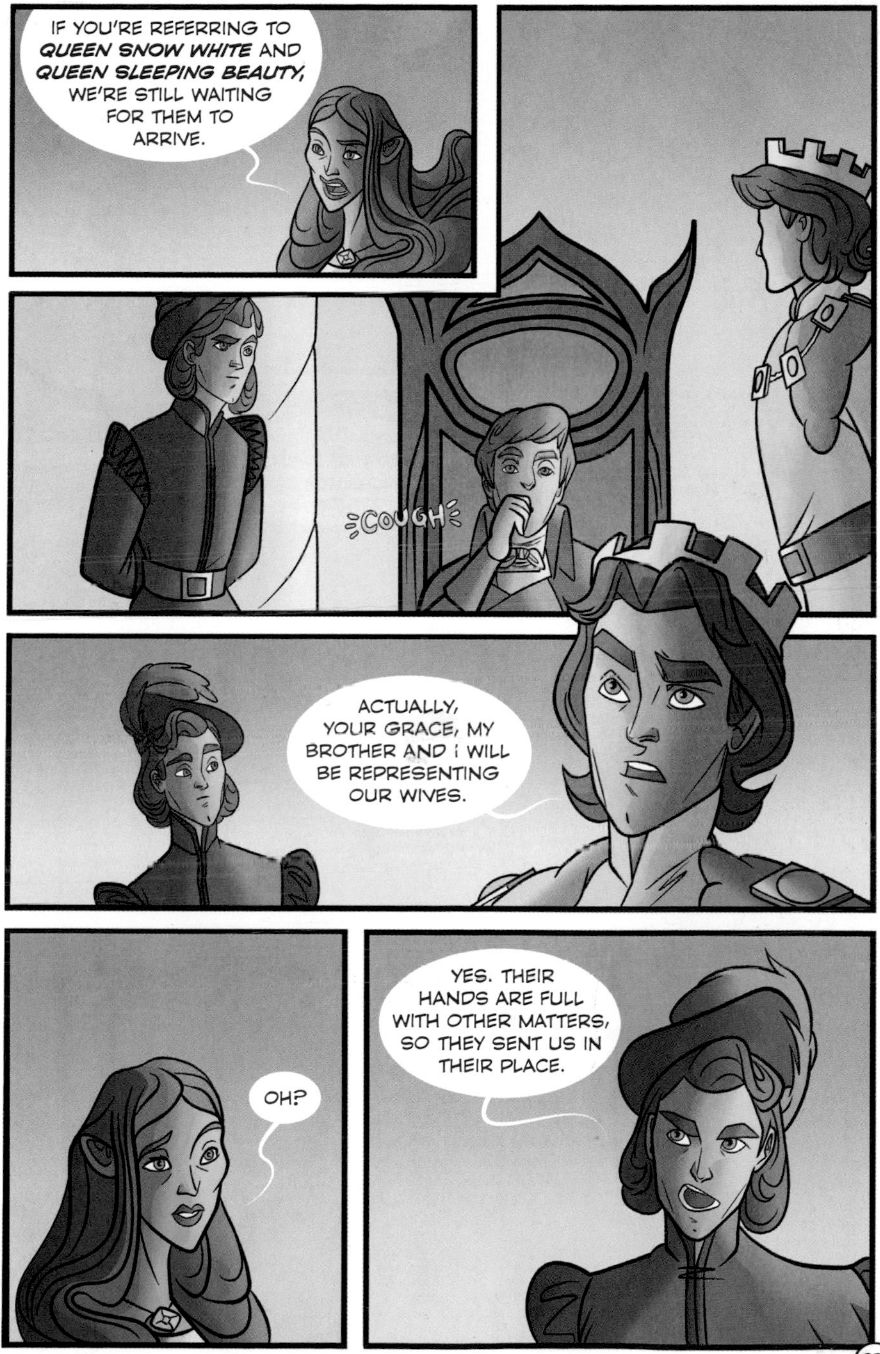
IF YOU'RE REFERRING TO *QUEEN SNOW WHITE* AND *QUEEN SLEEPING BEAUTY,* WE'RE STILL WAITING FOR THEM TO ARRIVE.
COUGH
ACTUALLY, YOUR GRACE, MY BROTHER AND I WILL BE REPRESENTING OUR WIVES.
OH?
YES. THEIR HANDS ARE FULL WITH OTHER MATTERS, SO THEY SENT US IN THEIR PLACE.

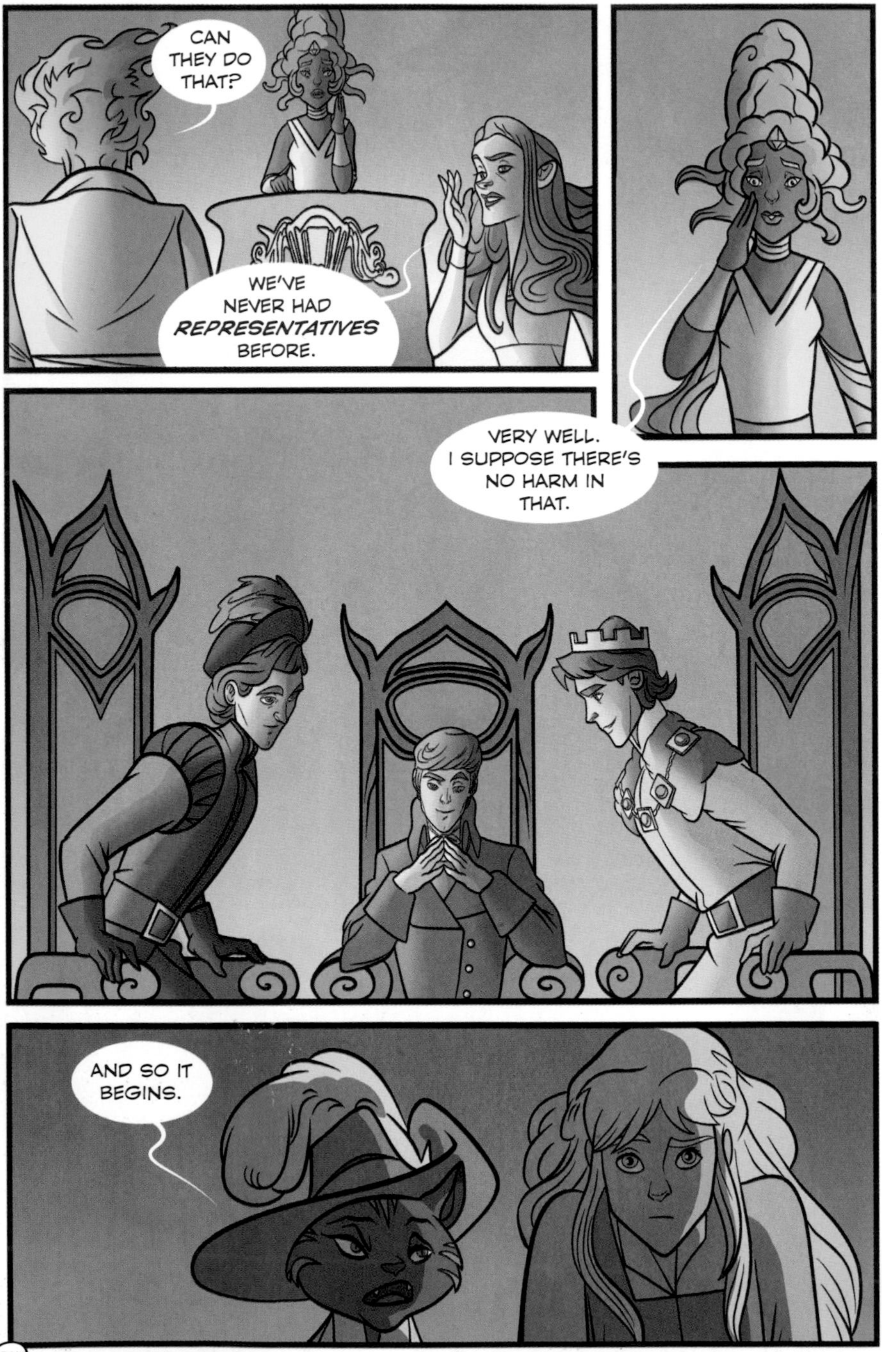
CAN THEY DO THAT?
WE'VE NEVER HAD *REPRESENTATIVES* BEFORE.
VERY WELL. I SUPPOSE THERE'S NO HARM IN THAT.
AND SO IT BEGINS.

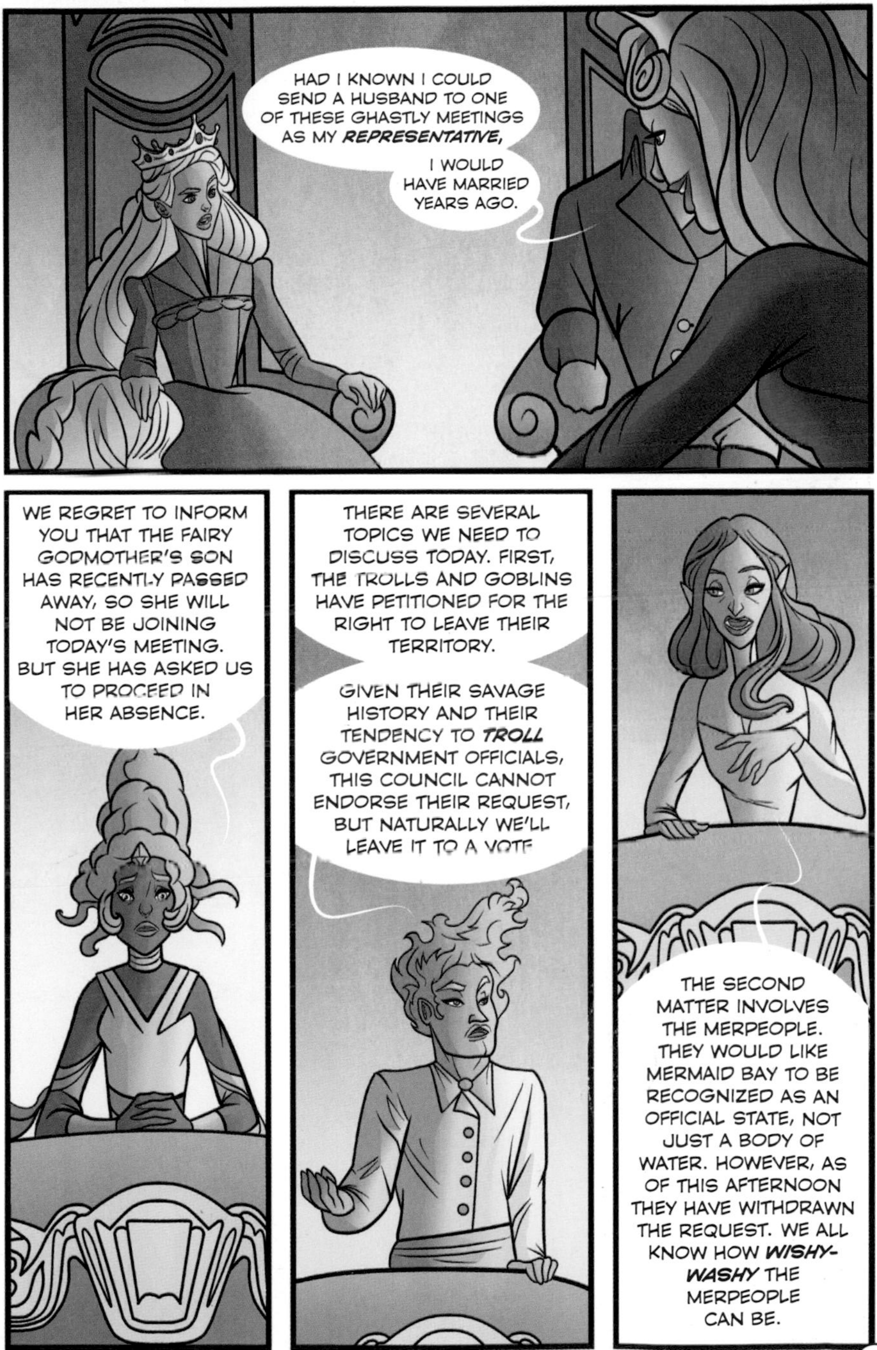
HAD I KNOWN I COULD SEND A HUSBAND TO ONE OF THESE GHASTLY MEETINGS AS MY *REPRESENTATIVE,*
I WOULD HAVE MARRIED YEARS AGO.
WE REGRET TO INFORM YOU THAT THE FAIRY GODMOTHER'S SON HAS RECENTLY PASSED AWAY, SO SHE WILL NOT BE JOINING TODAY'S MEETING. BUT SHE HAS ASKED US TO PROCEED IN HER ABSENCE.
THERE ARE SEVERAL TOPICS WE NEED TO DISCUSS TODAY. FIRST, THE TROLLS AND GOBLINS HAVE PETITIONED FOR THE RIGHT TO LEAVE THEIR TERRITORY.
GIVEN THEIR SAVAGE HISTORY AND THEIR TENDENCY TO *TROLL* GOVERNMENT OFFICIALS, THIS COUNCIL CANNOT ENDORSE THEIR REQUEST, BUT NATURALLY WE'LL LEAVE IT TO A VOTE
THE SECOND MATTER INVOLVES THE MERPEOPLE. THEY WOULD LIKE MERMAID BAY TO BE RECOGNIZED AS AN OFFICIAL STATE, NOT JUST A BODY OF WATER. HOWEVER, AS OF THIS AFTERNOON THEY HAVE WITHDRAWN THE REQUEST. WE ALL KNOW HOW *WISHY-WASHY* THE MERPEOPLE CAN BE.

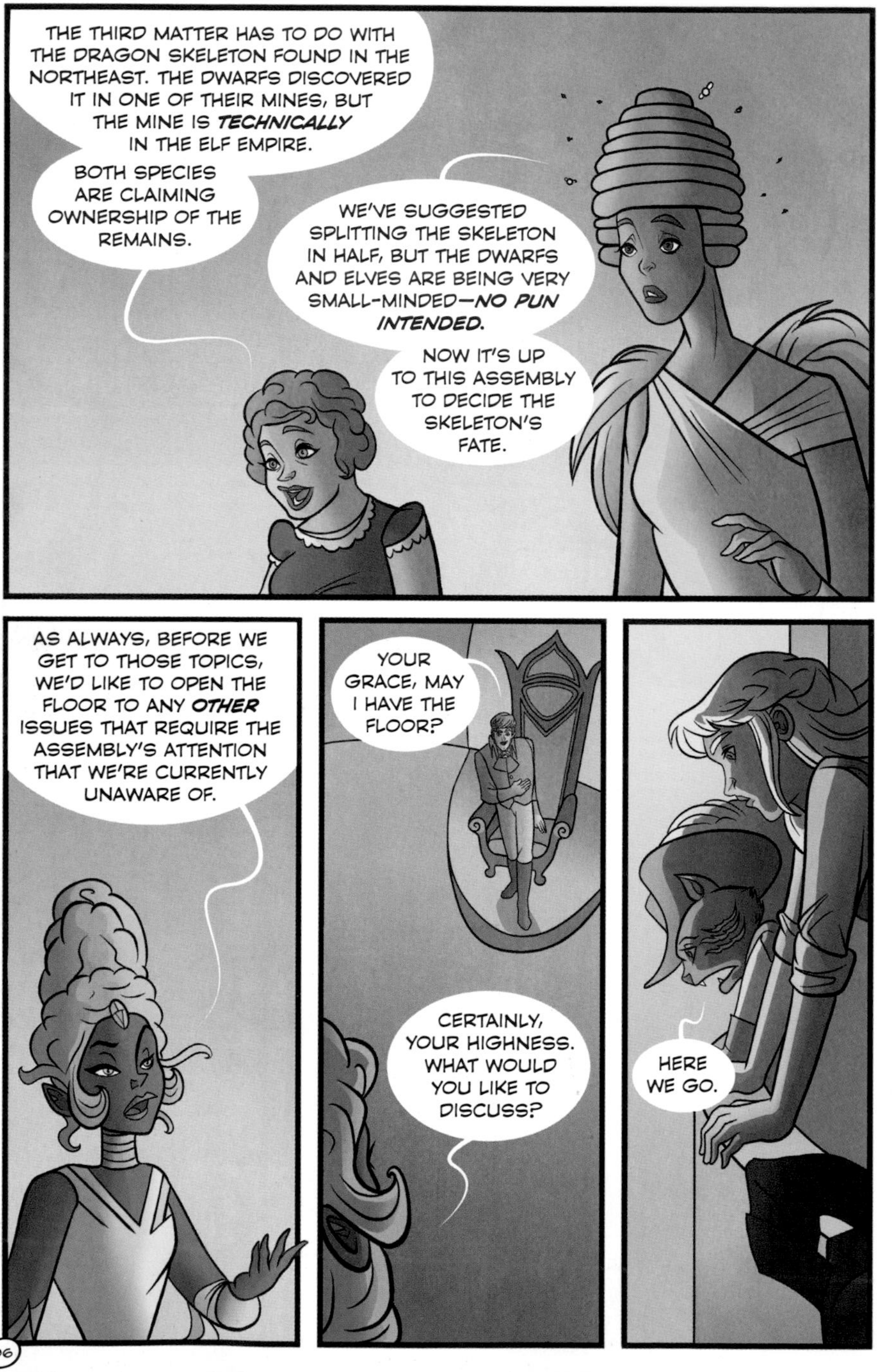
THE THIRD MATTER HAS TO DO WITH THE DRAGON SKELETON FOUND IN THE NORTHEAST. THE DWARFS DISCOVERED IT IN ONE OF THEIR MINES, BUT THE MINE IS *TECHNICALLY* IN THE ELF EMPIRE.
BOTH SPECIES ARE CLAIMING OWNERSHIP OF THE REMAINS.
WE'VE SUGGESTED SPLITTING THE SKELETON IN HALF, BUT THE DWARFS AND ELVES ARE BEING VERY SMALL-MINDED—***NO PUN INTENDED.***
NOW IT'S UP TO THIS ASSEMBLY TO DECIDE THE SKELETON'S FATE.
AS ALWAYS, BEFORE WE GET TO THOSE TOPICS, WE'D LIKE TO OPEN THE FLOOR TO ANY *OTHER* ISSUES THAT REQUIRE THE ASSEMBLY'S ATTENTION THAT WE'RE CURRENTLY UNAWARE OF.
YOUR GRACE, MAY I HAVE THE FLOOR?
CERTAINLY, YOUR HIGHNESS. WHAT WOULD YOU LIKE TO DISCUSS?
HERE WE GO.

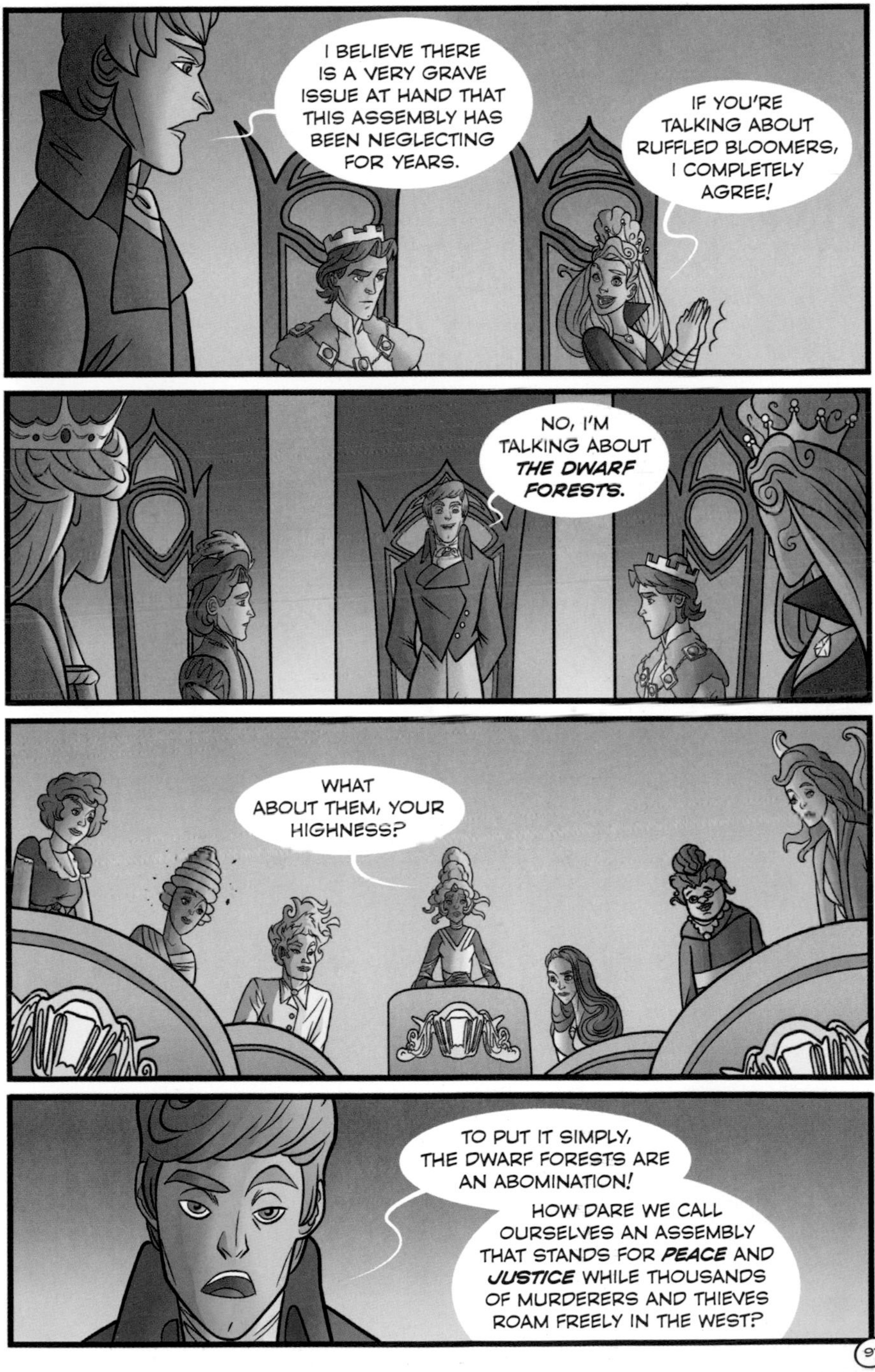
I BELIEVE THERE IS A VERY GRAVE ISSUE AT HAND THAT THIS ASSEMBLY HAS BEEN NEGLECTING FOR YEARS.
IF YOU'RE TALKING ABOUT RUFFLED BLOOMERS, I COMPLETELY AGREE!
NO, I'M TALKING ABOUT THE DWARF FORESTS.
WHAT ABOUT THEM, YOUR HIGHNESS?
TO PUT IT SIMPLY, THE DWARF FORESTS ARE AN ABOMINATION!
HOW DARE WE CALL OURSELVES AN ASSEMBLY THAT STANDS FOR PEACE AND JUSTICE WHILE THOUSANDS OF MURDERERS AND THIEVES ROAM FREELY IN THE WEST?

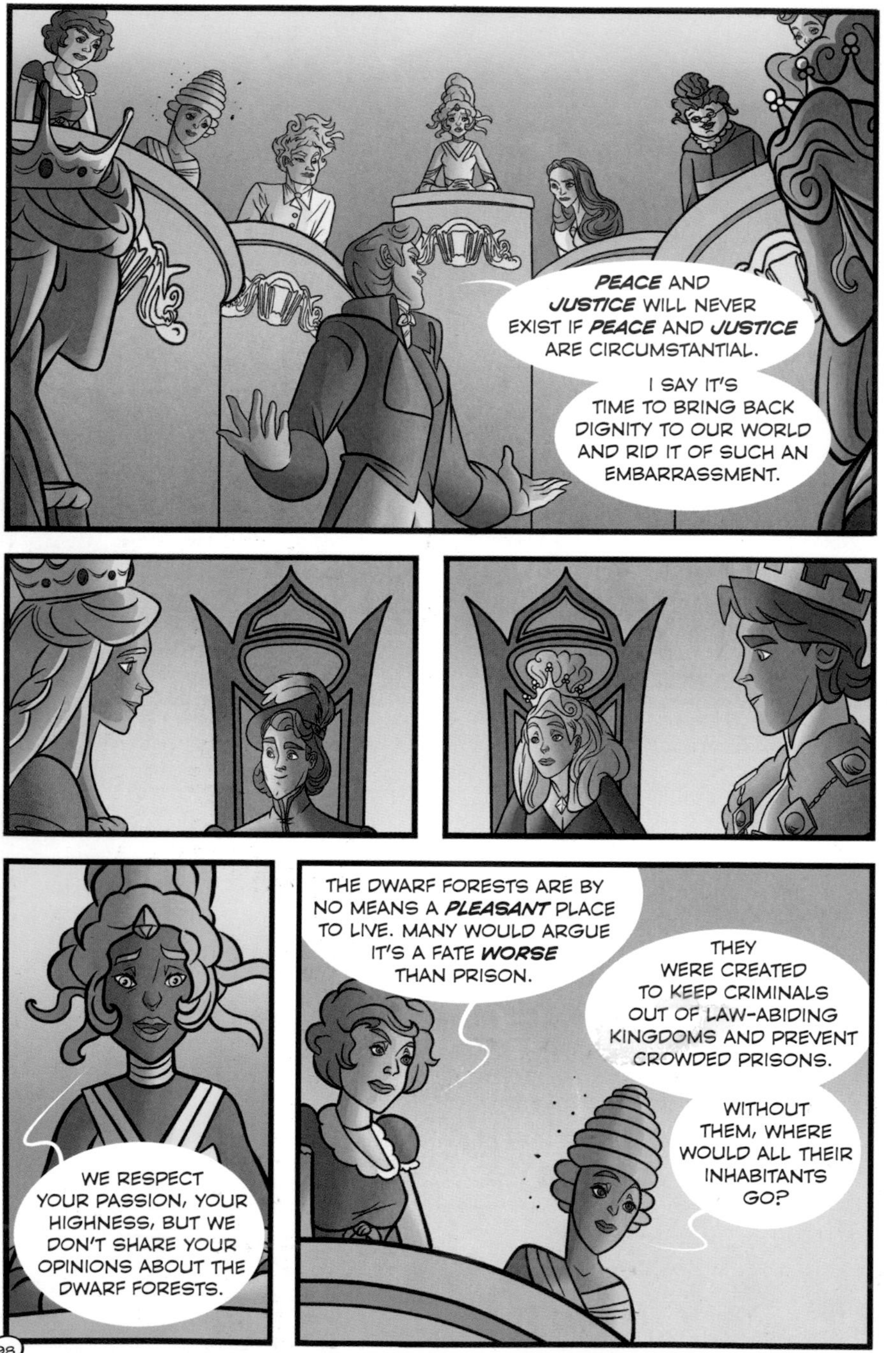
PEACE AND JUSTICE WILL NEVER EXIST IF PEACE AND JUSTICE ARE CIRCUMSTANTIAL.
I SAY IT'S TIME TO BRING BACK DIGNITY TO OUR WORLD AND RID IT OF SUCH AN EMBARRASSMENT.
WE RESPECT YOUR PASSION, YOUR HIGHNESS, BUT WE DON'T SHARE YOUR OPINIONS ABOUT THE DWARF FORESTS.
THE DWARF FORESTS ARE BY NO MEANS A PLEASANT PLACE TO LIVE. MANY WOULD ARGUE IT'S A FATE WORSE THAN PRISON.
THEY WERE CREATED TO KEEP CRIMINALS OUT OF LAW-ABIDING KINGDOMS AND PREVENT CROWDED PRISONS.
WITHOUT THEM, WHERE WOULD ALL THEIR INHABITANTS GO?

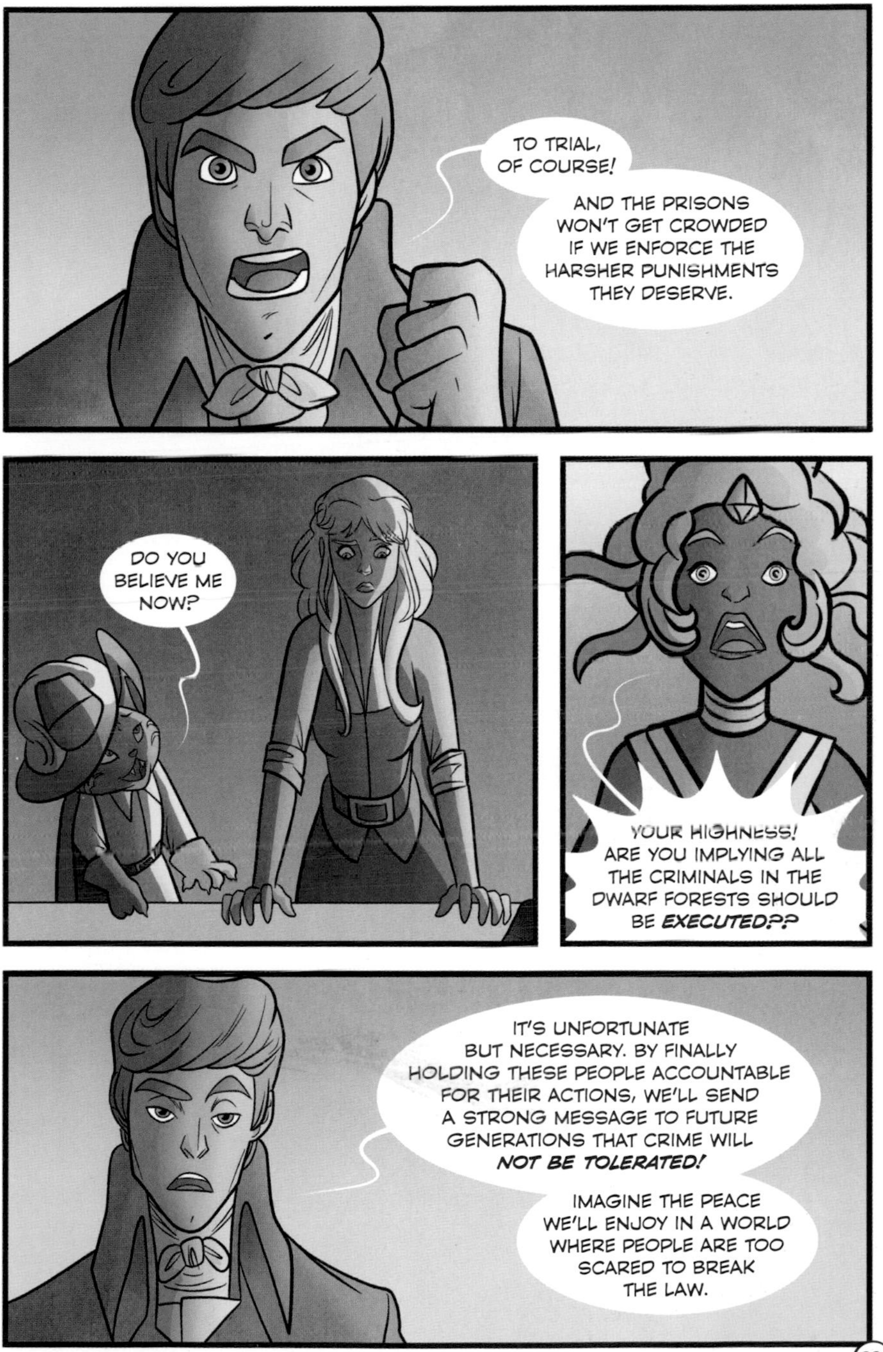
TO TRIAL, OF COURSE!
AND THE PRISONS WON'T GET CROWDED IF WE ENFORCE THE HARSHER PUNISHMENTS THEY DESERVE.
DO YOU BELIEVE ME NOW?
YOUR HIGHNESS! ARE YOU IMPLYING ALL THE CRIMINALS IN THE DWARF FORESTS SHOULD BE *EXECUTED??*
IT'S UNFORTUNATE BUT NECESSARY. BY FINALLY HOLDING THESE PEOPLE ACCOUNTABLE FOR THEIR ACTIONS, WE'LL SEND A STRONG MESSAGE TO FUTURE GENERATIONS THAT CRIME WILL ***NOT BE TOLERATED!***
IMAGINE THE PEACE WE'LL ENJOY IN A WORLD WHERE PEOPLE ARE TOO SCARED TO BREAK THE LAW.

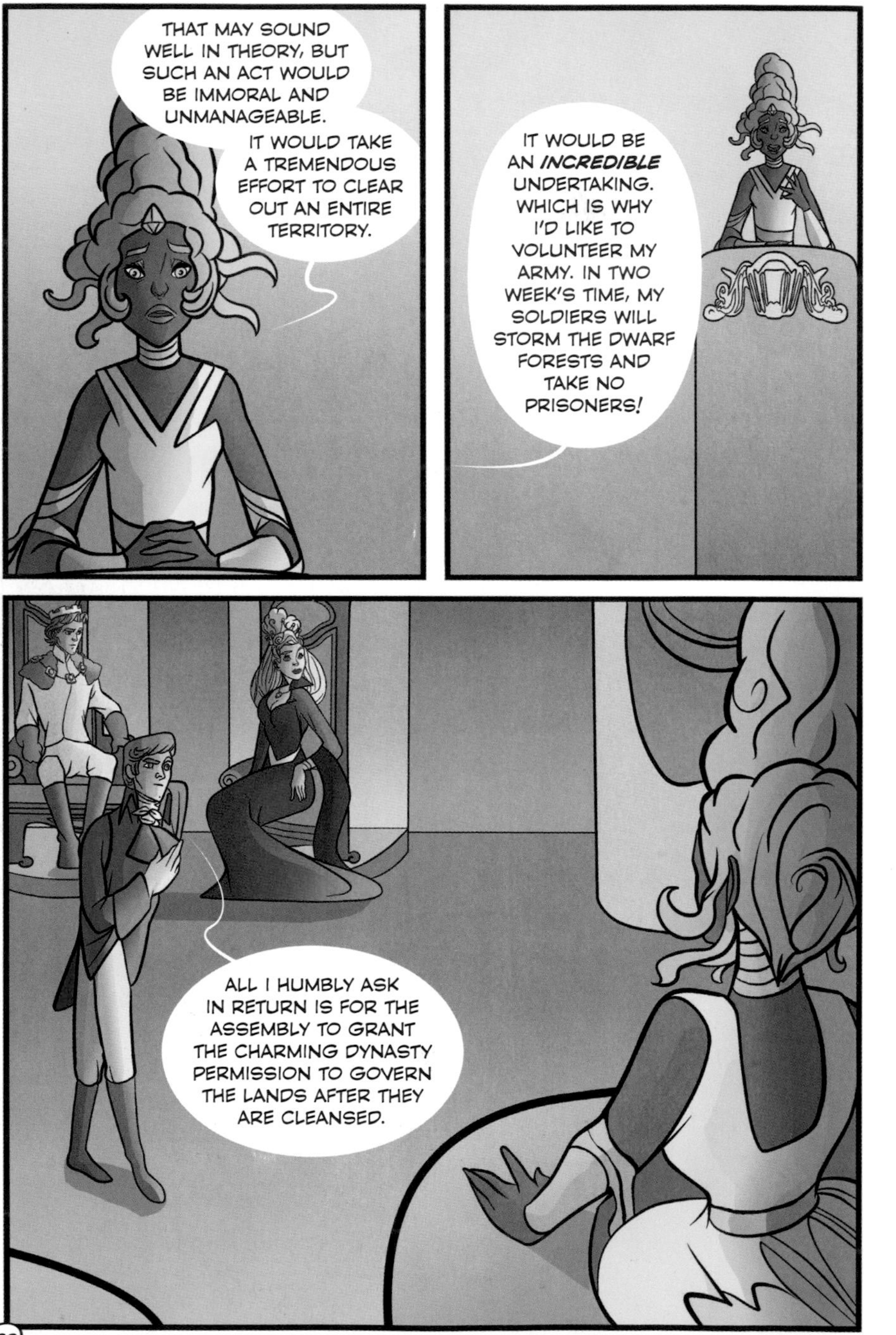
THAT MAY SOUND WELL IN THEORY, BUT SUCH AN ACT WOULD BE IMMORAL AND UNMANAGEABLE.
IT WOULD TAKE A TREMENDOUS EFFORT TO CLEAR OUT AN ENTIRE TERRITORY.
IT WOULD BE AN *INCREDIBLE* UNDERTAKING. WHICH IS WHY I'D LIKE TO VOLUNTEER MY ARMY. IN TWO WEEK'S TIME, MY SOLDIERS WILL STORM THE DWARF FORESTS AND TAKE NO PRISONERS!
ALL I HUMBLY ASK IN RETURN IS FOR THE ASSEMBLY TO GRANT THE CHARMING DYNASTY PERMISSION TO GOVERN THE LANDS AFTER THEY ARE CLEANSED.

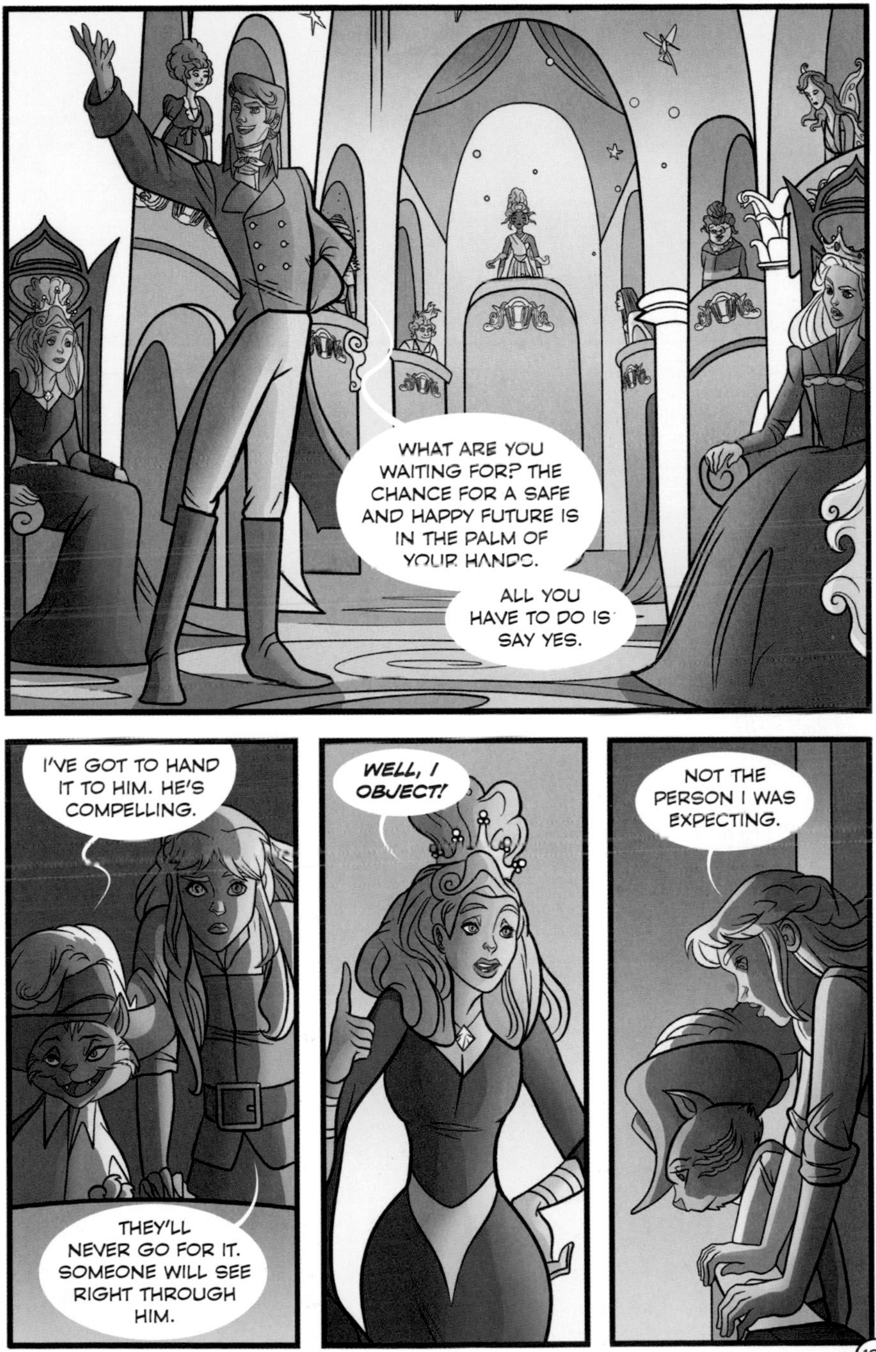
WHAT ARE YOU WAITING FOR? THE CHANCE FOR A SAFE AND HAPPY FUTURE IS IN THE PALM OF YOUR HANDS.
ALL YOU HAVE TO DO IS SAY YES.
I'VE GOT TO HAND IT TO HIM. HE'S COMPELLING.
THEY'LL NEVER GO FOR IT. SOMEONE WILL SEE RIGHT THROUGH HIM.
WELL, I OBJECT!
NOT THE PERSON I WAS EXPECTING.

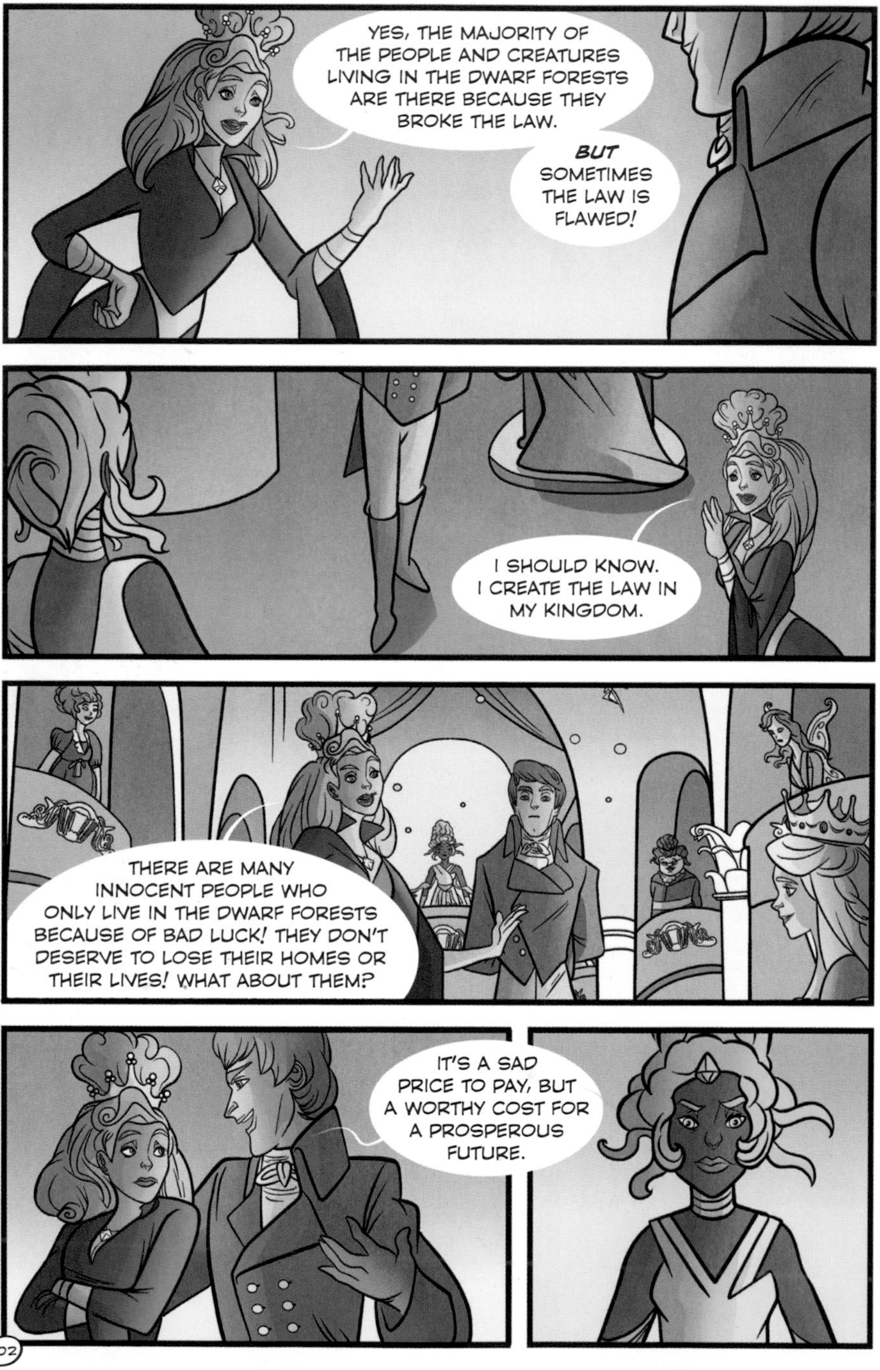
YES, THE MAJORITY OF THE PEOPLE AND CREATURES LIVING IN THE DWARF FORESTS ARE THERE BECAUSE THEY BROKE THE LAW.
BUT SOMETIMES THE LAW IS FLAWED!
I SHOULD KNOW. I CREATE THE LAW IN MY KINGDOM.
THERE ARE MANY INNOCENT PEOPLE WHO ONLY LIVE IN THE DWARF FORESTS BECAUSE OF BAD LUCK! THEY DON'T DESERVE TO LOSE THEIR HOMES OR THEIR LIVES! WHAT ABOUT THEM?
IT'S A SAD PRICE TO PAY, BUT A WORTHY COST FOR A PROSPEROUS FUTURE.

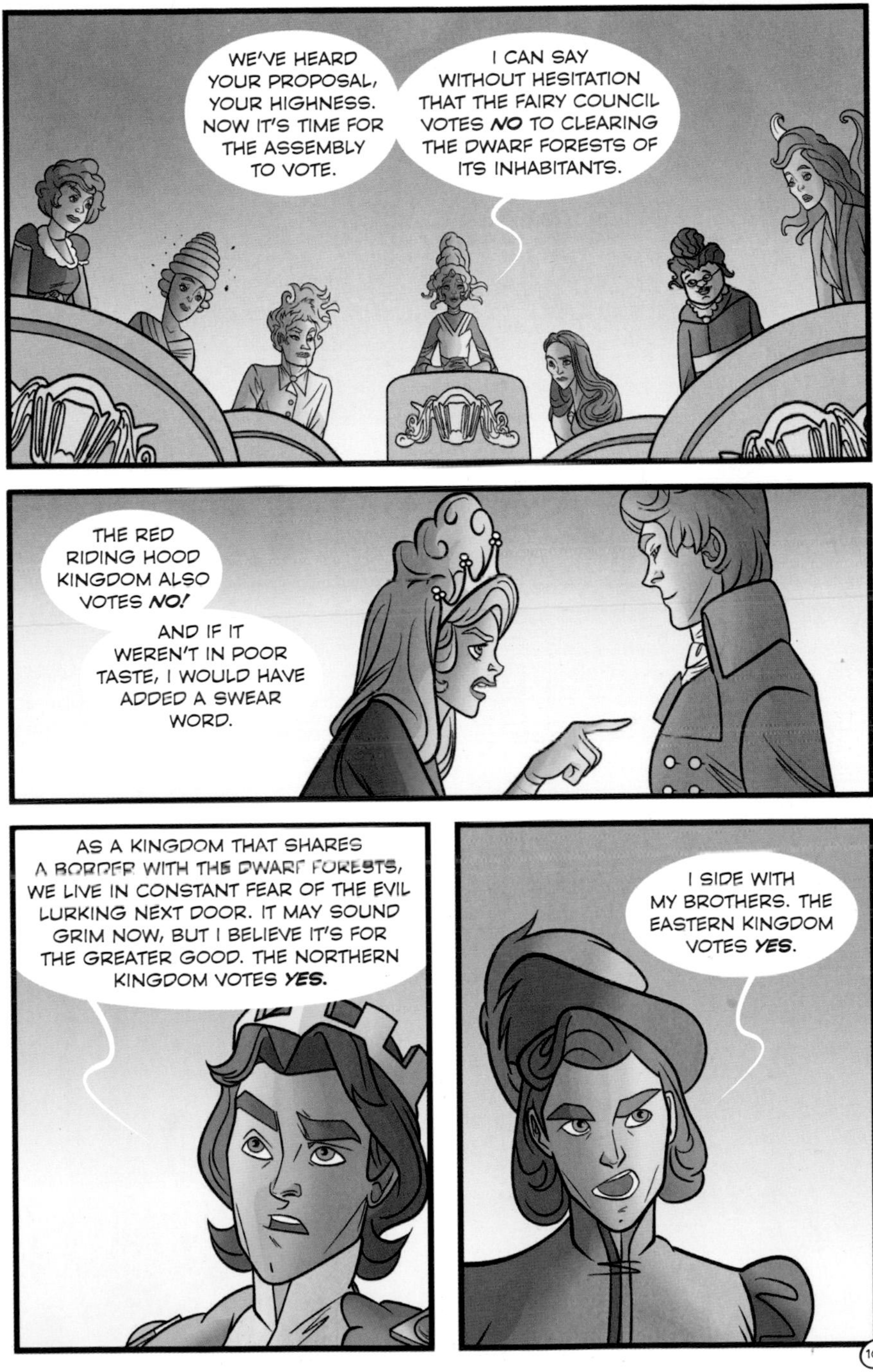
WE'VE HEARD YOUR PROPOSAL, YOUR HIGHNESS. NOW IT'S TIME FOR THE ASSEMBLY TO VOTE.
I CAN SAY WITHOUT HESITATION THAT THE FAIRY COUNCIL VOTES NO TO CLEARING THE DWARF FORESTS OF ITS INHABITANTS.
THE RED RIDING HOOD KINGDOM ALSO VOTES NO!
AND IF IT WEREN'T IN POOR TASTE, I WOULD HAVE ADDED A SWEAR WORD.
AS A KINGDOM THAT SHARES A BORDER WITH THE DWARF FORESTS, WE LIVE IN CONSTANT FEAR OF THE EVIL LURKING NEXT DOOR. IT MAY SOUND GRIM NOW, BUT I BELIEVE IT'S FOR THE GREATER GOOD. THE NORTHERN KINGDOM VOTES YES.
I SIDE WITH MY BROTHERS. THE EASTERN KINGDOM VOTES YES.

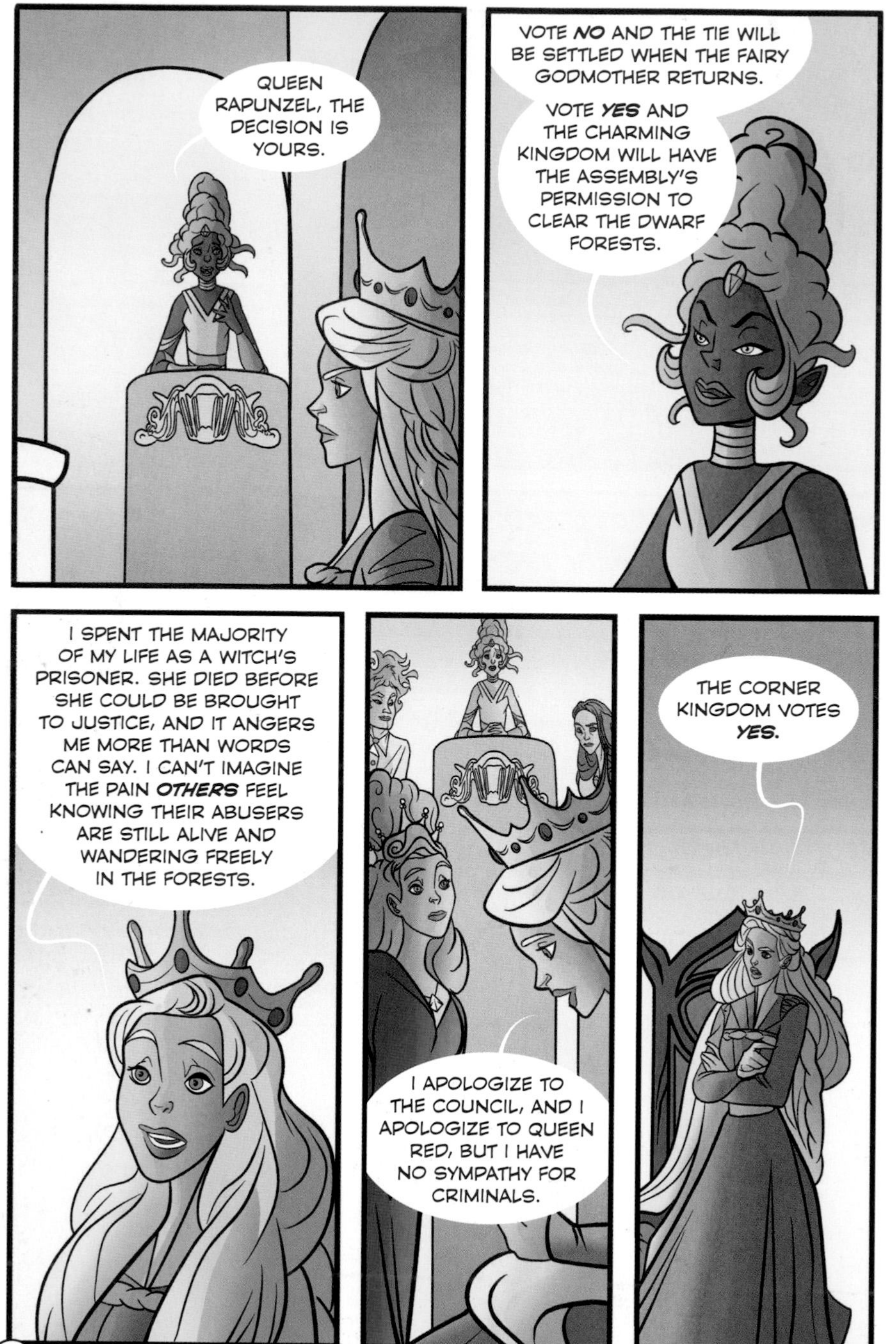
QUEEN RAPUNZEL, THE DECISION IS YOURS.
VOTE **NO** AND THE TIE WILL BE SETTLED WHEN THE FAIRY GODMOTHER RETURNS.
VOTE ***YES*** AND THE CHARMING KINGDOM WILL HAVE THE ASSEMBLY'S PERMISSION TO CLEAR THE DWARF FORESTS.
I SPENT THE MAJORITY OF MY LIFE AS A WITCH'S PRISONER. SHE DIED BEFORE SHE COULD BE BROUGHT TO JUSTICE, AND IT ANGERS ME MORE THAN WORDS CAN SAY. I CAN'T IMAGINE THE PAIN ***OTHERS*** FEEL KNOWING THEIR ABUSERS ARE STILL ALIVE AND WANDERING FREELY IN THE FORESTS.
I APOLOGIZE TO THE COUNCIL, AND I APOLOGIZE TO QUEEN RED, BUT I HAVE NO SYMPATHY FOR CRIMINALS.
THE CORNER KINGDOM VOTES ***YES***.

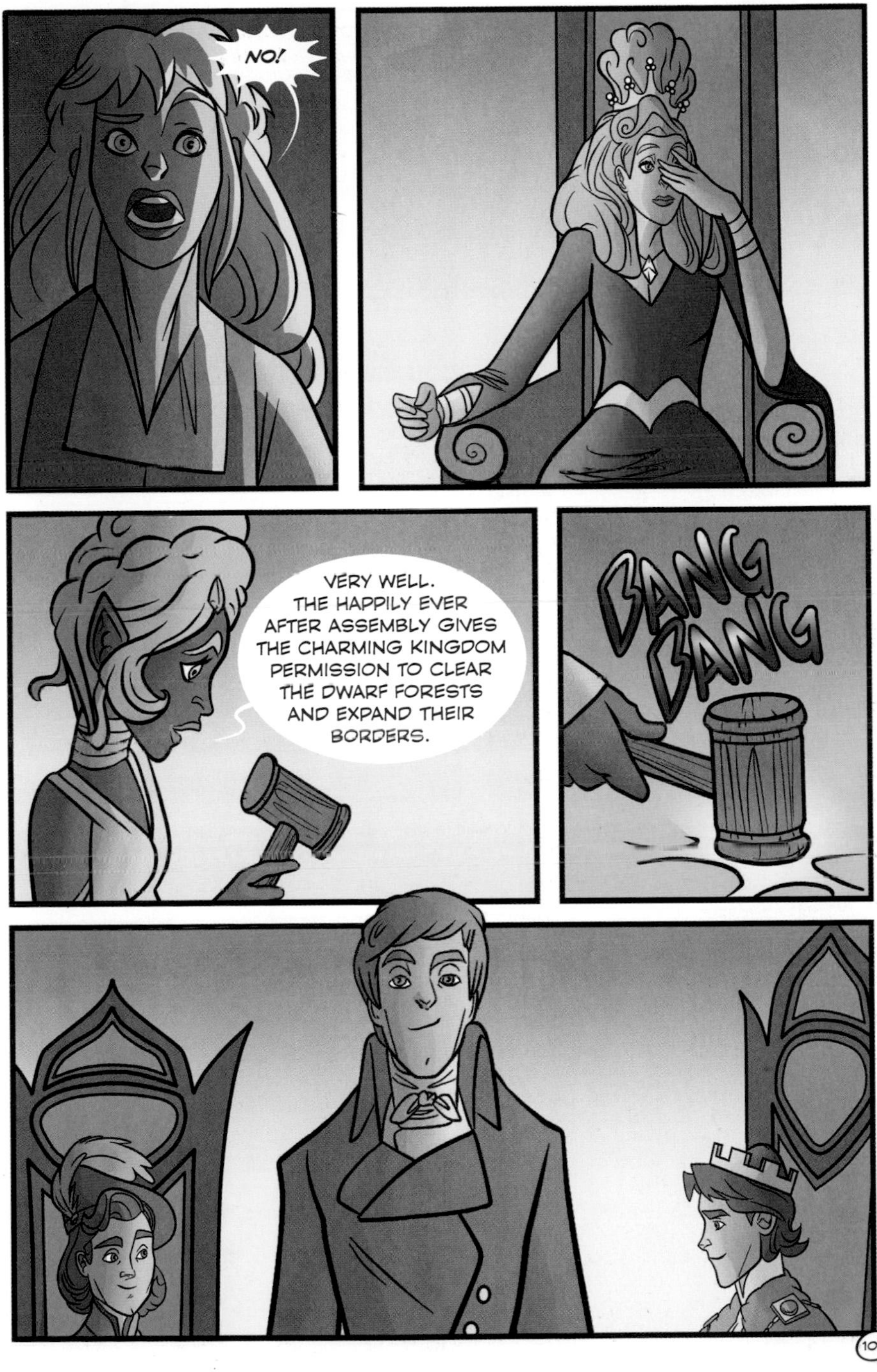
NO!
VERY WELL. THE HAPPILY EVER AFTER ASSEMBLY GIVES THE CHARMING KINGDOM PERMISSION TO CLEAR THE DWARF FORESTS AND EXPAND THEIR BORDERS.
BANG BANG

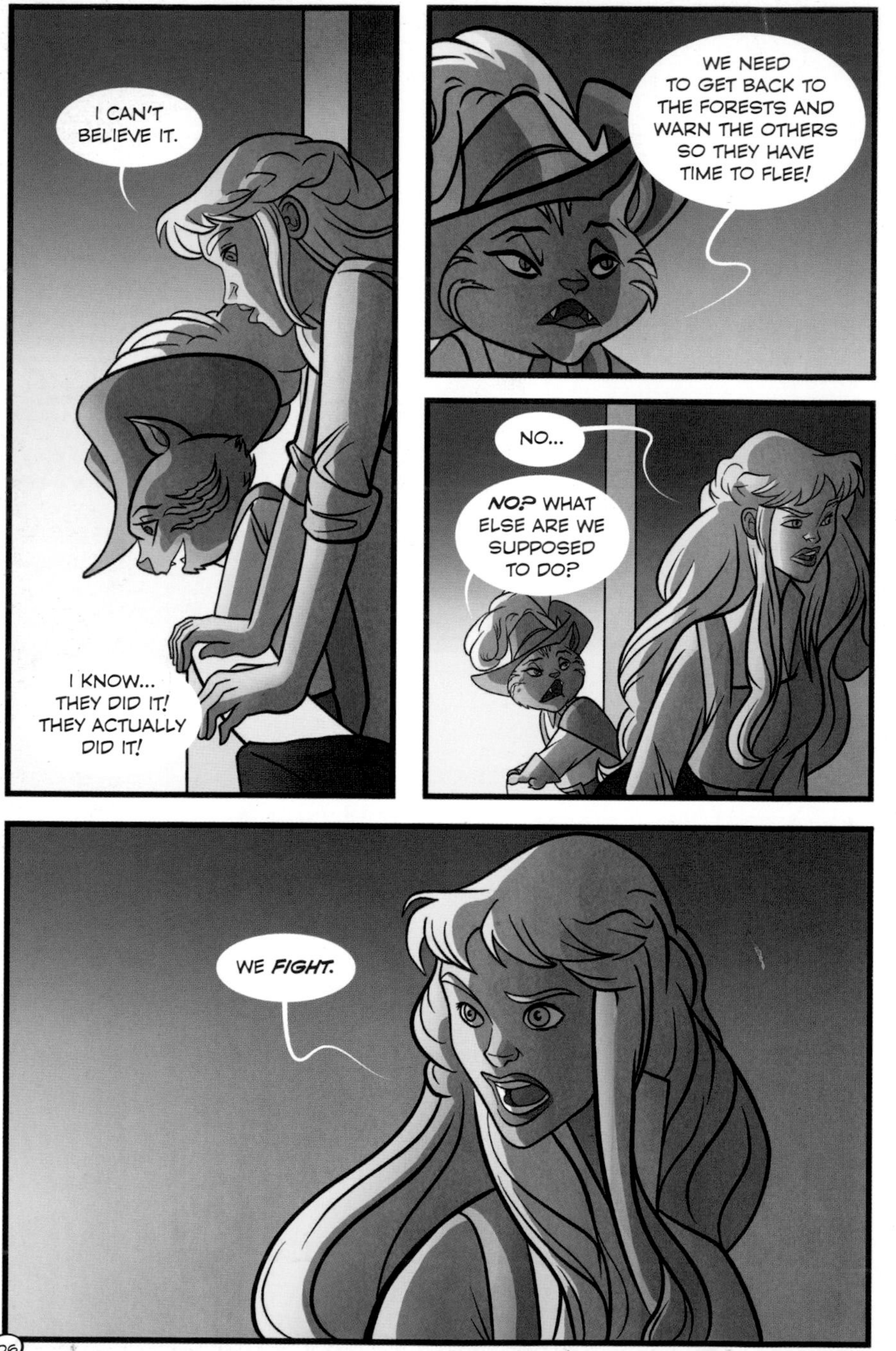
I CAN'T BELIEVE IT.
I KNOW... THEY DID IT! THEY ACTUALLY DID IT!
WE NEED TO GET BACK TO THE FORESTS AND WARN THE OTHERS SO THEY HAVE TIME TO FLEE!
NO...
NO? WHAT ELSE ARE WE SUPPOSED TO DO?
WE FIGHT.

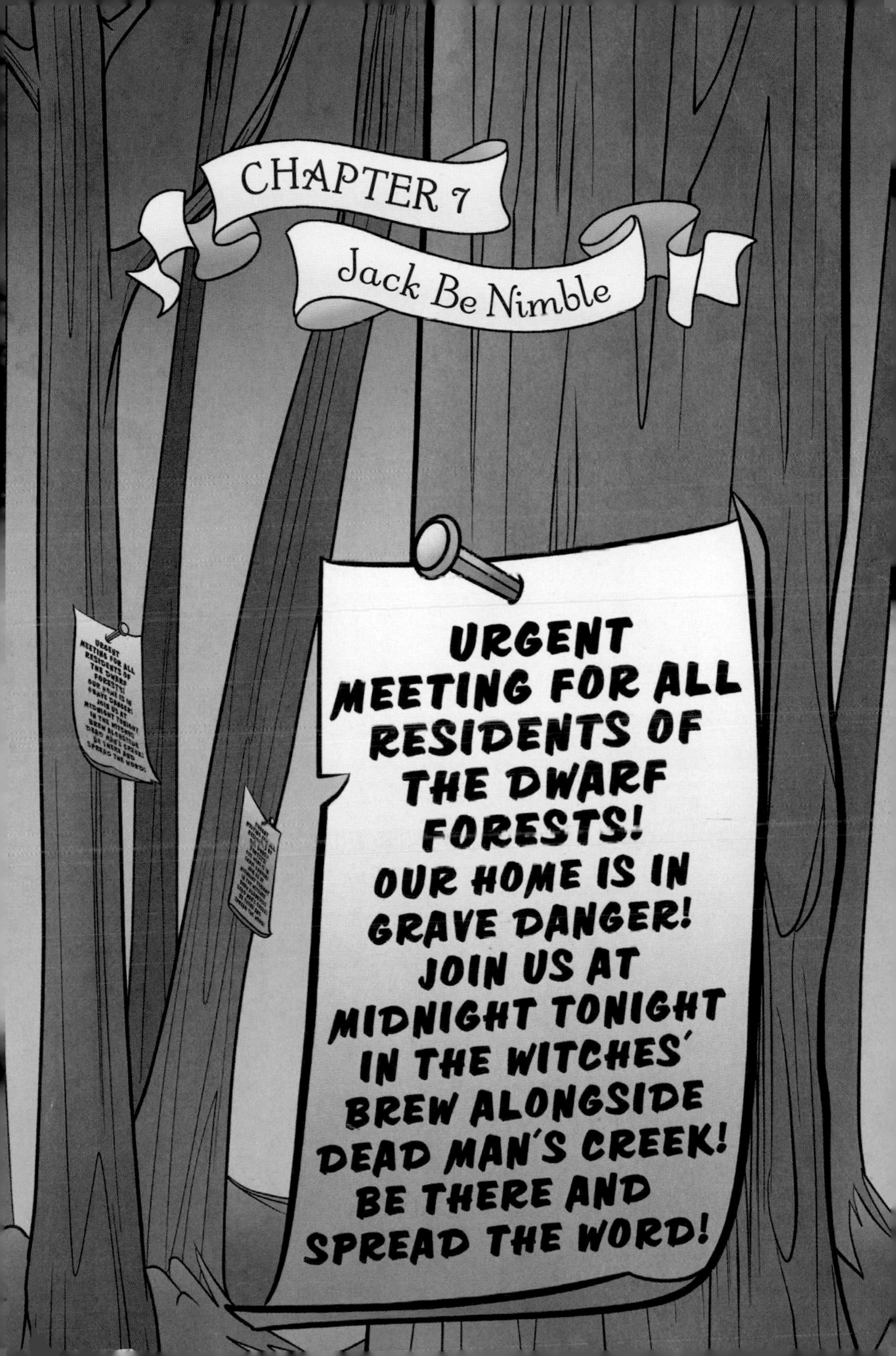
CHAPTER 7
Jack Be Nimble
URGENT
MEETING FOR ALL
RESIDENTS OF
THE DWARF
FORESTS!
OUR HOME IS IN
GRAVE DANGER!
JOIN US AT
MIDNIGHT TONIGHT
IN THE WITCHES'
BREW ALONGSIDE
DEAD MAN'S CREEK!
BE THERE AND
SPREAD THE WORD!

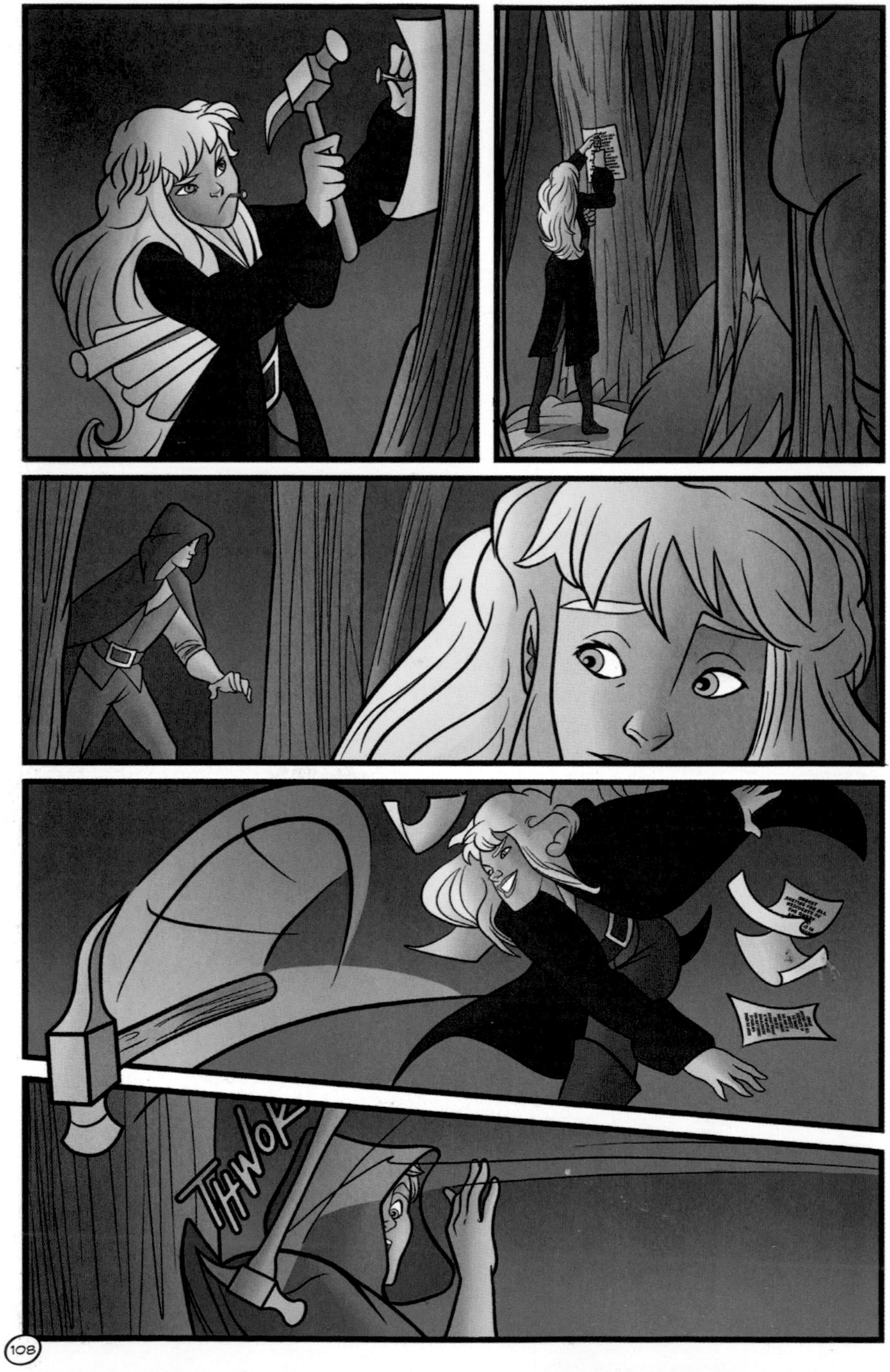
THWOK

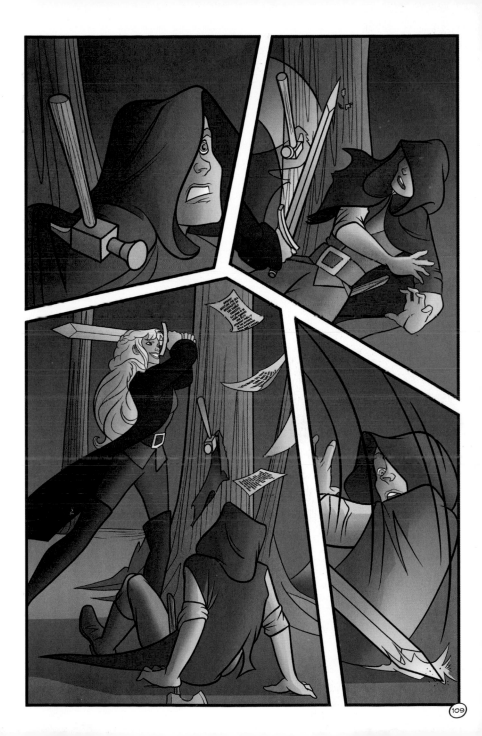

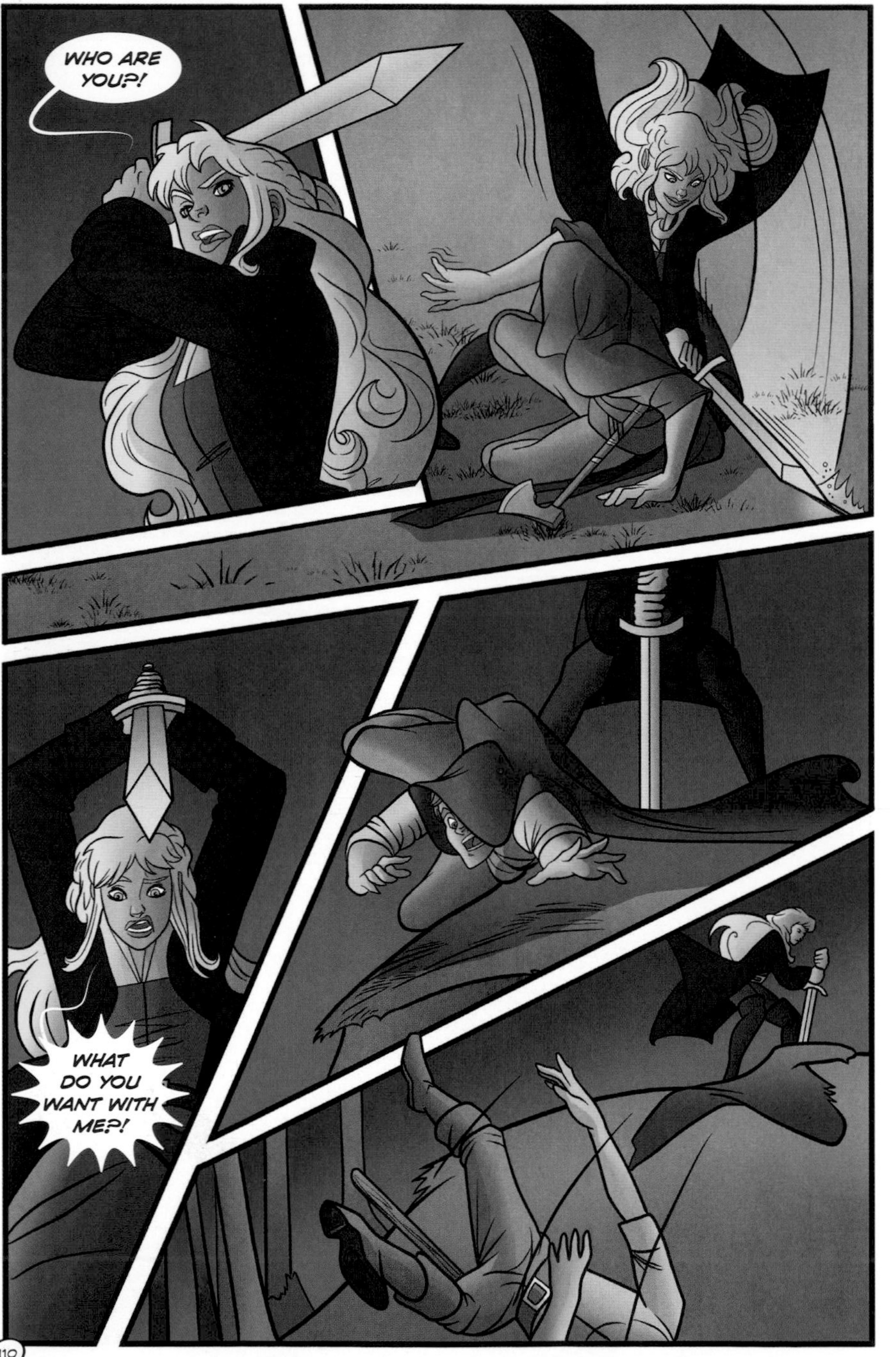
WHO ARE YOU?!
WHAT DO YOU WANT WITH ME?!

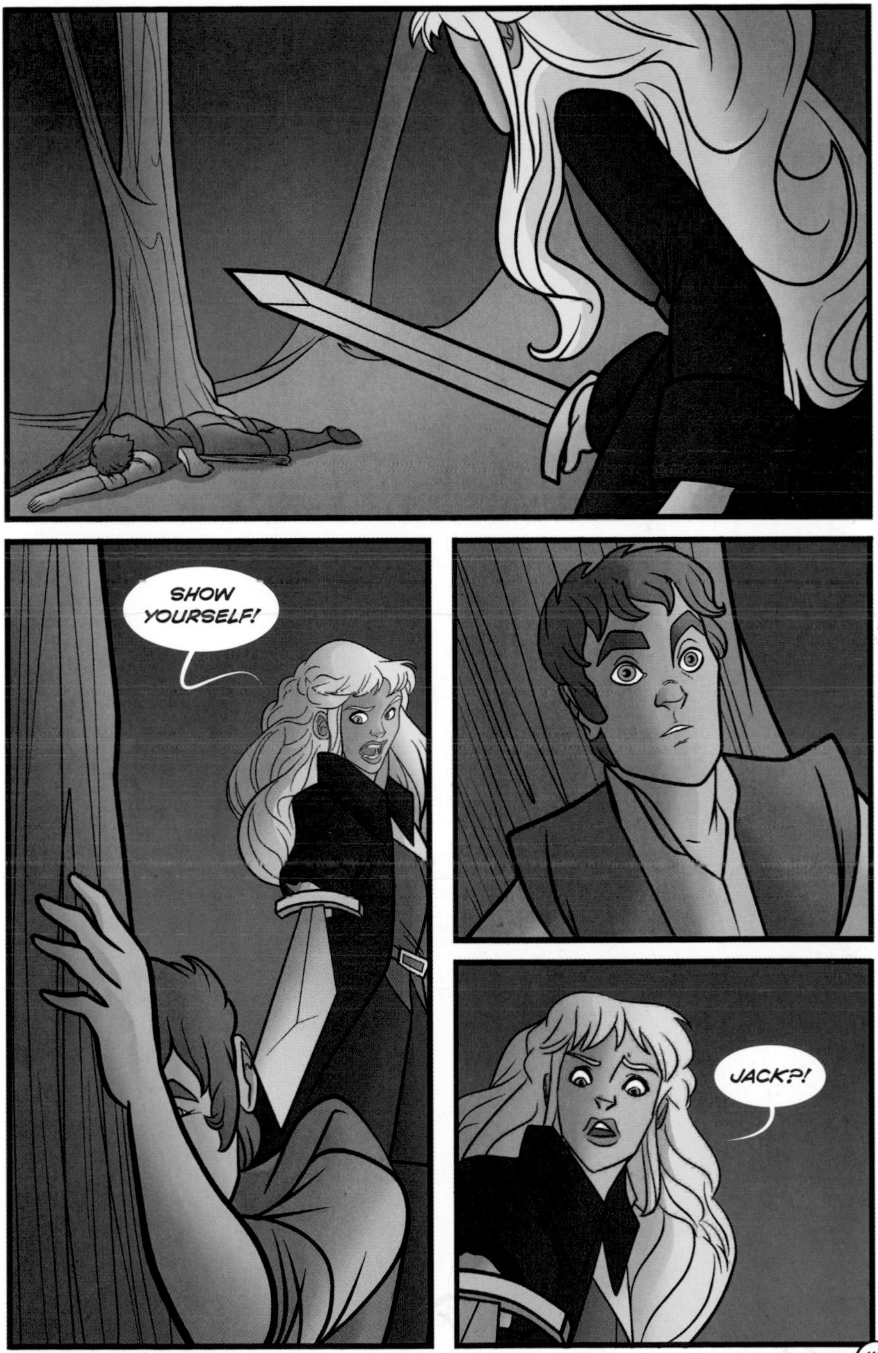
SHOW YOURSELF!
JACK?!

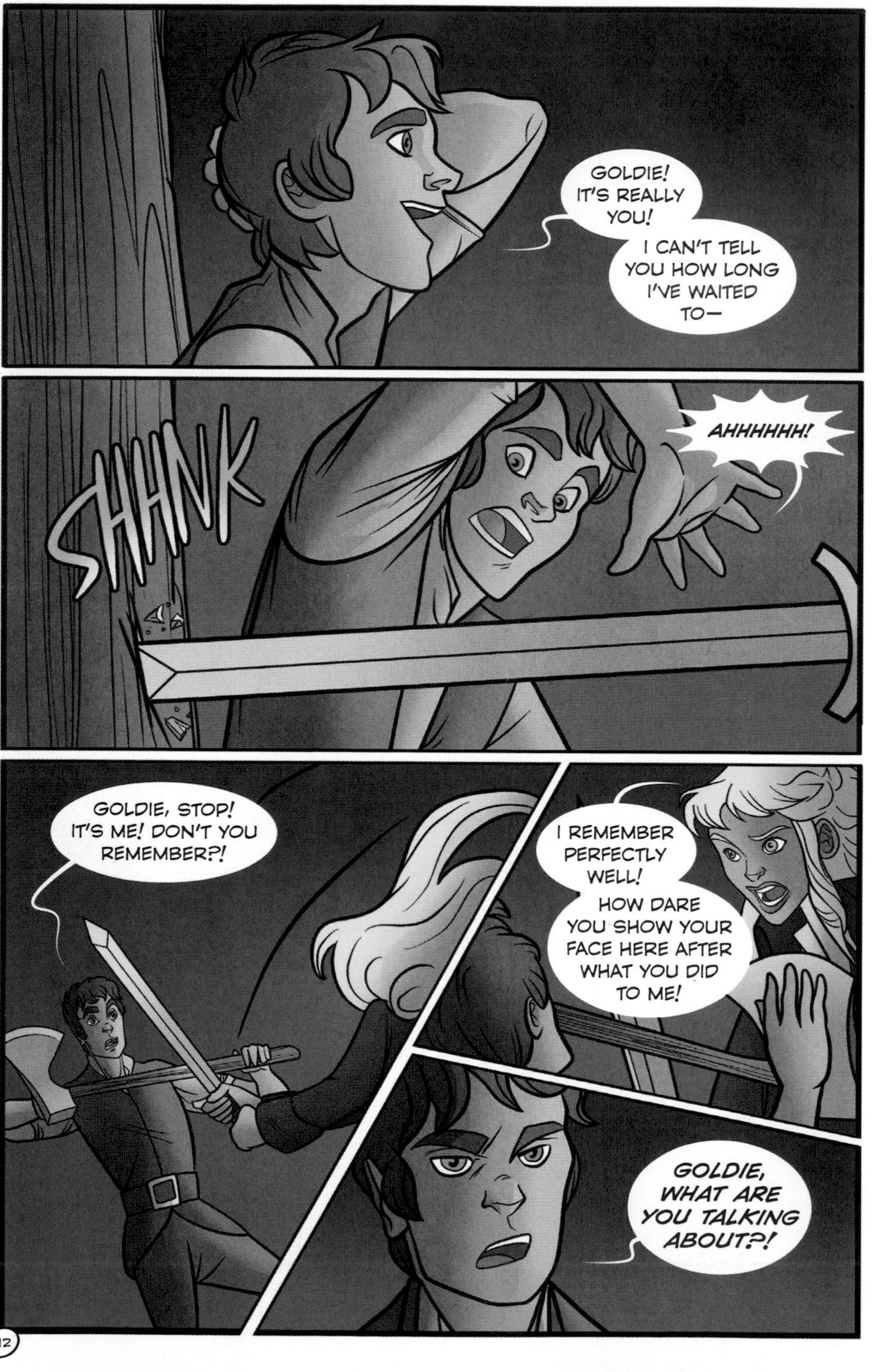

GOLDIE! IT'S REALLY YOU!
I CAN'T TELL YOU HOW LONG I'VE WAITED TO—
SHHNK
AHHHHHH!
GOLDIE, STOP! IT'S ME! DON'T YOU REMEMBER?!
I REMEMBER PERFECTLY WELL!
HOW DARE YOU SHOW YOUR FACE HERE AFTER WHAT YOU DID TO ME!
GOLDIE, WHAT ARE YOU TALKING ABOUT?!

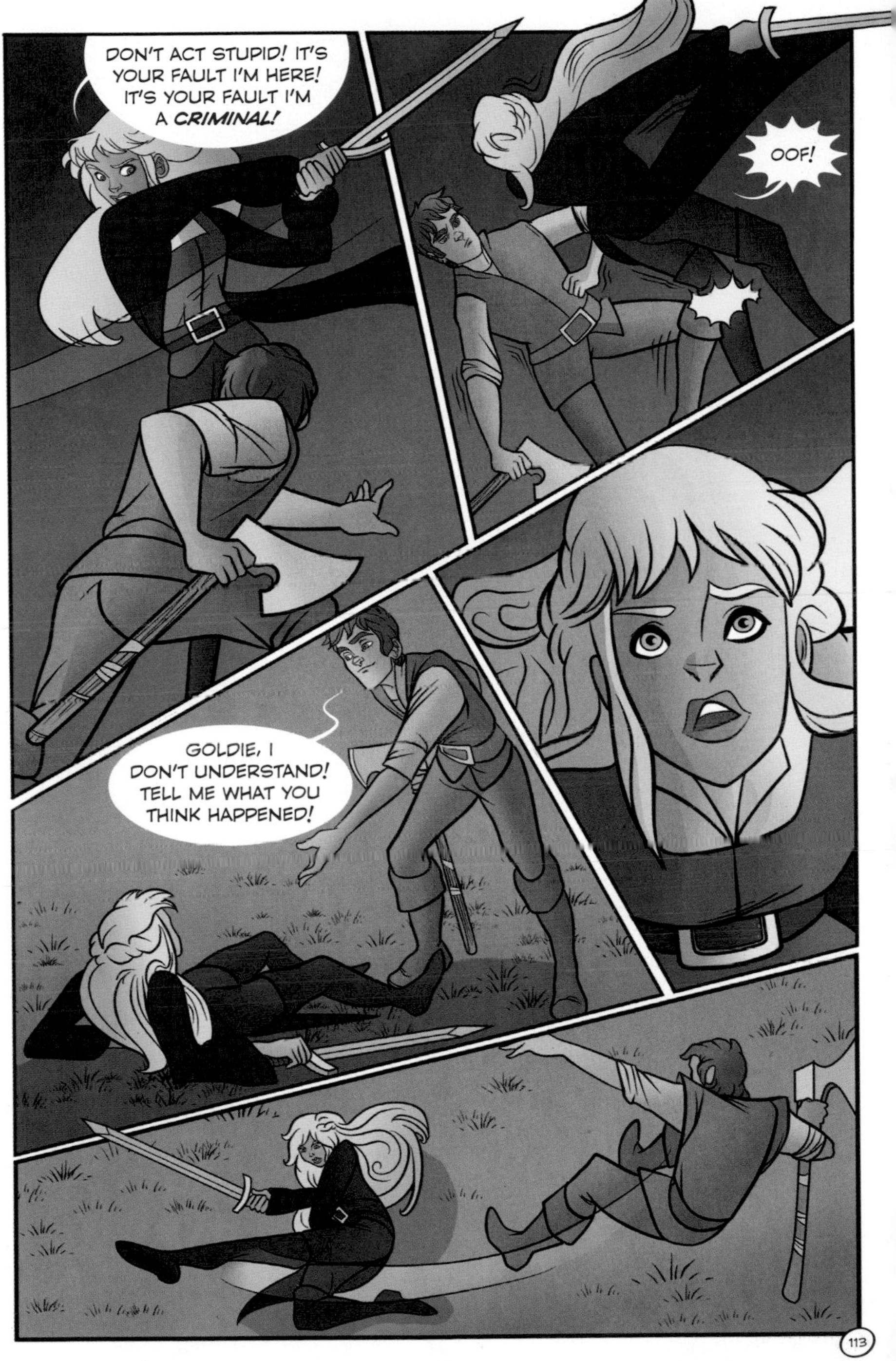
DON'T ACT STUPID! IT'S YOUR FAULT I'M HERE! IT'S YOUR FAULT I'M A *CRIMINAL!*
OOF!
GOLDIE, I DON'T UNDERSTAND! TELL ME WHAT YOU THINK HAPPENED!

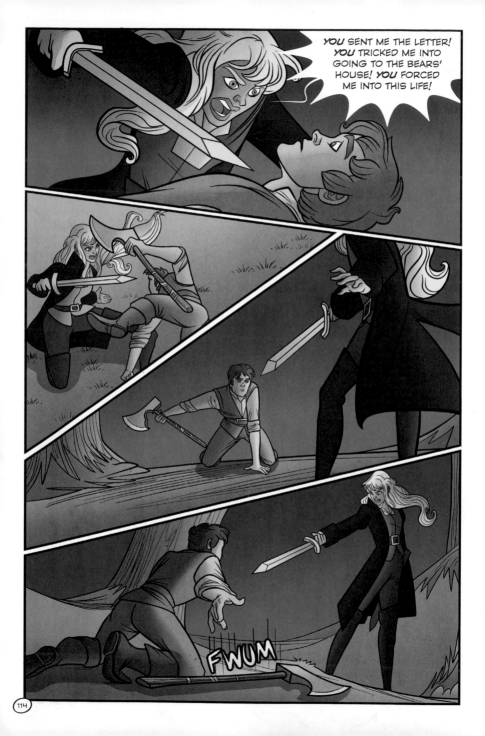

YOU SENT ME THE LETTER! YOU TRICKED ME INTO GOING TO THE BEARS' HOUSE! YOU FORCED ME INTO THIS LIFE!

FWUM

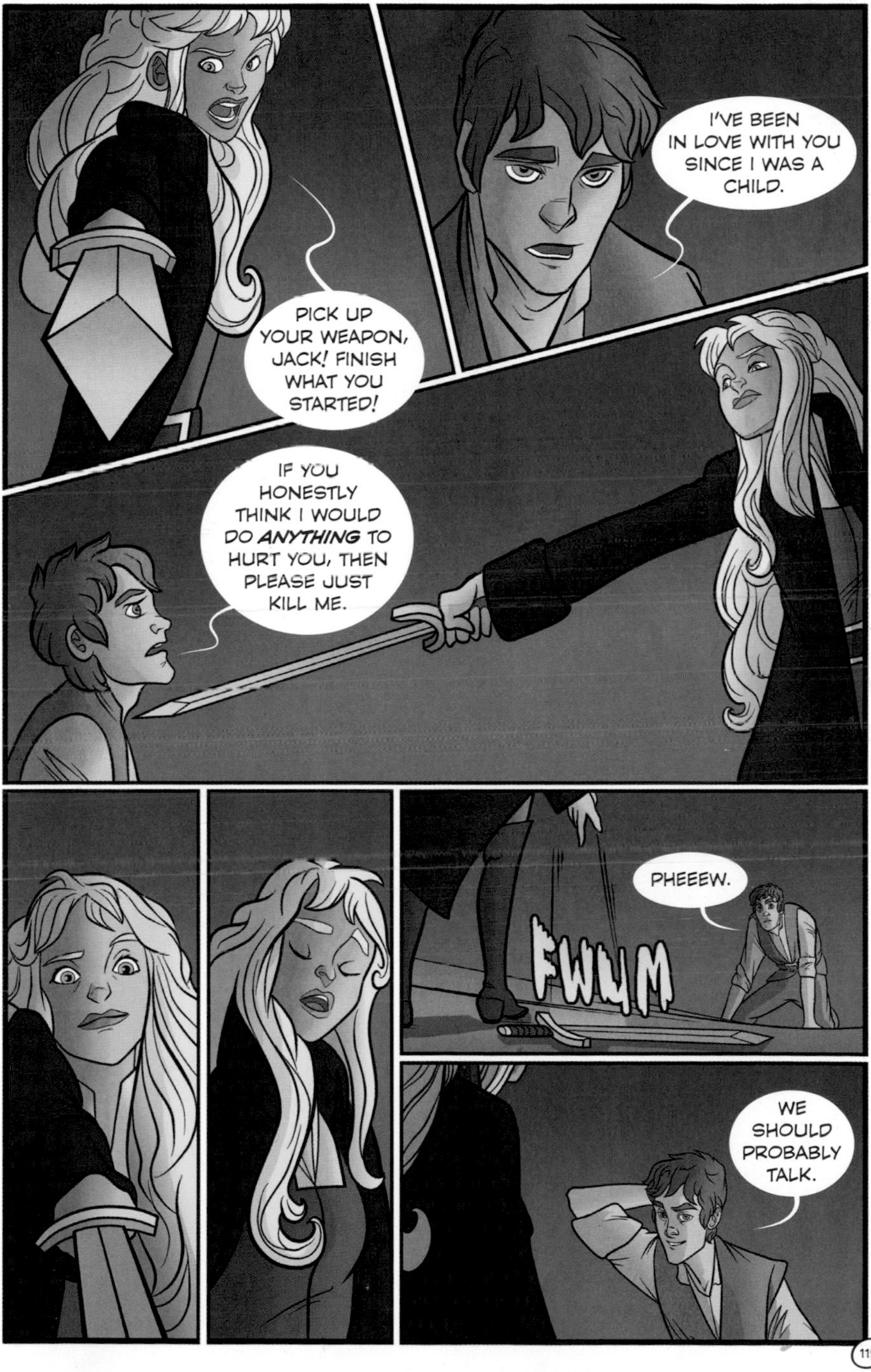
PICK UP YOUR WEAPON, JACK! FINISH WHAT YOU STARTED!
I'VE BEEN IN LOVE WITH YOU SINCE I WAS A CHILD.
IF YOU HONESTLY THINK I WOULD DO ANYTHING TO HURT YOU, THEN PLEASE JUST KILL ME.
FWUM
PHEEEW.
WE SHOULD PROBABLY TALK.

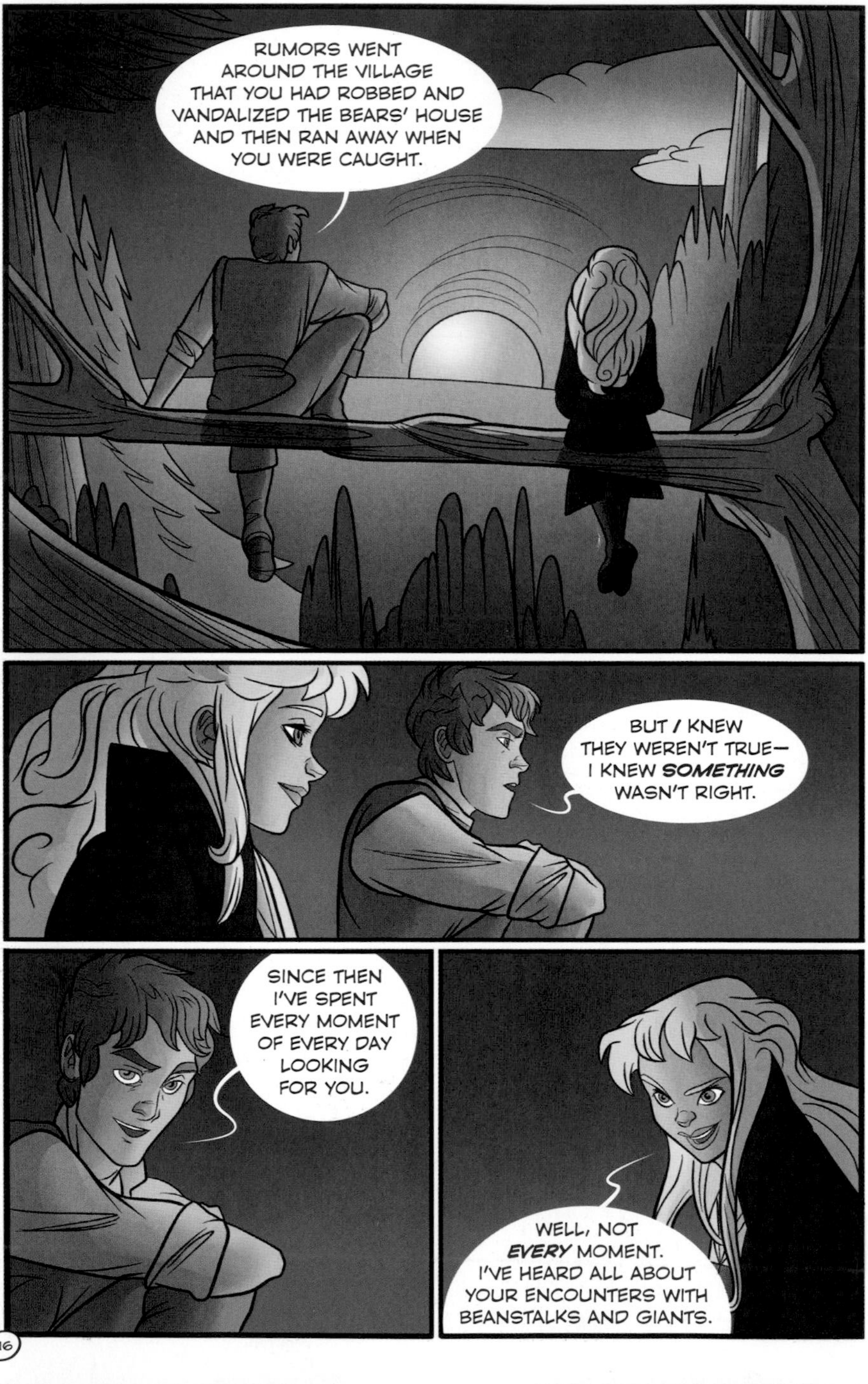
RUMORS WENT AROUND THE VILLAGE THAT YOU HAD ROBBED AND VANDALIZED THE BEARS' HOUSE AND THEN RAN AWAY WHEN YOU WERE CAUGHT.
BUT *I* KNEW THEY WEREN'T TRUE— I KNEW ***SOMETHING*** WASN'T RIGHT.
SINCE THEN I'VE SPENT EVERY MOMENT OF EVERY DAY LOOKING FOR YOU.
WELL, NOT ***EVERY*** MOMENT. I'VE HEARD ALL ABOUT YOUR ENCOUNTERS WITH BEANSTALKS AND GIANTS.

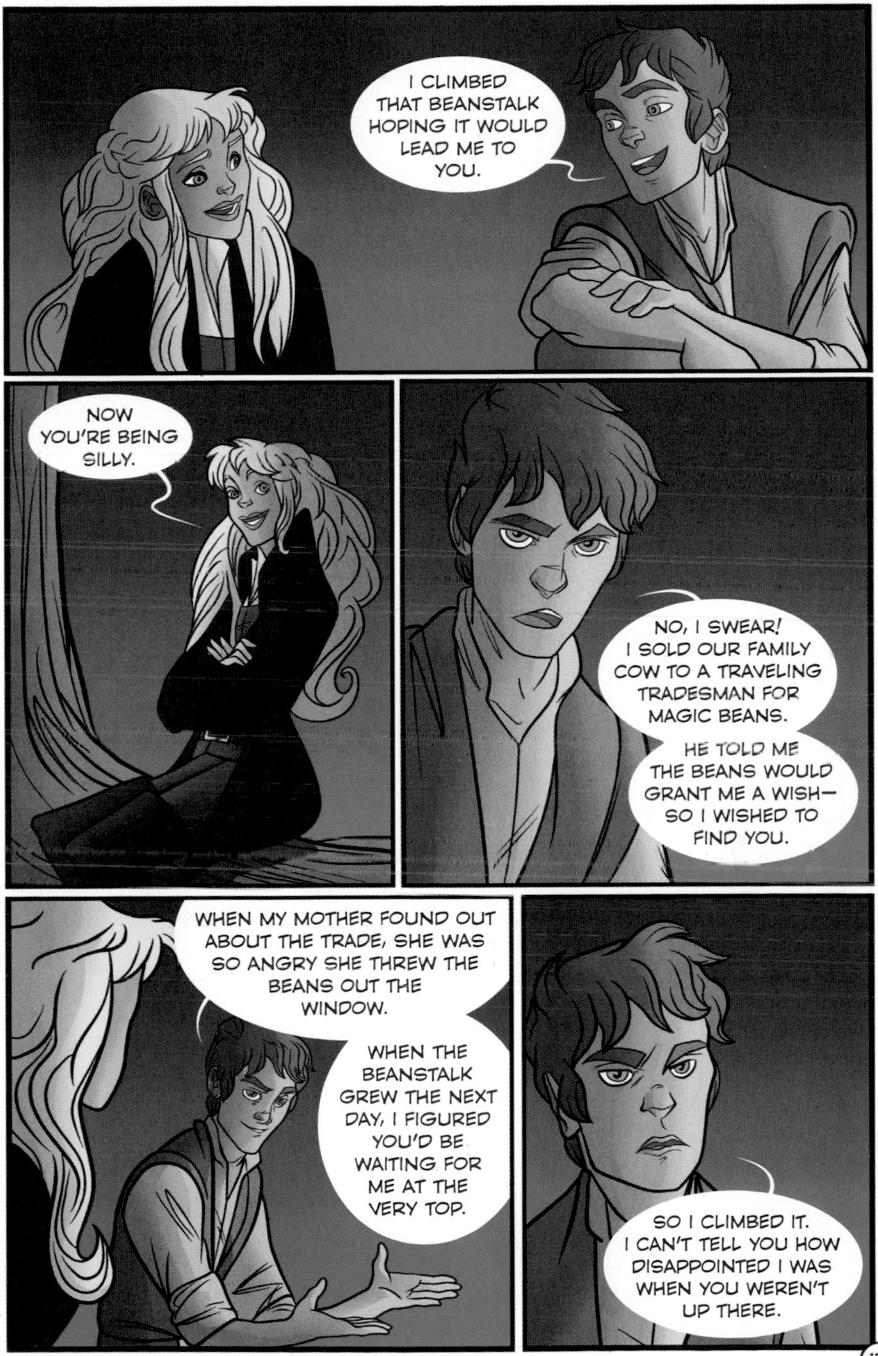

I CLIMBED THAT BEANSTALK HOPING IT WOULD LEAD ME TO YOU.
NOW YOU'RE BEING SILLY.
NO, I SWEAR! I SOLD OUR FAMILY COW TO A TRAVELING TRADESMAN FOR MAGIC BEANS.
HE TOLD ME THE BEANS WOULD GRANT ME A WISH— SO I WISHED TO FIND YOU.
WHEN MY MOTHER FOUND OUT ABOUT THE TRADE, SHE WAS SO ANGRY SHE THREW THE BEANS OUT THE WINDOW.
WHEN THE BEANSTALK GREW THE NEXT DAY, I FIGURED YOU'D BE WAITING FOR ME AT THE VERY TOP.
SO I CLIMBED IT. I CAN'T TELL YOU HOW DISAPPOINTED I WAS WHEN YOU WEREN'T UP THERE.

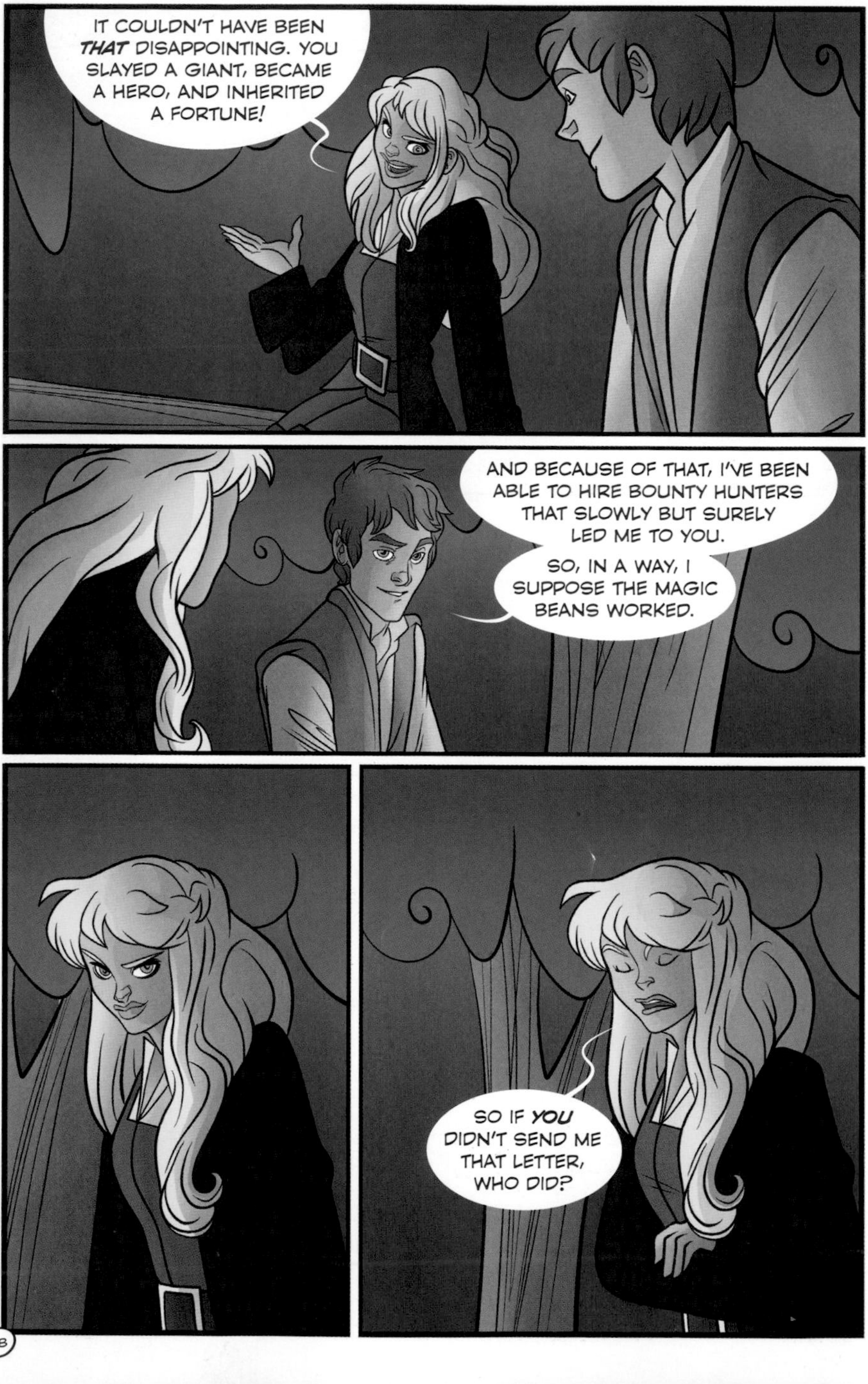
IT COULDN'T HAVE BEEN *THAT* DISAPPOINTING. YOU SLAYED A GIANT, BECAME A HERO, AND INHERITED A FORTUNE!
AND BECAUSE OF THAT, I'VE BEEN ABLE TO HIRE BOUNTY HUNTERS THAT SLOWLY BUT SURELY LED ME TO YOU.
SO, IN A WAY, I SUPPOSE THE MAGIC BEANS WORKED.
SO IF *YOU* DIDN'T SEND ME THAT LETTER, WHO DID?

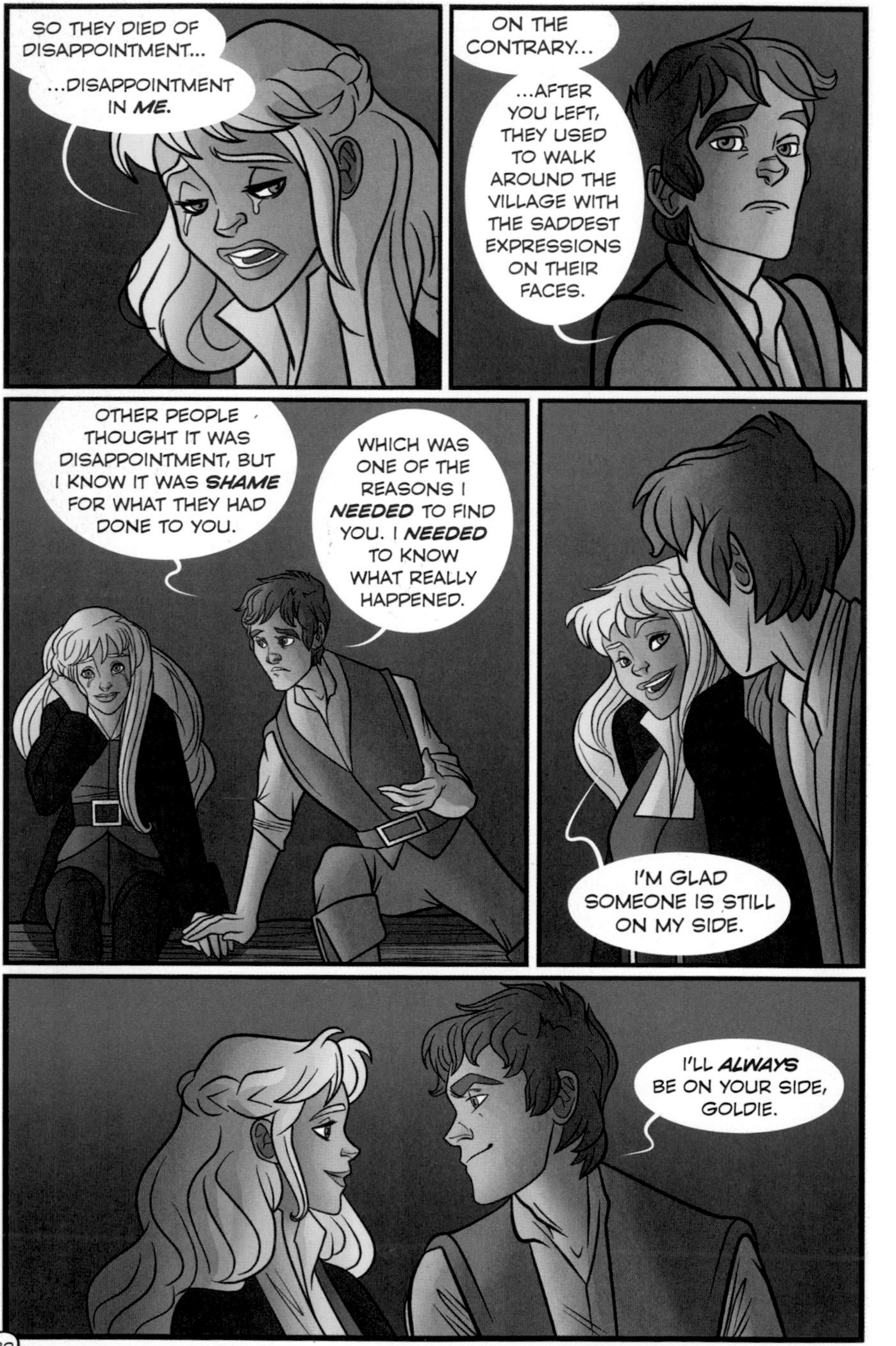
SO THEY DIED OF DISAPPOINTMENT...
...DISAPPOINTMENT IN *ME*.
ON THE CONTRARY...
...AFTER YOU LEFT, THEY USED TO WALK AROUND THE VILLAGE WITH THE SADDEST EXPRESSIONS ON THEIR FACES.
OTHER PEOPLE THOUGHT IT WAS DISAPPOINTMENT, BUT I KNOW IT WAS *SHAME* FOR WHAT THEY HAD DONE TO YOU.
WHICH WAS ONE OF THE REASONS I *NEEDED* TO FIND YOU. I *NEEDED* TO KNOW WHAT REALLY HAPPENED.
I'M GLAD SOMEONE IS STILL ON MY SIDE.
I'LL *ALWAYS* BE ON YOUR SIDE, GOLDIE.

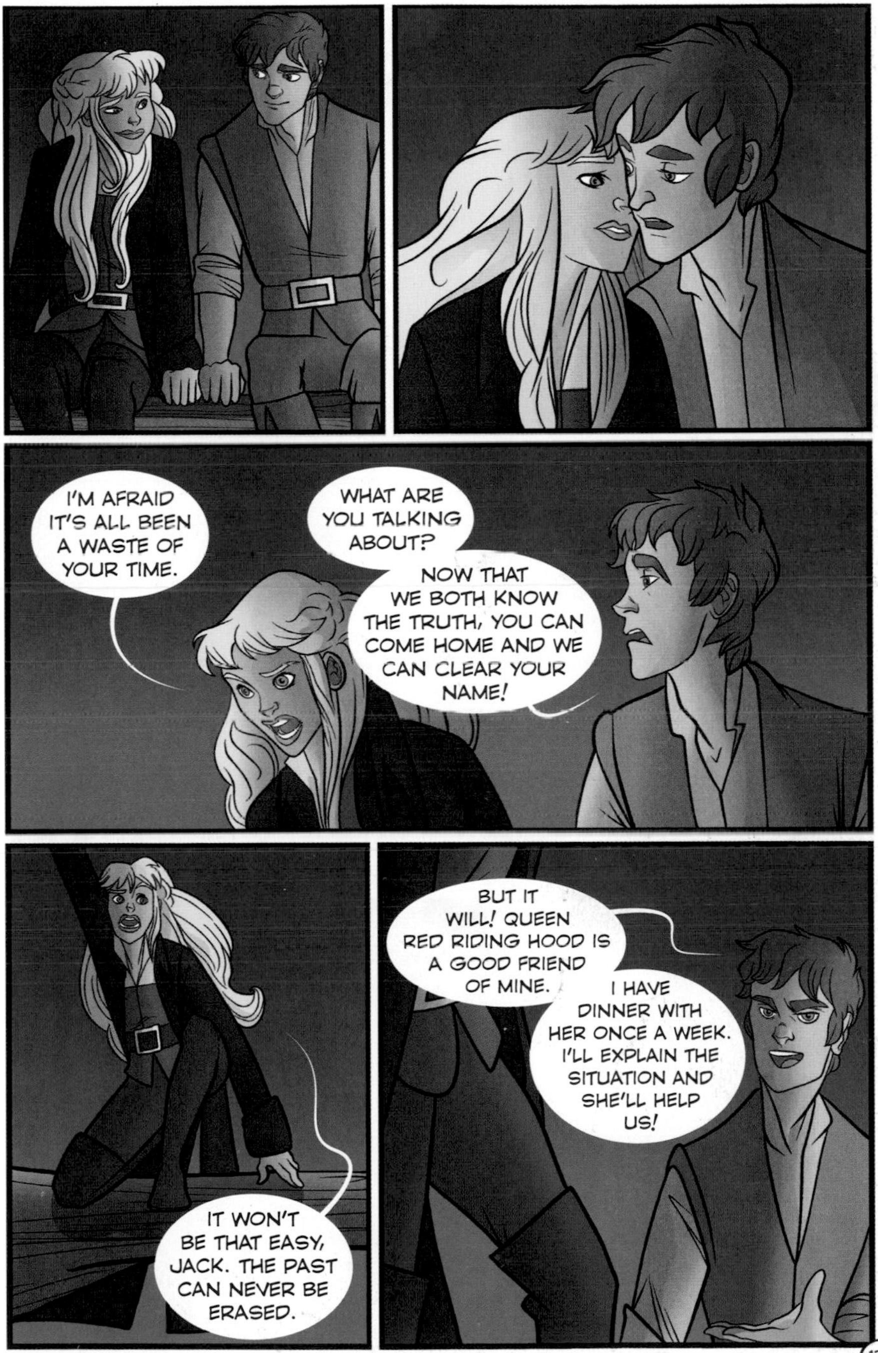
I'M AFRAID IT'S ALL BEEN A WASTE OF YOUR TIME.
WHAT ARE YOU TALKING ABOUT?
NOW THAT WE BOTH KNOW THE TRUTH, YOU CAN COME HOME AND WE CAN CLEAR YOUR NAME!
IT WON'T BE THAT EASY, JACK. THE PAST CAN NEVER BE ERASED.
BUT IT WILL! QUEEN RED RIDING HOOD IS A GOOD FRIEND OF MINE.
I HAVE DINNER WITH HER ONCE A WEEK. I'LL EXPLAIN THE SITUATION AND SHE'LL HELP US!

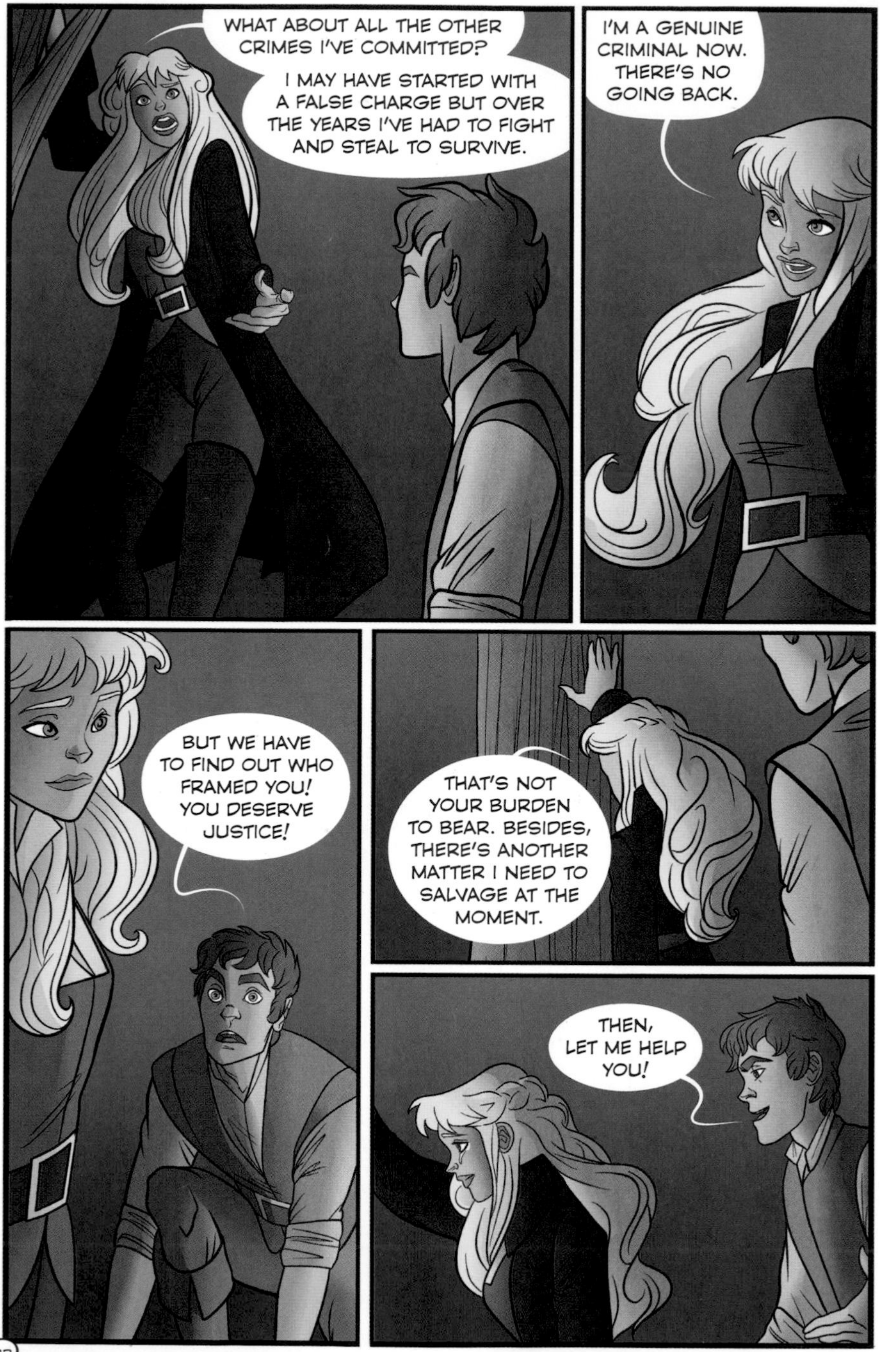
WHAT ABOUT ALL THE OTHER CRIMES I'VE COMMITTED?
I MAY HAVE STARTED WITH A FALSE CHARGE BUT OVER THE YEARS I'VE HAD TO FIGHT AND STEAL TO SURVIVE.
I'M A GENUINE CRIMINAL NOW. THERE'S NO GOING BACK.
BUT WE HAVE TO FIND OUT WHO FRAMED YOU! YOU DESERVE JUSTICE!
THAT'S NOT YOUR BURDEN TO BEAR. BESIDES, THERE'S ANOTHER MATTER I NEED TO SALVAGE AT THE MOMENT.
THEN, LET ME HELP YOU!

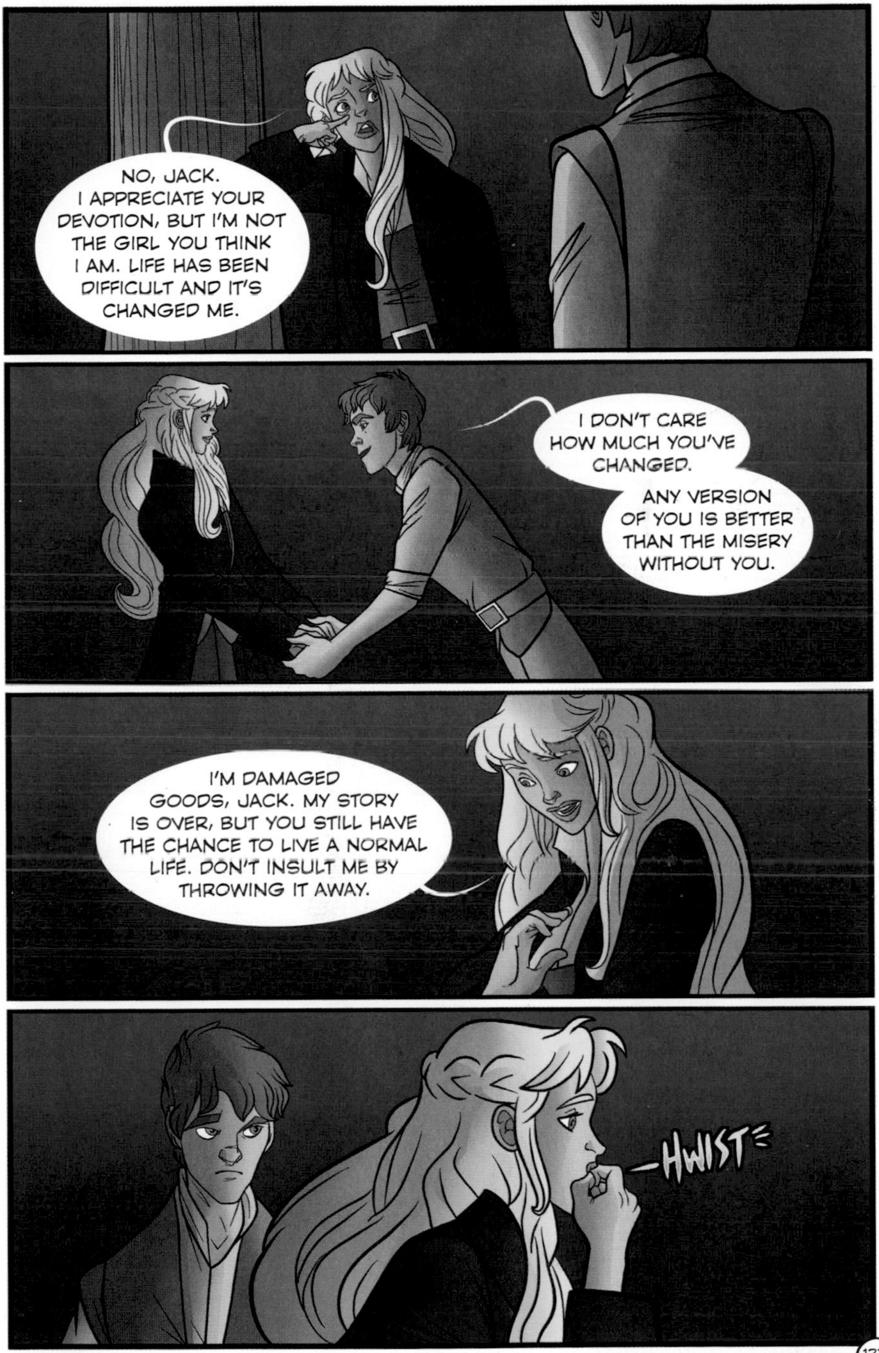
NO, JACK. I APPRECIATE YOUR DEVOTION, BUT I'M NOT THE GIRL YOU THINK I AM. LIFE HAS BEEN DIFFICULT AND IT'S CHANGED ME.
I DON'T CARE HOW MUCH YOU'VE CHANGED.
ANY VERSION OF YOU IS BETTER THAN THE MISERY WITHOUT YOU.
I'M DAMAGED GOODS, JACK. MY STORY IS OVER, BUT YOU STILL HAVE THE CHANCE TO LIVE A NORMAL LIFE. DON'T INSULT ME BY THROWING IT AWAY.
HWIST

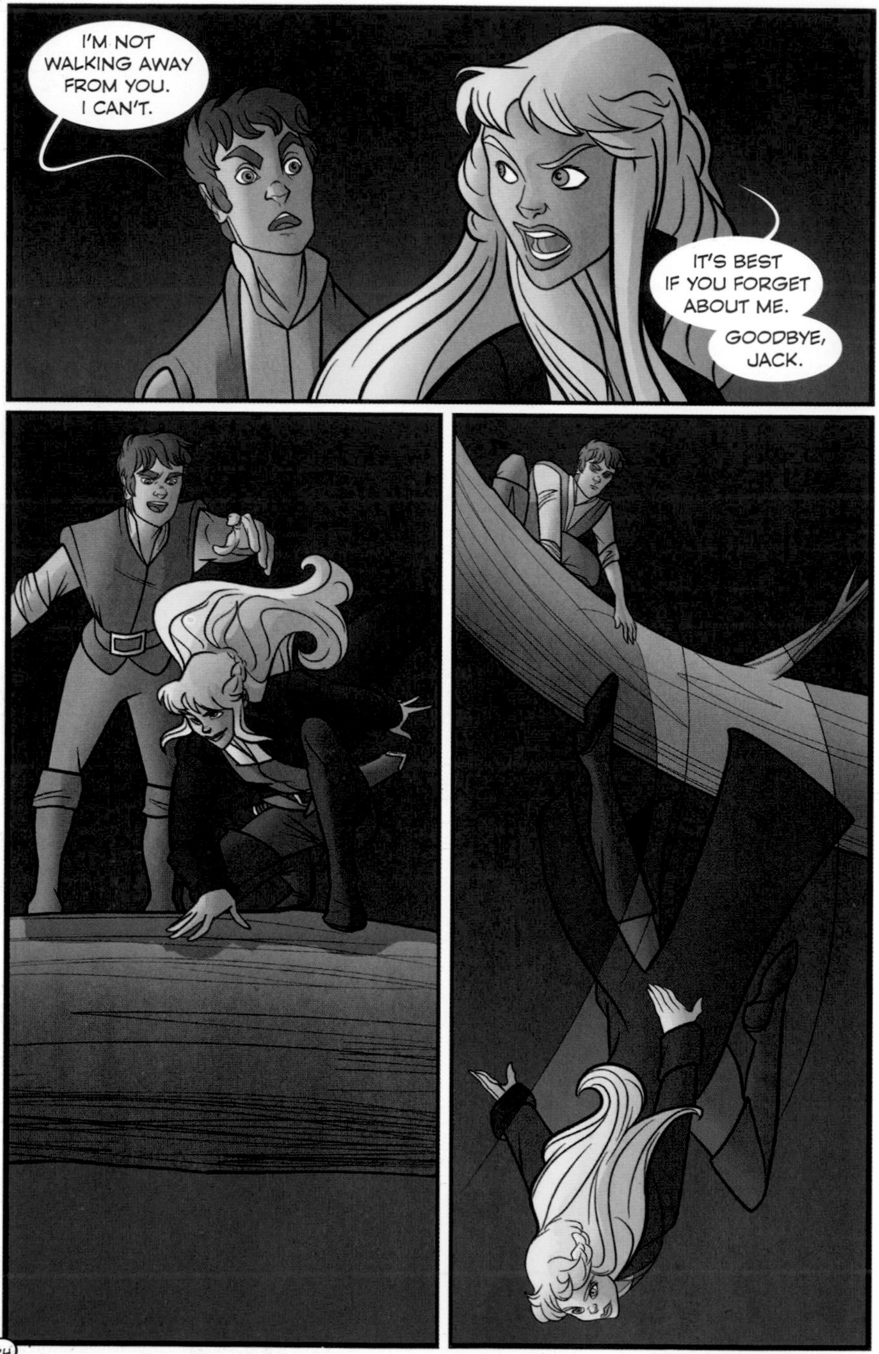
I'M NOT WALKING AWAY FROM YOU. I CAN'T.
IT'S BEST IF YOU FORGET ABOUT ME.
GOODBYE, JACK.

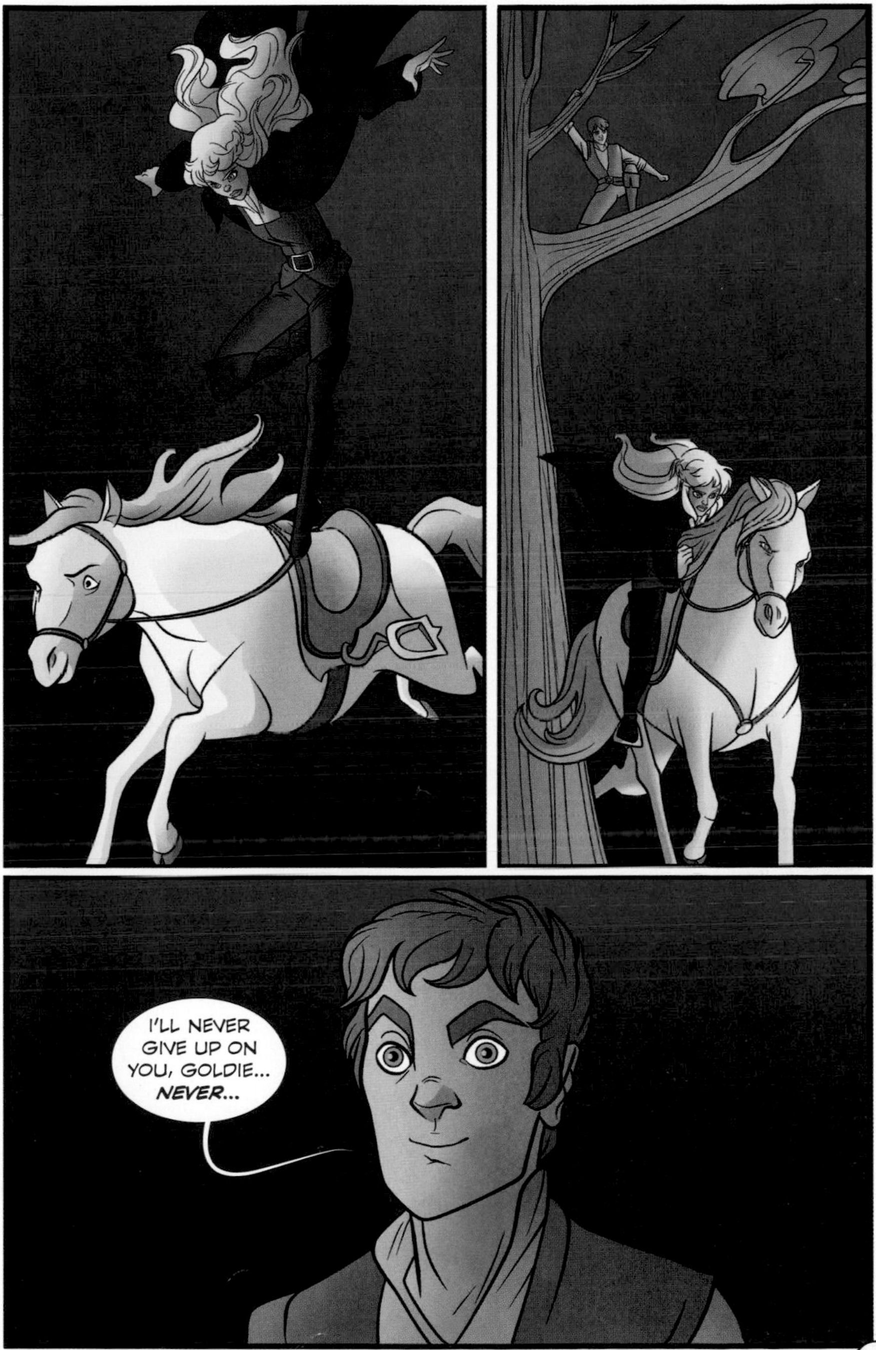
I'LL NEVER GIVE UP ON YOU, GOLDIE... ***NEVER...***

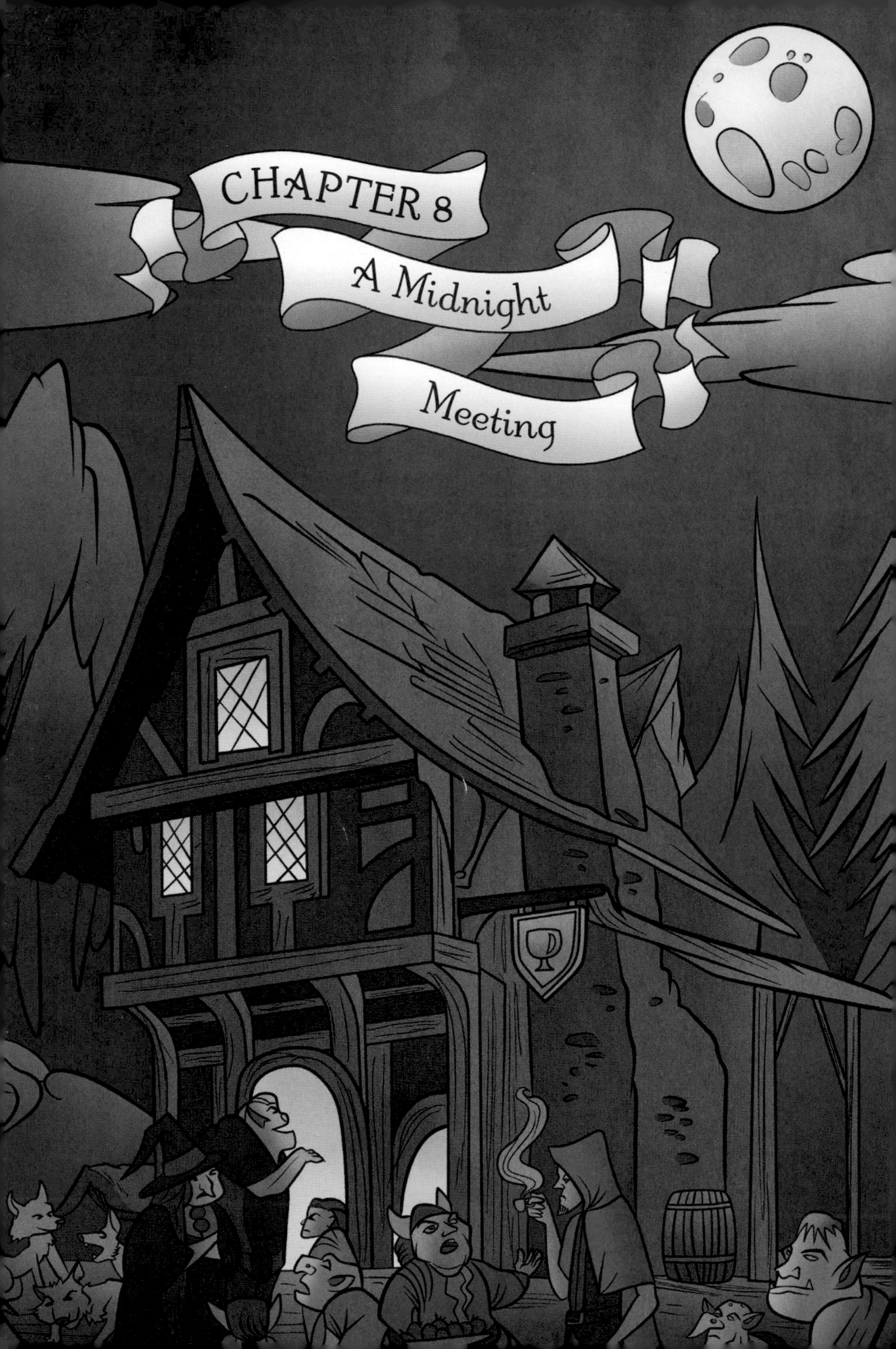
CHAPTER 8
A Midnight
Meeting

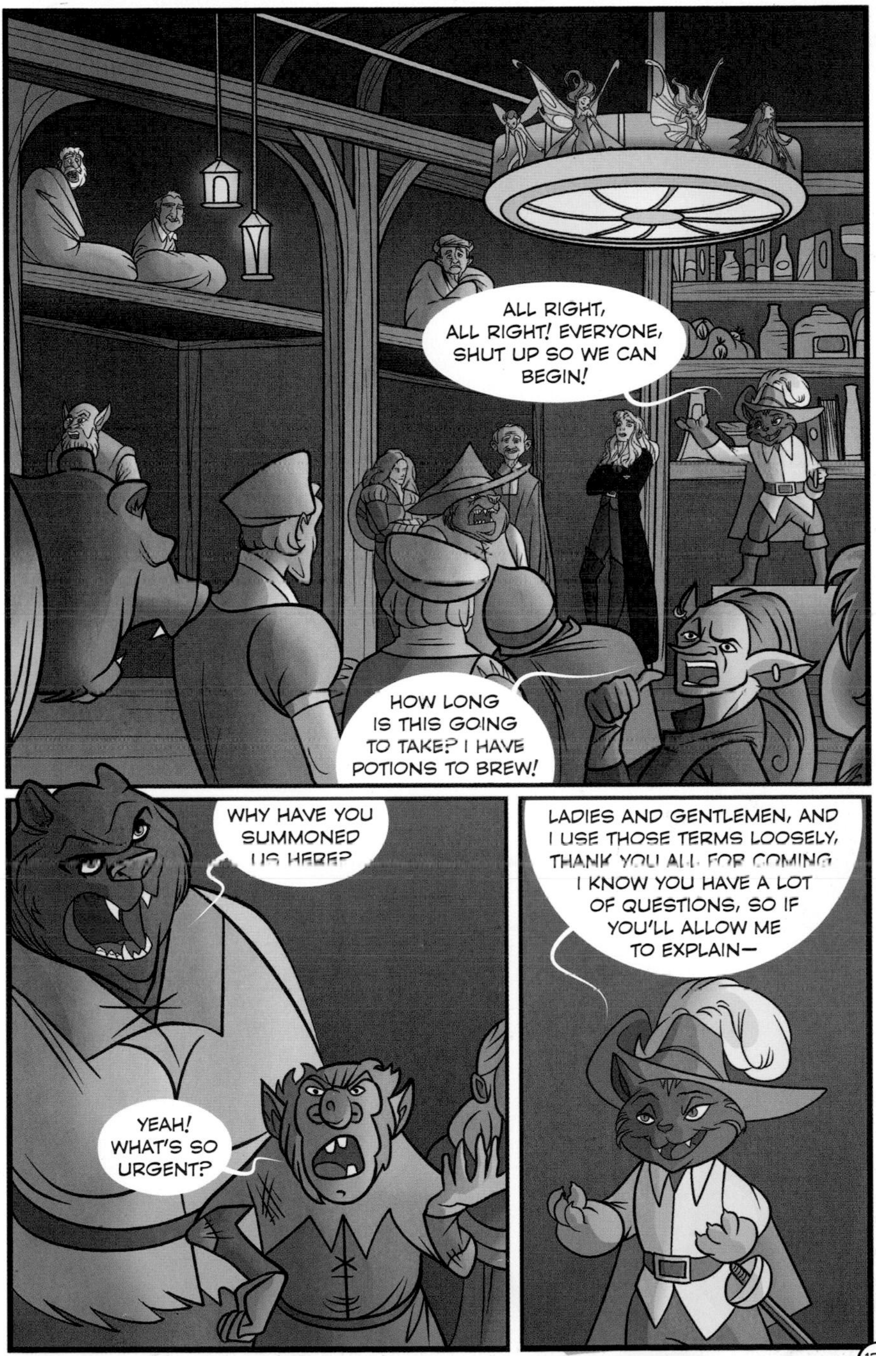
ALL RIGHT, ALL RIGHT! EVERYONE, SHUT UP SO WE CAN BEGIN!
HOW LONG IS THIS GOING TO TAKE? I HAVE POTIONS TO BREW!
WHY HAVE YOU SUMMONED US HERE?
YEAH! WHAT'S SO URGENT?
LADIES AND GENTLEMEN, AND I USE THOSE TERMS LOOSELY, THANK YOU ALL FOR COMING. I KNOW YOU HAVE A LOT OF QUESTIONS, SO IF YOU'LL ALLOW ME TO EXPLAIN—

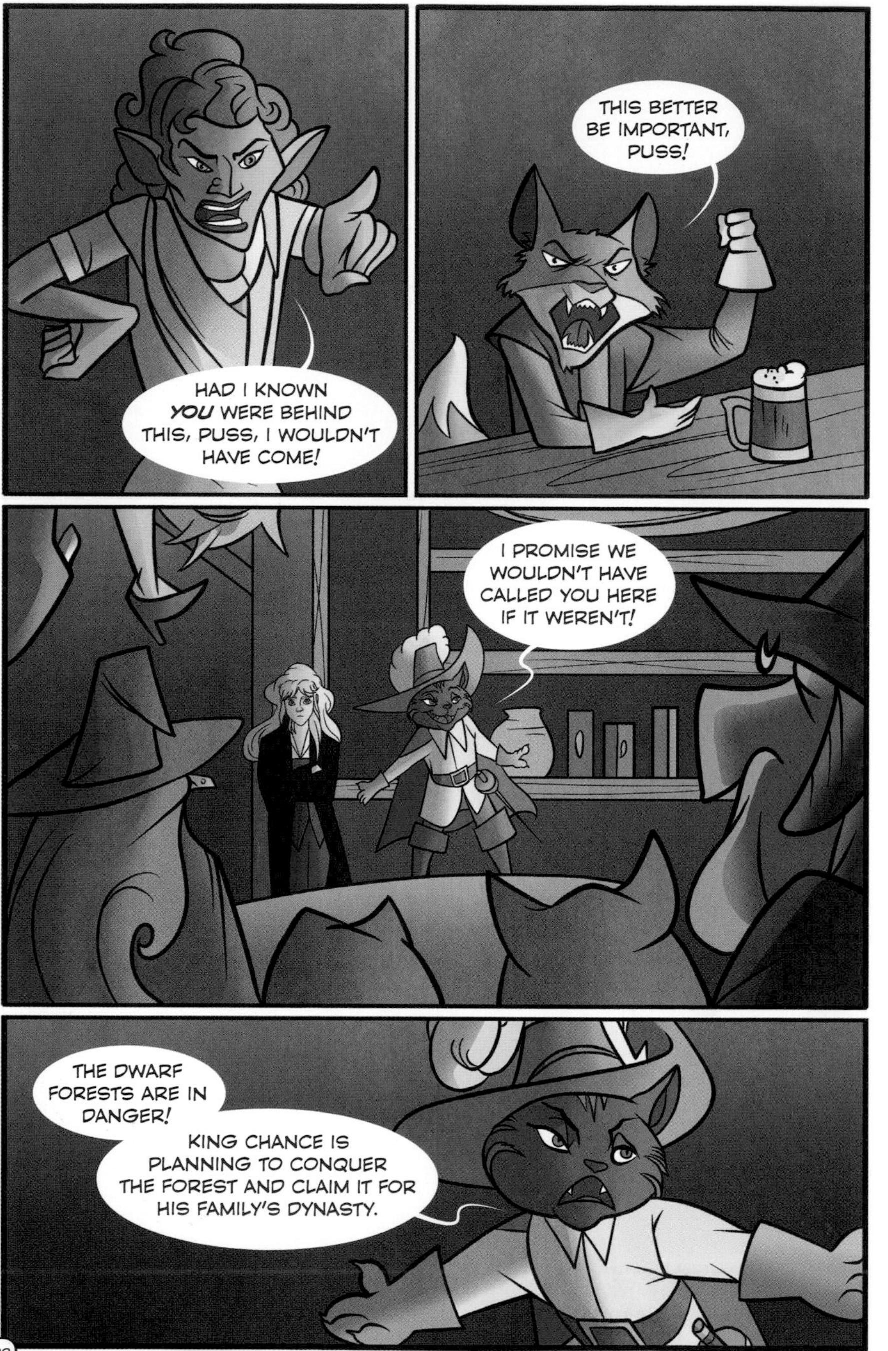
HAD I KNOWN *YOU* WERE BEHIND THIS, PUSS, I WOULDN'T HAVE COME!
THIS BETTER BE IMPORTANT, PUSS!
I PROMISE WE WOULDN'T HAVE CALLED YOU HERE IF IT WEREN'T!
THE DWARF FORESTS ARE IN DANGER!
KING CHANCE IS PLANNING TO CONQUER THE FOREST AND CLAIM IT FOR HIS FAMILY'S DYNASTY.

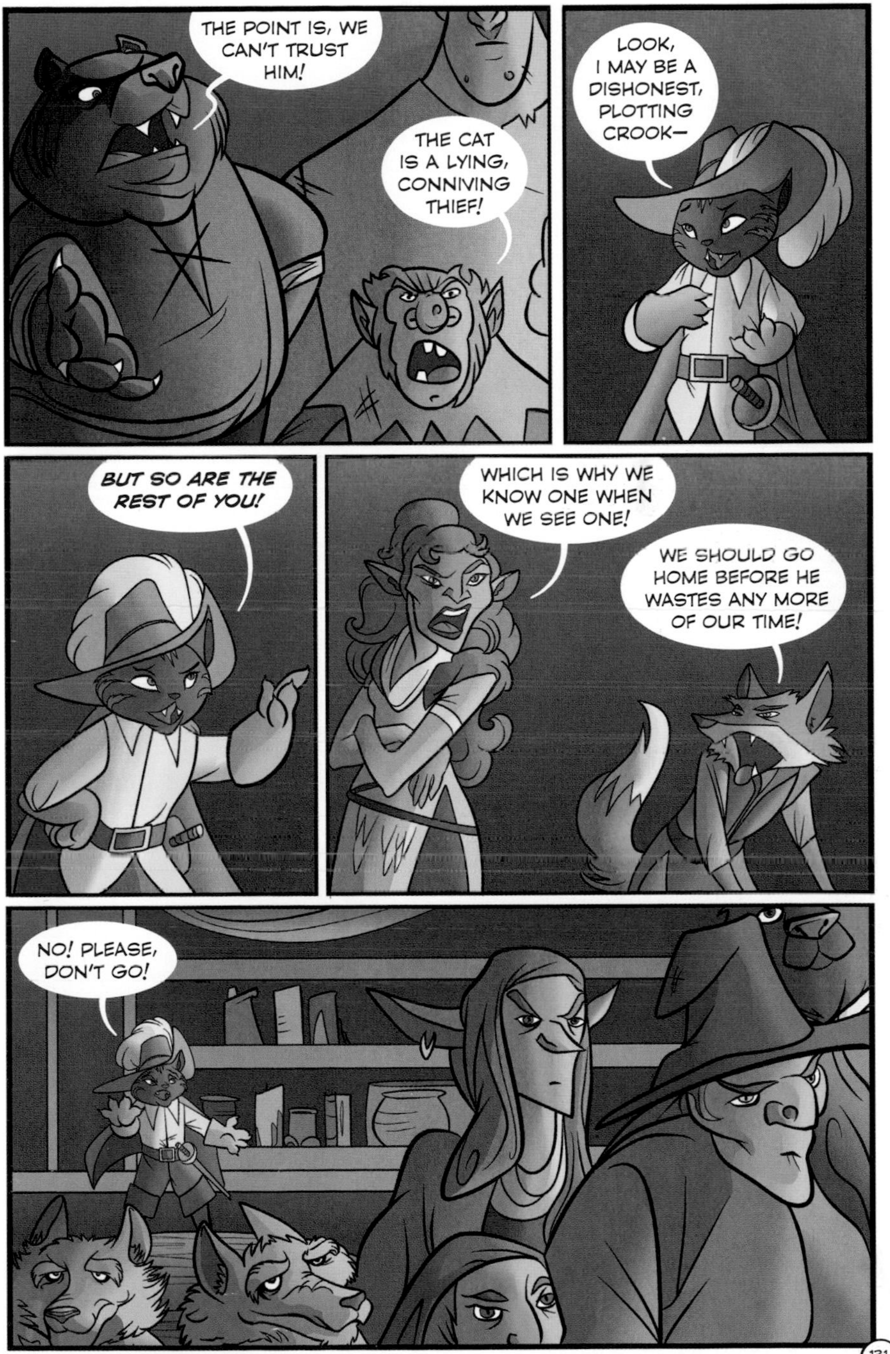
THE POINT IS, WE CAN'T TRUST HIM!
THE CAT IS A LYING, CONNIVING THIEF!
LOOK, I MAY BE A DISHONEST, PLOTTING CROOK—
BUT SO ARE THE REST OF YOU!
WHICH IS WHY WE KNOW ONE WHEN WE SEE ONE!
WE SHOULD GO HOME BEFORE HE WASTES ANY MORE OF OUR TIME!
NO! PLEASE, DON'T GO!

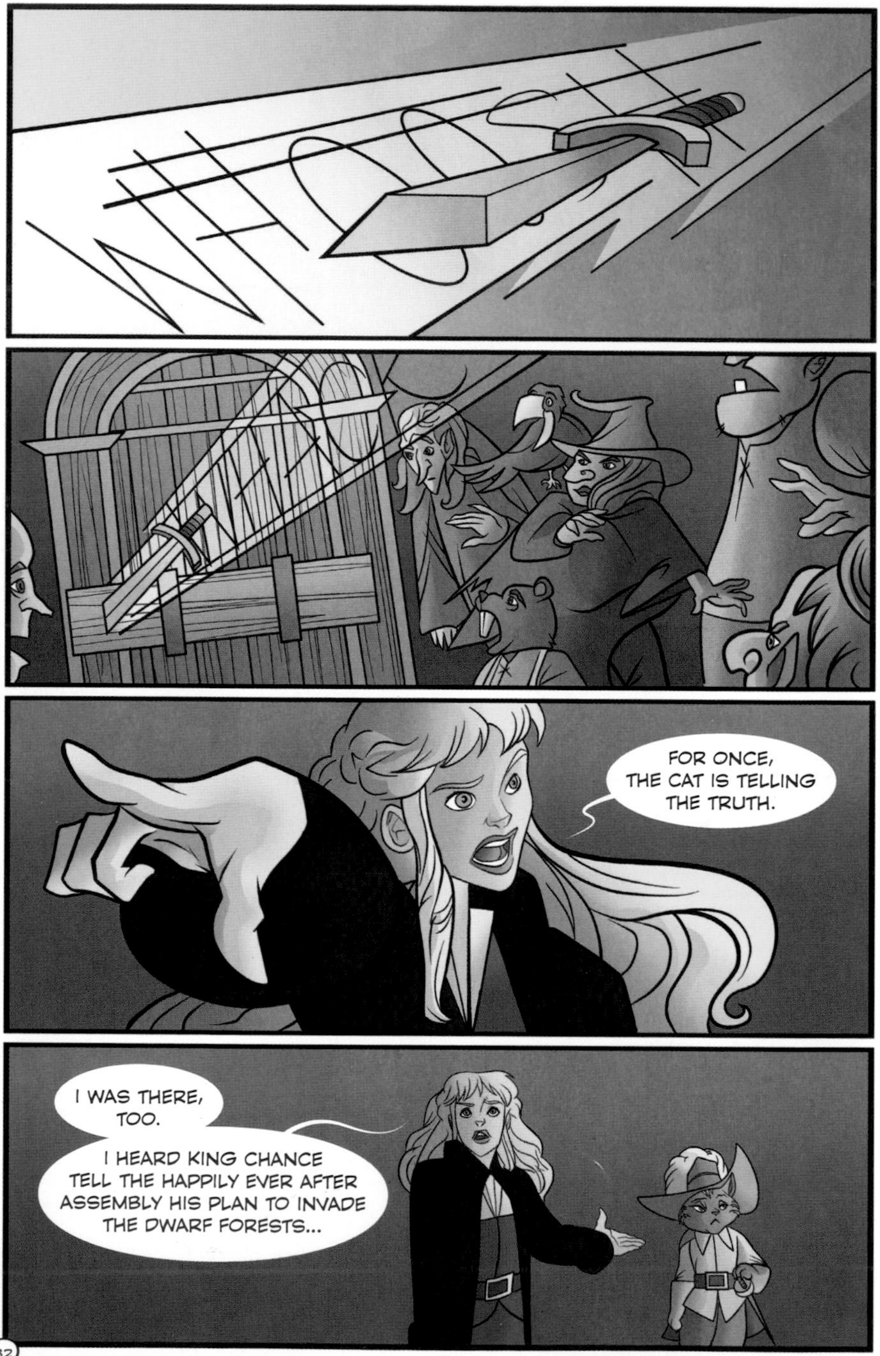
FOR ONCE, THE CAT IS TELLING THE TRUTH.
I WAS THERE, TOO.
I HEARD KING CHANCE TELL THE HAPPILY EVER AFTER ASSEMBLY HIS PLAN TO INVADE THE DWARF FORESTS...

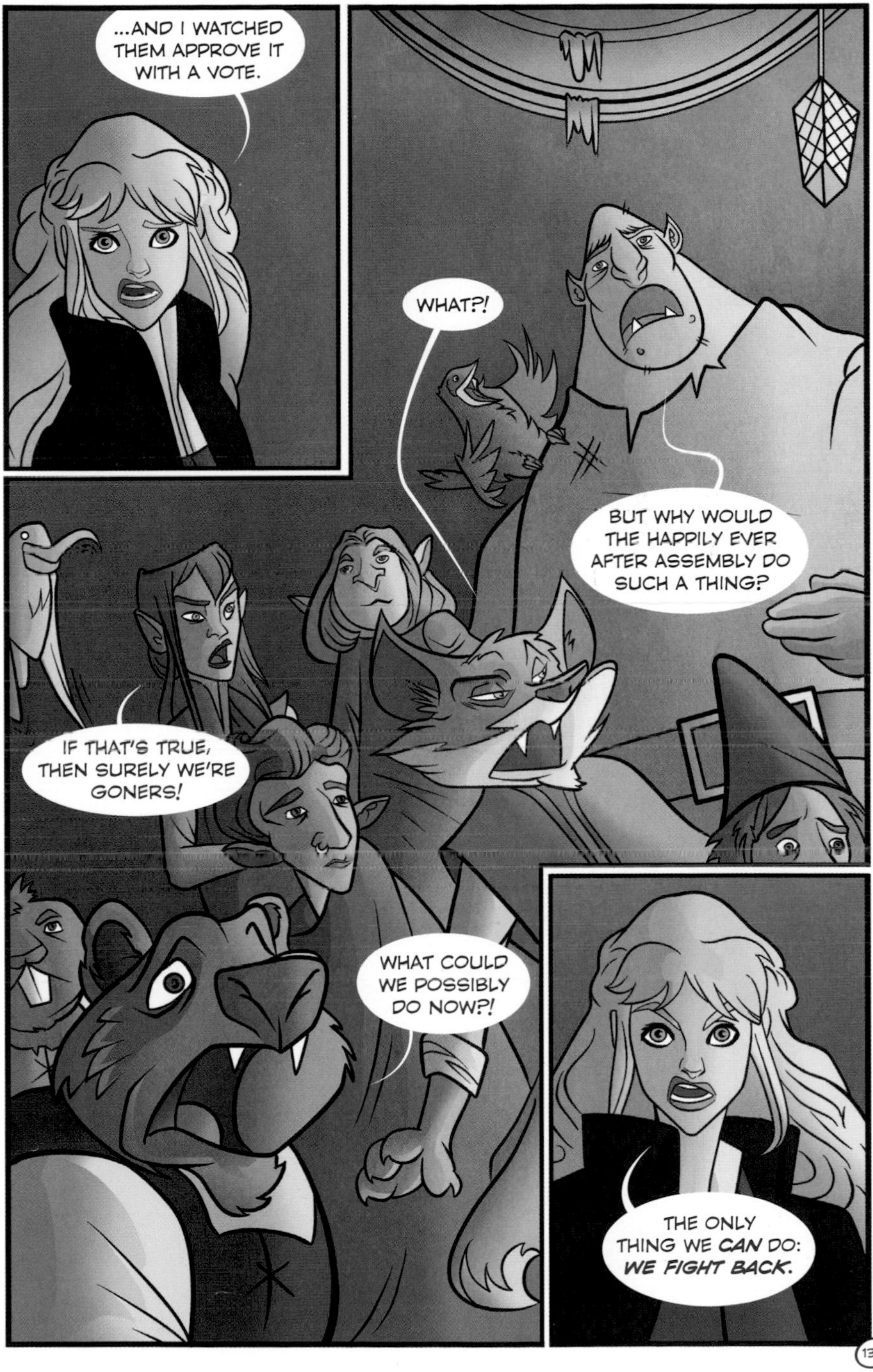
...AND I WATCHED THEM APPROVE IT WITH A VOTE.
WHAT?!
BUT WHY WOULD THE HAPPILY EVER AFTER ASSEMBLY DO SUCH A THING?
IF THAT'S TRUE, THEN SURELY WE'RE GONERS!
WHAT COULD WE POSSIBLY DO NOW?!
THE ONLY THING WE CAN DO: WE FIGHT BACK.

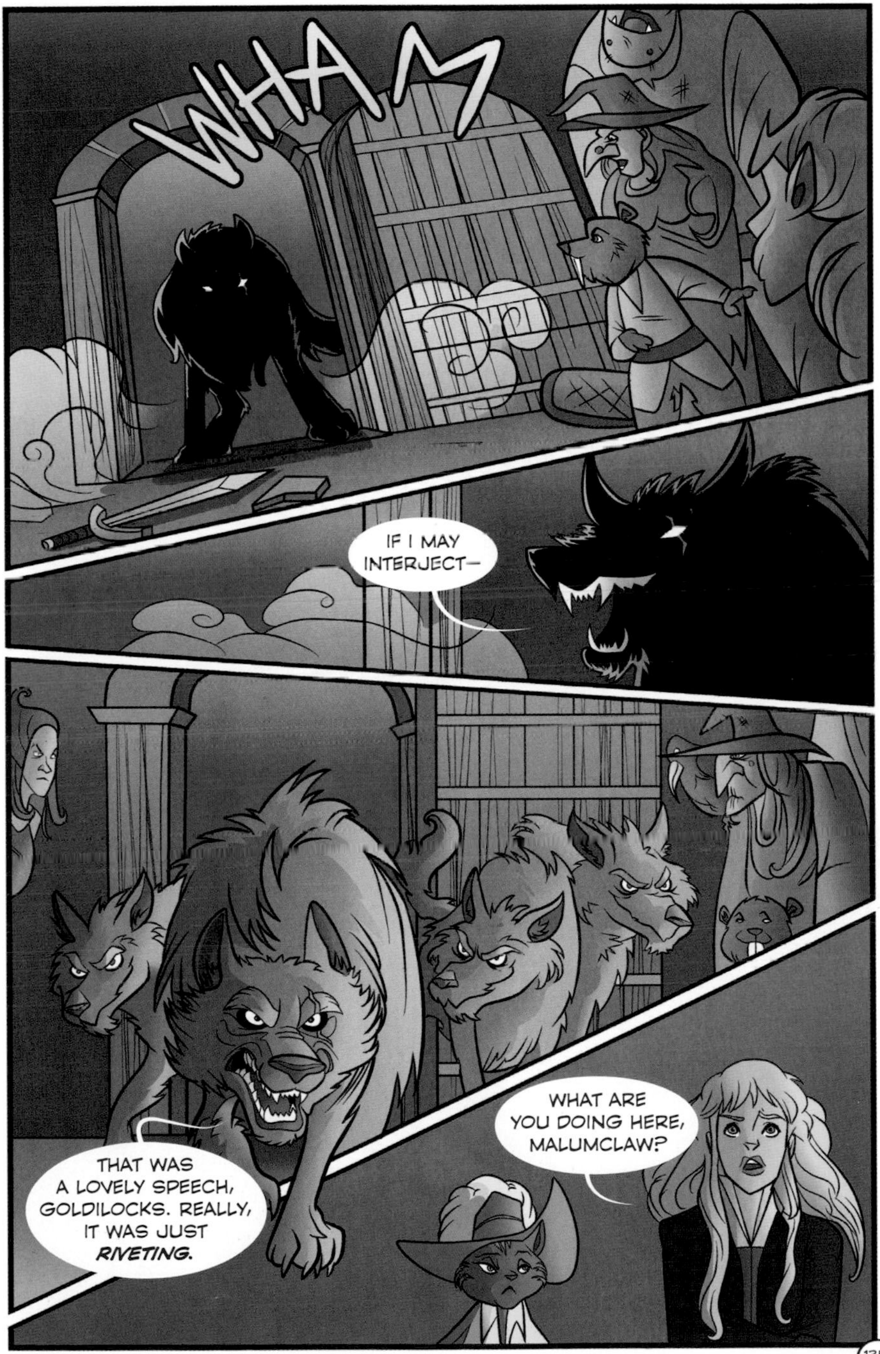
WHAM
IF I MAY INTERJECT—
THAT WAS A LOVELY SPEECH, GOLDILOCKS. REALLY, IT WAS JUST *RIVETING*.
WHAT ARE YOU DOING HERE, MALUMCLAW?

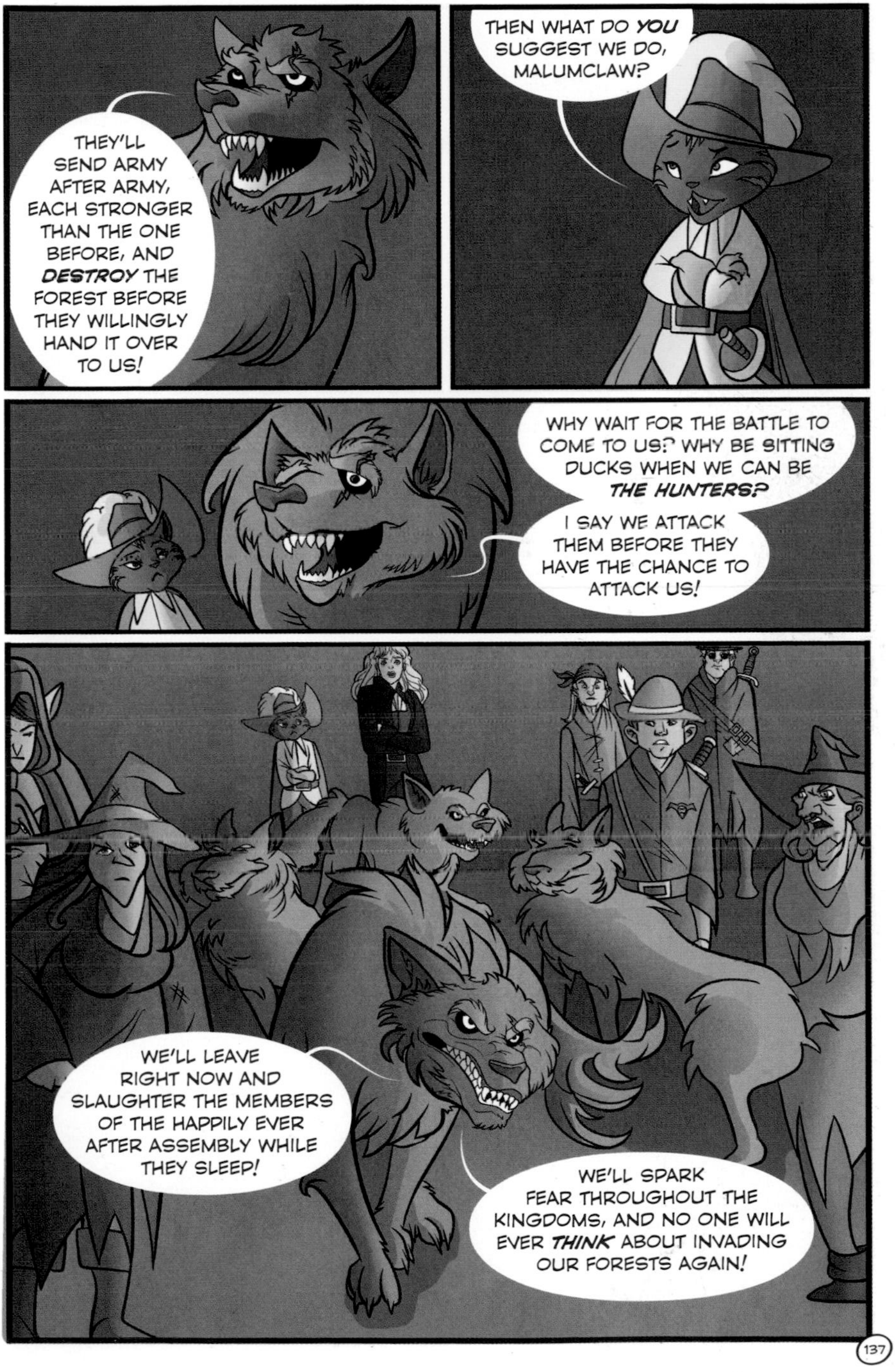
THEY'LL SEND ARMY AFTER ARMY, EACH STRONGER THAN THE ONE BEFORE, AND ***DESTROY*** THE FOREST BEFORE THEY WILLINGLY HAND IT OVER TO US!
THEN WHAT DO ***YOU*** SUGGEST WE DO, MALUMCLAW?
WHY WAIT FOR THE BATTLE TO COME TO US? WHY BE SITTING DUCKS WHEN WE CAN BE ***THE HUNTERS?***
I SAY WE ATTACK THEM BEFORE THEY HAVE THE CHANCE TO ATTACK US!
WE'LL LEAVE RIGHT NOW AND SLAUGHTER THE MEMBERS OF THE HAPPILY EVER AFTER ASSEMBLY WHILE THEY SLEEP!
WE'LL SPARK FEAR THROUGHOUT THE KINGDOMS, AND NO ONE WILL EVER ***THINK*** ABOUT INVADING OUR FORESTS AGAIN!

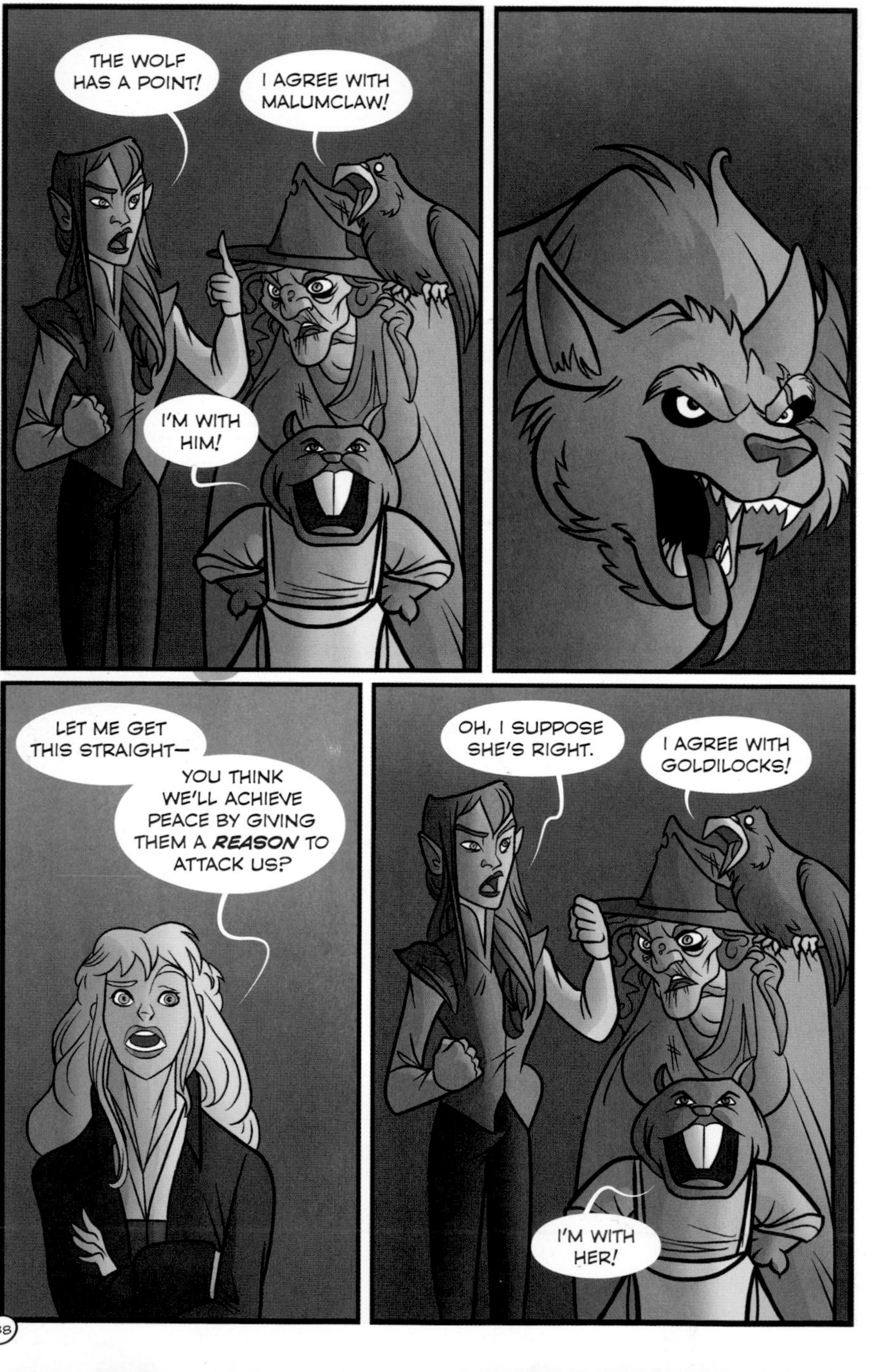
THE WOLF HAS A POINT!
I AGREE WITH MALUMCLAW!
I'M WITH HIM!
LET ME GET THIS STRAIGHT—
YOU THINK WE'LL ACHIEVE PEACE BY GIVING THEM A ***REASON*** TO ATTACK US?
OH, I SUPPOSE SHE'S RIGHT.
I AGREE WITH GOLDILOCKS!
I'M WITH HER!

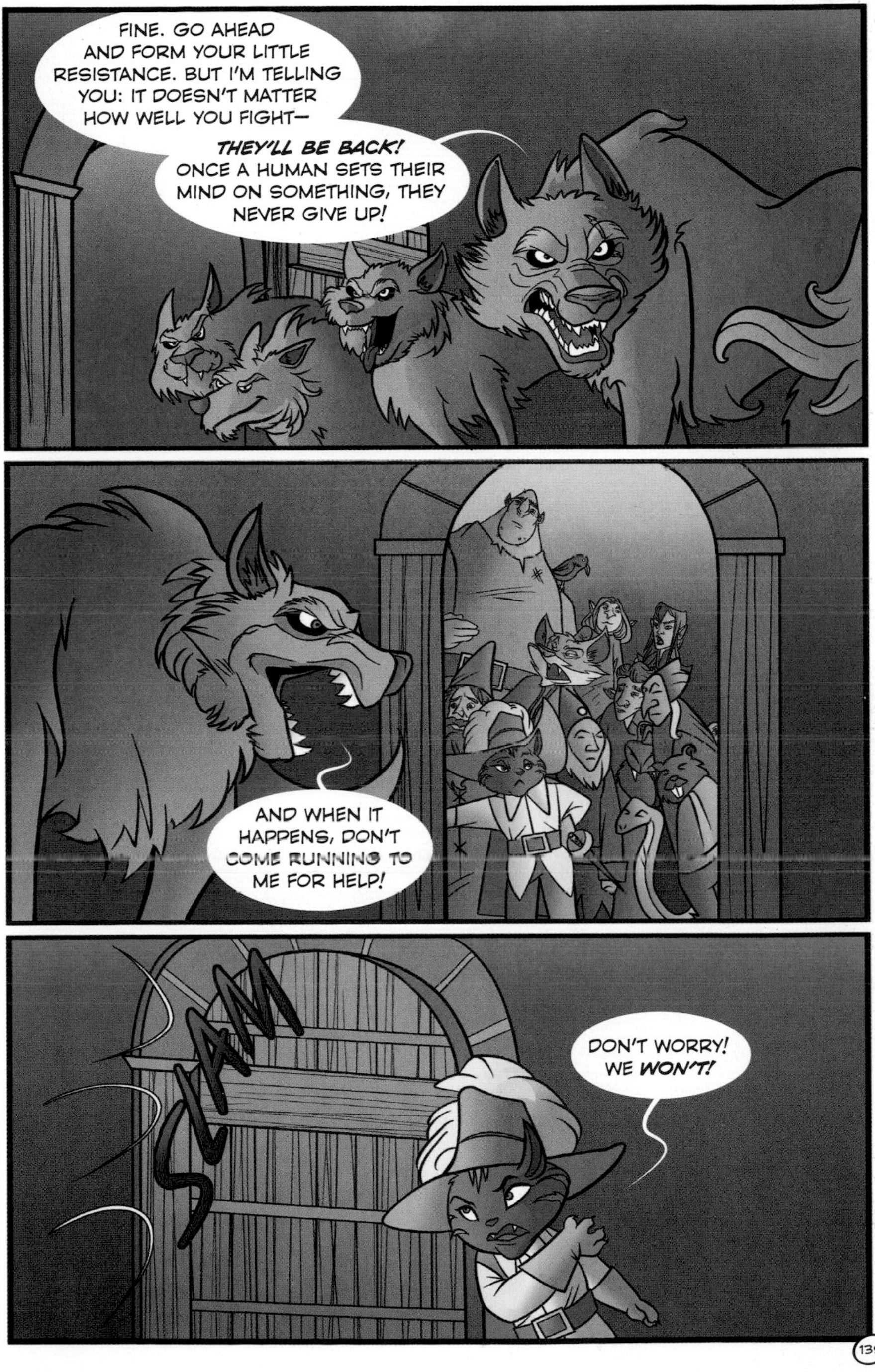
FINE. GO AHEAD AND FORM YOUR LITTLE RESISTANCE. BUT I'M TELLING YOU: IT DOESN'T MATTER HOW WELL YOU FIGHT—
THEY'LL BE BACK! ONCE A HUMAN SETS THEIR MIND ON SOMETHING, THEY NEVER GIVE UP!
AND WHEN IT HAPPENS, DON'T COME RUNNING TO ME FOR HELP!
SLAM
DON'T WORRY! WE WON'T!

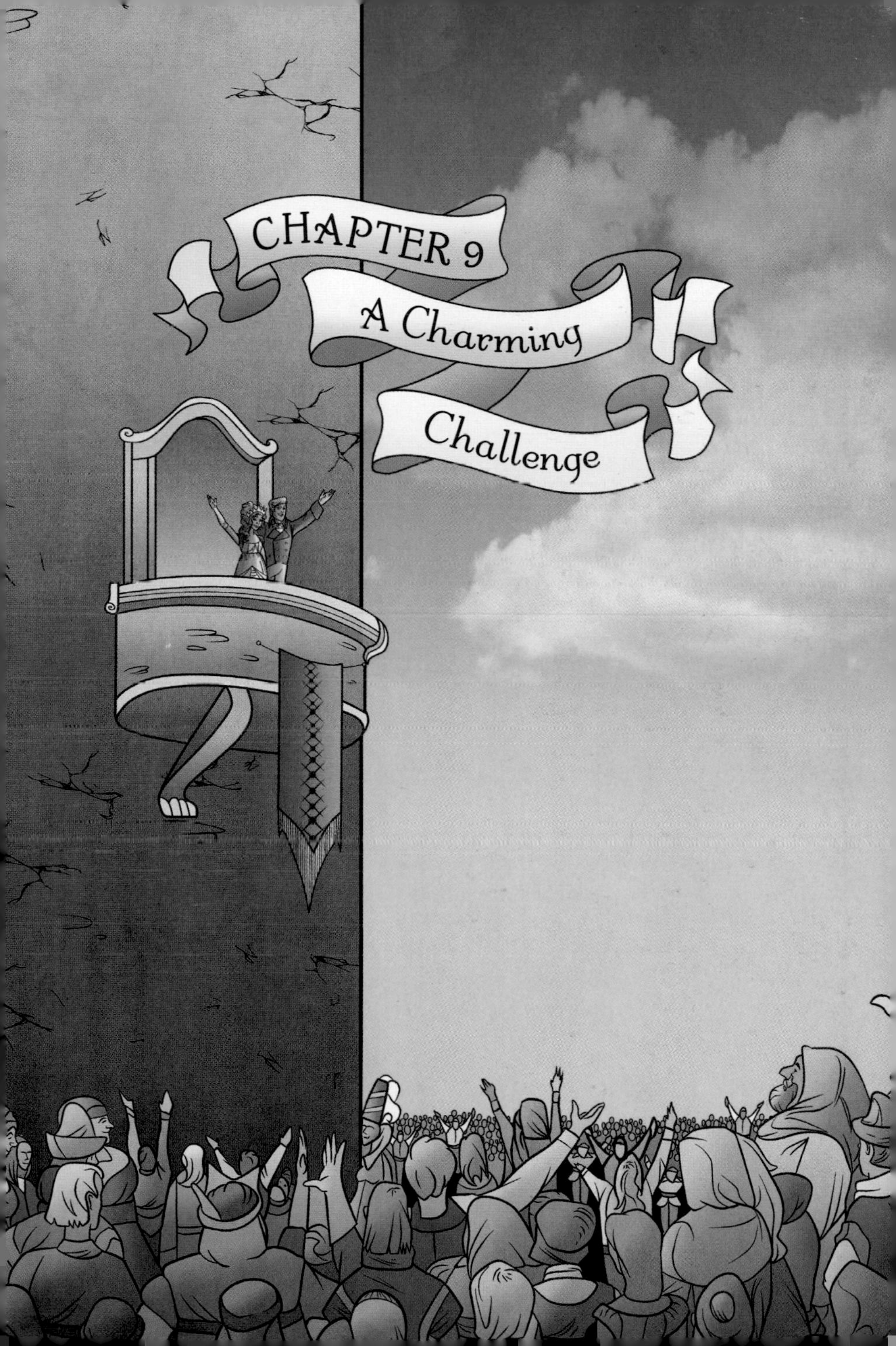
CHAPTER 9
A Charming
Challenge

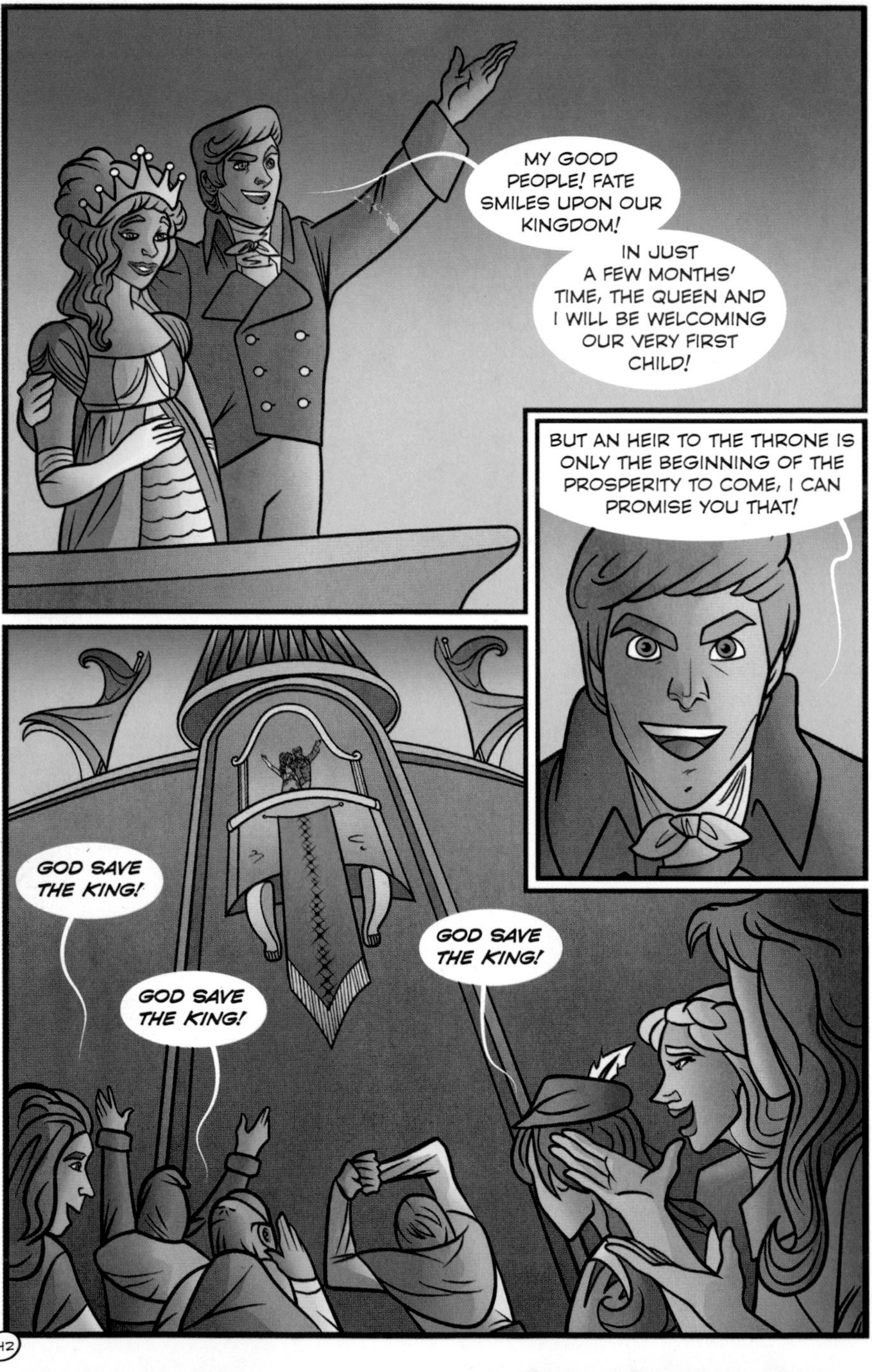

MY GOOD PEOPLE! FATE SMILES UPON OUR KINGDOM!
IN JUST A FEW MONTHS' TIME, THE QUEEN AND I WILL BE WELCOMING OUR VERY FIRST CHILD!
BUT AN HEIR TO THE THRONE IS ONLY THE BEGINNING OF THE PROSPERITY TO COME, I CAN PROMISE YOU THAT!
GOD SAVE THE KING!
GOD SAVE THE KING!
GOD SAVE THE KING!

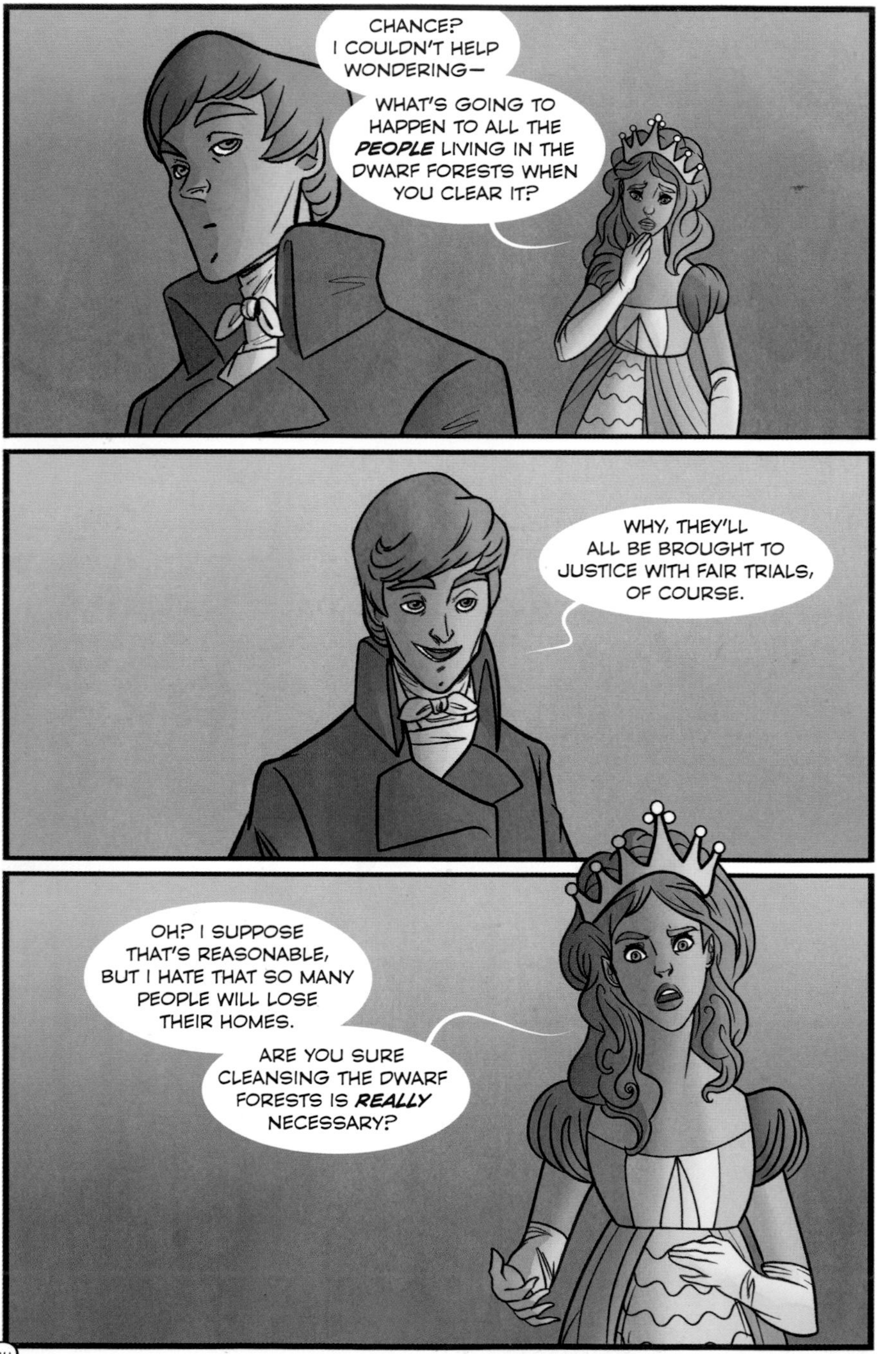
CHANCE? I COULDN'T HELP WONDERING—
WHAT'S GOING TO HAPPEN TO ALL THE *PEOPLE* LIVING IN THE DWARF FORESTS WHEN YOU CLEAR IT?
WHY, THEY'LL ALL BE BROUGHT TO JUSTICE WITH FAIR TRIALS, OF COURSE.
OH? I SUPPOSE THAT'S REASONABLE, BUT I HATE THAT SO MANY PEOPLE WILL LOSE THEIR HOMES.
ARE YOU SURE CLEANSING THE DWARF FORESTS IS *REALLY* NECESSARY?

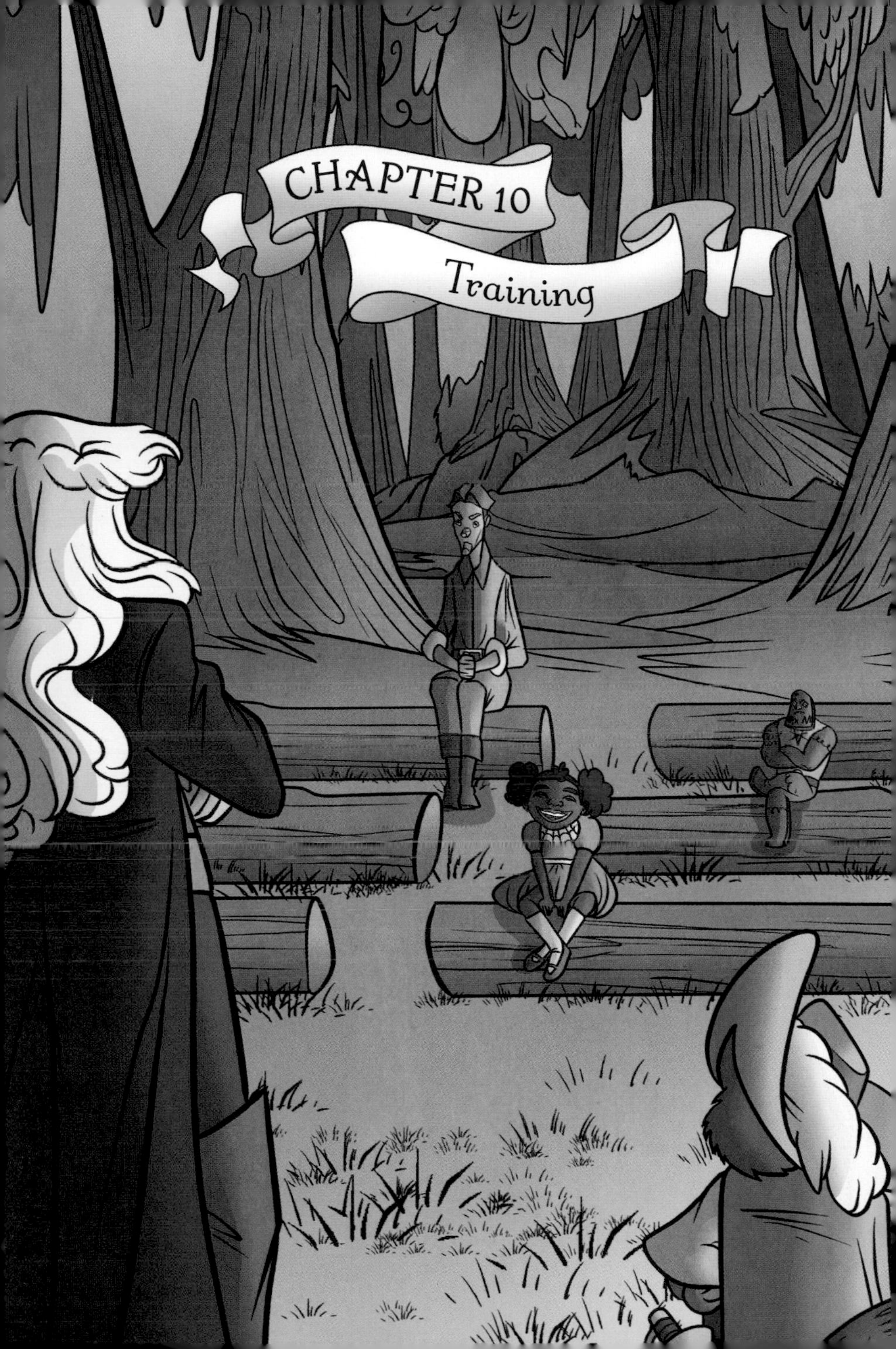
CHAPTER 10
Training

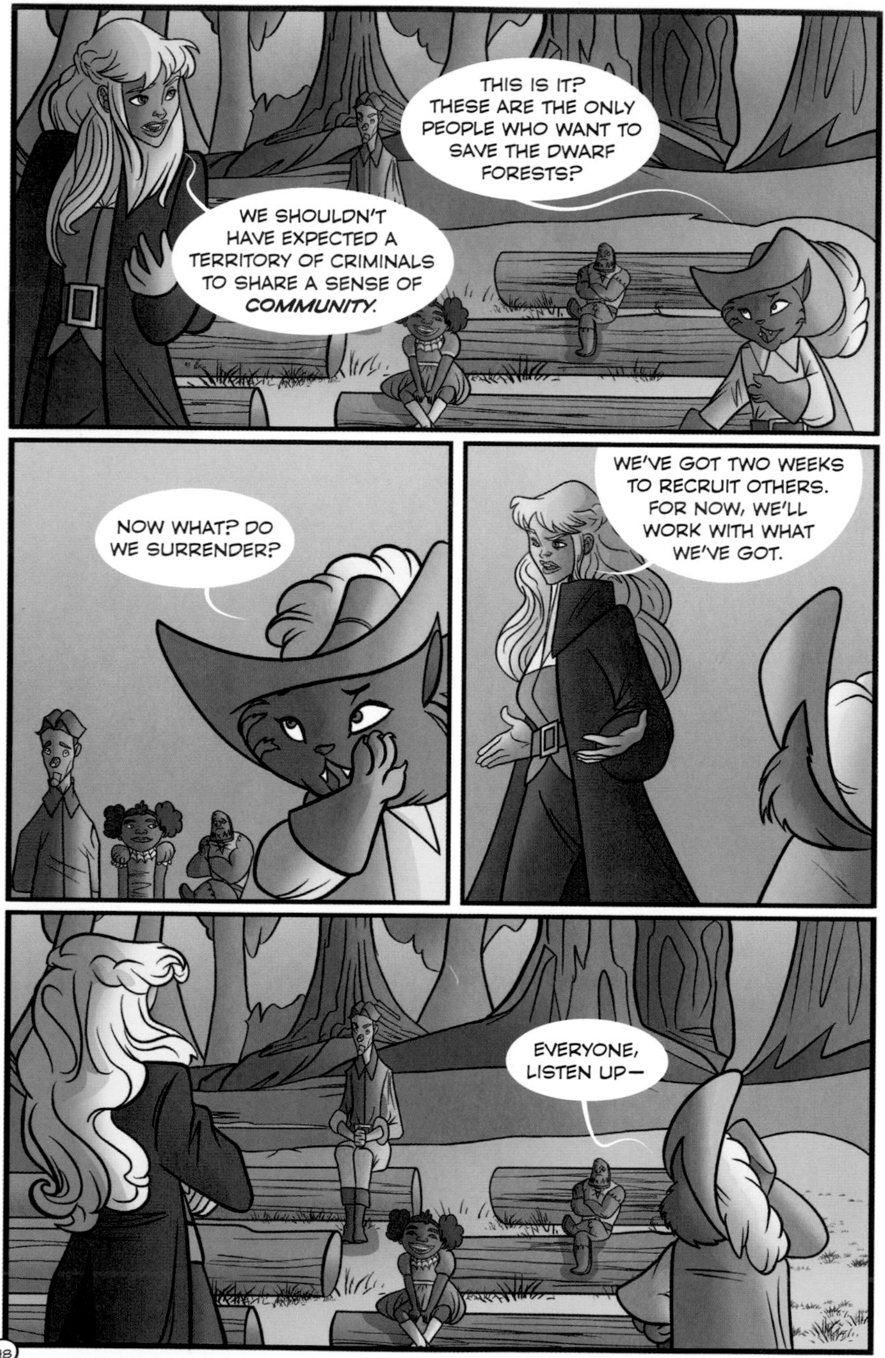
THIS IS IT? THESE ARE THE ONLY PEOPLE WHO WANT TO SAVE THE DWARF FORESTS?
WE SHOULDN'T HAVE EXPECTED A TERRITORY OF CRIMINALS TO SHARE A SENSE OF *COMMUNITY*.
NOW WHAT? DO WE SURRENDER?
WE'VE GOT TWO WEEKS TO RECRUIT OTHERS. FOR NOW, WE'LL WORK WITH WHAT WE'VE GOT.
EVERYONE, LISTEN UP—

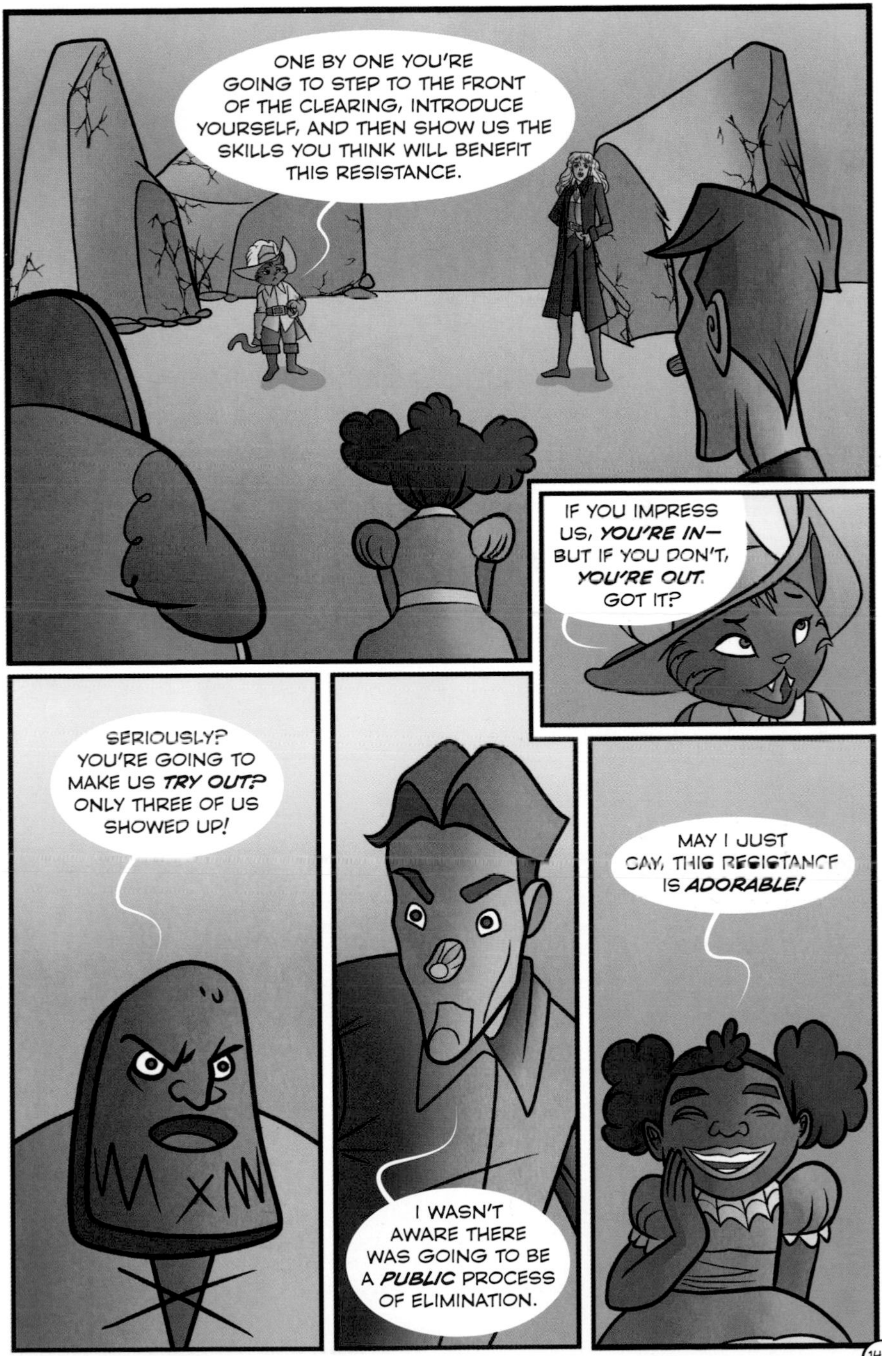
ONE BY ONE YOU'RE GOING TO STEP TO THE FRONT OF THE CLEARING, INTRODUCE YOURSELF, AND THEN SHOW US THE SKILLS YOU THINK WILL BENEFIT THIS RESISTANCE.
IF YOU IMPRESS US, ***YOU'RE IN***— BUT IF YOU DON'T, ***YOU'RE OUT.*** GOT IT?
SERIOUSLY? YOU'RE GOING TO MAKE US ***TRY OUT?*** ONLY THREE OF US SHOWED UP!
I WASN'T AWARE THERE WAS GOING TO BE A ***PUBLIC*** PROCESS OF ELIMINATION.
MAY I JUST SAY, THIS RESISTANCE IS ***ADORABLE!***

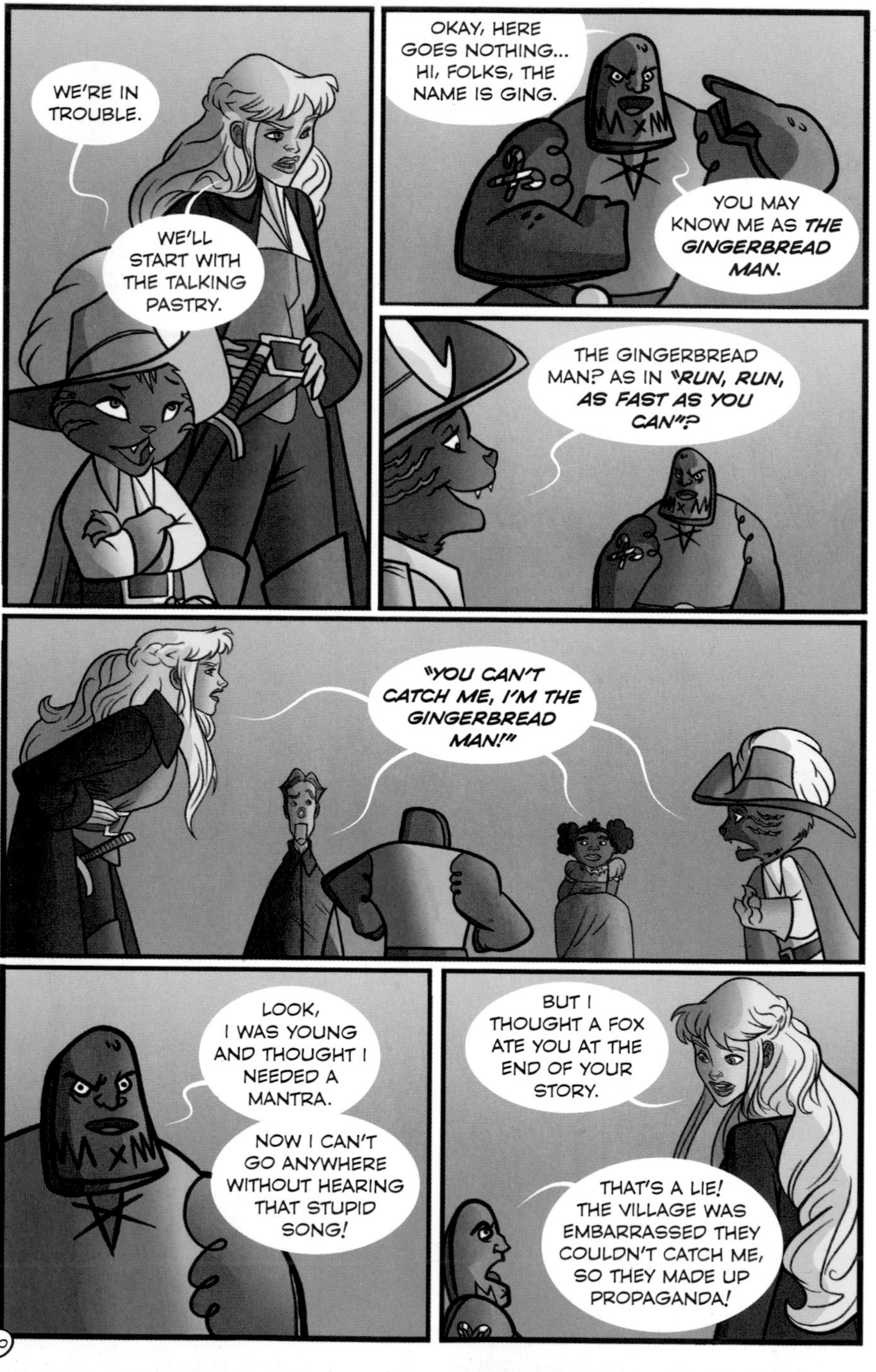
WE'RE IN TROUBLE.
WE'LL START WITH THE TALKING PASTRY.
OKAY, HERE GOES NOTHING... HI, FOLKS, THE NAME IS GING.
YOU MAY KNOW ME AS *THE GINGERBREAD MAN.*
THE GINGERBREAD MAN? AS IN *"RUN, RUN, AS FAST AS YOU CAN"?*
"YOU CAN'T CATCH ME, I'M THE GINGERBREAD MAN!"
LOOK, I WAS YOUNG AND THOUGHT I NEEDED A MANTRA.
NOW I CAN'T GO ANYWHERE WITHOUT HEARING THAT STUPID SONG!
BUT I THOUGHT A FOX ATE YOU AT THE END OF YOUR STORY.
THAT'S A LIE! THE VILLAGE WAS EMBARRASSED THEY COULDN'T CATCH ME, SO THEY MADE UP PROPAGANDA!

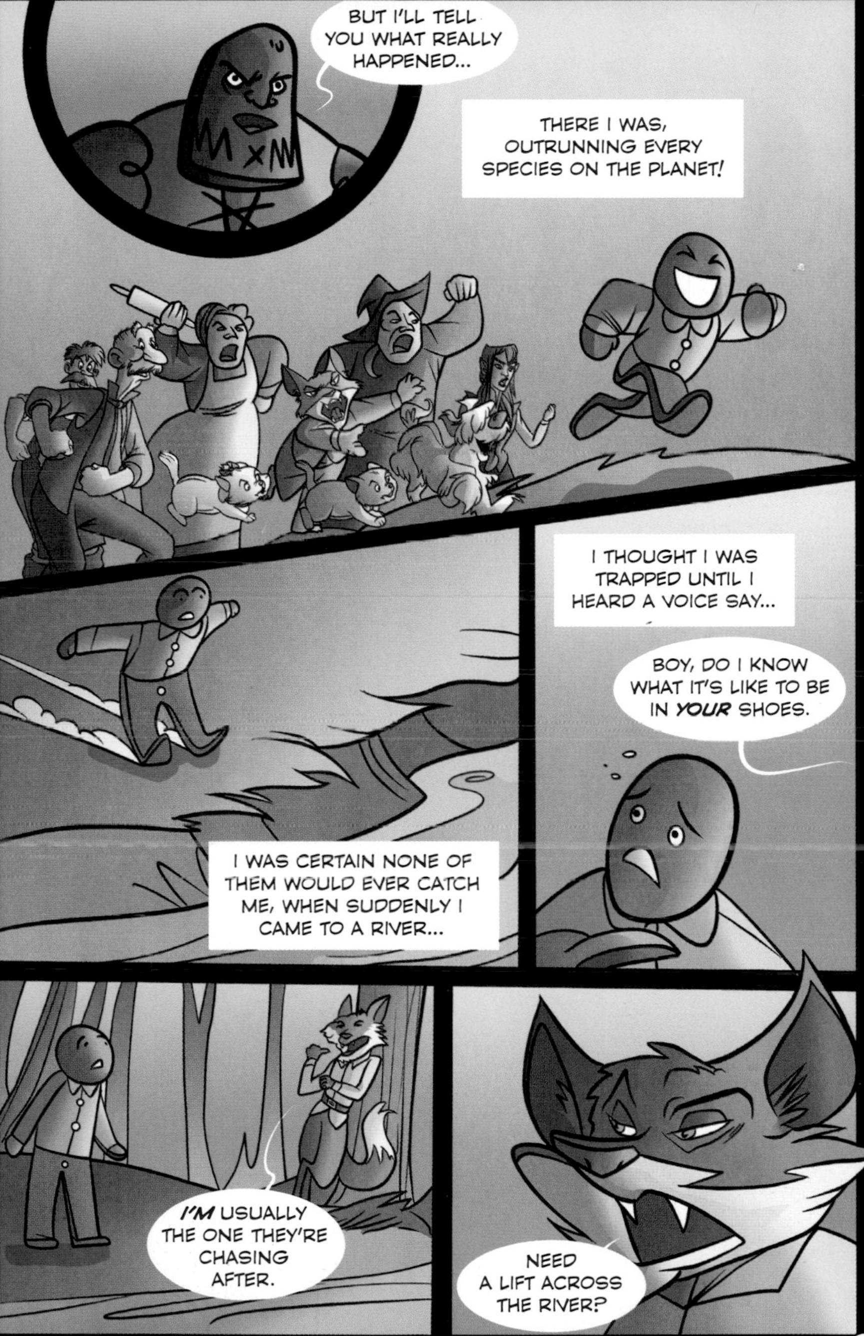
BUT I'LL TELL YOU WHAT REALLY HAPPENED...
THERE I WAS, OUTRUNNING EVERY SPECIES ON THE PLANET!
I WAS CERTAIN NONE OF THEM WOULD EVER CATCH ME, WHEN SUDDENLY I CAME TO A RIVER...
I THOUGHT I WAS TRAPPED UNTIL I HEARD A VOICE SAY...
BOY, DO I KNOW WHAT IT'S LIKE TO BE IN *YOUR* SHOES.
I'M USUALLY THE ONE THEY'RE CHASING AFTER.
NEED A LIFT ACROSS THE RIVER?

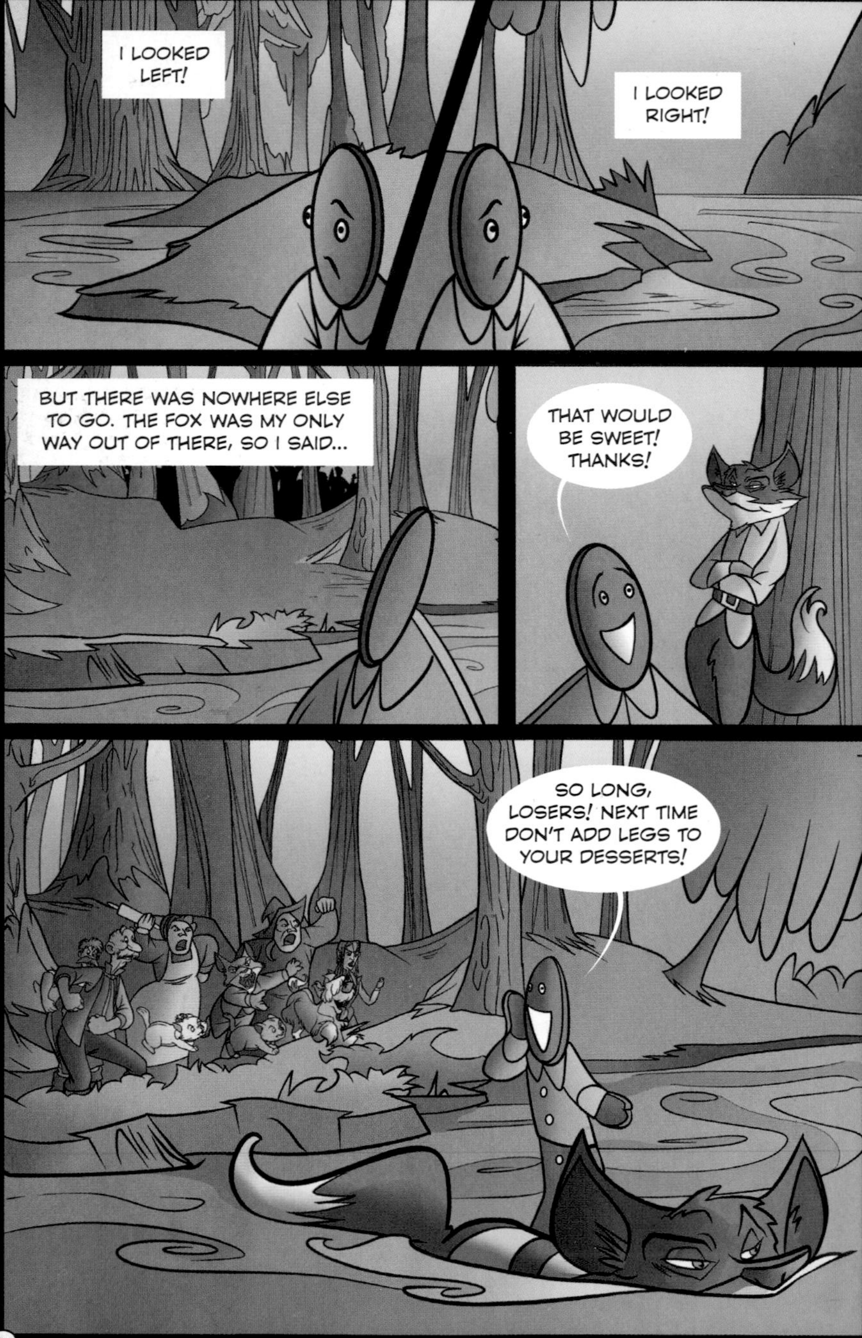
I LOOKED LEFT!
I LOOKED RIGHT!
BUT THERE WAS NOWHERE ELSE TO GO. THE FOX WAS MY ONLY WAY OUT OF THERE, SO I SAID...
THAT WOULD BE SWEET! THANKS!
SO LONG, LOSERS! NEXT TIME DON'T ADD LEGS TO YOUR DESSERTS!

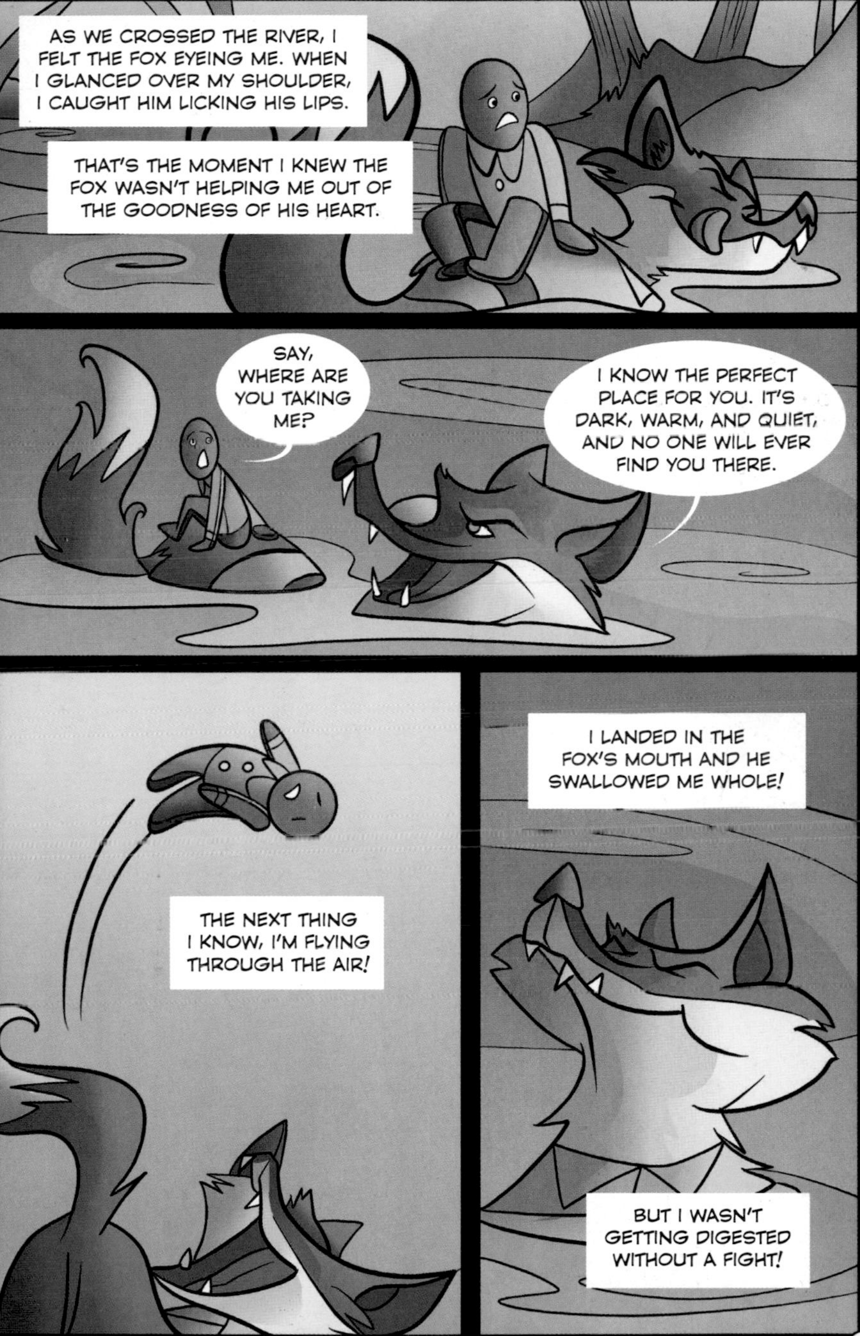
AS WE CROSSED THE RIVER, I FELT THE FOX EYEING ME. WHEN I GLANCED OVER MY SHOULDER, I CAUGHT HIM LICKING HIS LIPS.
THAT'S THE MOMENT I KNEW THE FOX WASN'T HELPING ME OUT OF THE GOODNESS OF HIS HEART.
SAY, WHERE ARE YOU TAKING ME?
I KNOW THE PERFECT PLACE FOR YOU. IT'S DARK, WARM, AND QUIET, AND NO ONE WILL EVER FIND YOU THERE.
THE NEXT THING I KNOW, I'M FLYING THROUGH THE AIR!
I LANDED IN THE FOX'S MOUTH AND HE SWALLOWED ME WHOLE!
BUT I WASN'T GETTING DIGESTED WITHOUT A FIGHT!

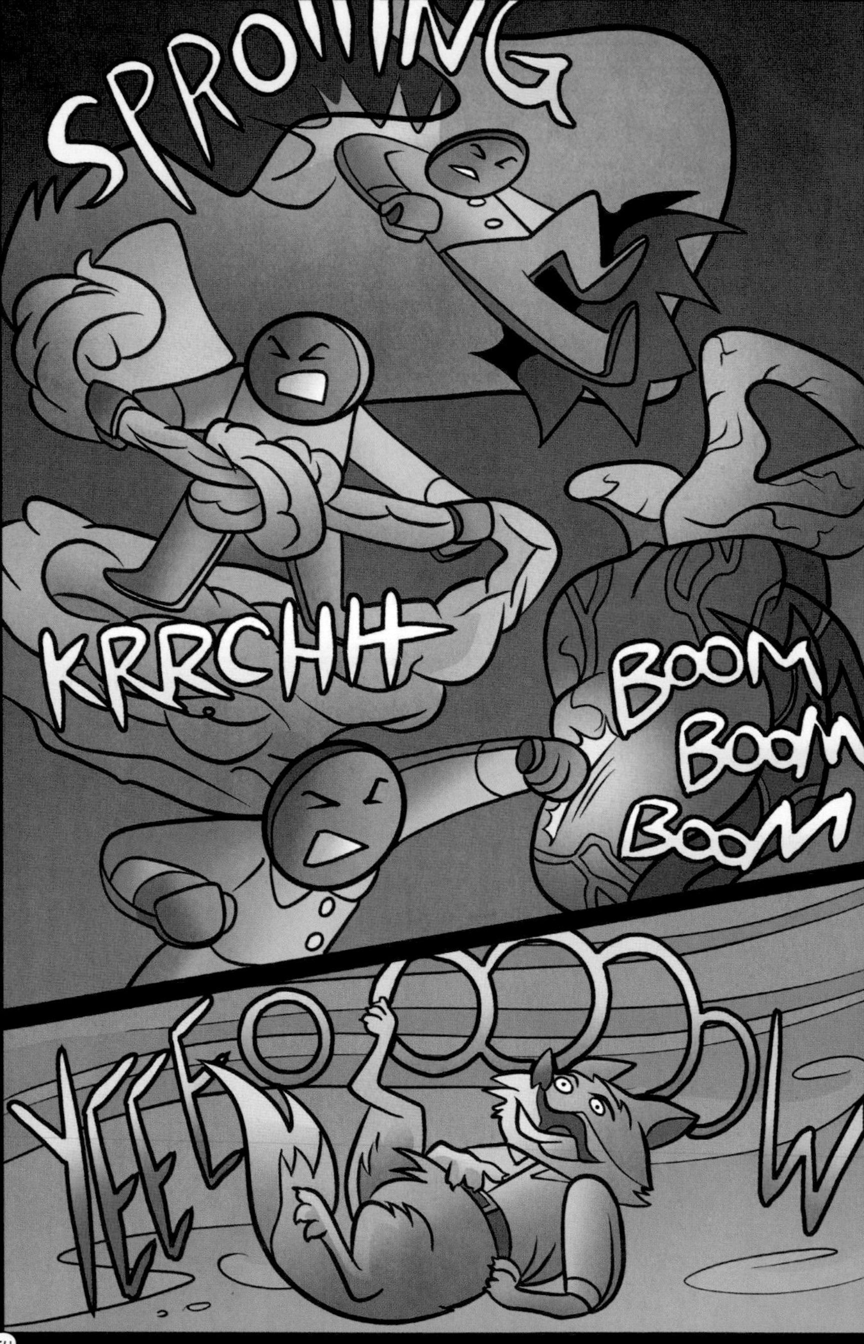
SPROIIING
KRRCHH
BOOM
BOOM
BOOM
YEEOOOOOW

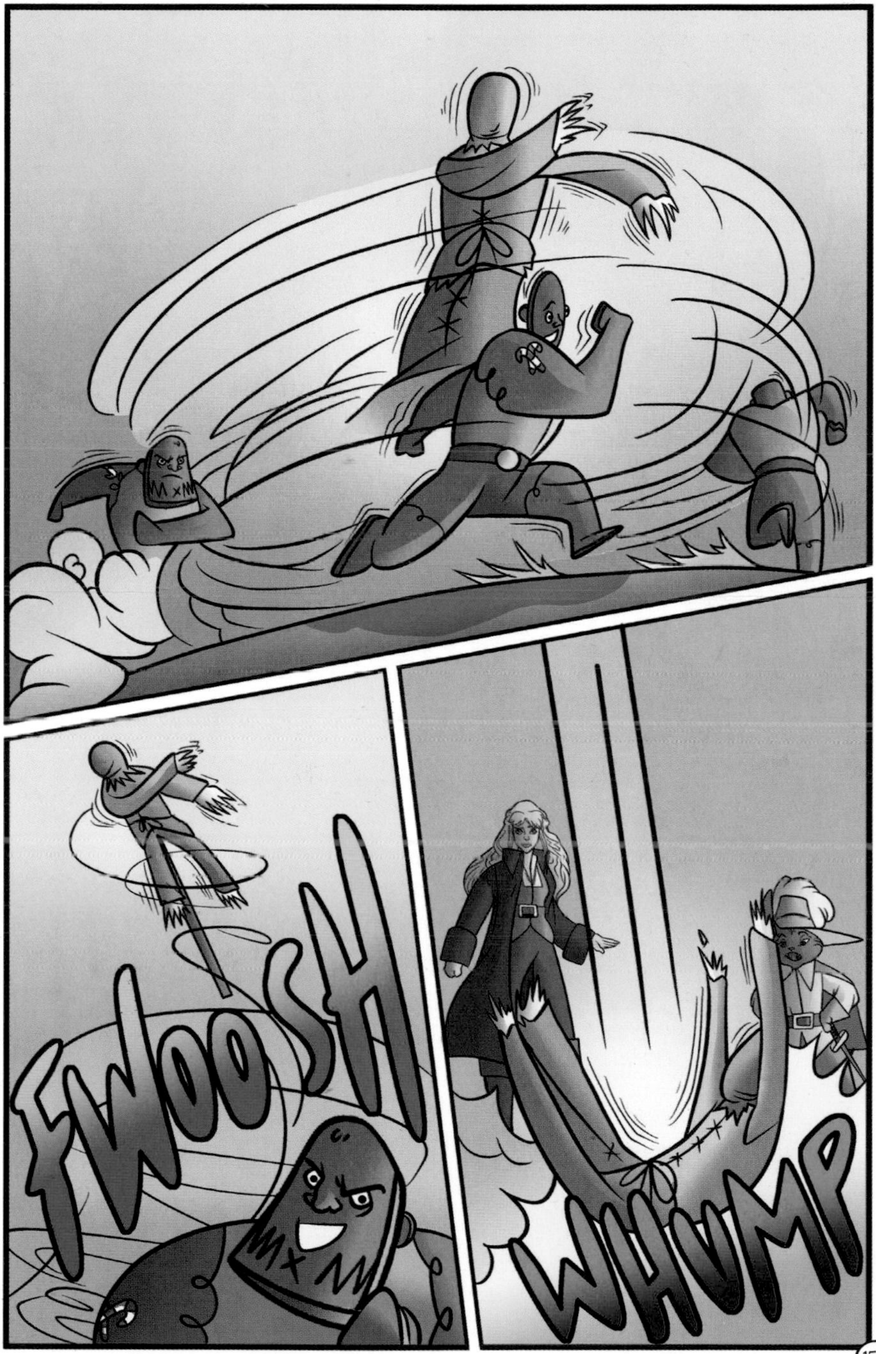
FWOOSH
WHUMP

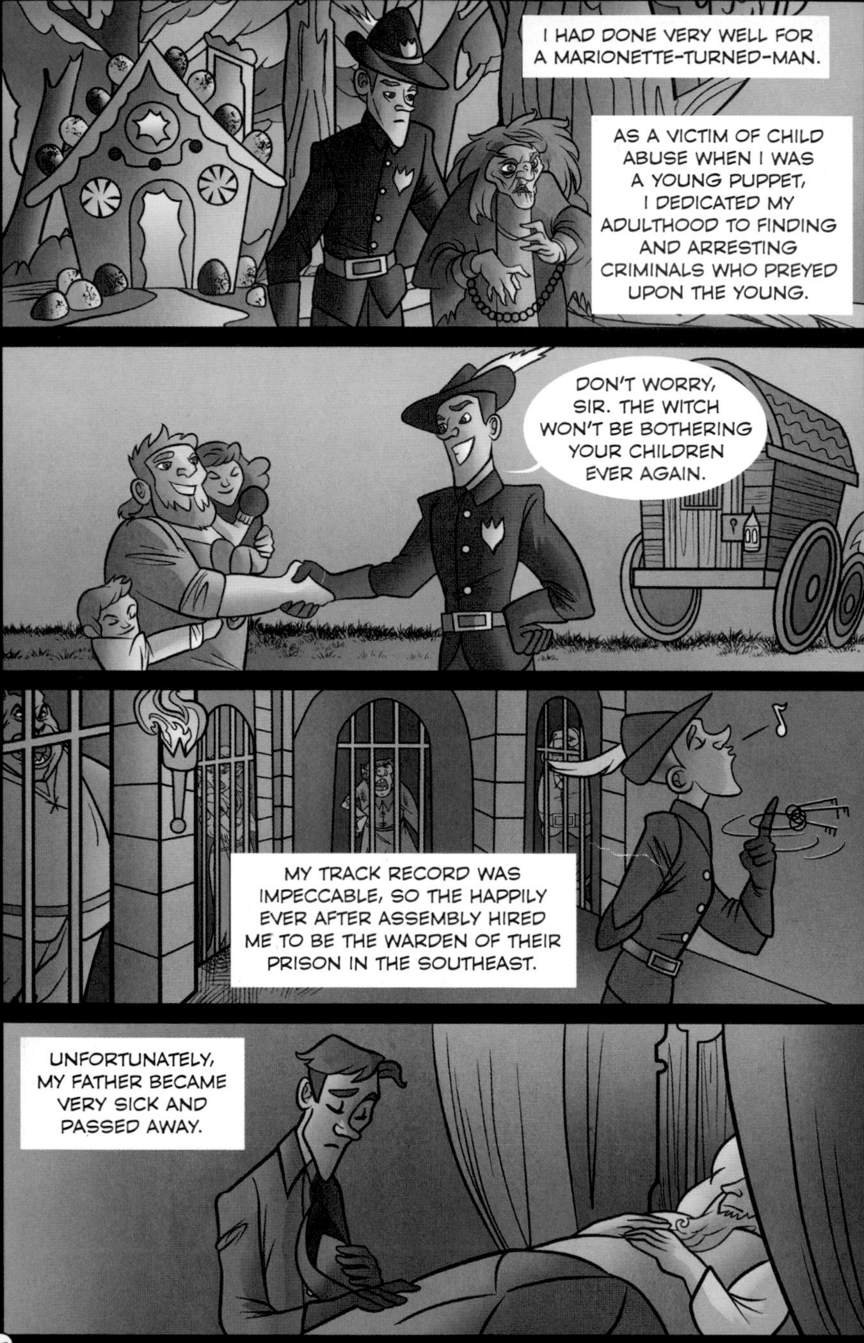
I HAD DONE VERY WELL FOR A MARIONETTE-TURNED-MAN.
AS A VICTIM OF CHILD ABUSE WHEN I WAS A YOUNG PUPPET, I DEDICATED MY ADULTHOOD TO FINDING AND ARRESTING CRIMINALS WHO PREYED UPON THE YOUNG.
DON'T WORRY, SIR. THE WITCH WON'T BE BOTHERING YOUR CHILDREN EVER AGAIN.
MY TRACK RECORD WAS IMPECCABLE, SO THE HAPPILY EVER AFTER ASSEMBLY HIRED ME TO BE THE WARDEN OF THEIR PRISON IN THE SOUTHEAST.
UNFORTUNATELY, MY FATHER BECAME VERY SICK AND PASSED AWAY.

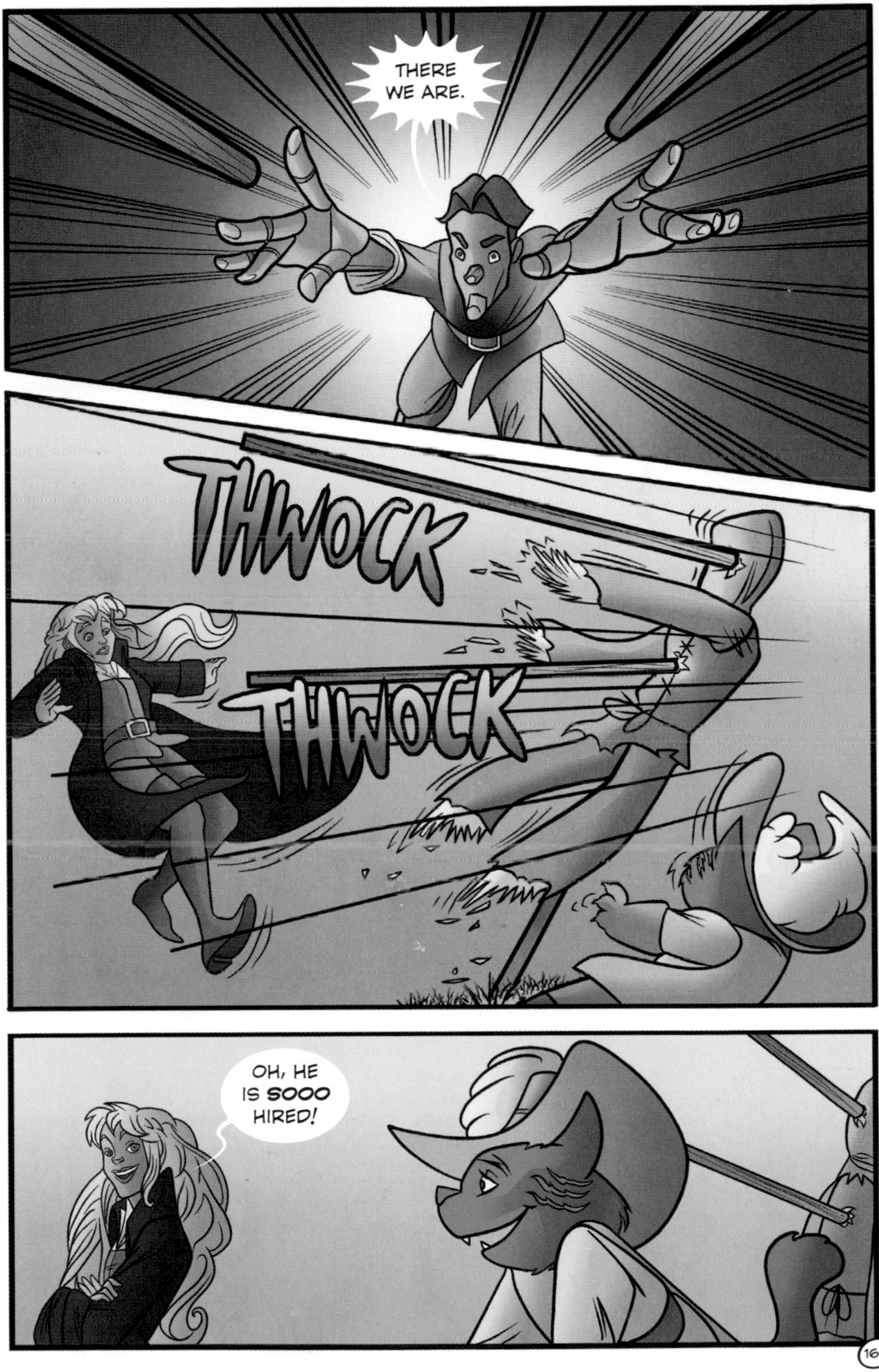
THERE WE ARE.
THWOCK
THWOCK
OH, HE IS **SOOO** HIRED!

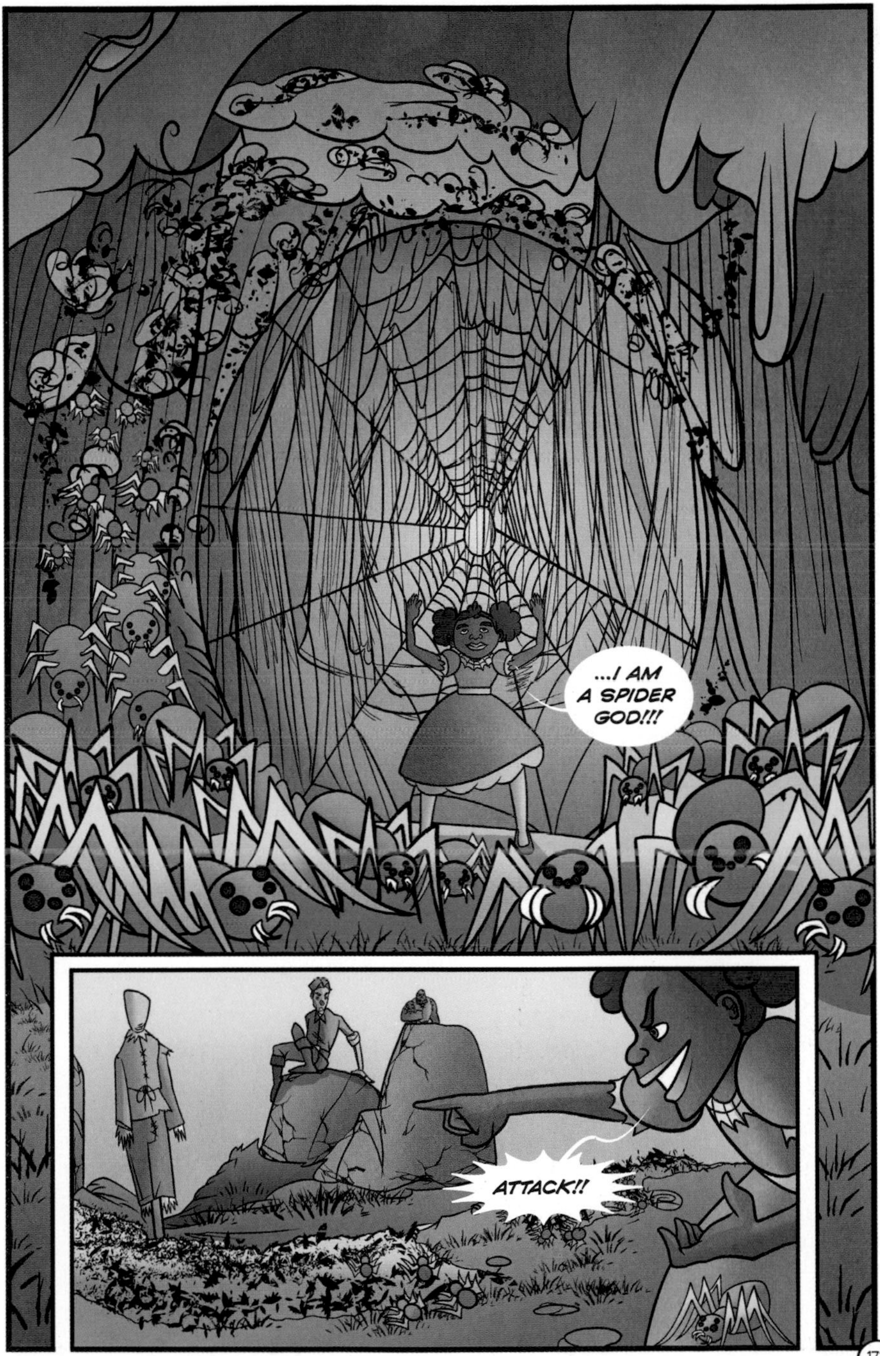
...I AM A SPIDER GOD!!!
ATTACK!!

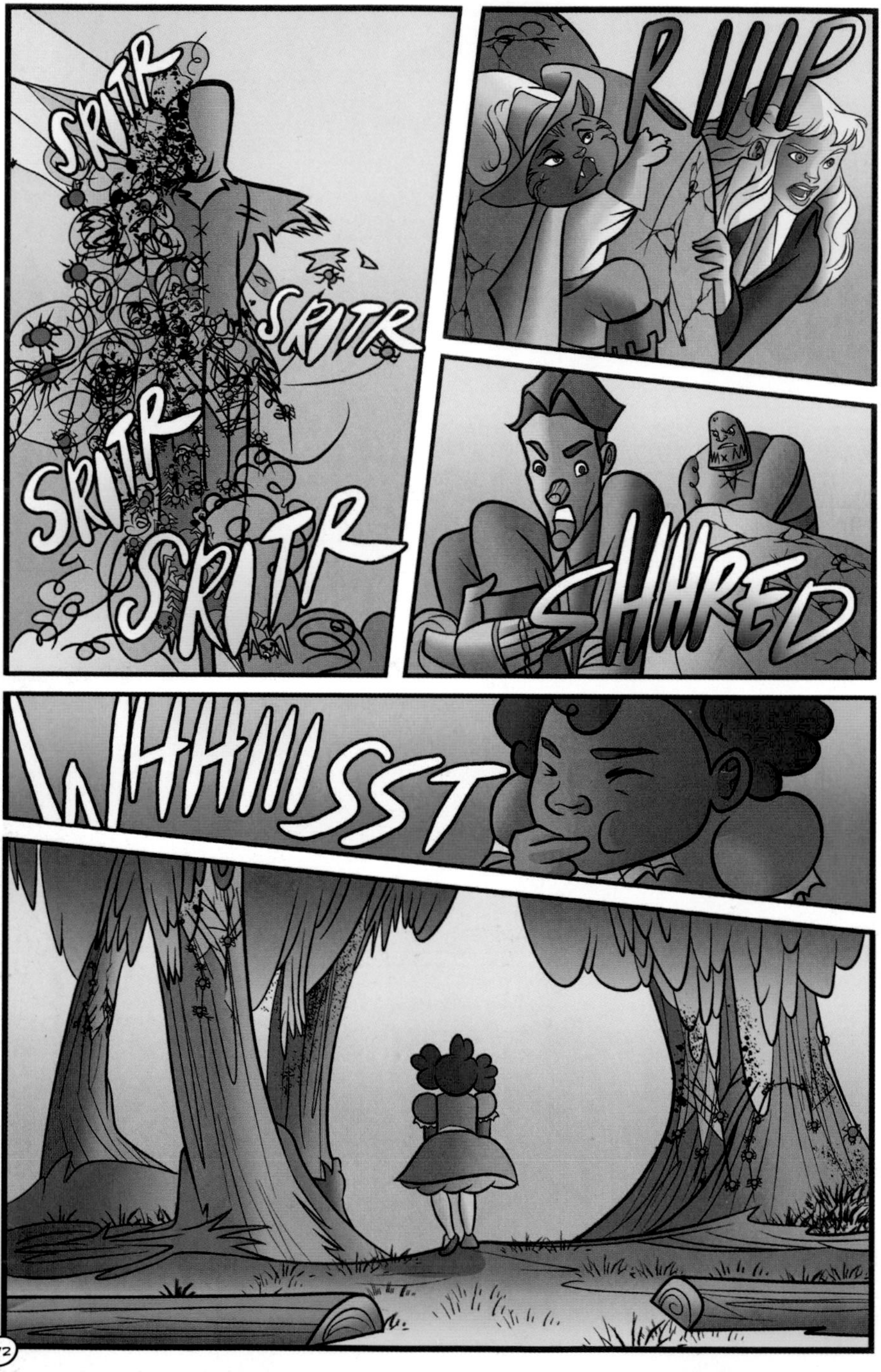
SRITR
SRITR
SRITR
SRITR
RIIIP
SHHRED
WHHIIISST

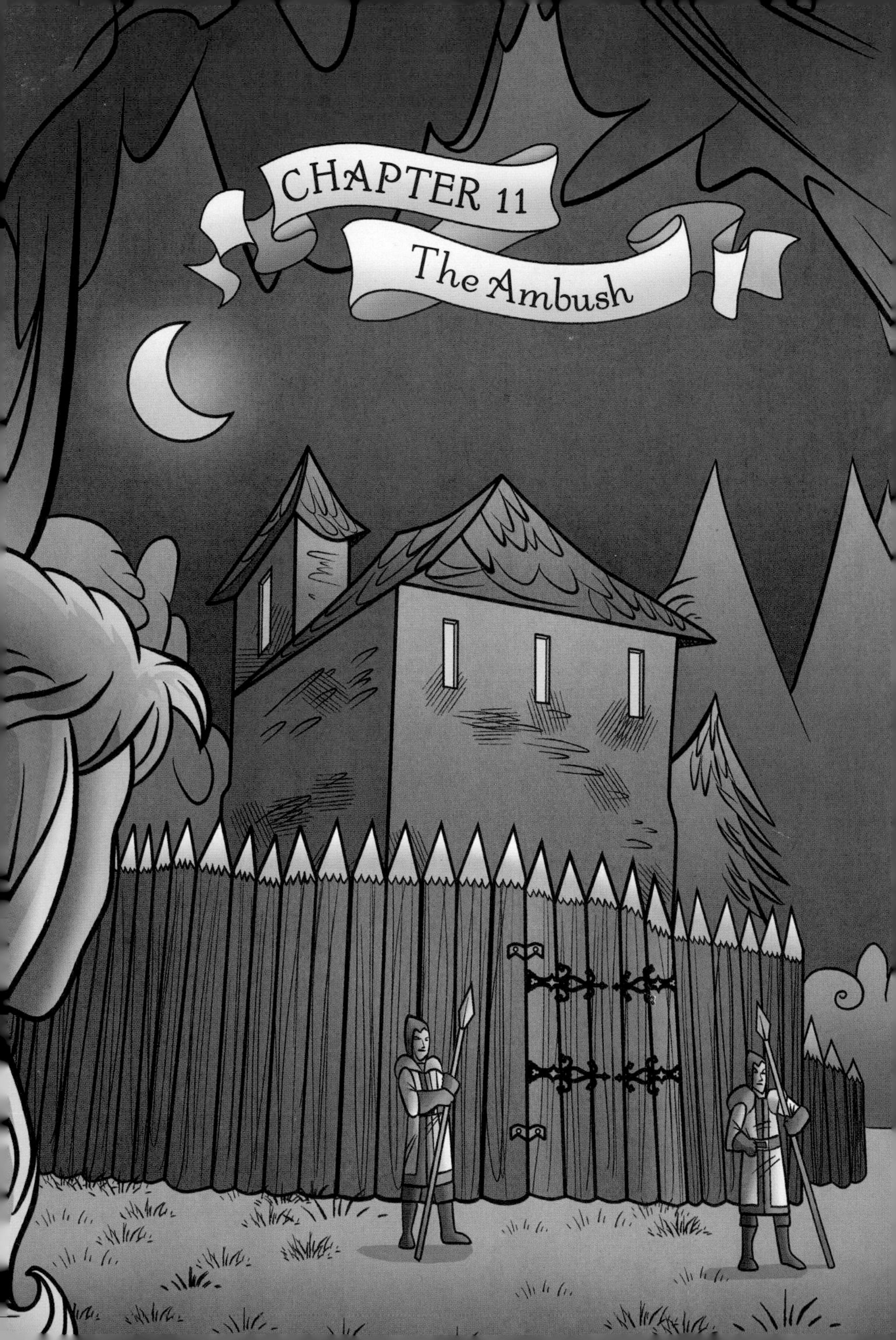
CHAPTER 11
The Ambush

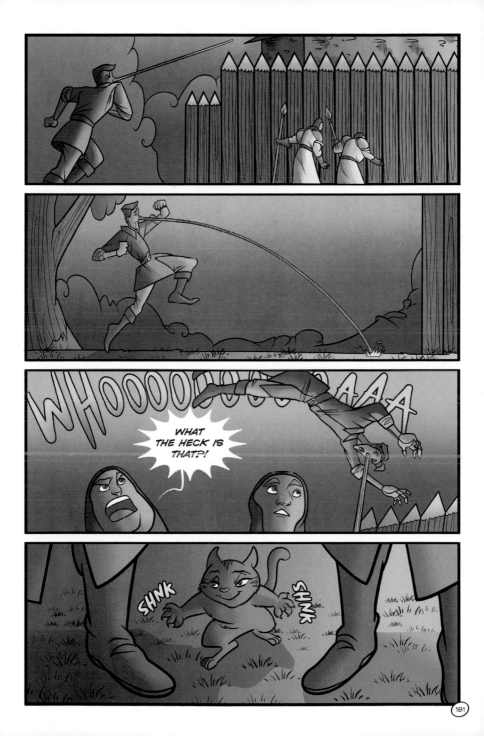

WHOOOOO AAAA

WHAT THE HECK IS THAT?!

SHNK SHNK

181

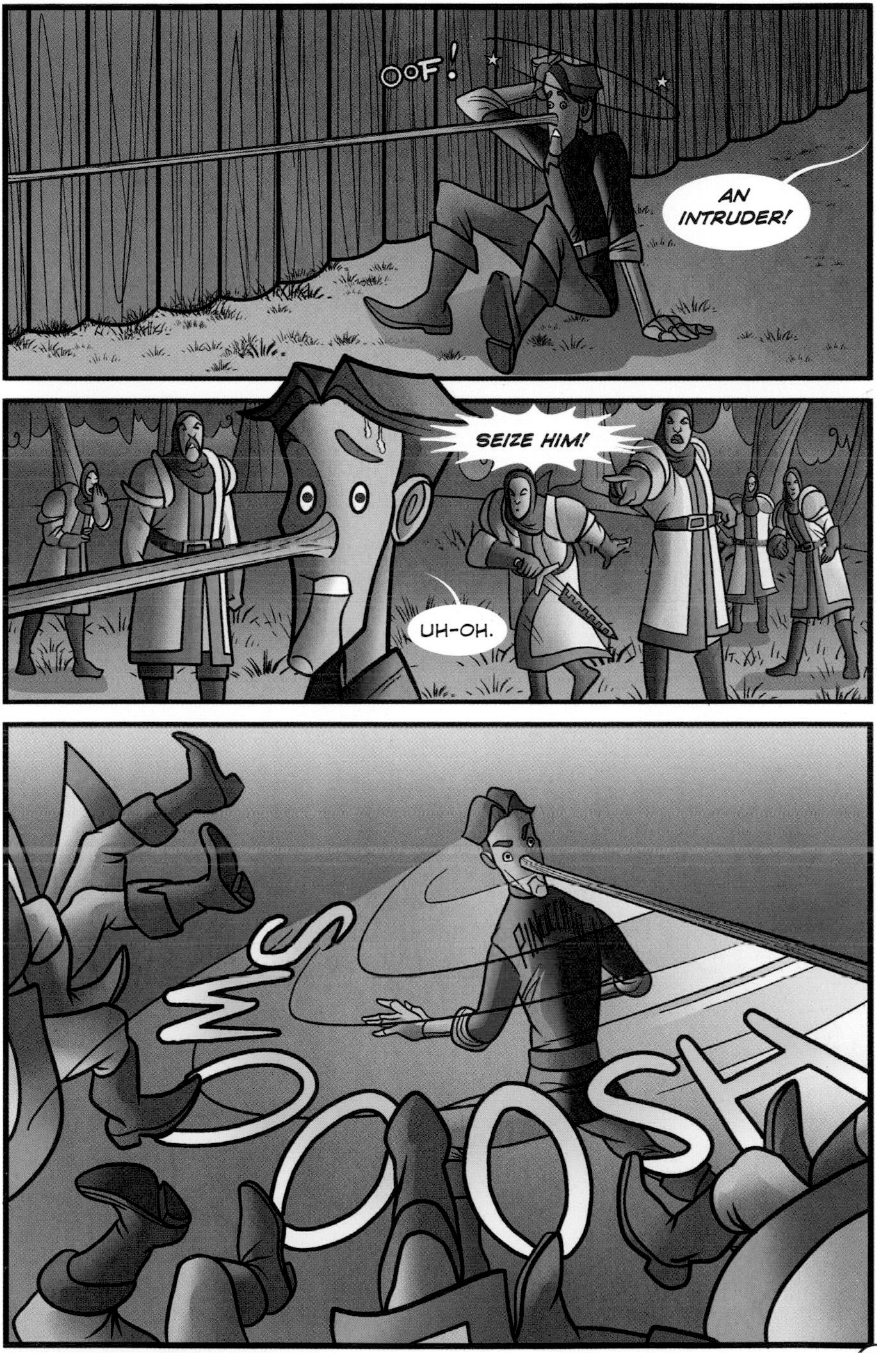
OOF!
AN INTRUDER!
SEIZE HIM!
UH-OH.
SWOOSH

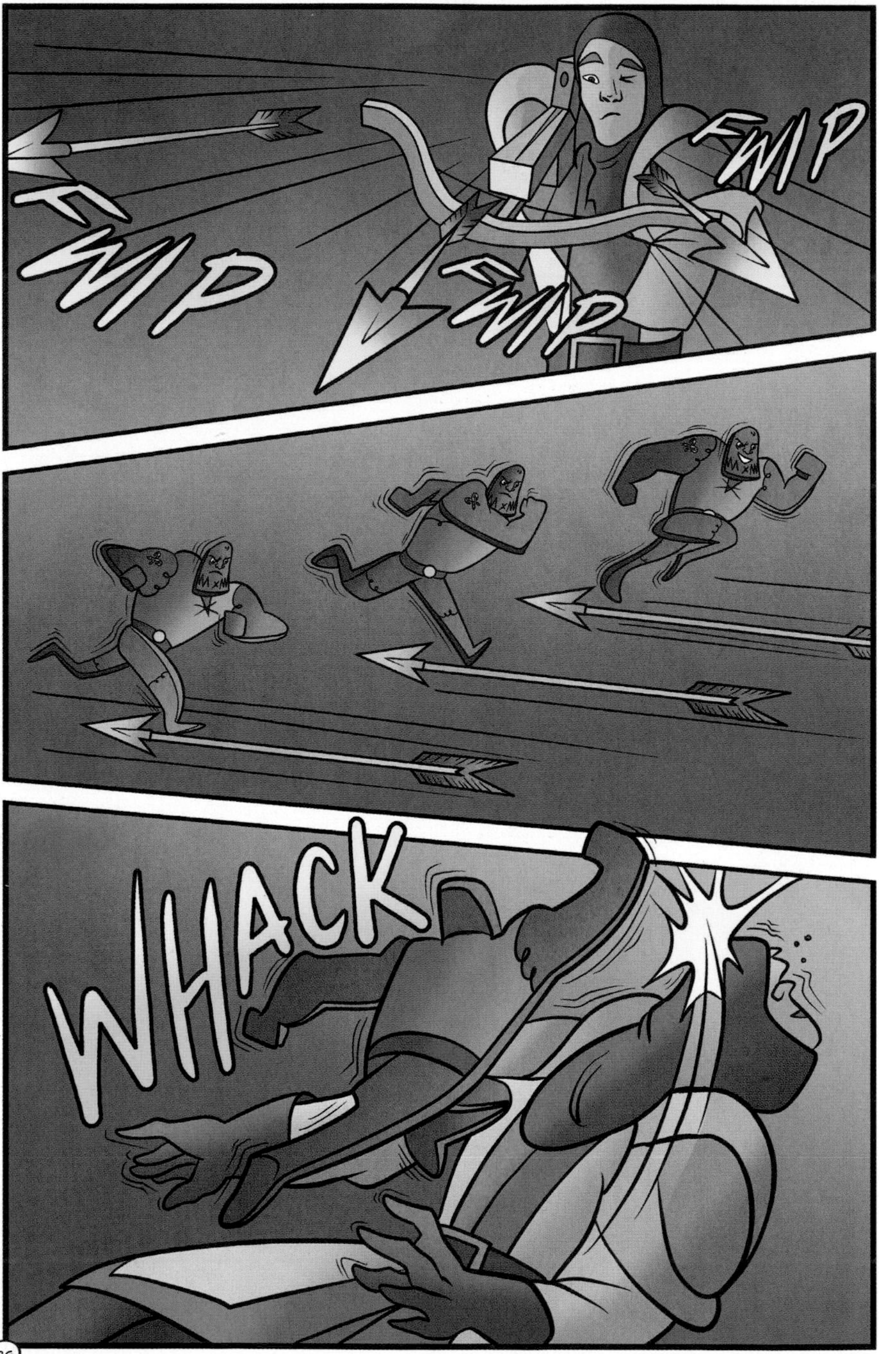
FWIP
FWIP
FWIP
WHACK

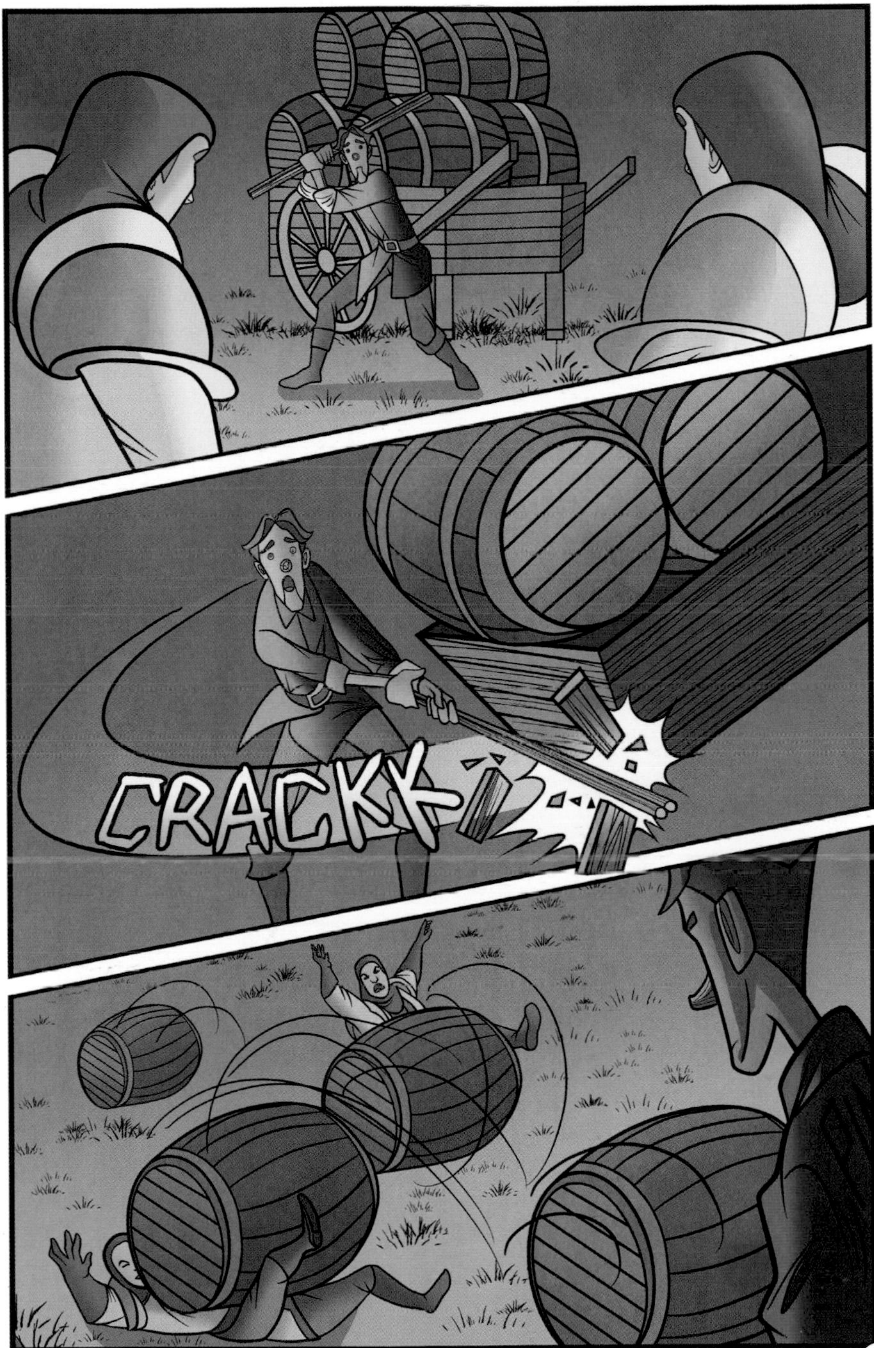
CRACKK

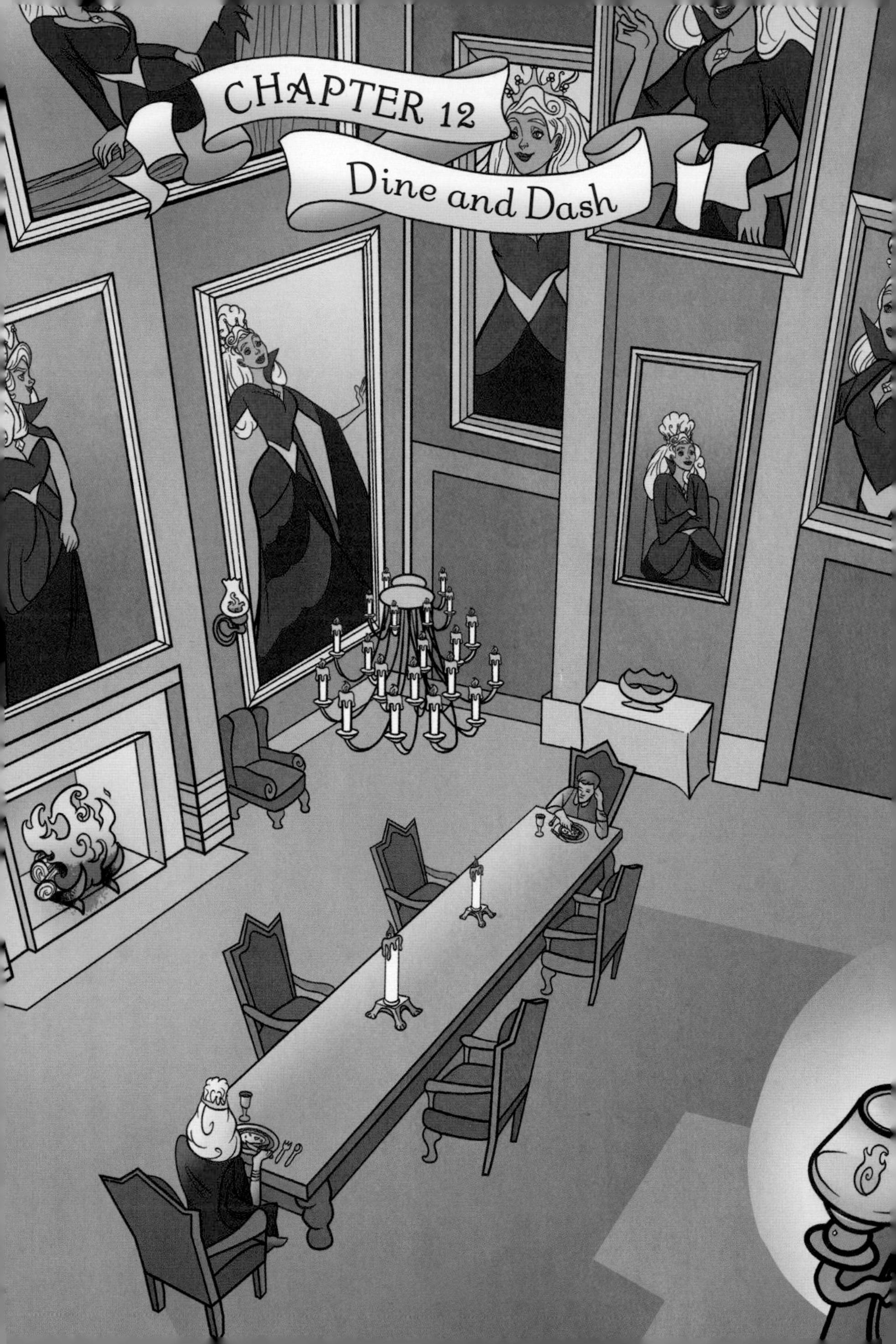
CHAPTER 12
Dine and Dash

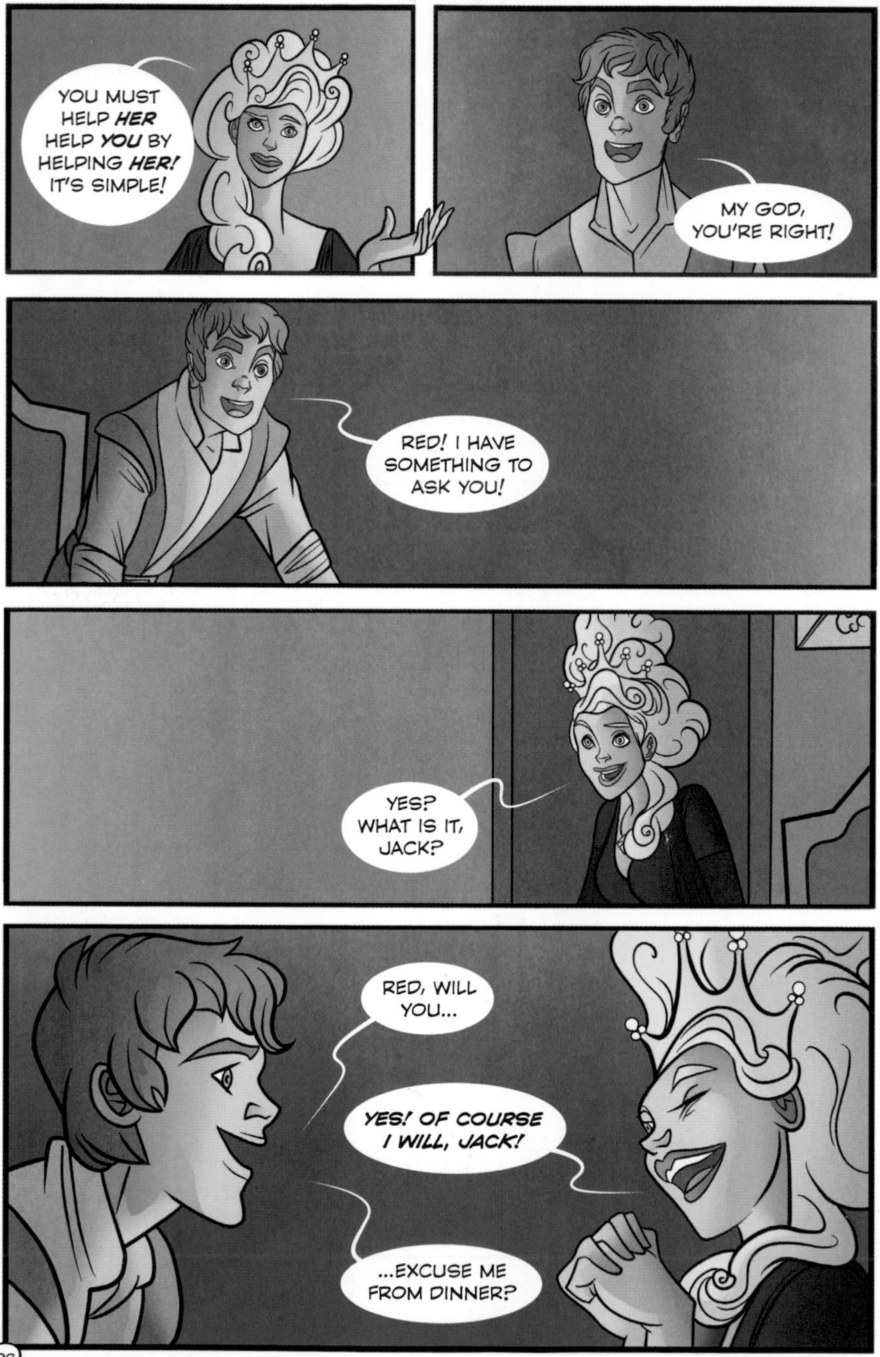
YOU MUST HELP ***HER*** HELP ***YOU*** BY HELPING ***HER!*** IT'S SIMPLE!
MY GOD, YOU'RE RIGHT!
RED! I HAVE SOMETHING TO ASK YOU!
YES? WHAT IS IT, JACK?
RED, WILL YOU...
YES! OF COURSE I WILL, JACK!
...EXCUSE ME FROM DINNER?

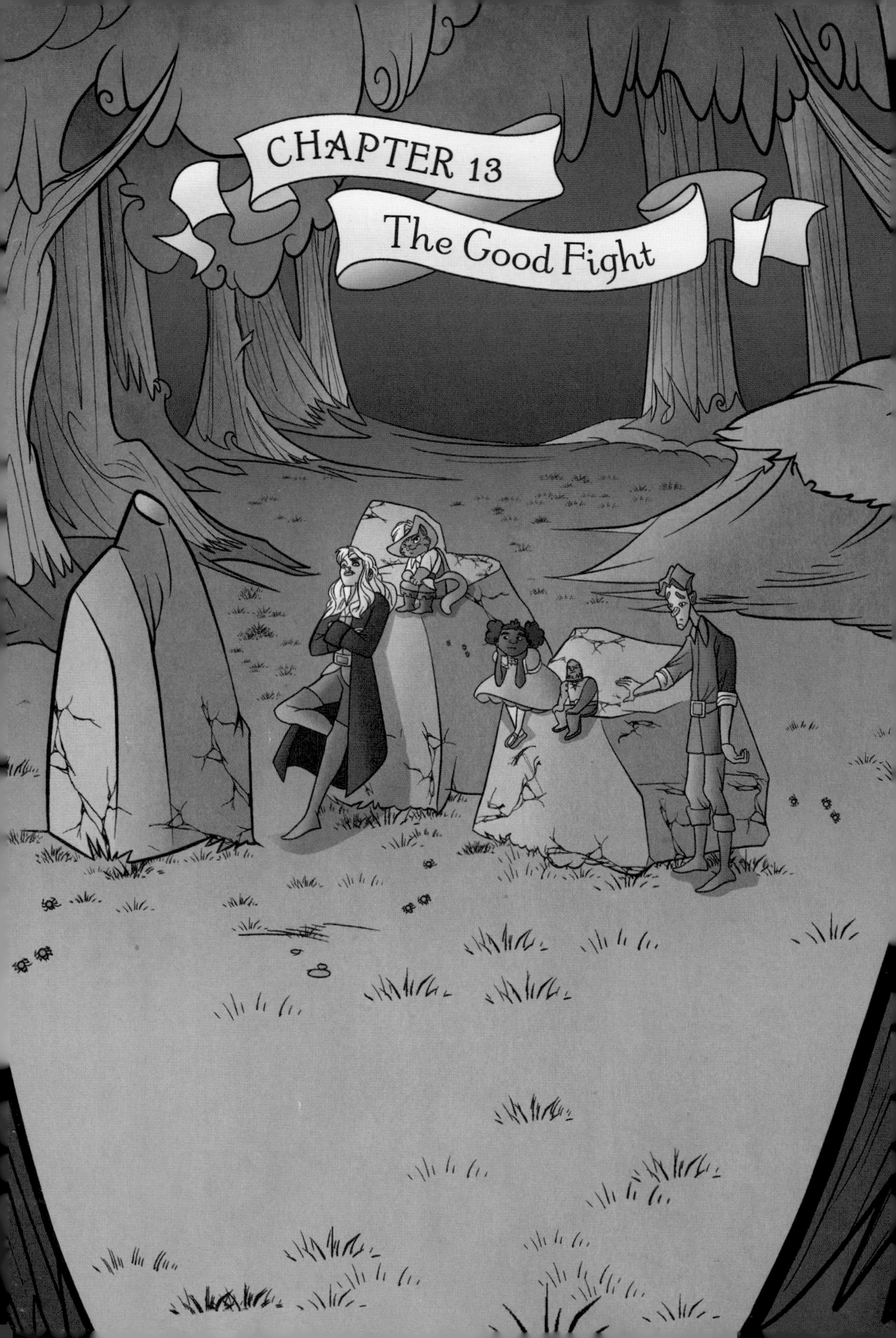
CHAPTER 13
The Good Fight

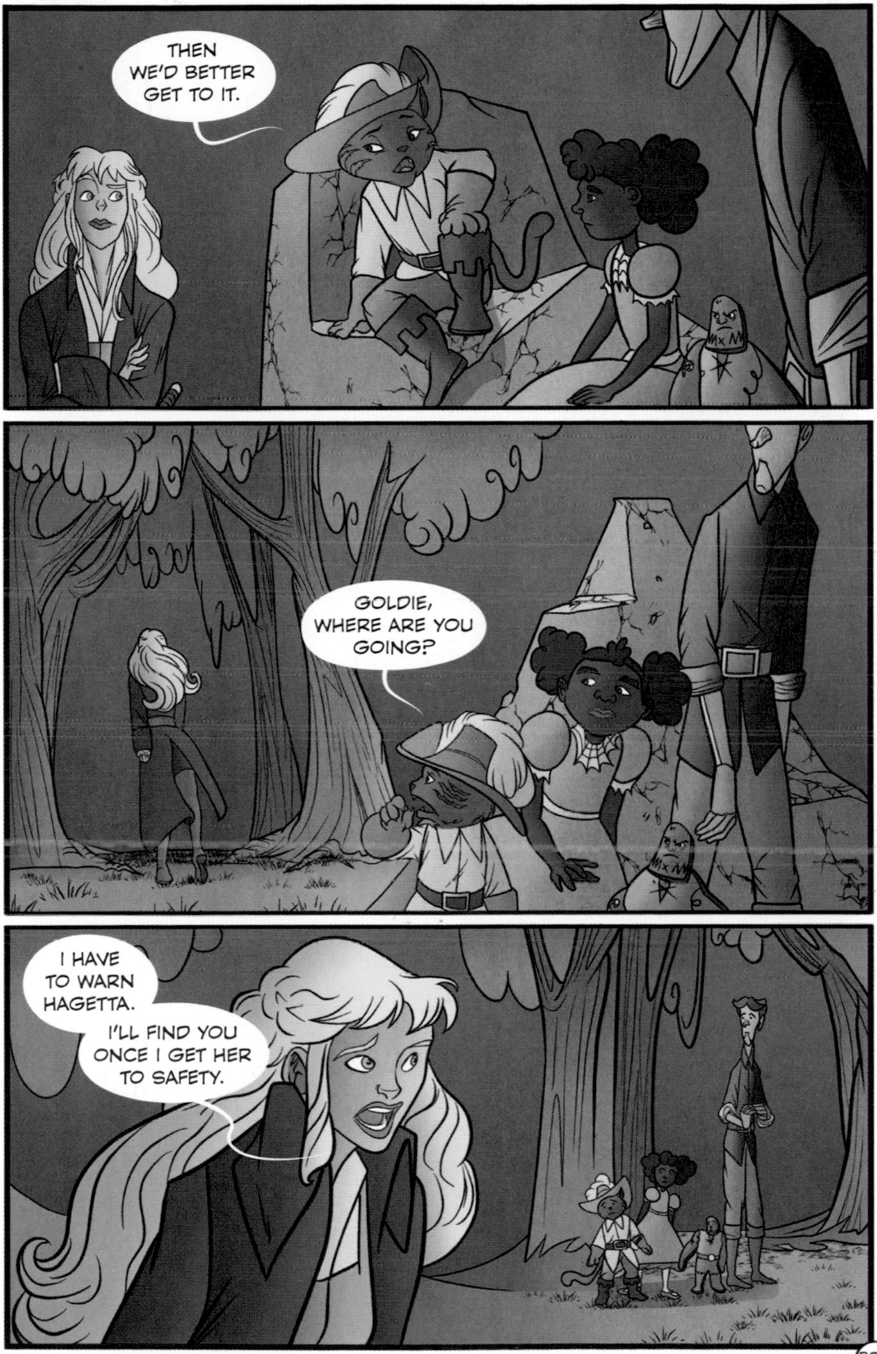
THEN WE'D BETTER GET TO IT.
GOLDIE, WHERE ARE YOU GOING?
I HAVE TO WARN HAGETTA.
I'LL FIND YOU ONCE I GET HER TO SAFETY.

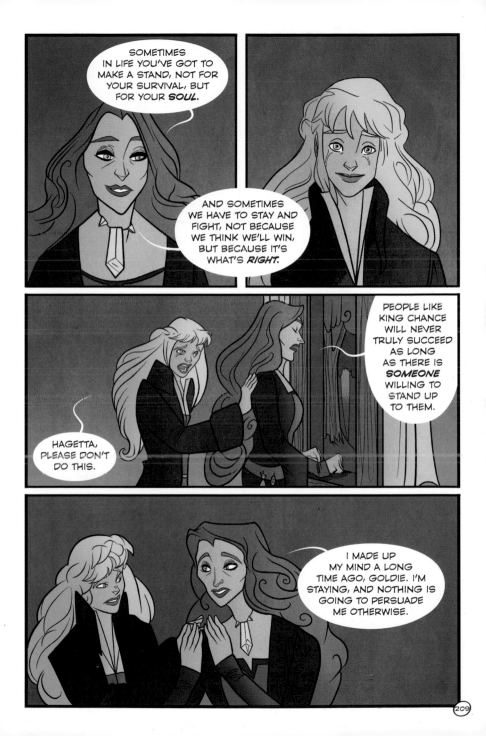

CHAPTER 14
The Evacuation

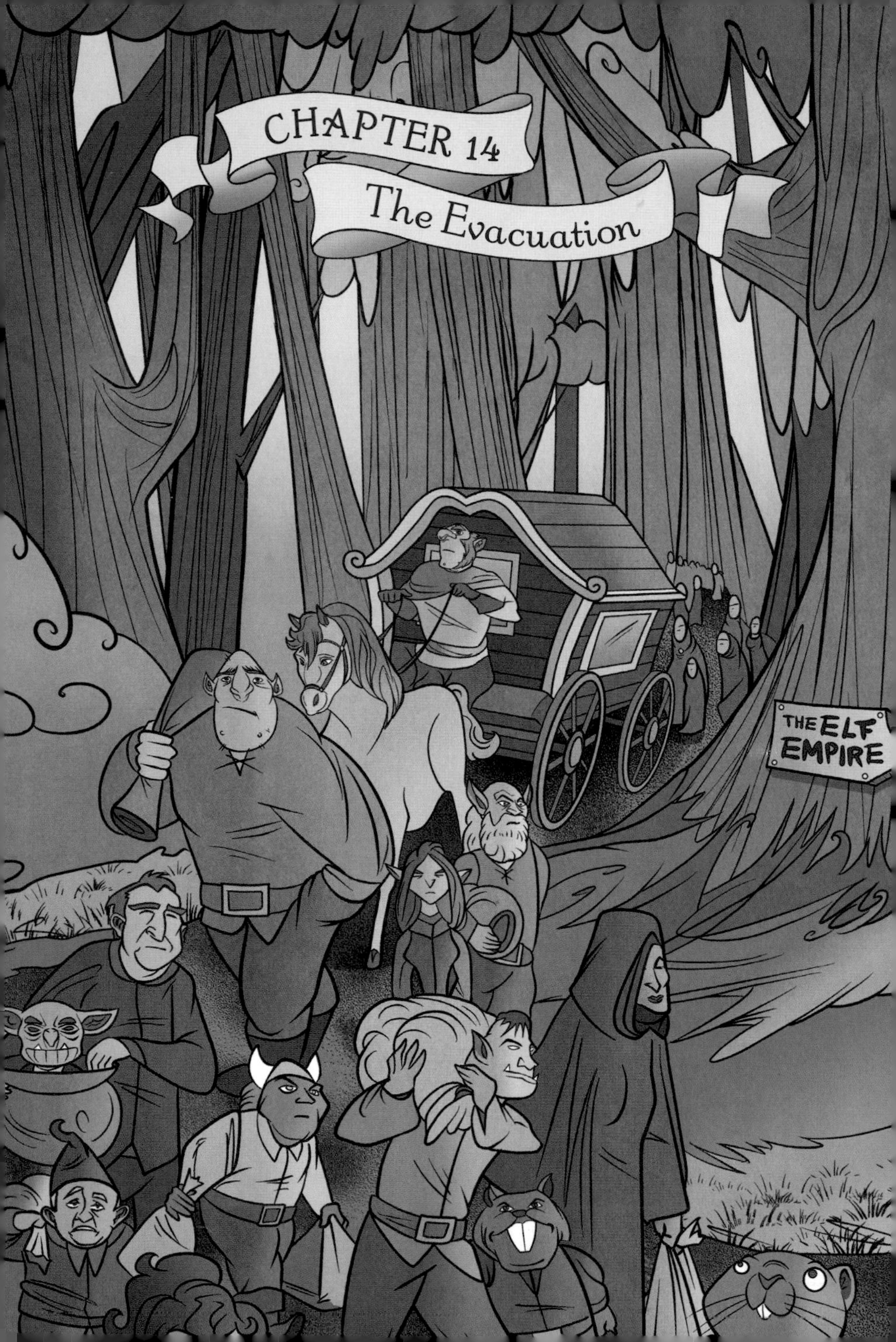
THE ELF EMPIRE

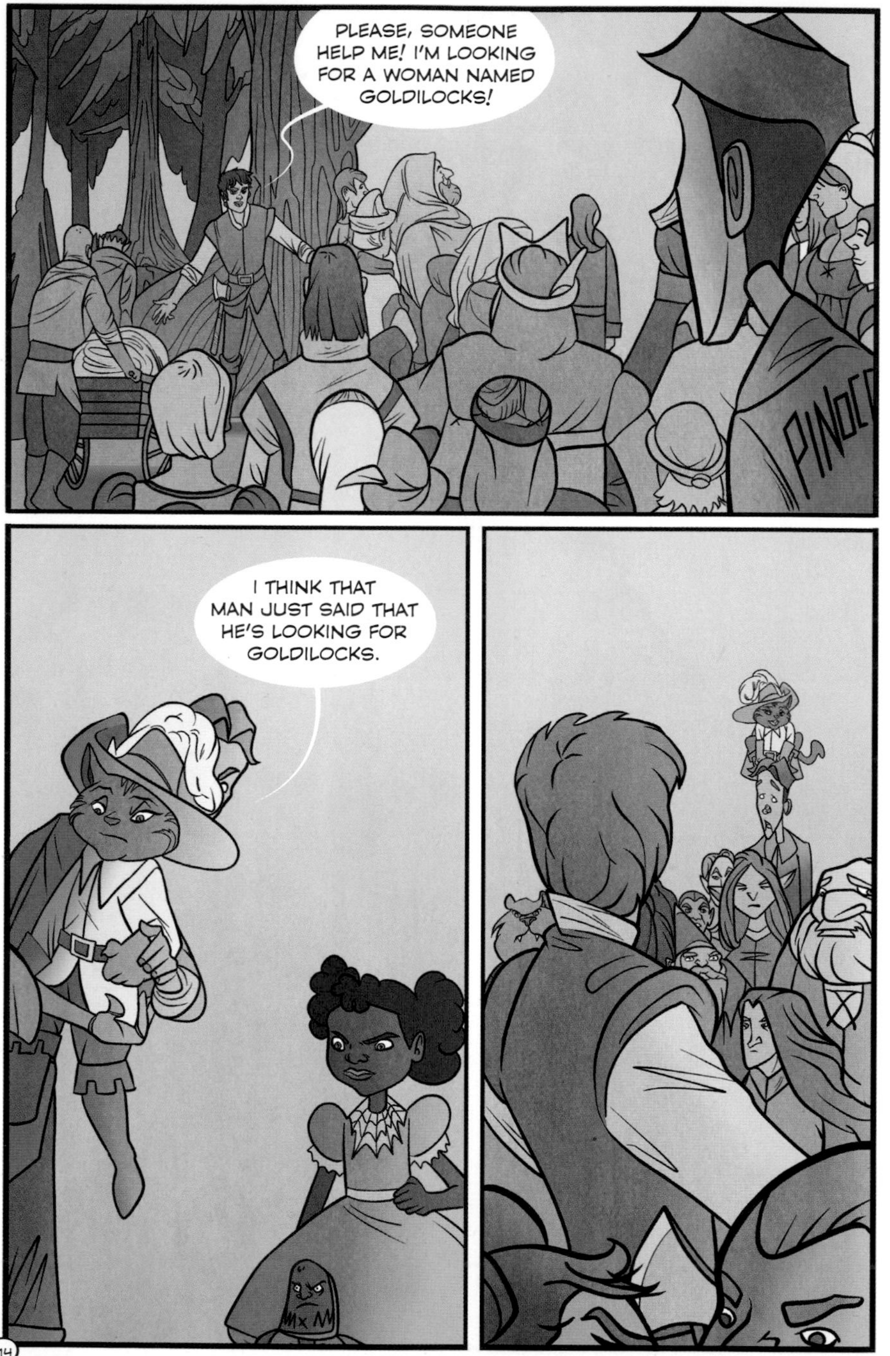
PLEASE, SOMEONE HELP ME! I'M LOOKING FOR A WOMAN NAMED GOLDILOCKS!
I THINK THAT MAN JUST SAID THAT HE'S LOOKING FOR GOLDILOCKS.

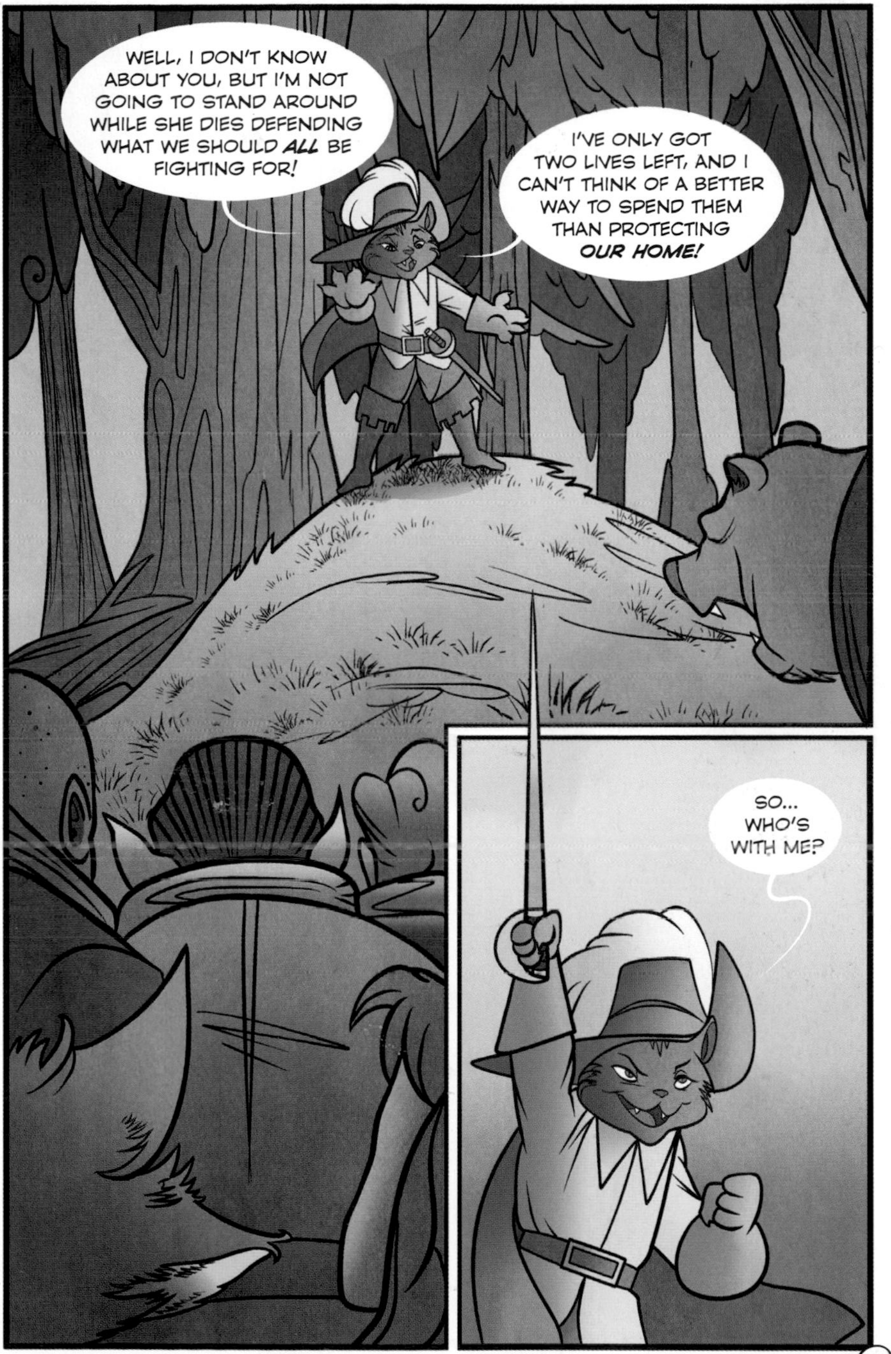
WELL, I DON'T KNOW ABOUT YOU, BUT I'M NOT GOING TO STAND AROUND WHILE SHE DIES DEFENDING WHAT WE SHOULD ALL BE FIGHTING FOR!
I'VE ONLY GOT TWO LIVES LEFT, AND I CAN'T THINK OF A BETTER WAY TO SPEND THEM THAN PROTECTING OUR HOME!
SO... WHO'S WITH ME?

CHAPTER 15
The Army Arrives

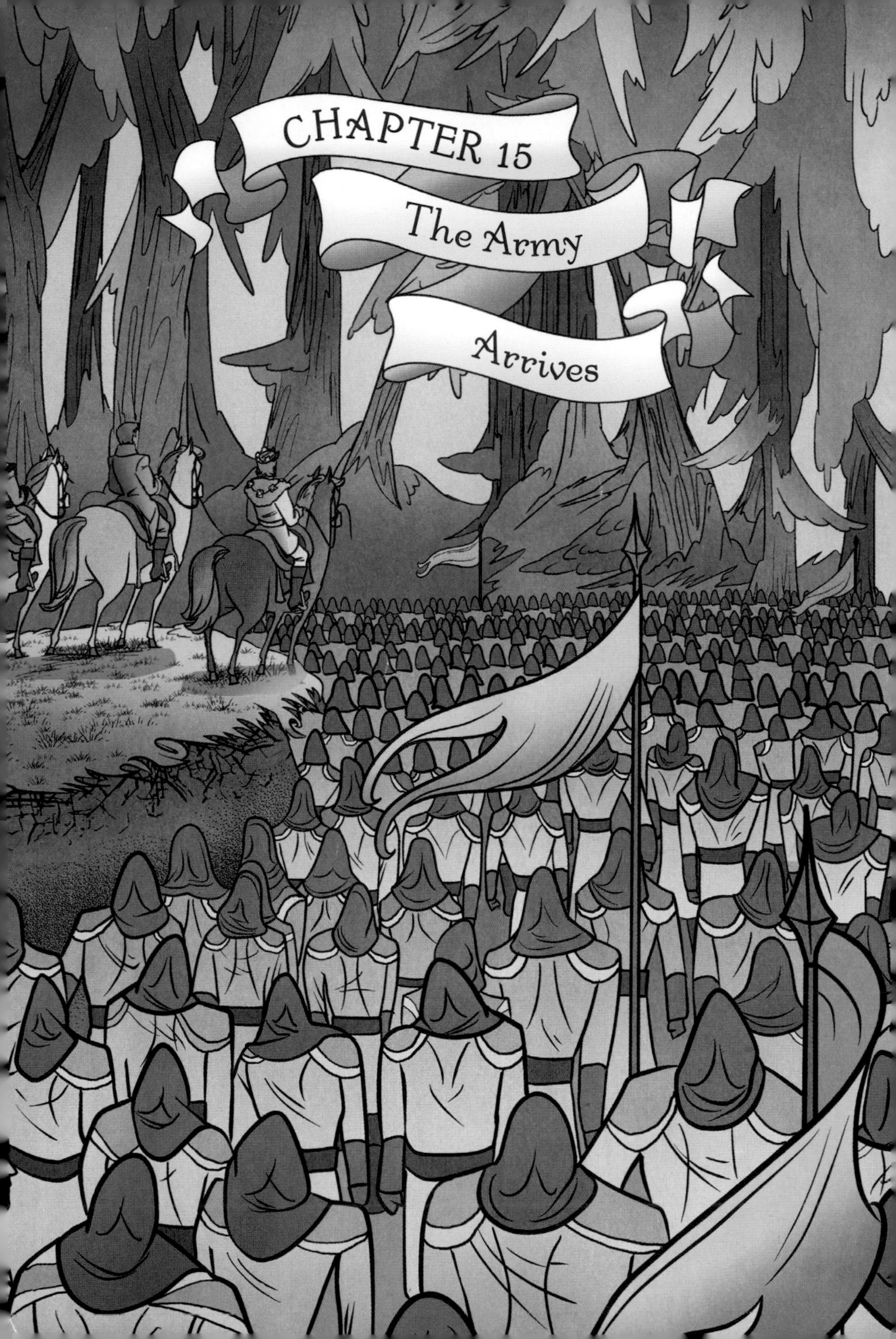

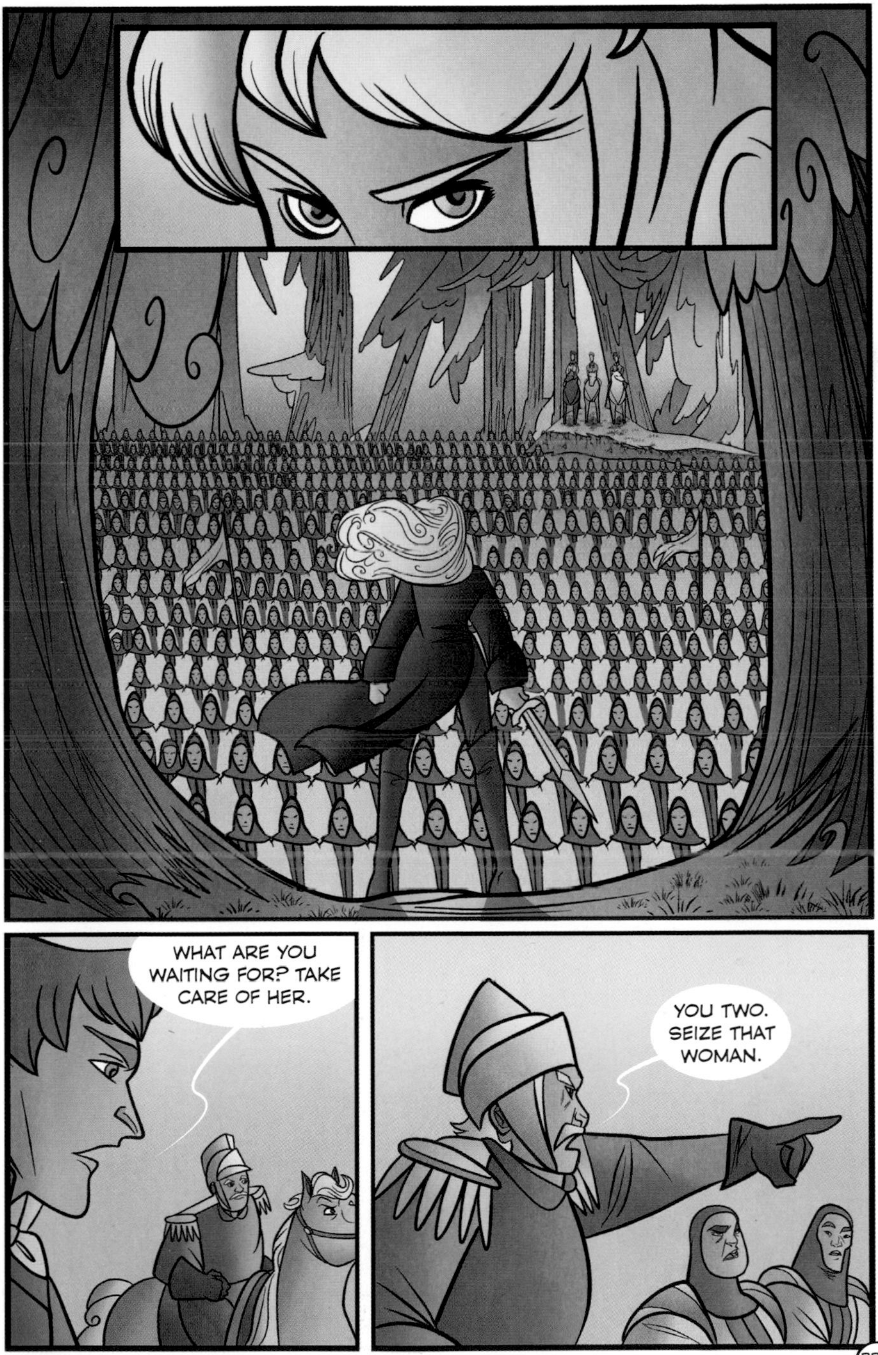
WHAT ARE YOU WAITING FOR? TAKE CARE OF HER.
YOU TWO. SEIZE THAT WOMAN.

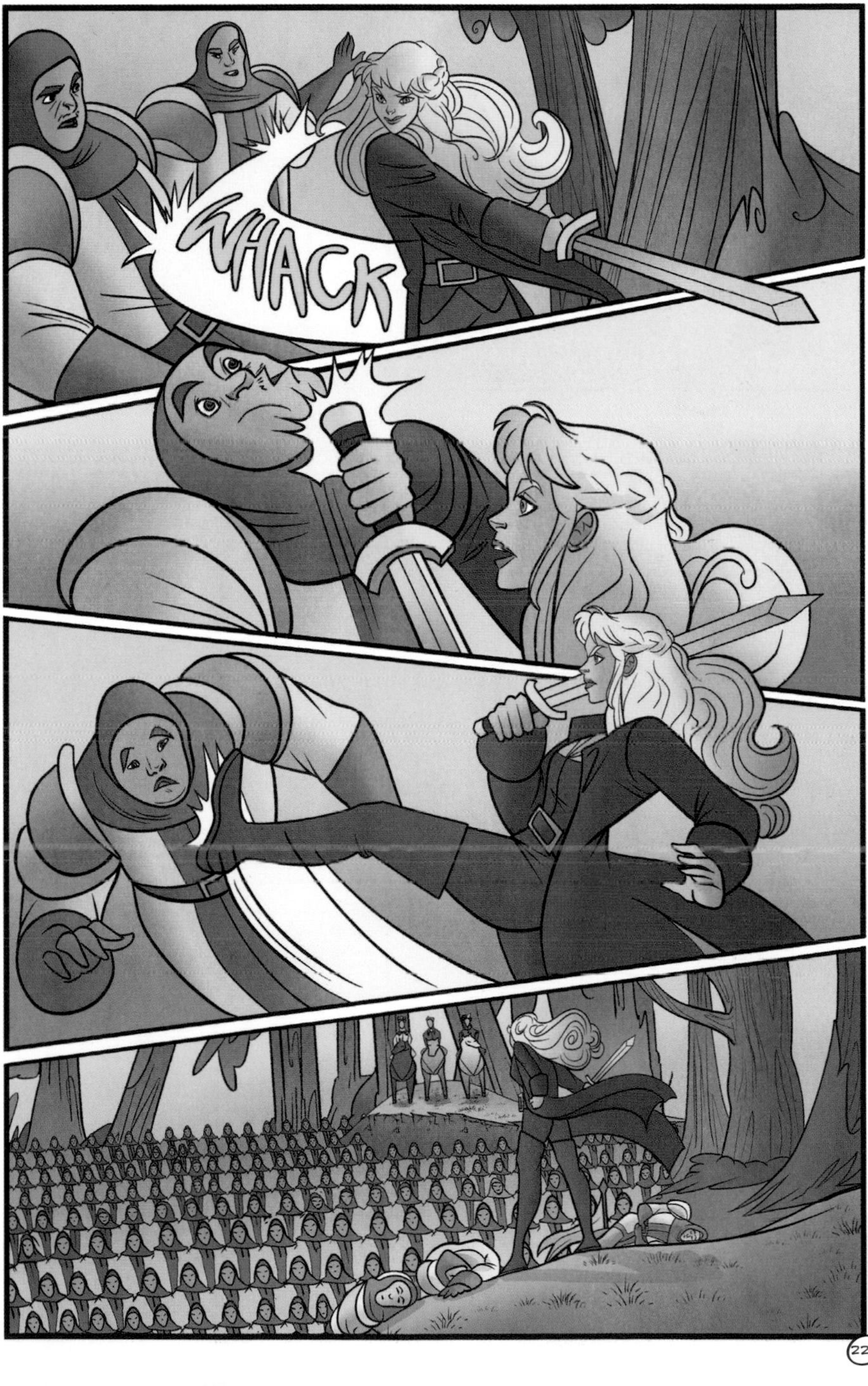
WHACK

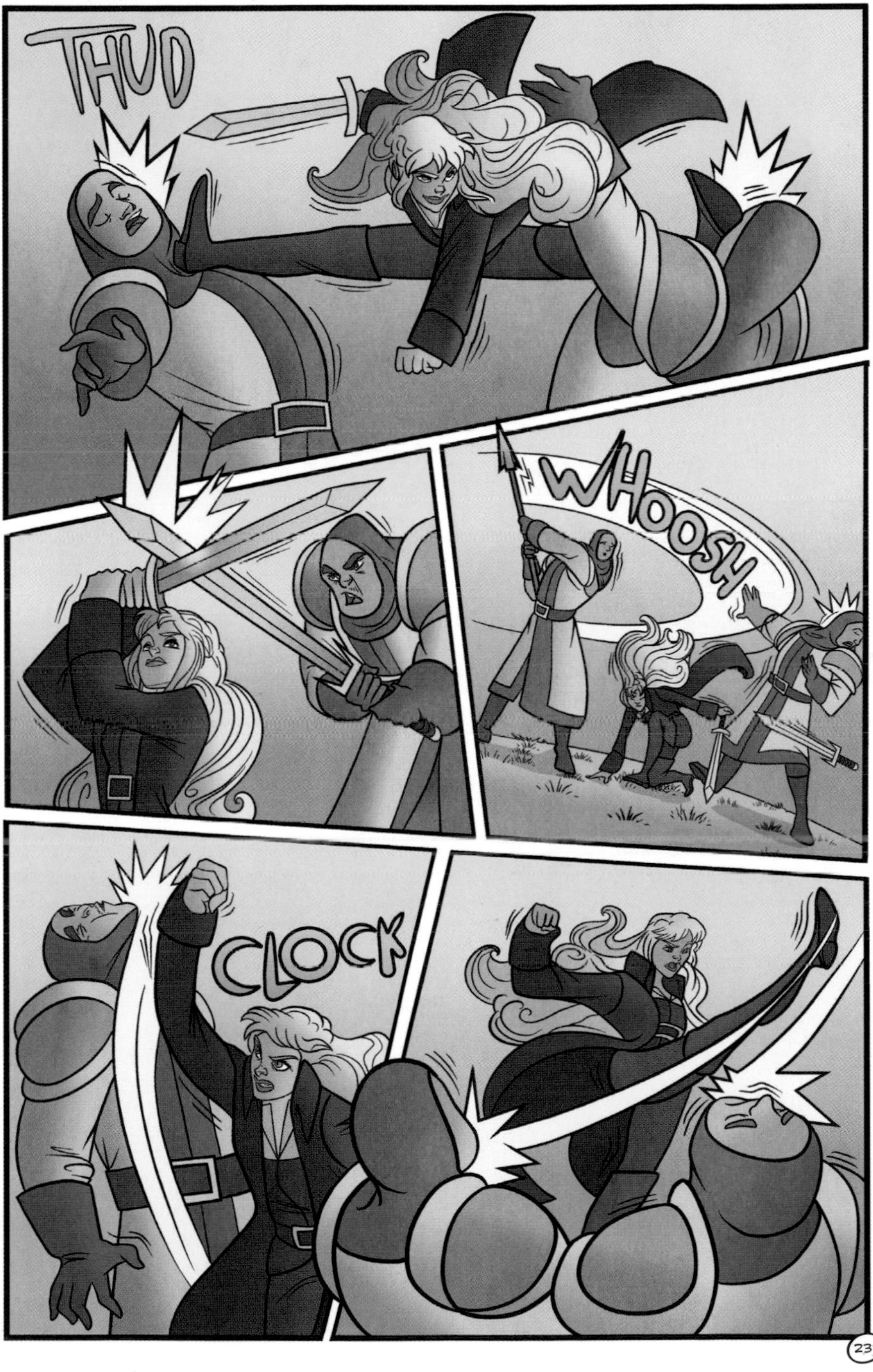
THUD
WHOOSH
CLOCK

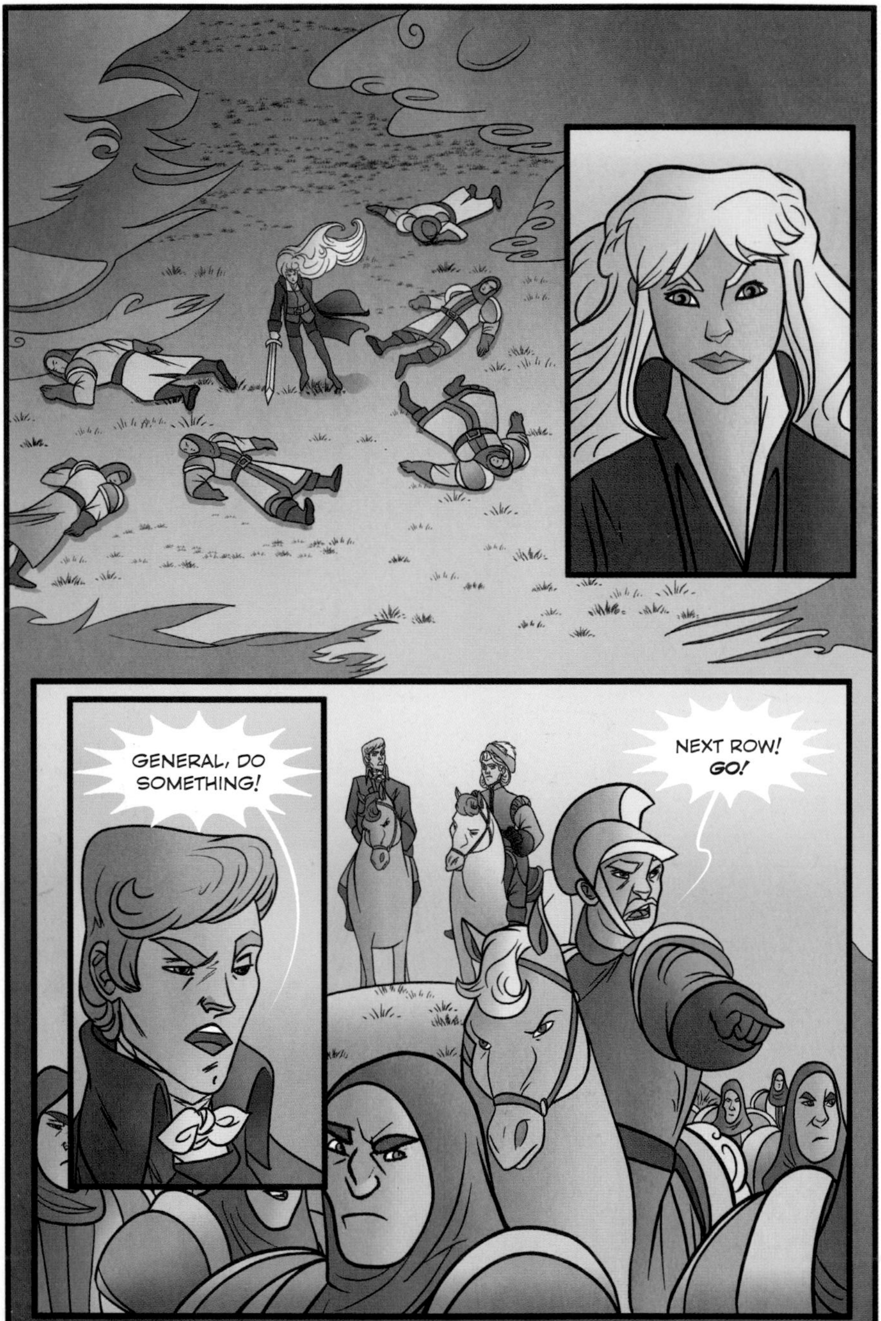
GENERAL, DO SOMETHING!
NEXT ROW! GO!

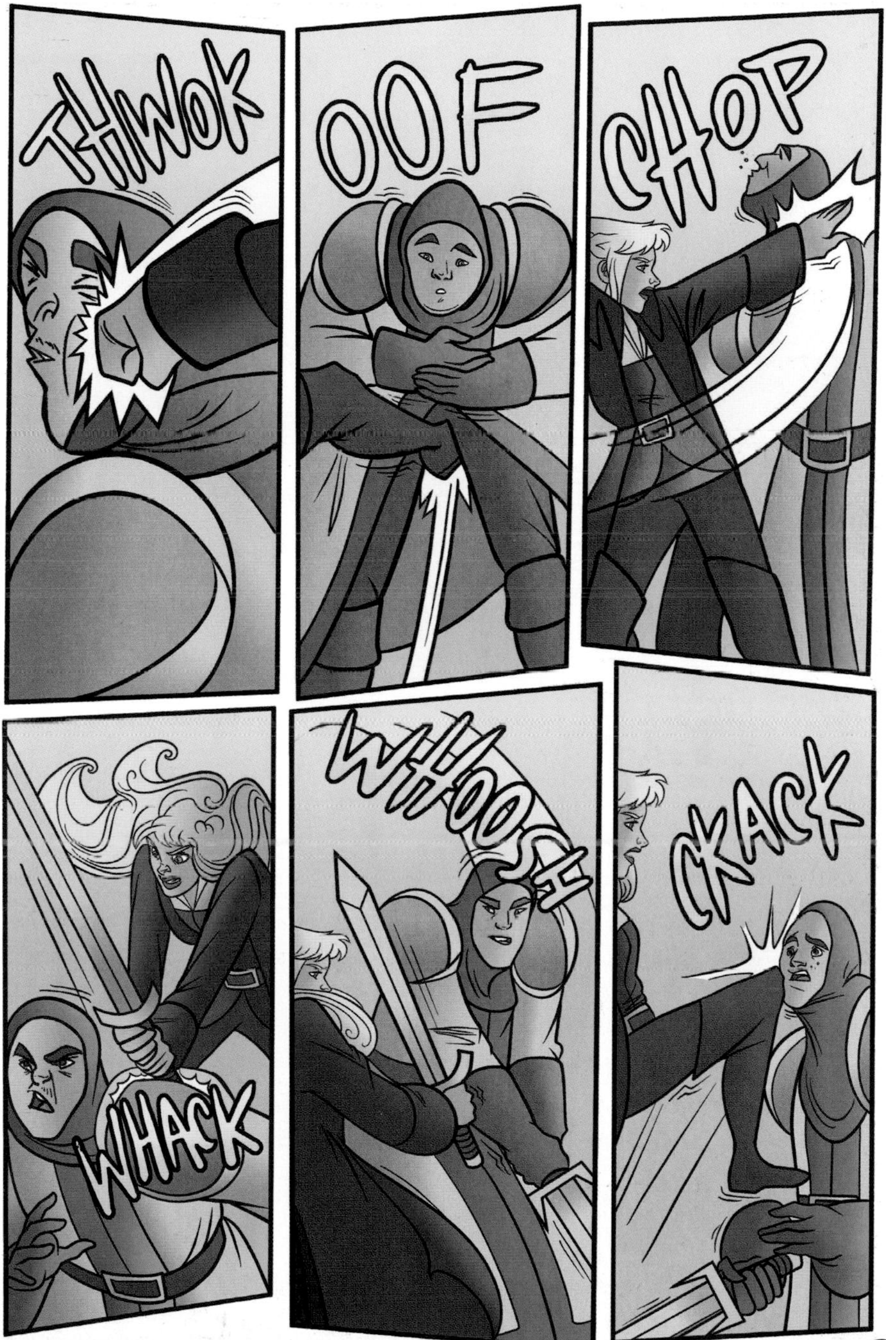
THWOK
OOF
CHOP
WHACK
WHOOSH
CRACK

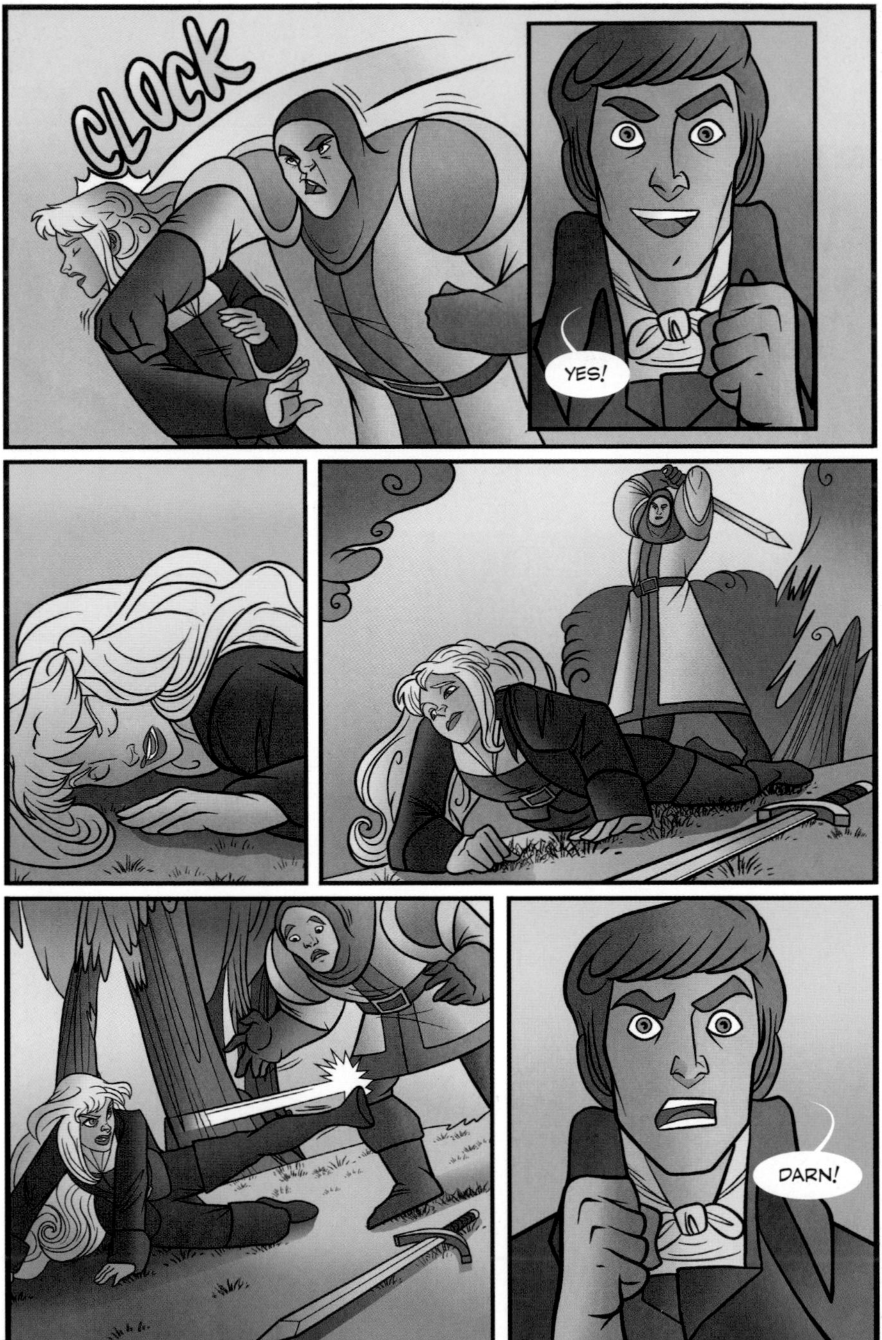
CLOCK
YES!
DARN!

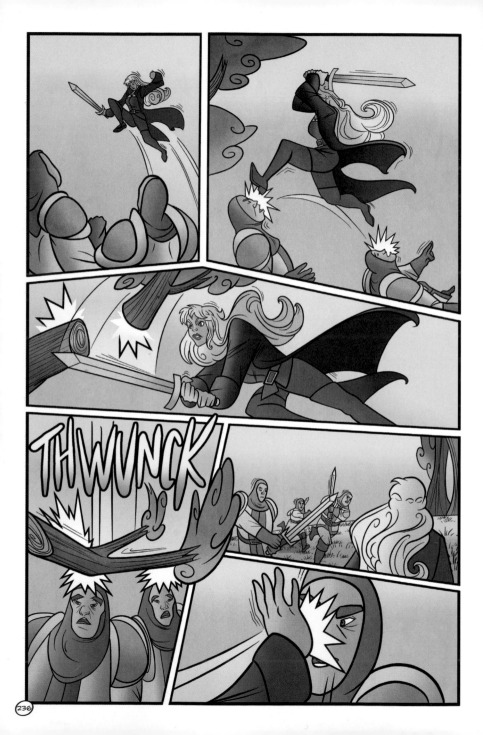

THWUNCK

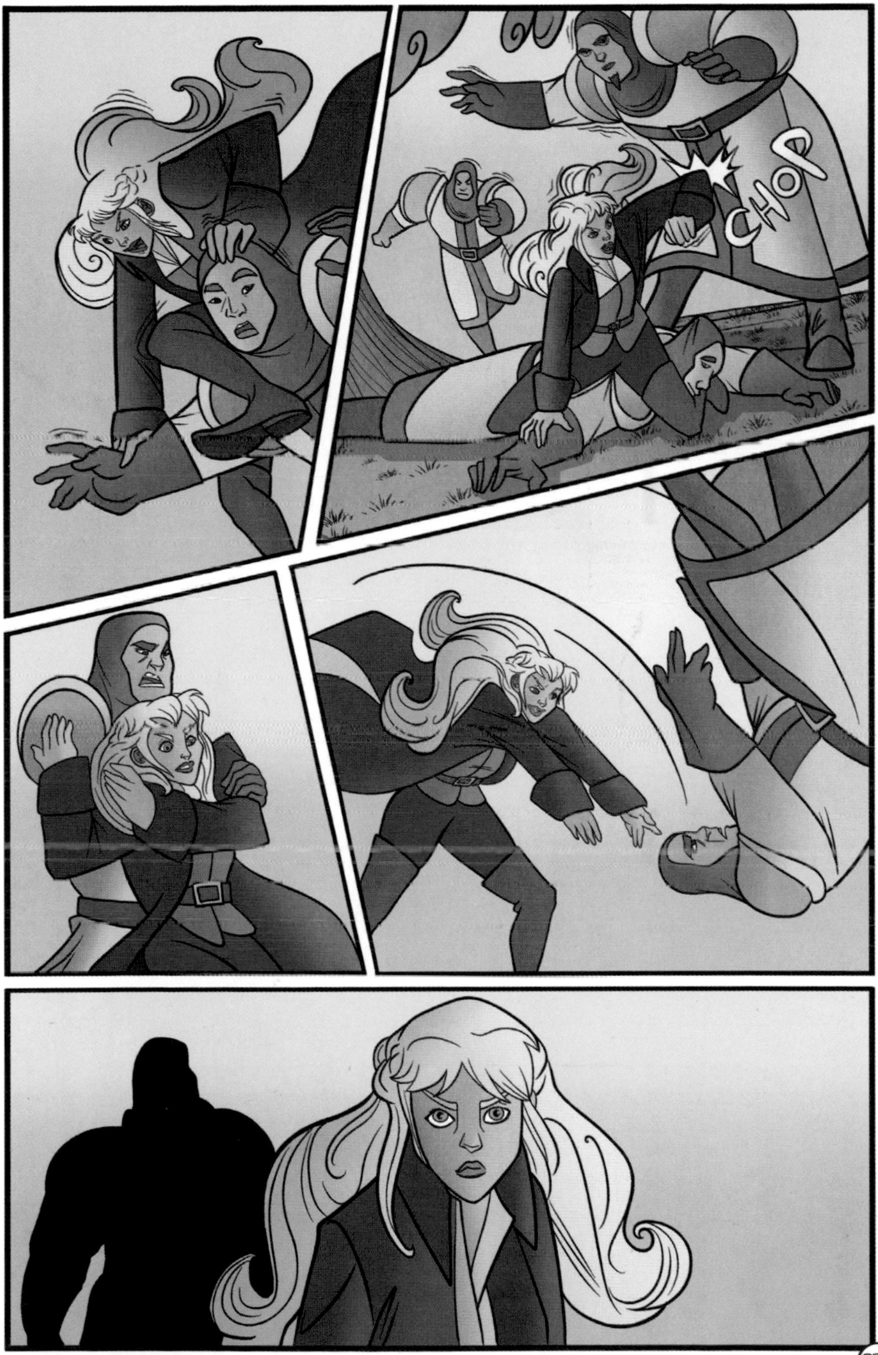
CHOP

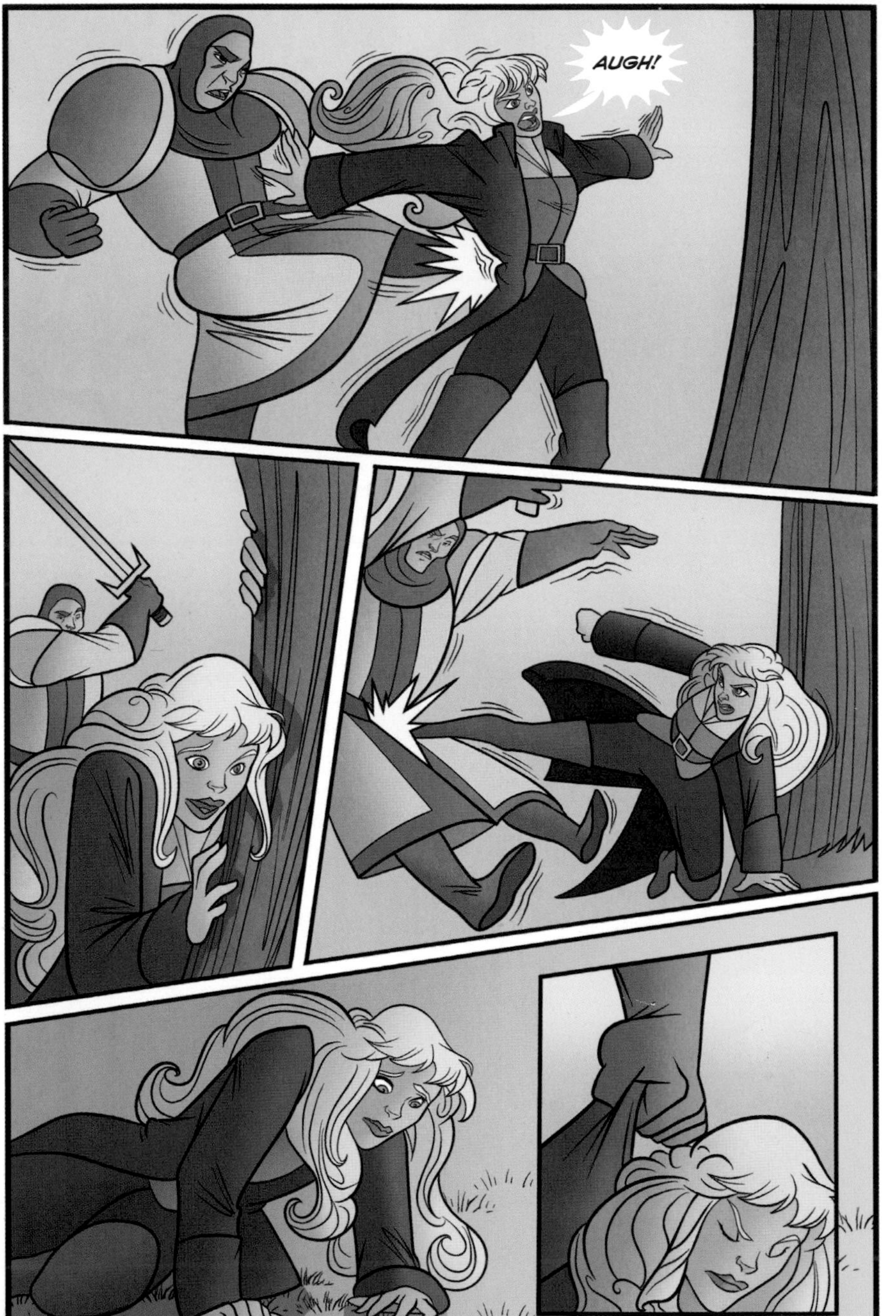
AUGH!

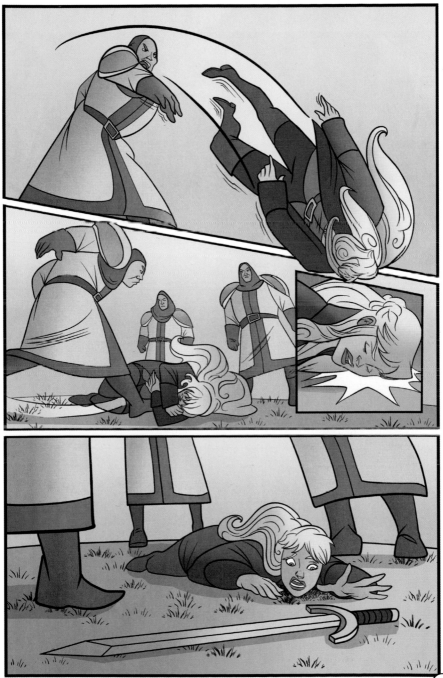

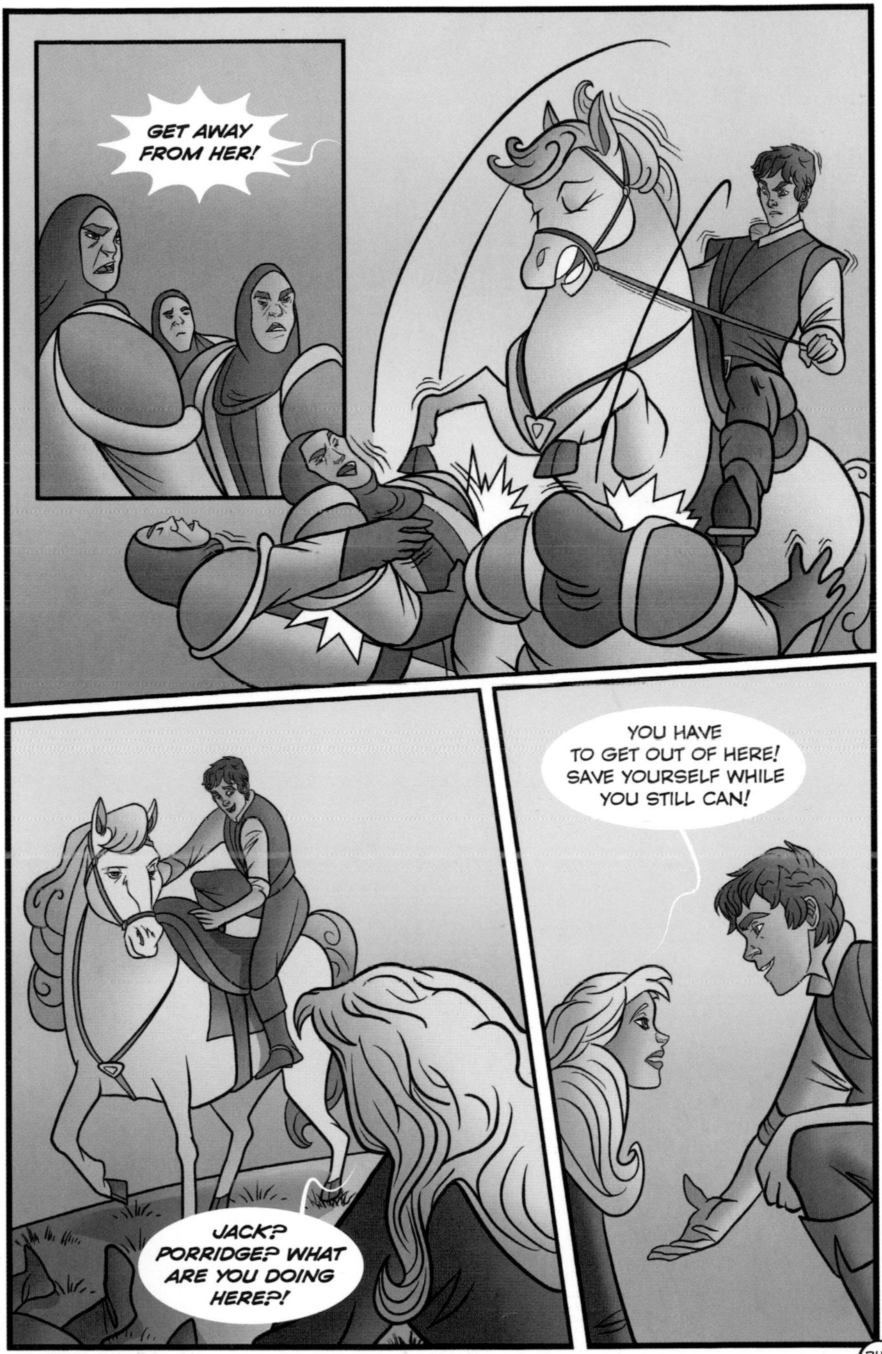
GET AWAY FROM HER!
JACK? PORRIDGE? WHAT ARE YOU DOING HERE?!
YOU HAVE TO GET OUT OF HERE! SAVE YOURSELF WHILE YOU STILL CAN!

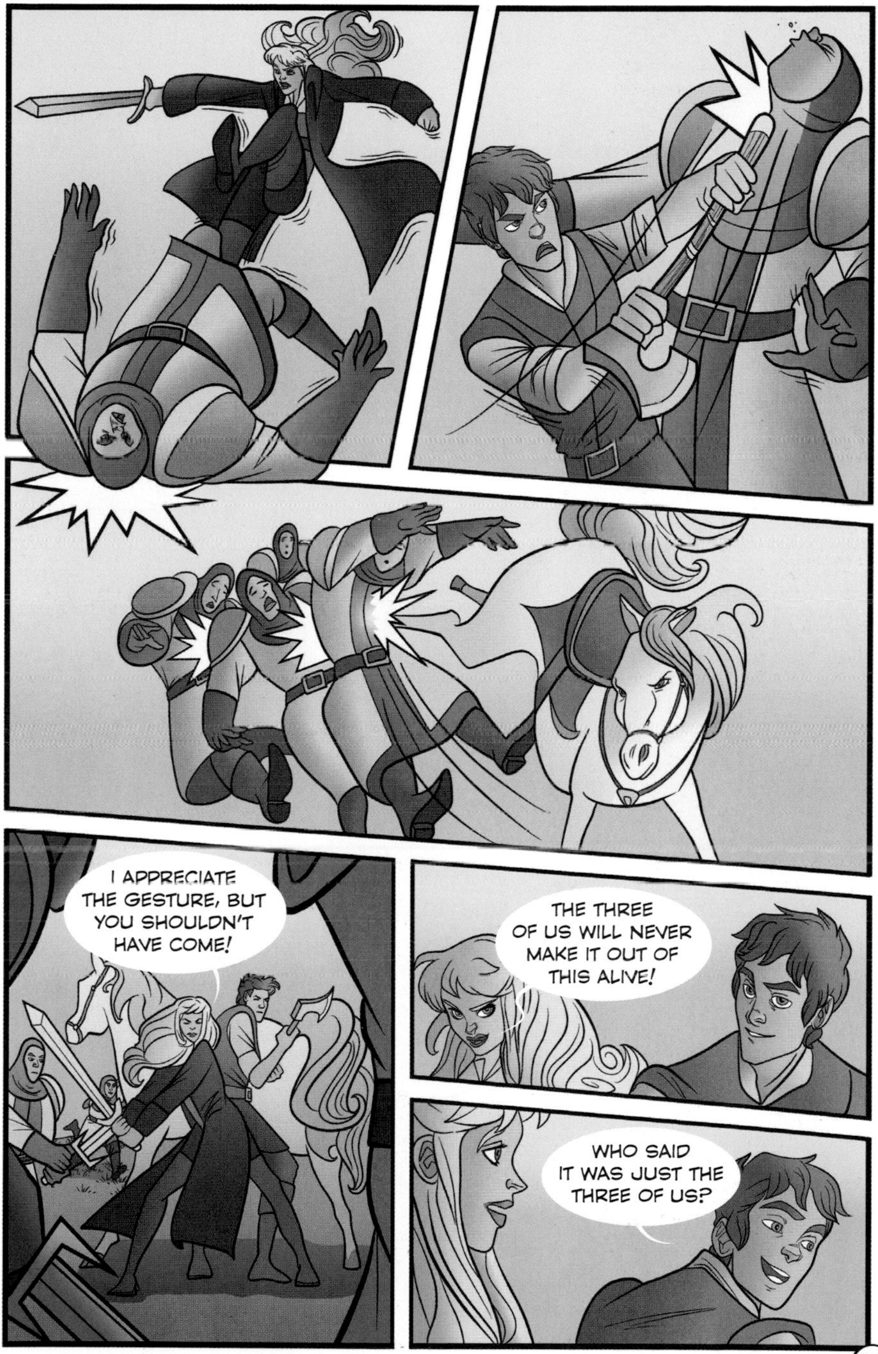
I APPRECIATE THE GESTURE, BUT YOU SHOULDN'T HAVE COME!
THE THREE OF US WILL NEVER MAKE IT OUT OF THIS ALIVE!
WHO SAID IT WAS JUST THE THREE OF US?

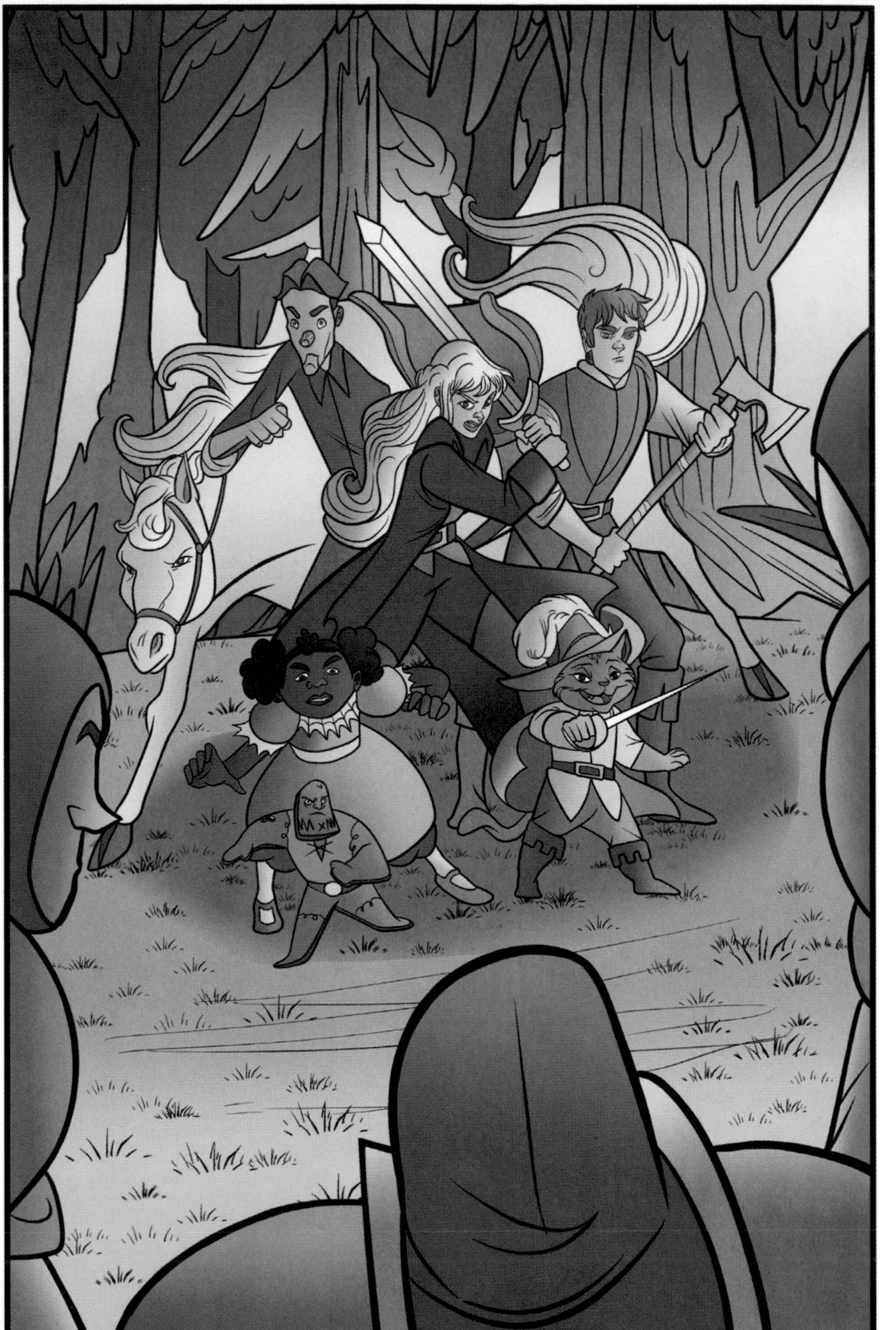

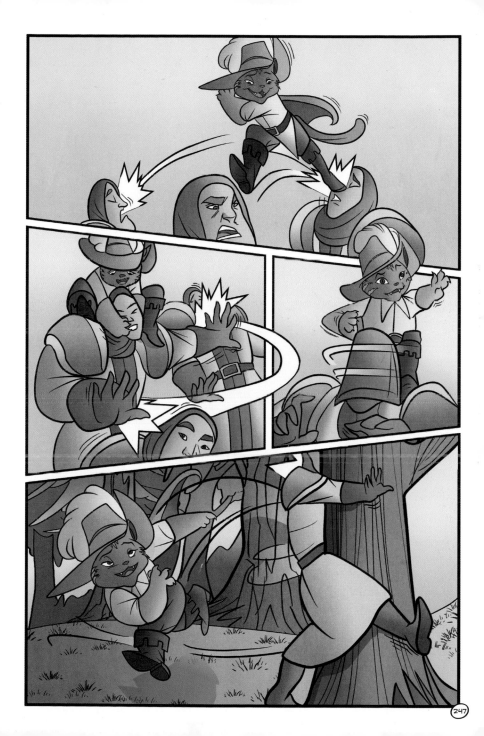

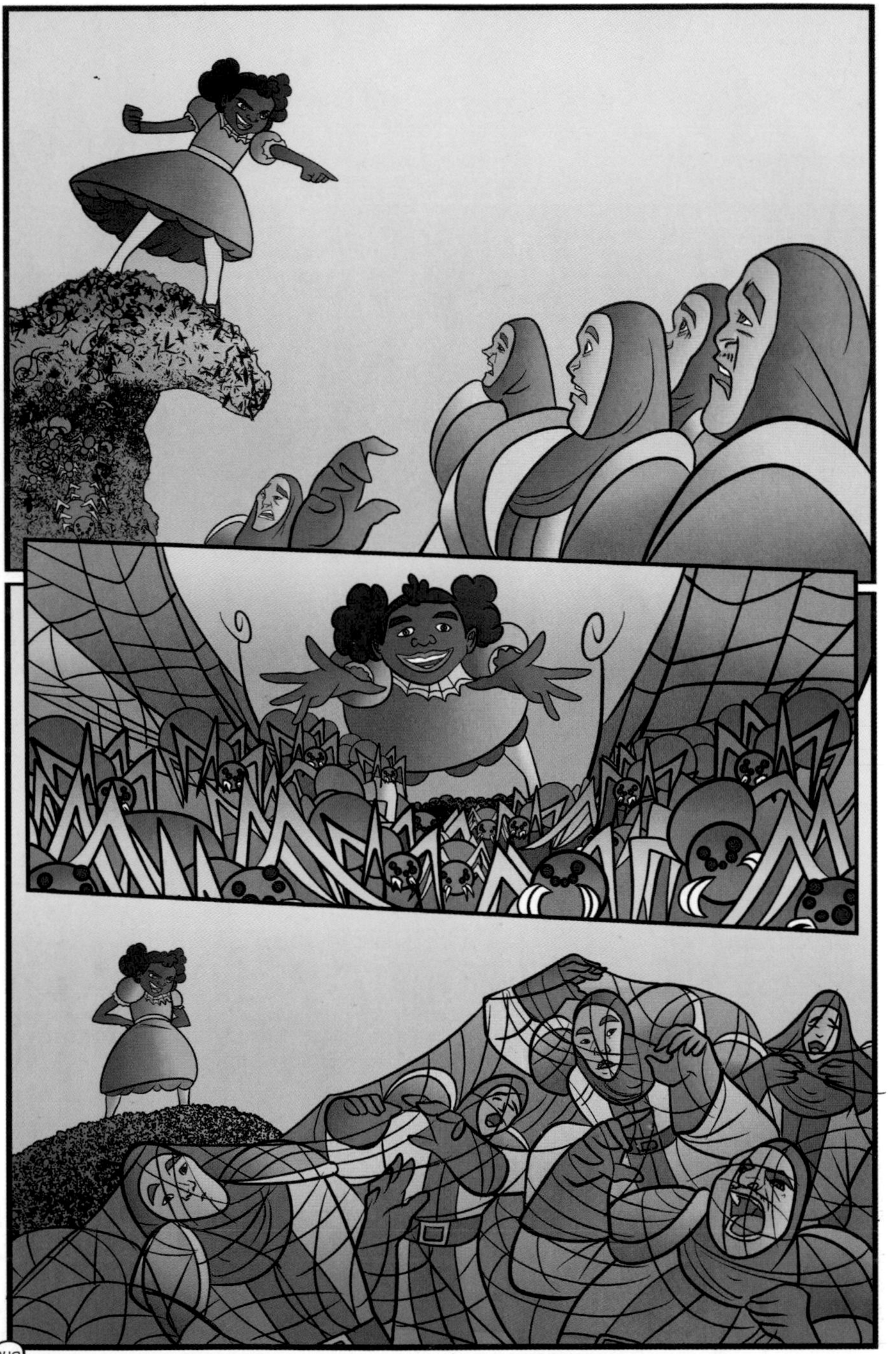

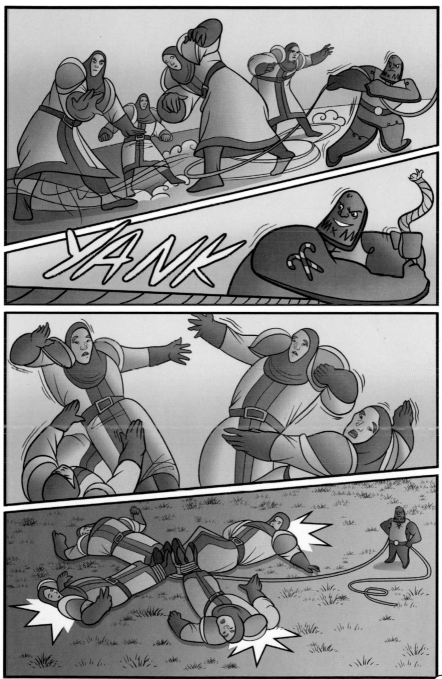

YANK

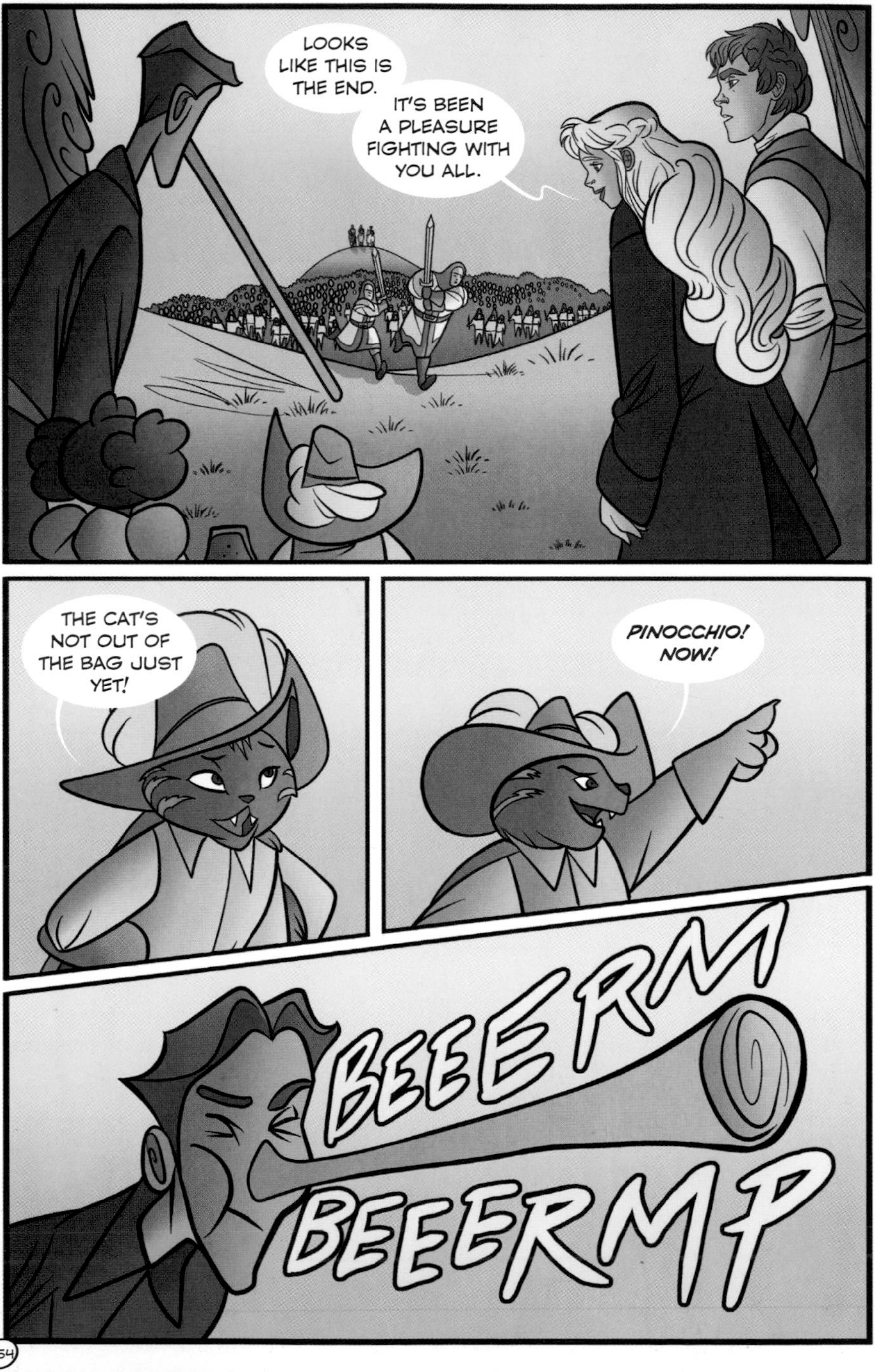
LOOKS LIKE THIS IS THE END.
IT'S BEEN A PLEASURE FIGHTING WITH YOU ALL.
THE CAT'S NOT OUT OF THE BAG JUST YET!
PINOCCHIO! NOW!
BEEERM
BEEERMP

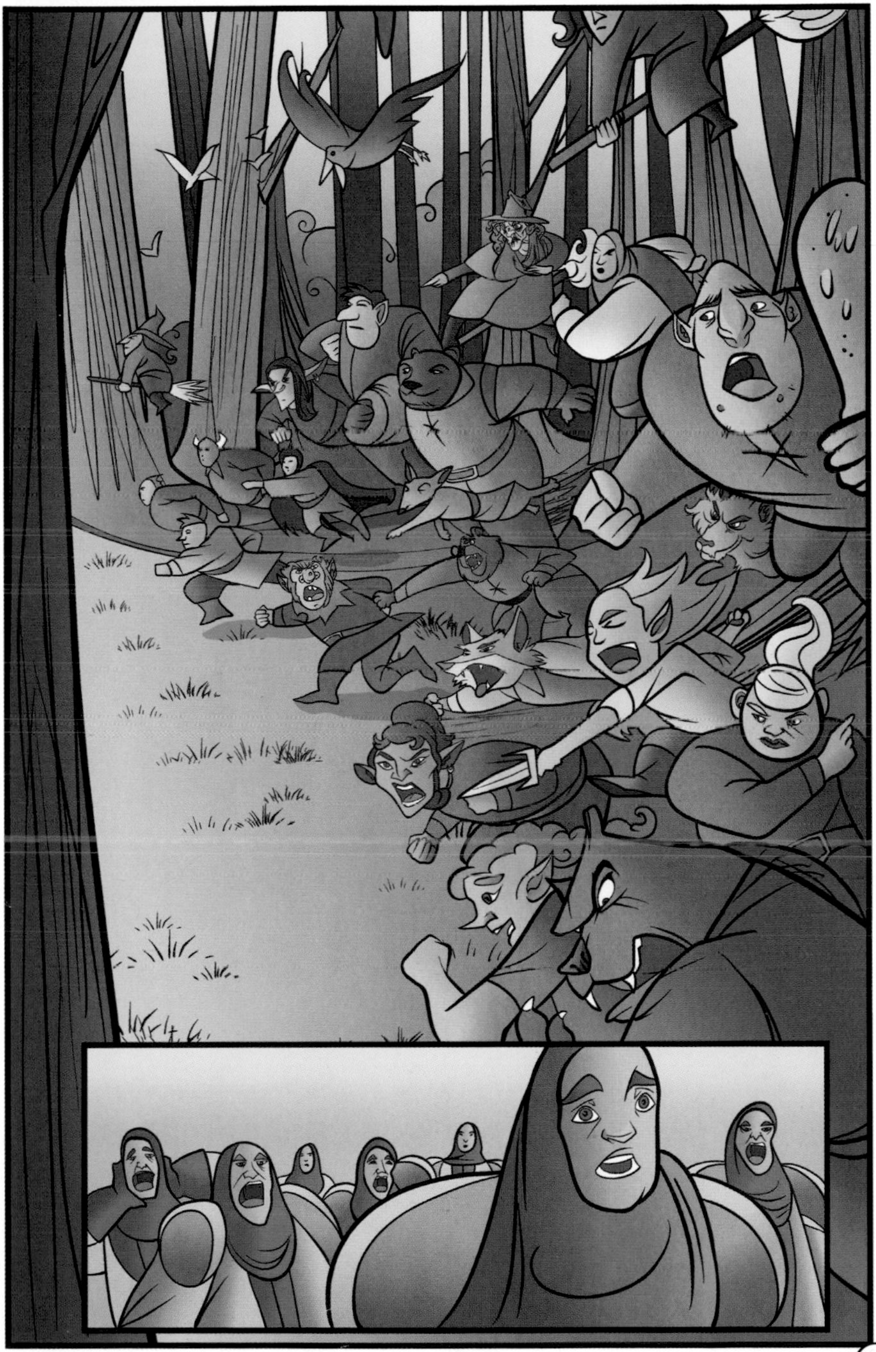

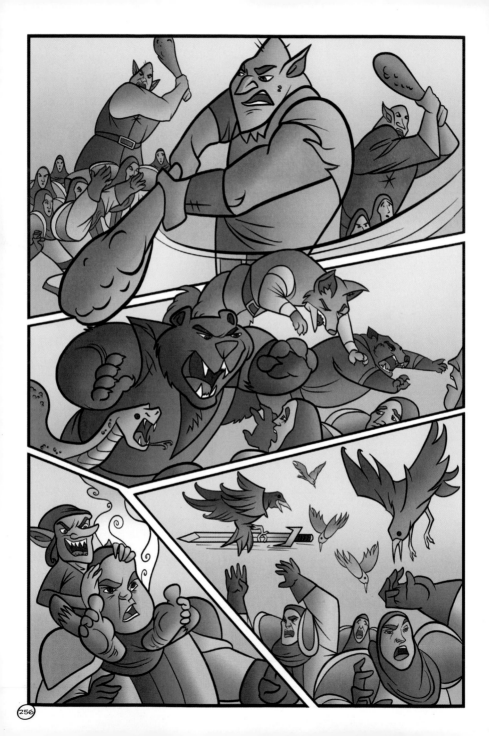

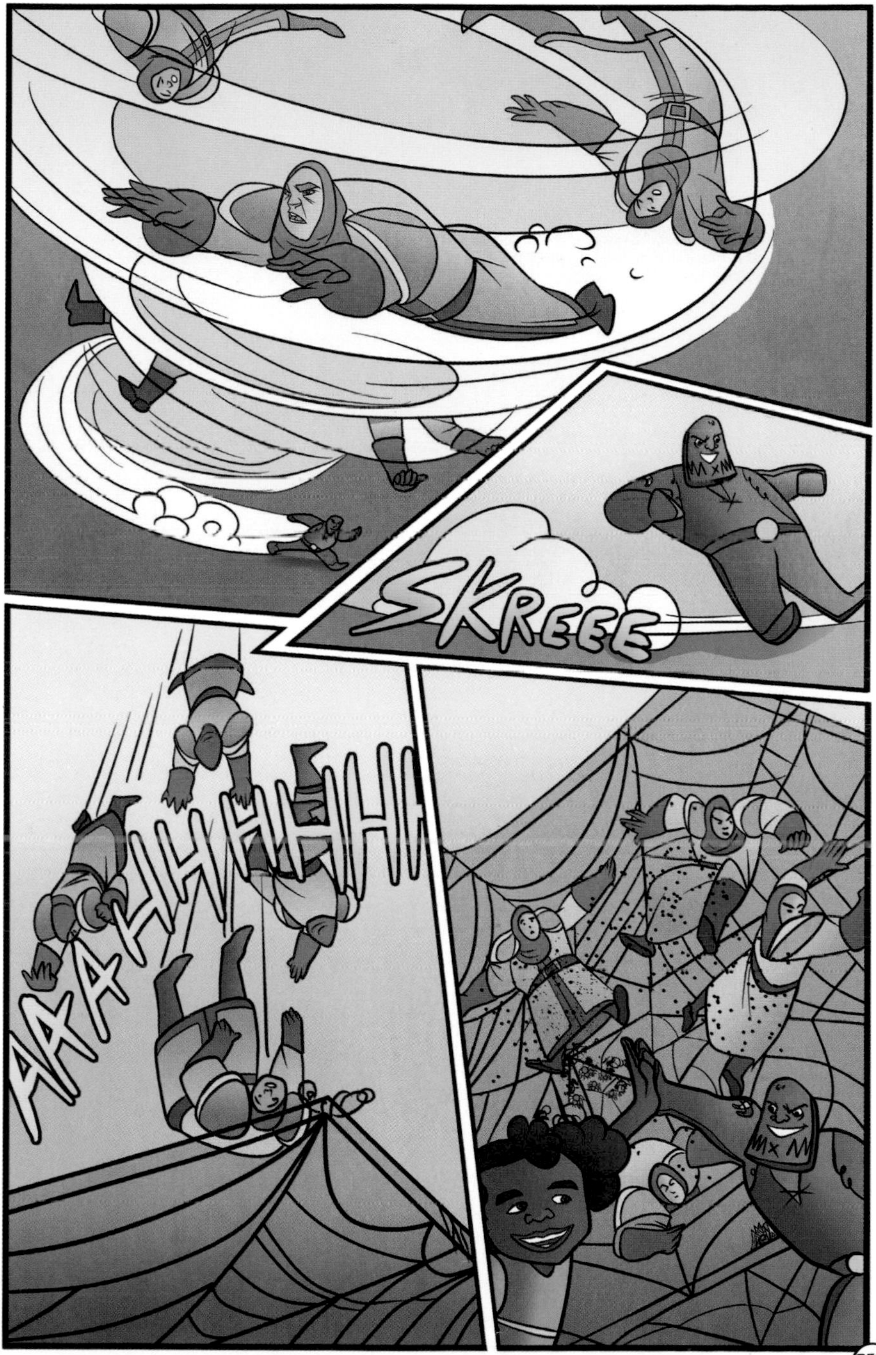
SKREEE
AAAHHHHHH

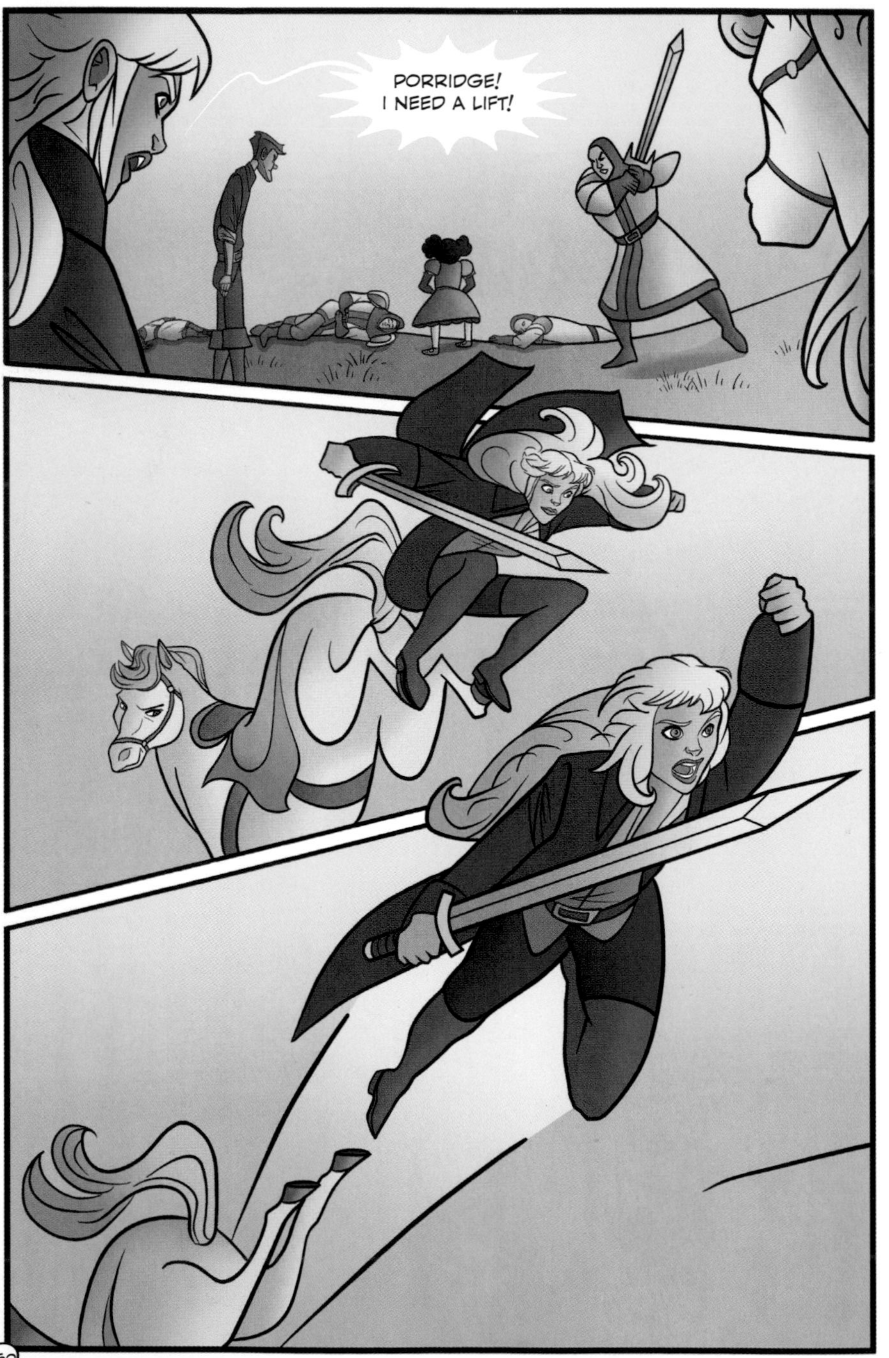
PORRIDGE!
I NEED A LIFT!

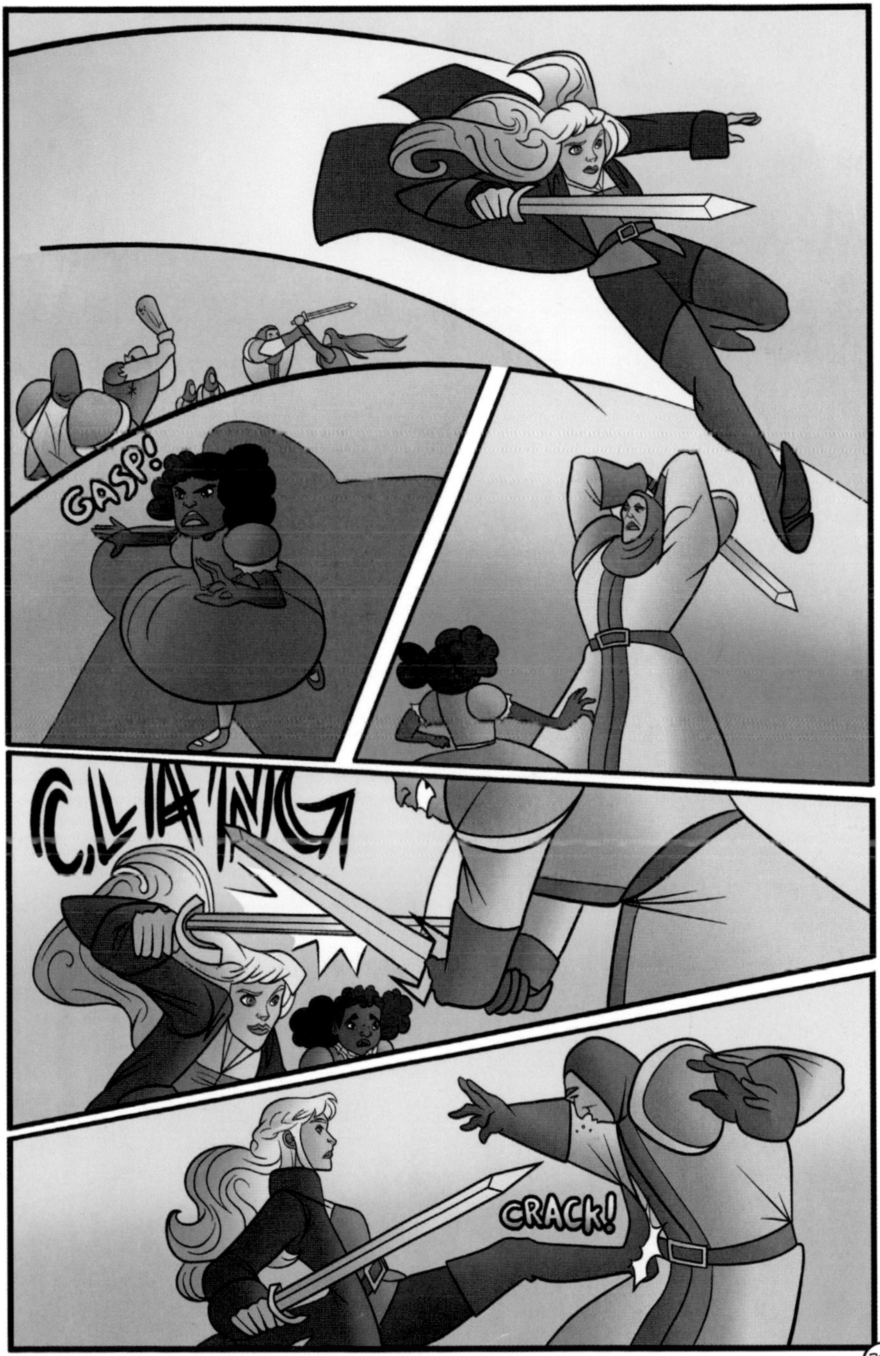
GASP!
CLANG
CRACK!

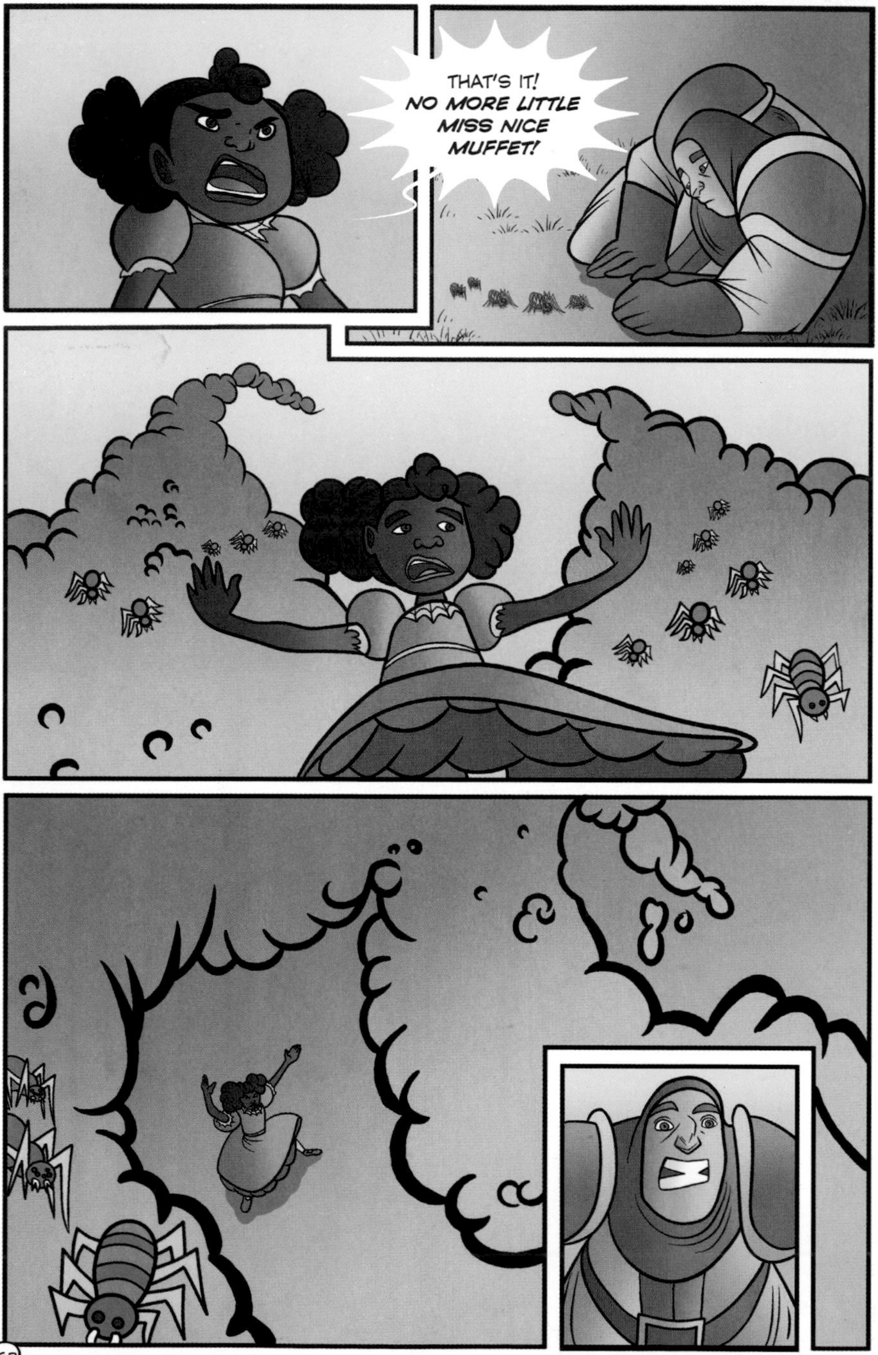
THAT'S IT!
NO MORE LITTLE MISS NICE MUFFET!

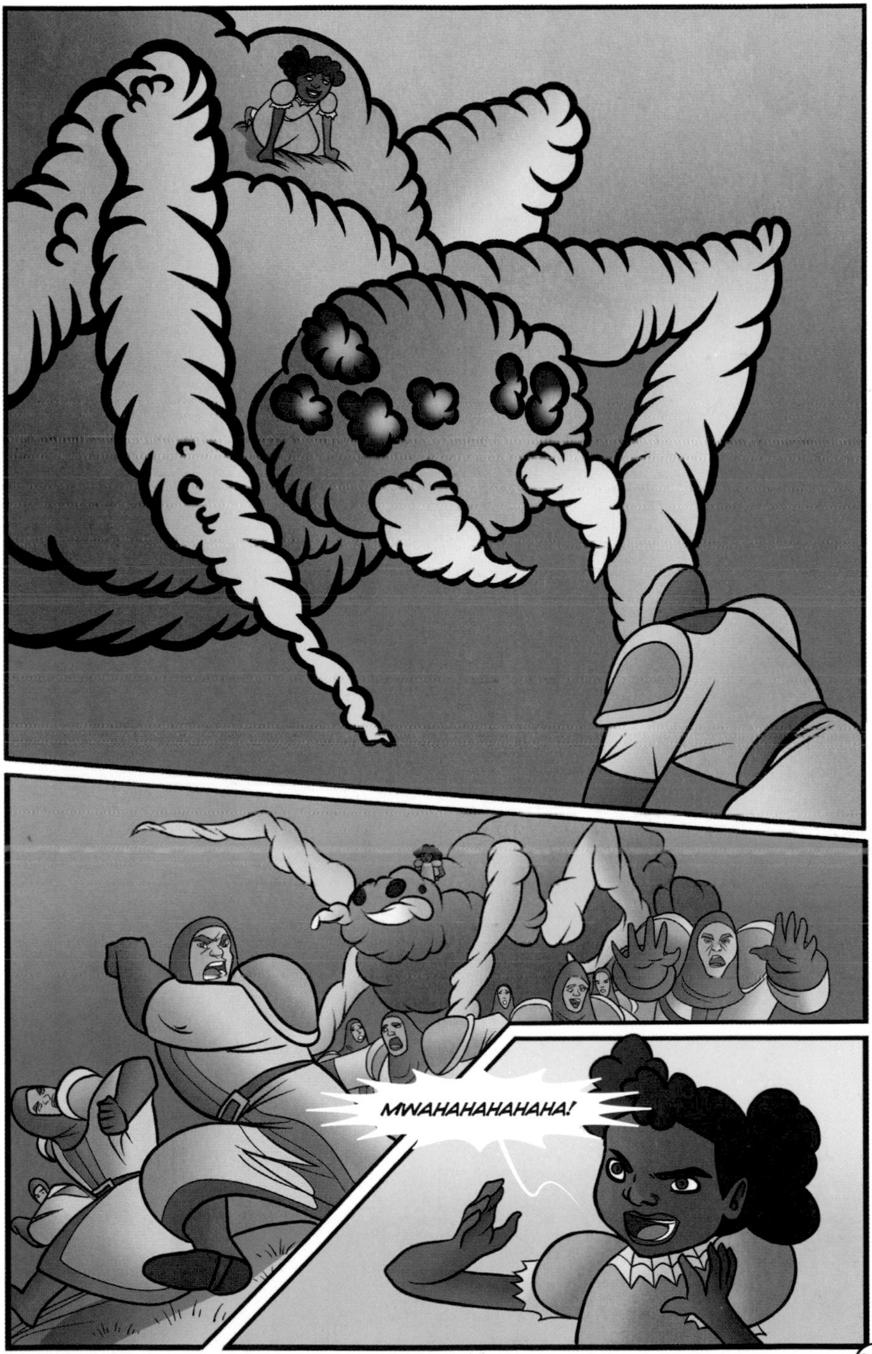
MWAHAHAHAHAHA!

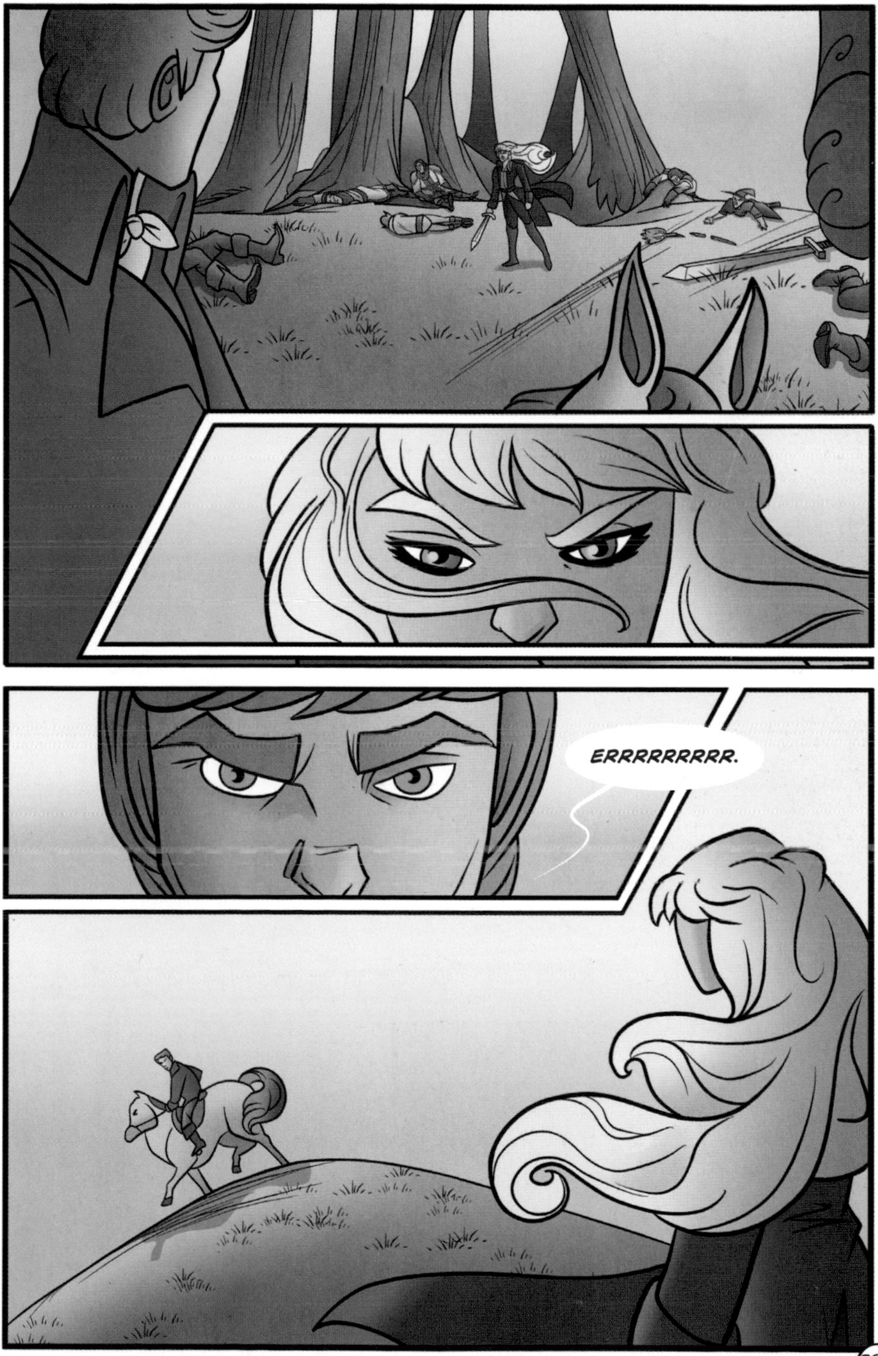
ERRRRRRRRR.

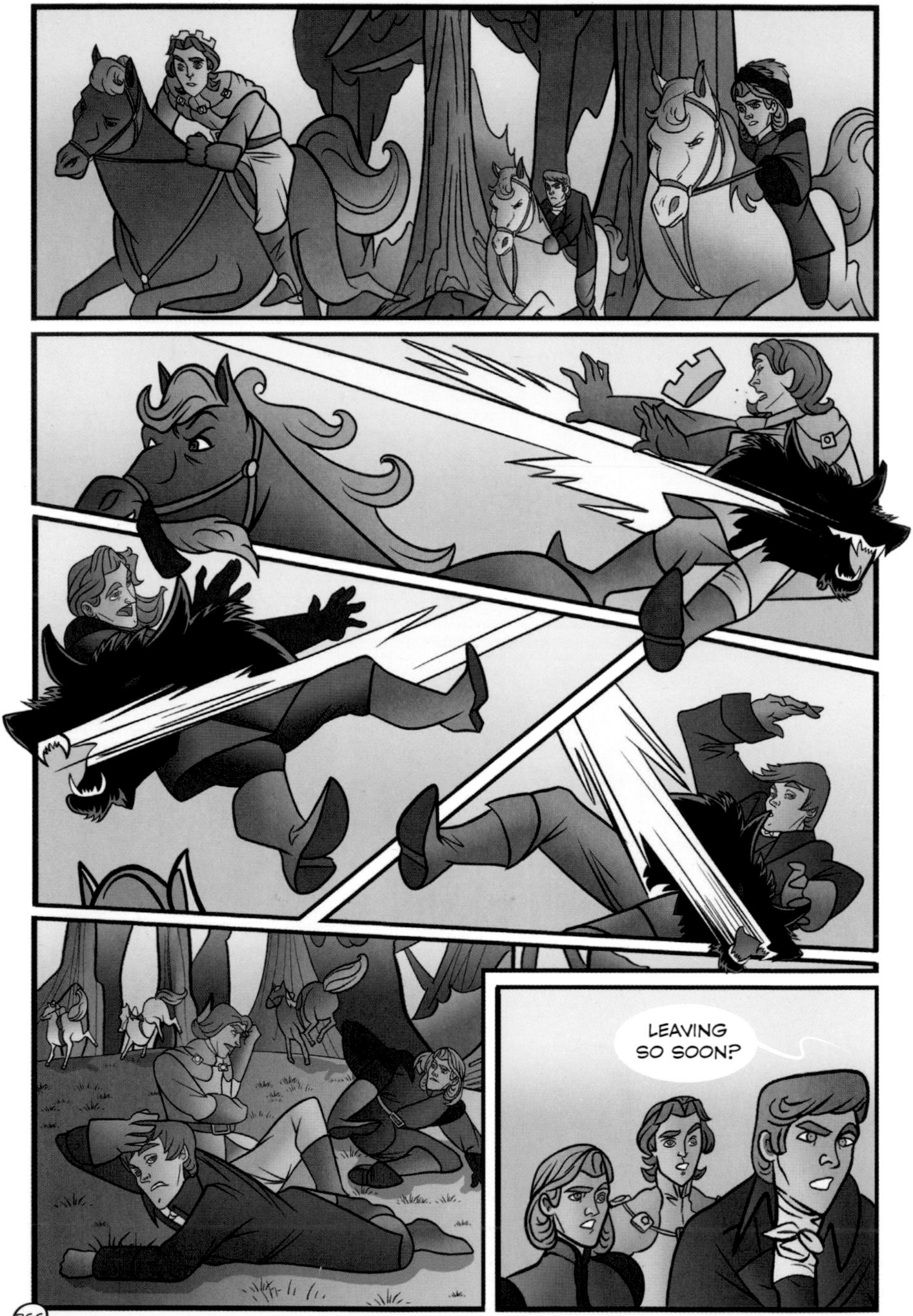
LEAVING SO SOON?

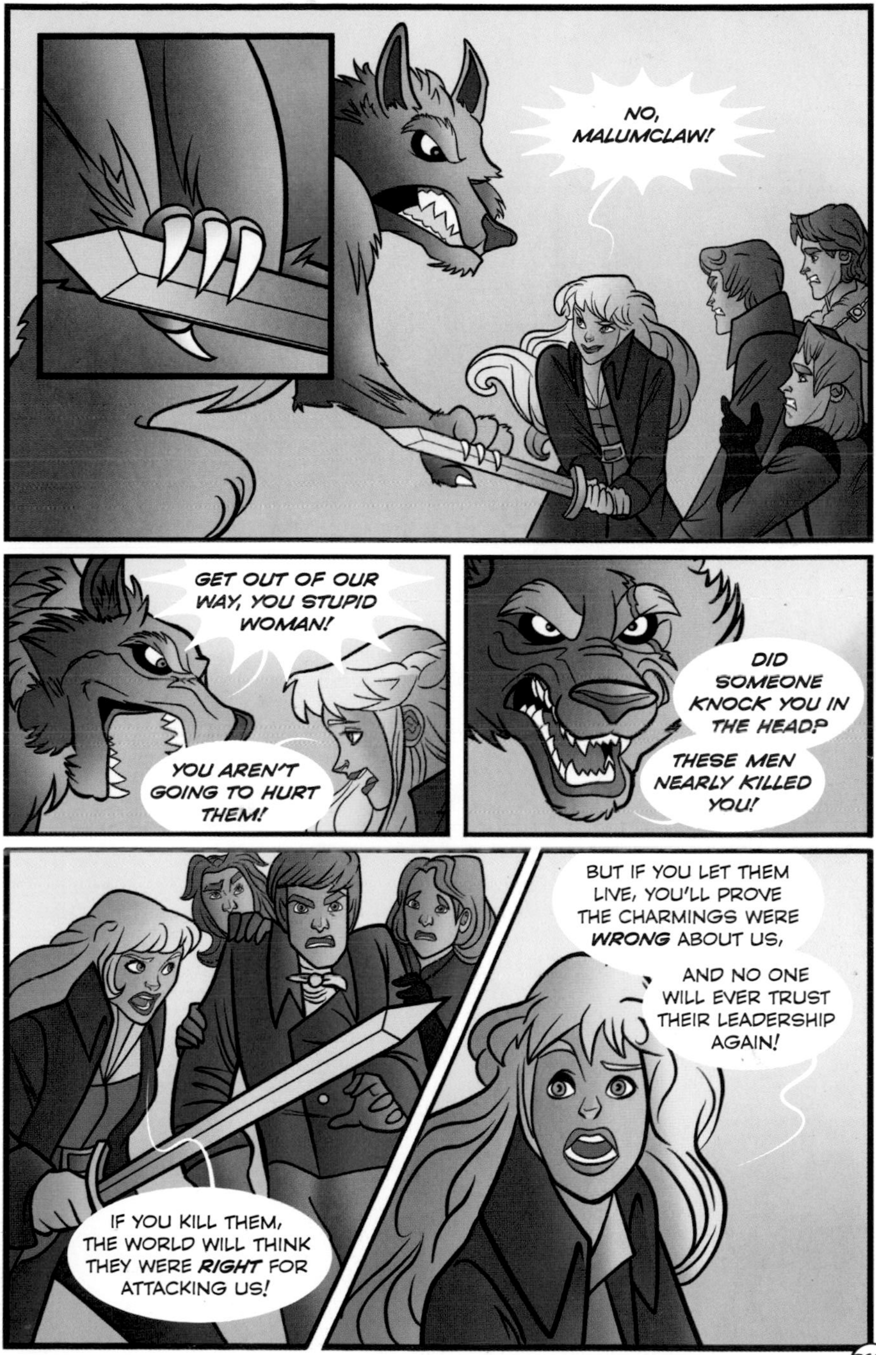
NO, MALUMCLAW!
GET OUT OF OUR WAY, YOU STUPID WOMAN!
YOU AREN'T GOING TO HURT THEM!
DID SOMEONE KNOCK YOU IN THE HEAD?
THESE MEN NEARLY KILLED YOU!
IF YOU KILL THEM, THE WORLD WILL THINK THEY WERE RIGHT FOR ATTACKING US!
BUT IF YOU LET THEM LIVE, YOU'LL PROVE THE CHARMINGS WERE WRONG ABOUT US,
AND NO ONE WILL EVER TRUST THEIR LEADERSHIP AGAIN!

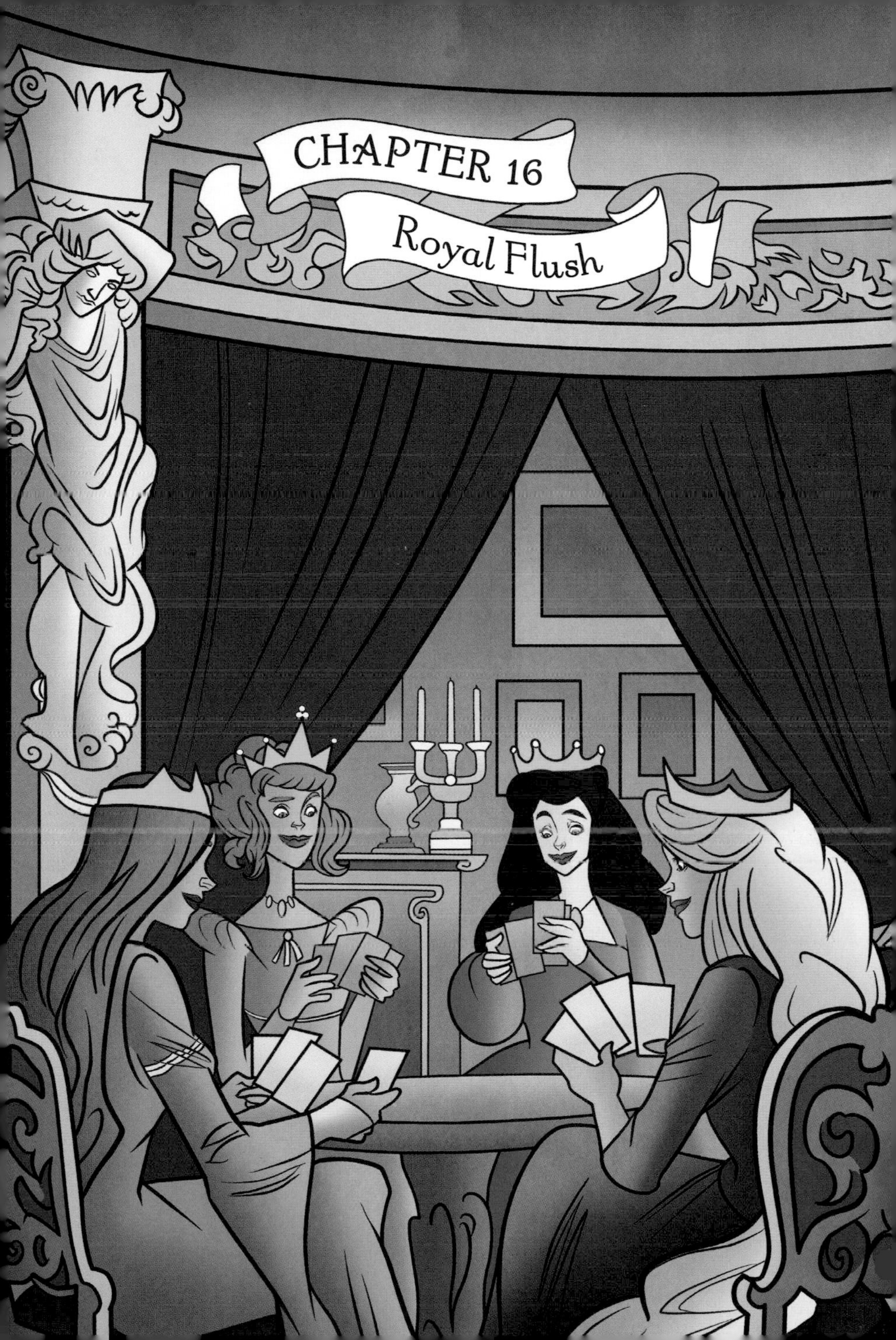
CHAPTER 16
Royal Flush

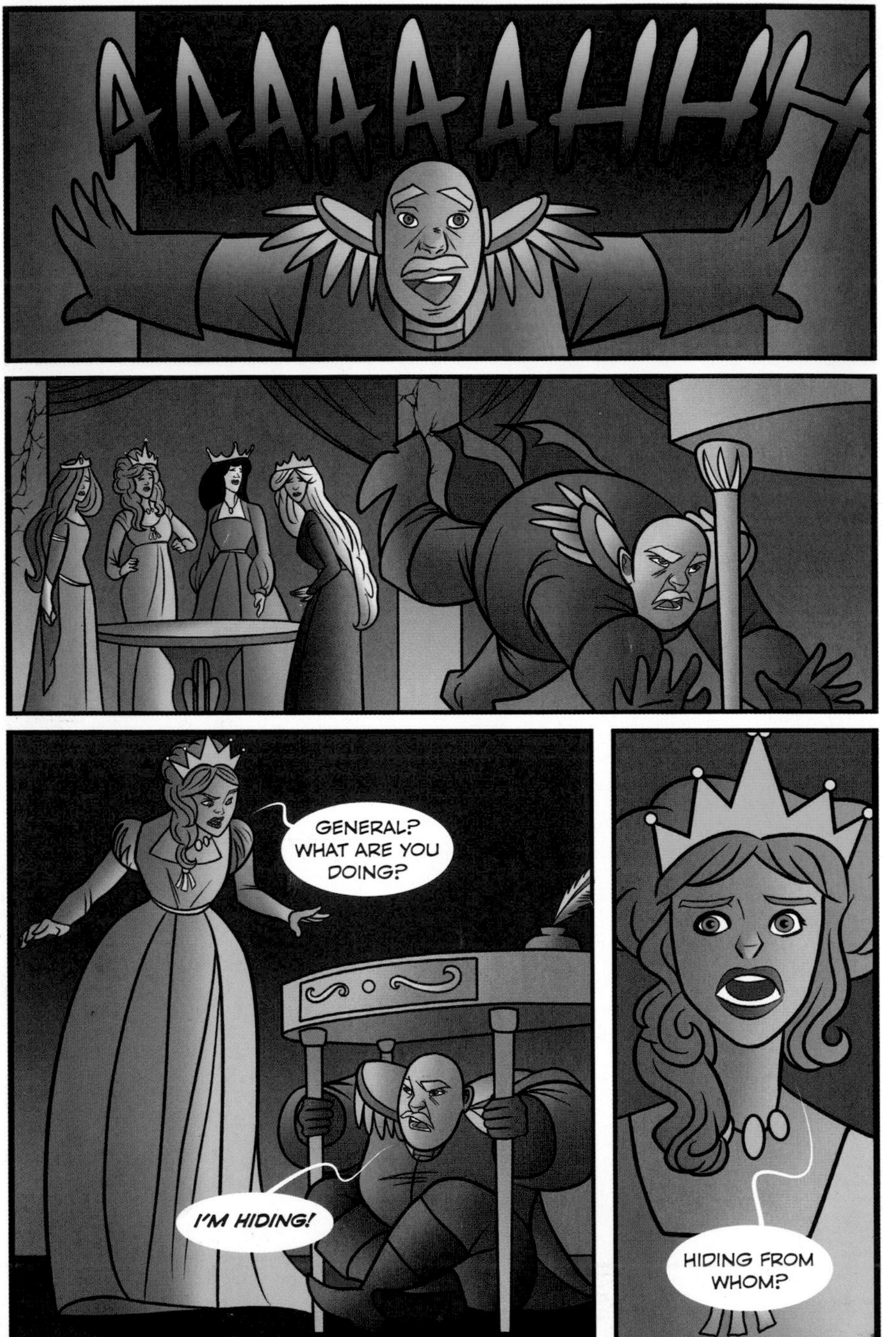
AAAAAAHHH
GENERAL? WHAT ARE YOU DOING?
I'M HIDING!
HIDING FROM WHOM?

CHAPTER 17

Just Beginning

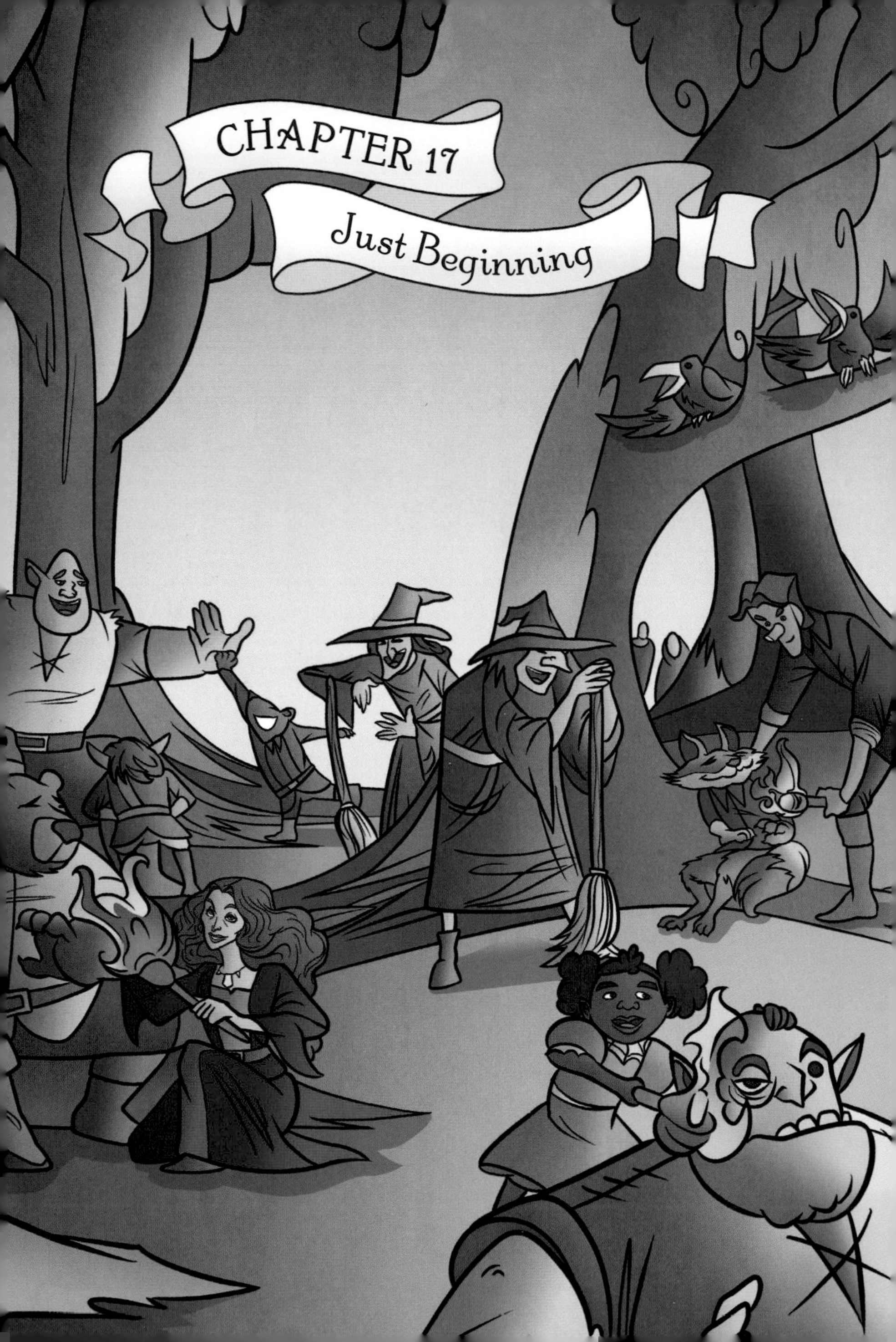

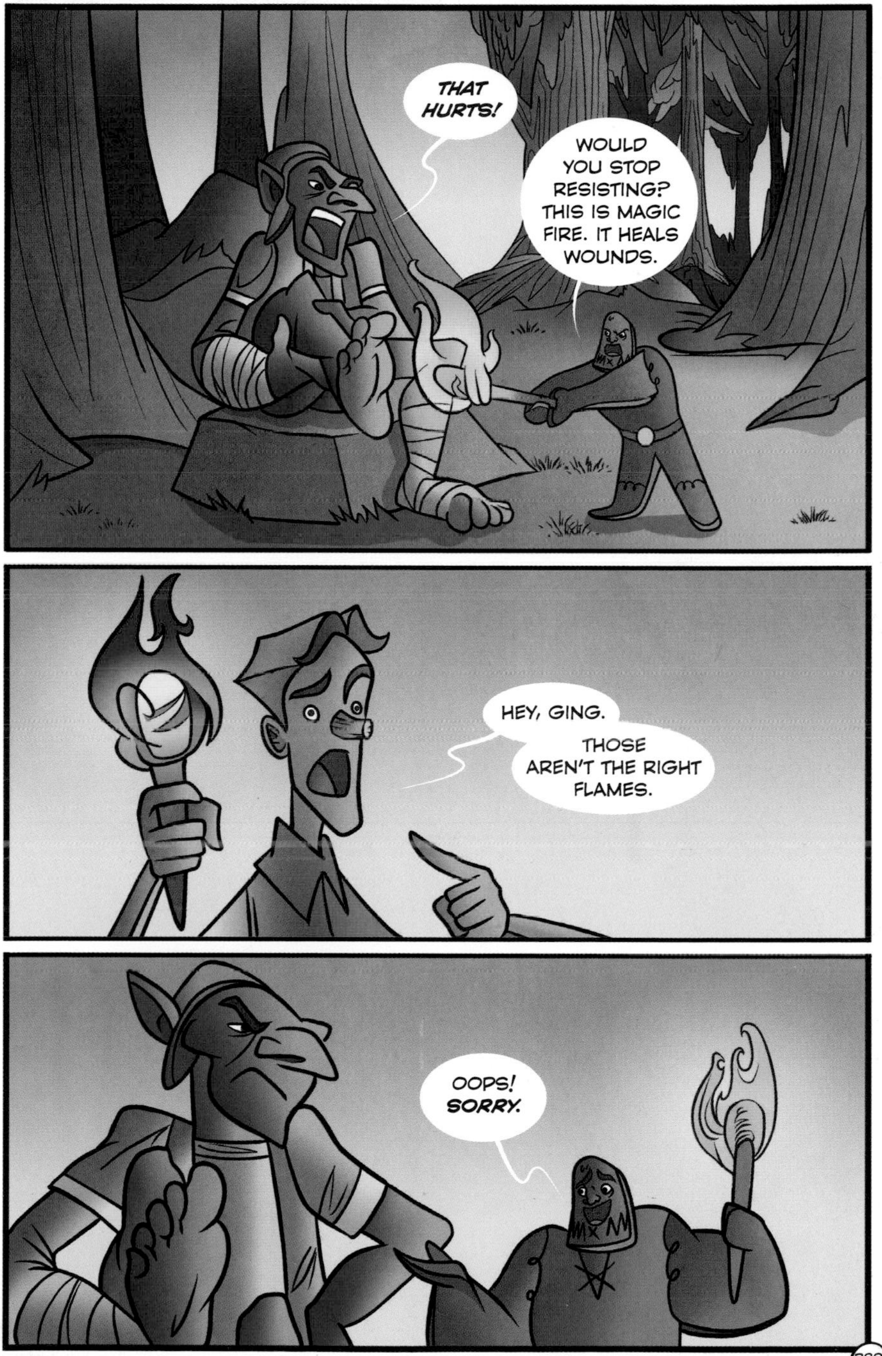

THAT HURTS!
WOULD YOU STOP RESISTING? THIS IS MAGIC FIRE. IT HEALS WOUNDS.
HEY, GING.
THOSE AREN'T THE RIGHT FLAMES.
OOPS! SORRY.

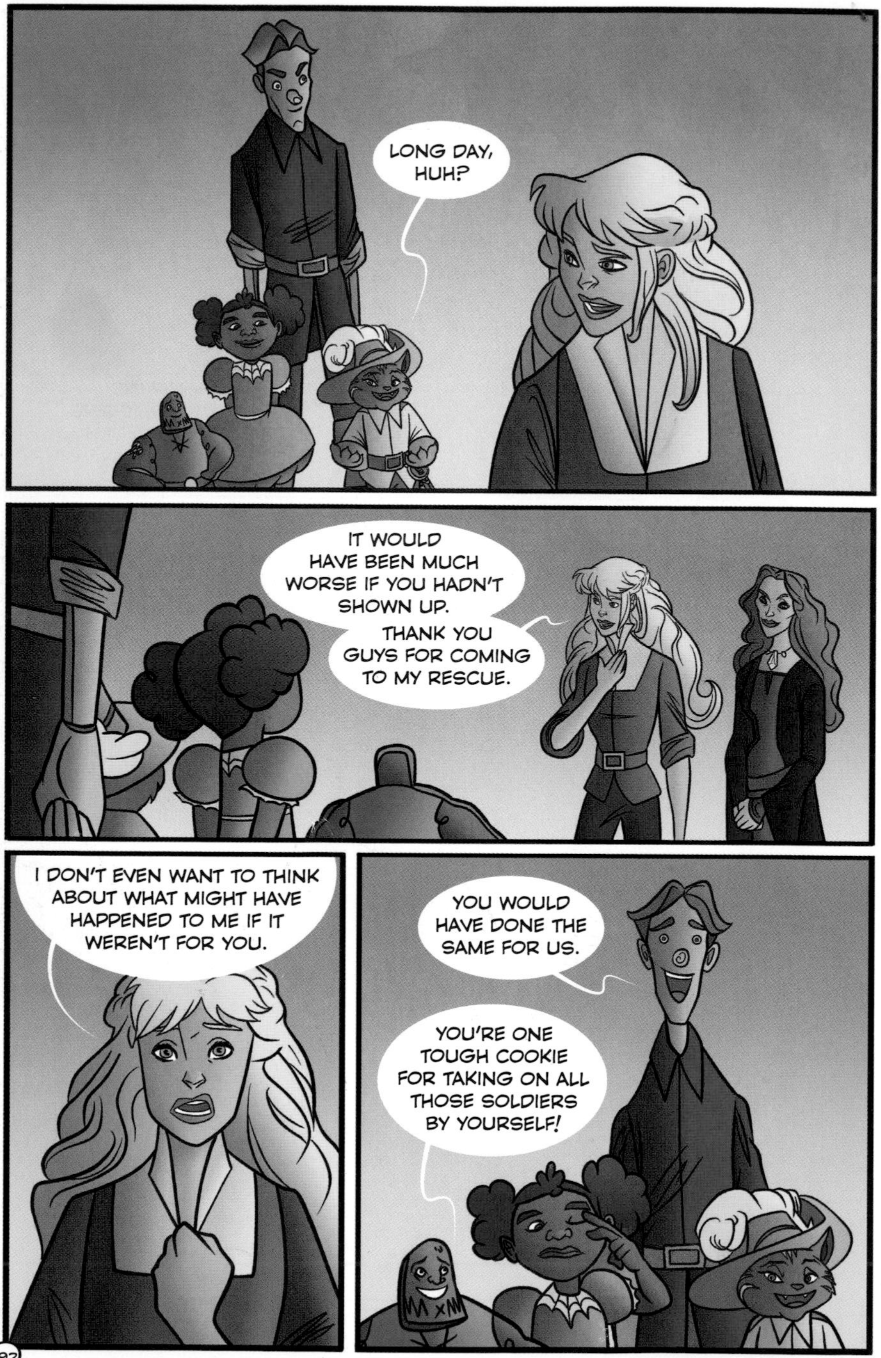
LONG DAY, HUH?
IT WOULD HAVE BEEN MUCH WORSE IF YOU HADN'T SHOWN UP.
THANK YOU GUYS FOR COMING TO MY RESCUE.
I DON'T EVEN WANT TO THINK ABOUT WHAT MIGHT HAVE HAPPENED TO ME IF IT WEREN'T FOR YOU.
YOU WOULD HAVE DONE THE SAME FOR US.
YOU'RE ONE TOUGH COOKIE FOR TAKING ON ALL THOSE SOLDIERS BY YOURSELF!

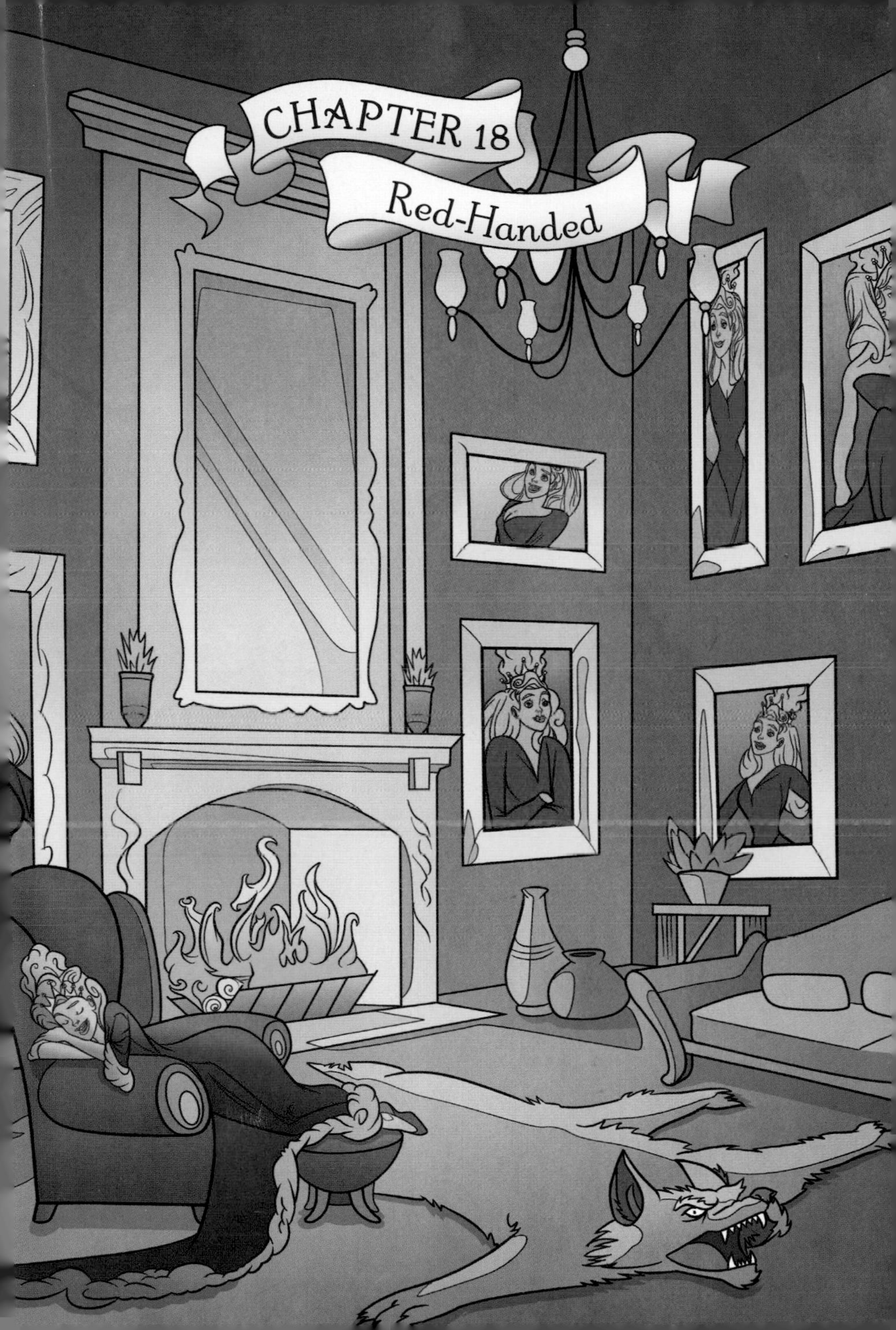
CHAPTER 18
Red-Handed

307

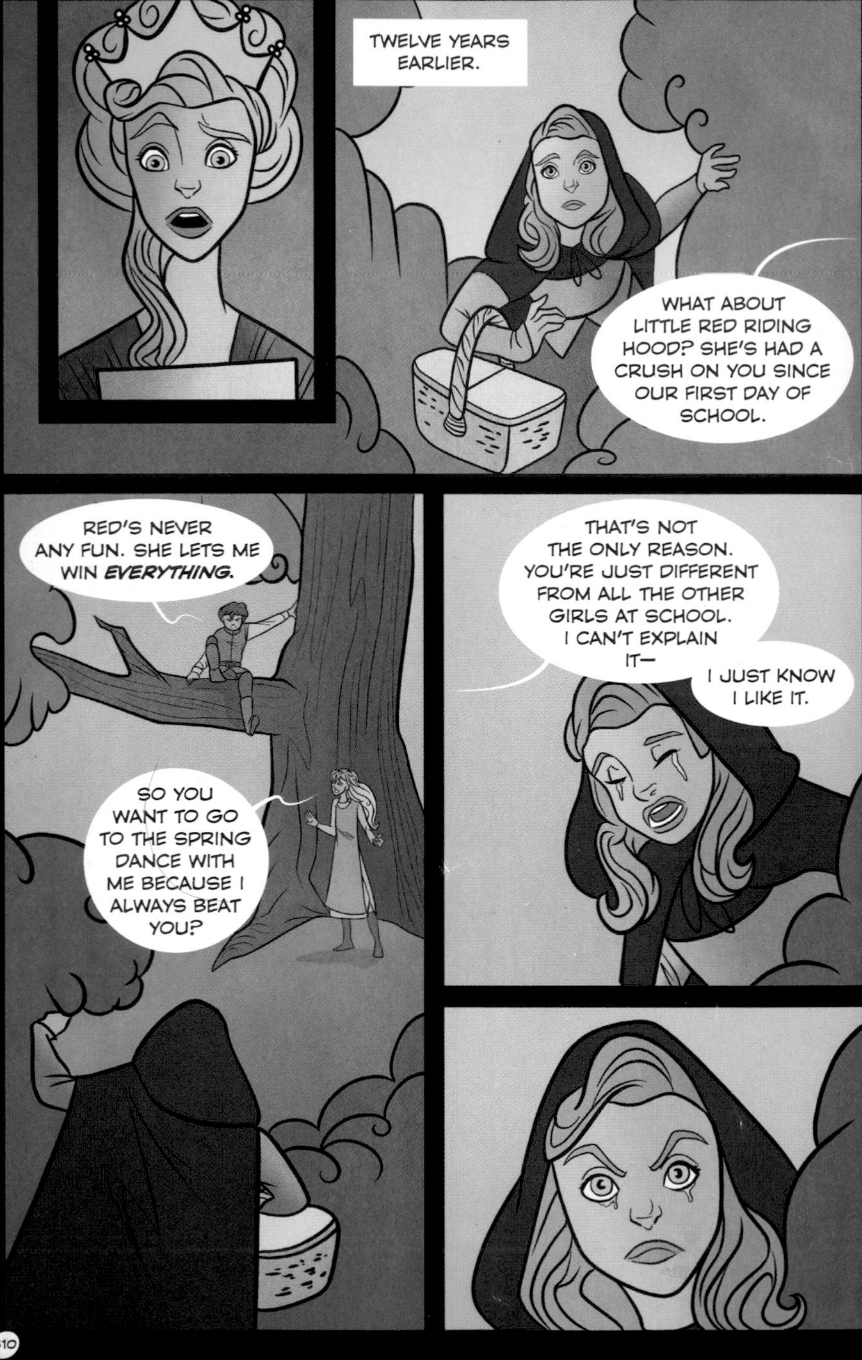
TWELVE YEARS EARLIER.
WHAT ABOUT LITTLE RED RIDING HOOD? SHE'S HAD A CRUSH ON YOU SINCE OUR FIRST DAY OF SCHOOL.
RED'S NEVER ANY FUN. SHE LETS ME WIN *EVERYTHING*.
SO YOU WANT TO GO TO THE SPRING DANCE WITH ME BECAUSE I ALWAYS BEAT YOU?
THAT'S NOT THE ONLY REASON. YOU'RE JUST DIFFERENT FROM ALL THE OTHER GIRLS AT SCHOOL. I CAN'T EXPLAIN IT—
I JUST KNOW I LIKE IT.

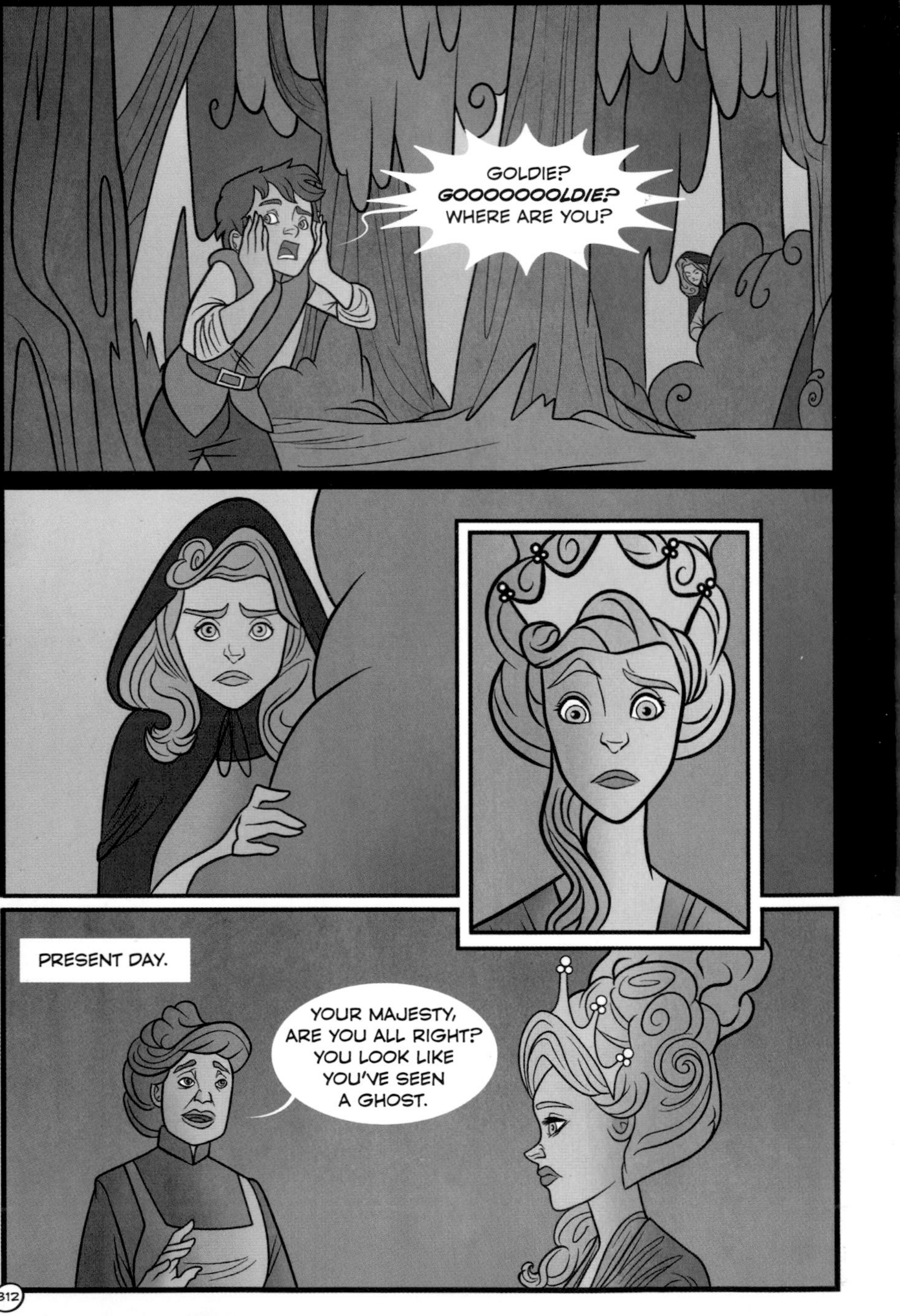
GOLDIE?
GOOOOOOOLDIE?
WHERE ARE YOU?
PRESENT DAY.
YOUR MAJESTY, ARE YOU ALL RIGHT? YOU LOOK LIKE YOU'VE SEEN A GHOST.

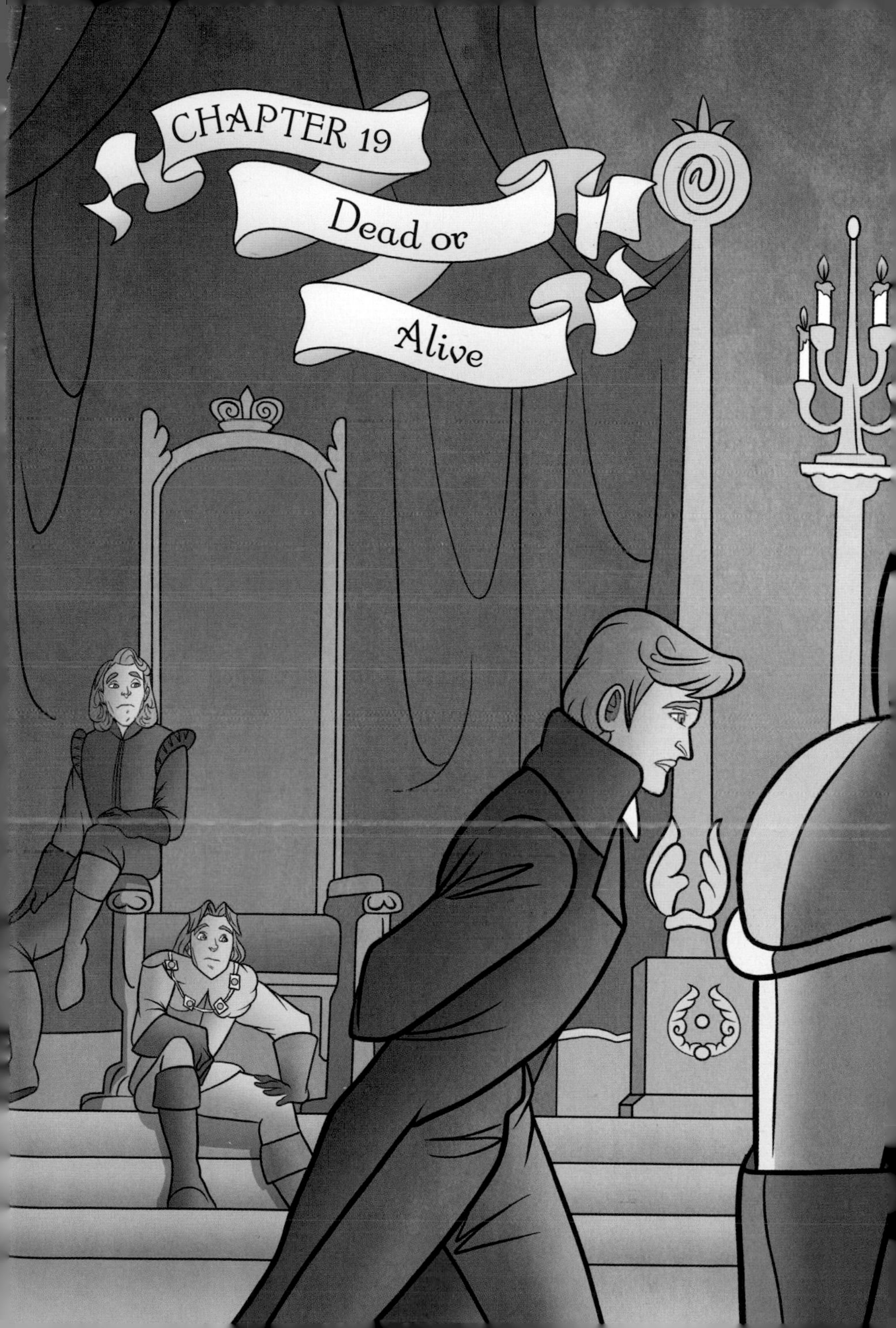
CHAPTER 19
Dead or
Alive

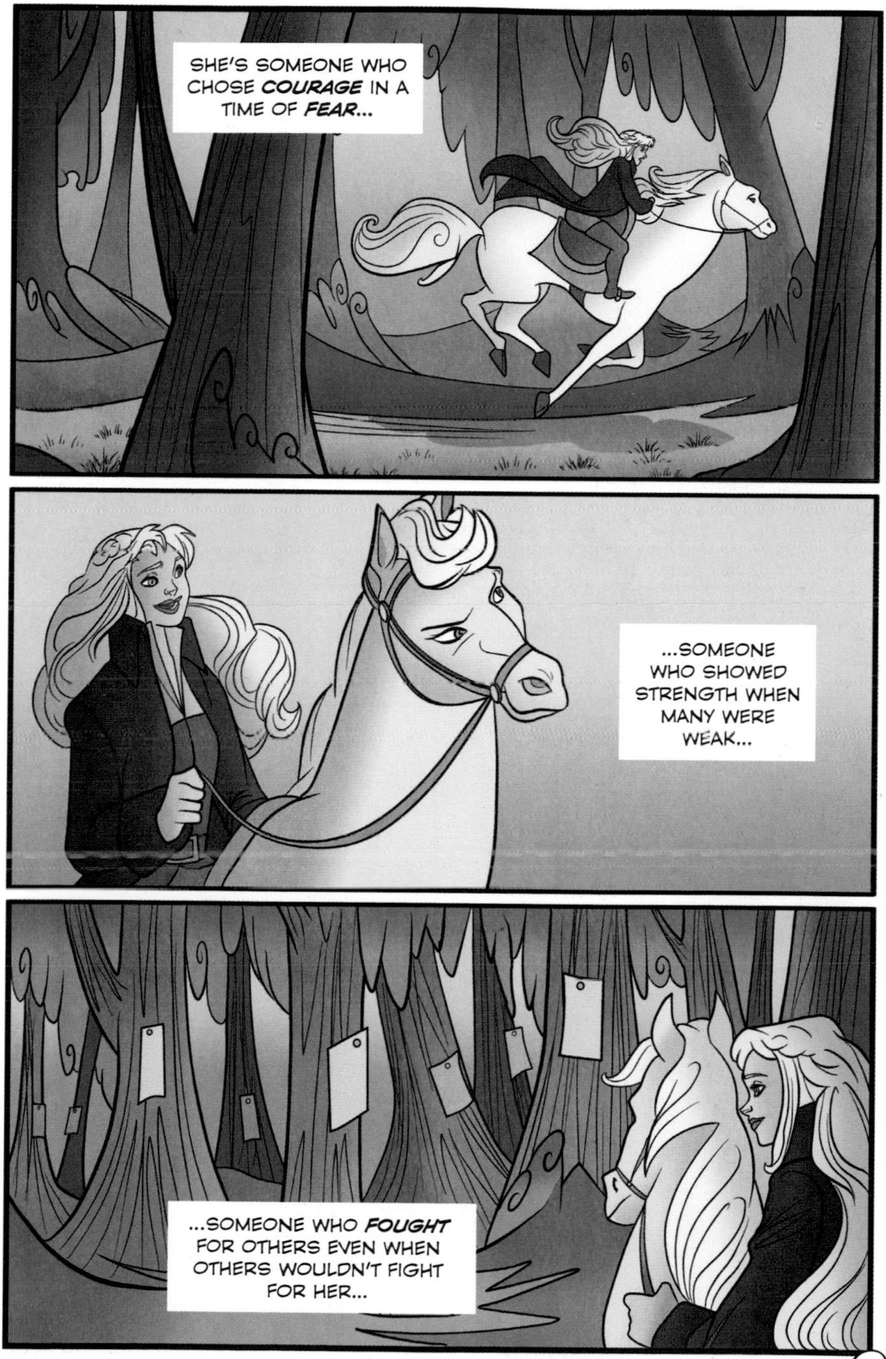
SHE'S SOMEONE WHO CHOSE ***COURAGE*** IN A TIME OF ***FEAR***...
...SOMEONE WHO SHOWED STRENGTH WHEN MANY WERE WEAK...
...SOMEONE WHO ***FOUGHT*** FOR OTHERS EVEN WHEN OTHERS WOULDN'T FIGHT FOR HER...

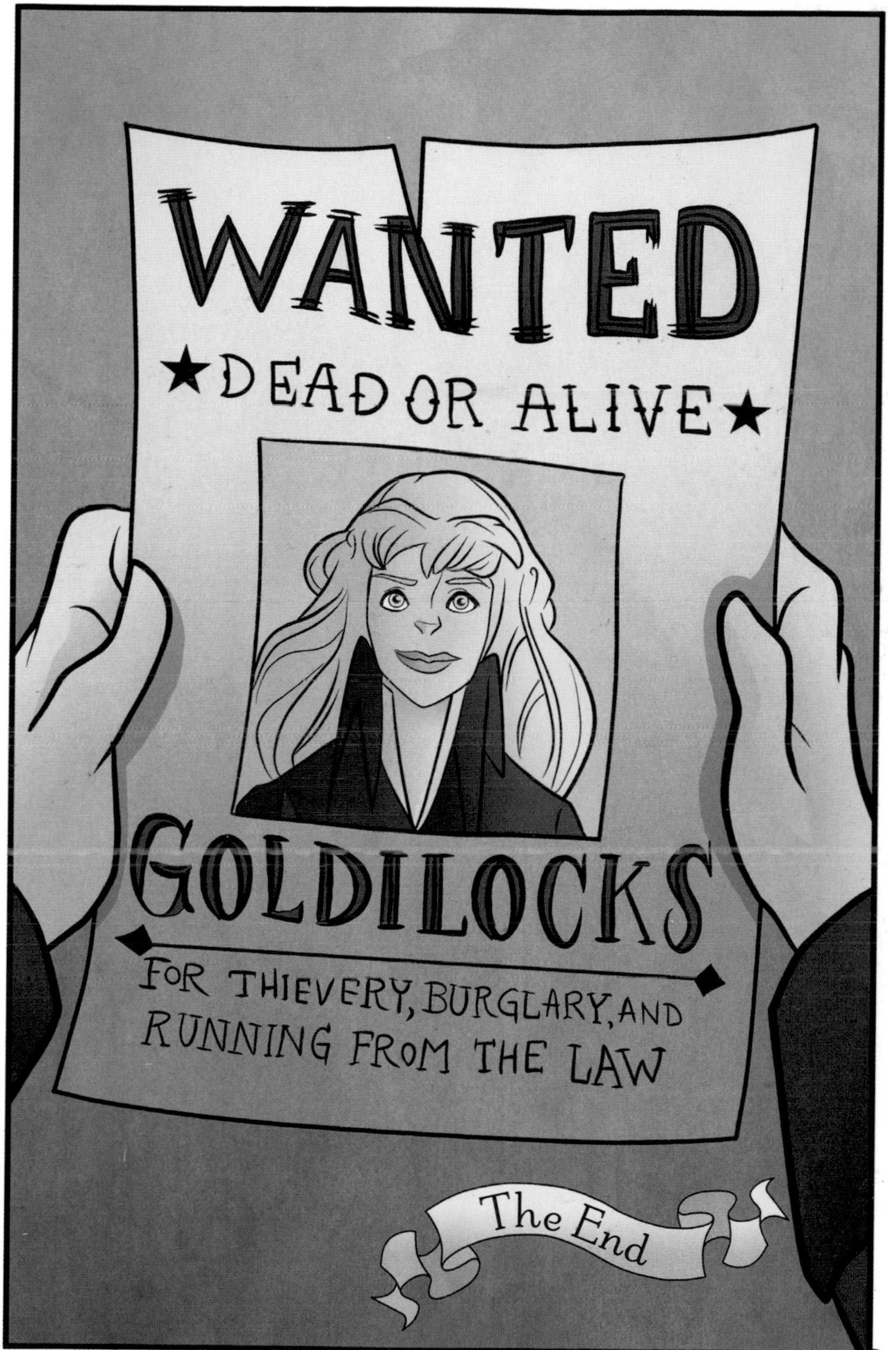
WANTED
DEAD OR ALIVE
GOLDILOCKS
FOR THIEVERY, BURGLARY, AND RUNNING FROM THE LAW
The End

Acknowledgments

I'd like to thank Rob Weisbach, Derek Kroeger, Alla Plotkin, Rachel Karten, Marcus Colen, ICM, and Heather Manzutto for making "Team CC" a well-oiled machine.

All the incredible people at Little, Brown, including Alvina Ling, Megan Tingley, Siena Koncsol, Stefanie Hoffman, Shawn Foster, Jackie Engel, Emilie Polster, Janelle DeLuise, Ruqayyah Daud, Jen Graham, Sasha Illingworth, Christina Quintero, Ching Chan, Lindsay Walter-Greaney, Andrea Colvin, Jake Regier, Virginia Lawther, and Regina Castillo. And Jon Proctor and Lisa K. Weber for bringing these characters to life.

Since this graphic novel features a heroine, I'd especially like to thank all the amazing women in my life for their continued encouragement and support. I hope you recognize the courage and compassion you've instilled in me, reflected in the characters throughout the story.